"We need to go in now because if we stay out here one moment longer, I'll be forced to kiss you."

And there it was, out in the open. This thing...

"And you don't want to?" It was a whisper, so low Matt thought he'd misheard. But he hadn't. Penny's whisper seemed to echo. Even the owls above their heads seemed to pause to listen.

Did he want to?

This was such a bad idea. This woman was his employee. She was trapped here for the next four days, or longer if she took him up on his offer to extend.

What was he doing? Standing in the dark talking of kissing a woman?

Did he want to?

"Yes," he said, because there was nothing else to say.

"Then what's stopping you?"

"Penny..."

"Just shut up, Matt Fraser, and kiss me."

And what was a man to say to that?

Matt took Penny into his arms and he kissed her.

STRANDED WITH THE SECRET BILLIONAIRE

BY
MARION LENNOX

First Published in Great Britain 2017
By Mills & Boon, an imprint of HarperCollins*Publishers*
1 London Bridge Street, London, SE1 9GF

© 2017 Marion Lennox

This work includes words based on "THE SERENITY PRAYER" by Reinhold Niebuhr.

ISBN: 978-0-263-92289-9

23-0417

Our policy is to use papers that are natural, renewable and recyclable products and made from wood grown in sustainable forests. The logging and manufacturing processes conform to the legal environmental regulations of the country of origin.

Printed and bound in Spain
by CPI, Barcelona

Marion Lennox has written more than a hundred romances and is published in over a hundred countries and thirty languages. Her multiple awards include the prestigious RITA® Award (twice) and the *RT Book Reviews* Career Achievement Award for "a body of work which makes us laugh and teaches us about love."

Marion adores her family, her kayak, her dog and lying on the beach with a book someone else has written. Heaven!

This book is dedicated to the memory of Grace,
the warmest, most generous mother-in-law
a woman could wish for—and the baker
of the world's best ginger fluff sponge!

CHAPTER ONE

THE IMPECCABLE ENGLISH ACCENT had directed Penelope
Hindmarsh-Firth twelve hundred kilometres across two
states without a problem. From 'Take the third exit after the
Harbour Tunnel', as Penny had navigated her way out of
Sydney, to 'Continue for two hundred kilometres until you
reach the next turn', as she'd crossed South Australia's vast
inland farming country, the cultured voice hadn't faltered.

True, the last turn had made Penny uneasy. The accent
had told her to proceed for thirty kilometres along the Innawarra Track, but it had hesitated over the pronunciation
of Innawarra. Penny had hesitated too. The country around
them was beautiful, lush and green from recent rains and
dotted with vast stands of river red gums. The road she'd
been on had been narrow, but solid and well used.

In contrast, the Innawarra Track looked hardly used. It
was rough and deeply rutted.

Penny's car wasn't built for rough. She was driving her
gorgeous little sports car. Pink. The car had been her father's engagement gift to her, a joyful signal to the world
that Penny had done something he approved of.

That hadn't lasted. Of course not—when had pleasing her father lasted? Right now she seemed to be doing
a whole lot wrong.

She was facing a creek crossing. It had been raining
hard up north. She'd heard reports of it on the radio but
hadn't taken much notice. Now, what looked to be a usu-

ally dry creek bed was running. She got out of the car, took off her pink sandals and walked across, testing the depth.

Samson was doing no testing. Her little white poodle stood in the back seat and whined, and Penny felt a bit like whining too.

'It's okay,' she told Samson. 'Look, it only comes up to my ankles, and the nice lady on the satnav says this is the quickest way to Malley's Corner.'

Samson still whined, but Penny climbed back behind the wheel and steered her little car determinedly through the water. There were stones underneath. It felt solid and the water barely reached the centre of her tyres. So far so good.

Her qualms were growing by the minute.

She'd estimated it'd take her two hours tops to reach Malley's, but it was already four in the afternoon and the road ahead looked like an obstacle course.

'If worst comes to worst we can sleep in the car,' she told Samson. 'And we're getting used to worst, right?'

Samson whined again but Penny didn't. The time for whining was over.

'Malley's Corner, here I come,' she muttered. 'Floods or not, I'm never turning back.'

Matt Fraser was a man in control. He didn't depend on luck. Early in life, luck had played him a sour hand and he hadn't trusted in it since.

When he was twelve, Matt's mother had taken a job as a farmer's housekeeper. For Matt, who'd spent his young life tugged from one emotional disaster to another, the farm had seemed heaven and farming had been his life ever since. With only one—admittedly major—hiccup to impede his progress he'd done spectacularly well, but here was another hiccup and it was a big one. He was staring out from his veranda at his massive shearing shed. It was set up for a five a.m. start. His team of crack shearers was ready but his planning had let him down.

He needed to break the news soon, and it wouldn't be pretty.

Hiring gun shearers was half the trick to success in this business. Over the years Matt had worked hard to make sure he had everything in place to attract the best, and he'd succeeded.

But this afternoon's phone call had floored him.

'Sorry, Matt, can't do. The water's already cut the Innawarra Track to your north and they're saying the floodwaters will cut you off from the south by tomorrow. You want to hire me a helicopter? It's the only alternative.'

A helicopter would cut into his profits from the wool clip but that wouldn't bother him. It was keeping his shearers happy that was the problem. No matter whose fault it was, an unhappy shed meant he'd slip down the shearers' roster next year. He'd be stuck with a winter shear rather than the spring shears that kept his flocks in such great shape.

So he needed a chopper, but there were none for hire. The flooding up north had all available helicopters either hauling idiots out of floodwater or, more mundanely, dropping feed to stranded stock.

He should go and tell them now, he thought.

He'd cop a riot.

He had to tell them some time.

Dinner was easy. They had to provide their own. It was only at first smoko tomorrow that the proverbial would hit the fan.

'They might as well sleep in ignorance,' he muttered and headed out the back of the sheds to find his horse. Nugget didn't care about shearing and shearing shed politics. His two kelpies, Reg and Bluey, flew out from under the house the moment they heard the clink of his riding gear. They didn't care either.

And, for the moment, neither did Matt.

'Courage to change the things that can be changed, strength to accept those things that can't be changed and the wisdom to know the difference...' It was a good mantra. He couldn't hire a chopper. Shearing would be a surly, ill-tempered disaster but it was tomorrow's worry.

For now he led Nugget out of the home paddock and whistled the dogs to follow.

He might be in trouble but for now he had every intention of forgetting about it.

She was in so much trouble.

'You'd think if there were stones at the bottom of one creek there'd be stones at the bottom of every creek.' She was standing on the far side of the second creek crossing. Samson was still in the car.

Her car was in the middle of the creek.

It wasn't deep. She'd checked. Once more she'd climbed out of the car and waded through, and it was no deeper than the last.

What she hadn't figured was that the bottom of this section of the creek was soft, loose sand. Sand that sucked a girl's tyres down.

Was it her imagination or was the water rising?

She'd checked the important things a girl should know before coming out here—like telephone reception. It was lousy so she'd spent serious money fitting herself out with a satellite phone, but who could she ring? Her father? *Dad, come and get me out of a river.* He'd swear at her, tell her she was useless and tell his assistant to organize a chopper to bring her home.

That assistant would probably be Brett.

She'd rather burn in hell.

So who? Her friends?

They'd think it was a blast, a joke to be bruited all over the Internet. Penelope Hindmarsh-Firth, indulged daughter of a billionaire, stuck in the outback in her new pink car. A broken engagement. A scandal. Her first ever decision to revolt.

There wasn't one she would trust not to sell the story to the media.

Her new employer?

She'd tried to sound competent in her phone interview. Maybe it would come to that, but he'd need to come by truck and no truck could reach her by dark.

Aargh.

Samson was watching from the car, whimpering as the water definitely rose.

'Okay,' she said wearily. 'I didn't much like this car anyway. We have lots of supplies. I have half a kitchen worth of cooking gear and specialist ingredients in those boxes. Let's get everything unloaded, including you. If no one comes before the car goes under I guess we're camping here while my father's engagement gift floats down the river.'

There was a car in the middle of the creek.

A pink car. A tiny sports car. Cute.

Wet. Getting closer to being swept away by the minute.

Of all the dumb...

There was a woman heaving boxes from some sort of luggage rack she'd rigged onto the back. She was hauling them to safety.

A little dog was watching from the riverbank, yapping with anxiety.

Matt reined to a halt and stared incredulously. Reg and Bluey stopped too, quivering with shock, and then hurled themselves down towards what Matt thought must surely be a hallucination. A poodle? They'd never seen such a thing.

The woman in the water turned and saw the two dogs, then ran, trying to launch herself between the killer dogs and her pooch.

She was little and blonde, and her curls twisted to her shoulders. She was wearing a short denim skirt, a bright pink blouse and oversized pink earrings. She was nicely curved—very nicely curved.

Her sunglasses were propped on her head. She looked as if she was dressed for sipping Chardonnay at some beachside café.

She reached the bank, slipped in the soft sand and her crate fell out of her hands.

A teapot fell out and rolled into the water.

'Samson!' She hauled herself to her feet, yelling to her poodle, but Reg and Bluey had reached their target.

Matt was too stunned to call them off, but there was no need. His dogs weren't vicious. This small mutt must look like a lone sheep, needing to be returned to the flock. Rounding up stray sheep was what his dogs did best.

But Matt could almost see what they were thinking as they reached the white bit of fluff, skidded to a halt and started the universal sniffing of both ends. *It looks like a sheep but...what...?*

He grinned. The troubles of the day took a back seat for the moment and he nudged Nugget forward.

There wasn't a thing he could do about his shearing problems. What he needed was distraction, and this looked just what the doctor ordered.

She needed a knight on a white charger. This was no white charger, though. The horse was huge and black as night. And the guy on it?

Instead of armour, he wore the almost universal uniform of the farmer. Moleskin pants. A khaki shirt, open at the throat, sleeves rolled to the elbows. A wide Akubra hat. As he edged his horse carefully down the embankment she had the impression of a weathered face, lean, dark, strong. Not so old. In his thirties?

His mouth was curving into a smile. He was laughing? At her?

'In a spot of bother, ma'am?'

What she would have given to be able to say: *No bother—everything's under control, thank you.*

But her car was sinking and Samson was somewhere under his dogs.

'Yeah,' she said grimly. 'I tried to cross but the creek doesn't have stones in it.'

His lips twitched. 'How inconsiderate.'

'The last creek did.'

He put his hands up, as if in surrender. 'I cannot tell a lie,' he told her. 'I dropped stones in the first crossing but not this one. The first floods all the time. This one not so much. There's a lot of water coming down. I doubt you'd get back over the first crossing now.'

'You put the stones in…'

'Yes, ma'am.'

She stood and thought about it. She had bare feet—a pair of bright pink sandals had been tossed onto the bank on this side. Obviously she'd waded through first, which was intelligent. Driving into a flooded creek with a sandy base was the opposite.

But now wasn't the time for judging. The water was rising by the minute. 'Would you like me to help you get your car out?'

And any hint of belligerence died. 'Could you? Do you know how?'

'You have cushions on your passenger seat,' he said. He'd been checking out the car while they talked. A big car might be a problem but this looked small enough to push, and with the traction of cushions… 'We could use those.'

'They're Samson's.'

'Samson?'

'My poodle.'

'I see.' He was still having trouble keeping a straight face. 'Is he likely to bite my arm off if I use his cushions?'

She glanced to where Reg and Bluey were still warily circling Samson. Samson was wisely standing still. Very still.

'Your dogs…'

'Are meeting a poodle for the very first time. They won't take a piece out of him, if that's what you're worried about. So Samson won't take a piece out of me if I borrow his cushion?'

'No. Please… If you could…'

'My pleasure, ma'am. I haven't pushed a pink car out of floodwaters for a very long time.'

And then he got bossy.

He swung himself down from his horse. He didn't bother tying it up—the assumption, she guessed, was that it'd stay where he left it and the assumption seemed correct. Then he strode out into the water to her car. He removed the cushions, then stooped and wedged them underwater, in front of the back wheels.

'Rear-wheel drive is useful,' he told her. 'Four-wheel drive is better—it's pretty much essential out here. You didn't think to borrow something a little more useful before driving off-road?'

'This *is* a road.'

'This is a track,' he told her.

He was standing almost thigh-deep in water and he was soaked from pushing the cushions into place.

'I should push,' she offered.

The lips twitched again. 'I'm thinking I might just have a bit more muscle. Could you hop in and switch on the ignition? When I tell you to accelerate, go for it. Straight forward, and as soon as you feel the car get a grip, keep going.'

She thought about it for a moment and saw a problem. A big one. 'Um...'

He paused. 'Um?'

'Are there any more creeks?' she asked, her voice filled with trepidation.

'Any more creeks where?'

'Between here and Malley's Corner.'

'You're headed for Malley's Corner?'

'Yes.' She tilted her chin at the note of incredulity in his voice. It was the same incredulity she'd heard from every one of her family and friends.

He paused for a moment. The water level rose an inch.

'We'll talk about it later,' he said curtly. 'We have minutes to get your car clear before she's properly swamped. Get in and turn it on.'

'But are there more creeks?'

'A dozen or so.'

'Then I can't get to Malley's Corner,' she wailed. 'I need to go back the way I came. Can you push me back to the other side?'

'You want to do a U-turn in the middle of the creek?'

'No, but I don't want to be trapped.'

'I have news for you, lady,' he told her. 'You're already trapped. The only hope we have of getting your car out of this water is to go straight forward and do it now. Get in your car and I'll push or it'll be washed away. Move!'

She gave a yelp of fright—and moved.

She was in such a mess.

Actually, if she was honest, she wasn't in a mess at all.

She was perfectly dry. Her little car was on dry land, still drivable. Samson had jumped back up into the passenger seat and was looking around for his cushions. It looked as if she could drive happily away. There were more creeks but for now she was safe.

But she had a cowboy to thank, the guy who'd saved her car—and he was the mess.

Though actually… She *should* be able to describe him as a mess, she thought. He'd shoved the cushions under her back wheels to get traction and then, as she'd touched the accelerator, he'd put his hands under the back of her car and pushed.

She'd felt the strength of him, the sheer muscle. With the acceleration behind him he'd practically heaved the little car free.

She'd stopped and looked back, and her cowboy—her rescuer—was sprawled full length in the water.

When he stood up he almost looked scary. He was seriously big, he was soaked and he was spitting sand. He did not look happy.

When he reached the bank she backed off a little.

'Th…thank you,' she ventured. 'That was very good of you.'

'My pleasure, ma'am,' he said with obvious sarcasm and she winced.

'I'm sorry.'

'All in a day's work. I've heaved stock from bogs before this. Your car's not much bigger than a decent bull.' He wiped away some sand and she had a clearer view of his face. He had deep brown eyes set in a strongly boned face. Strength and capability and toughness was written on every inch of him. This wasn't the sort of guy she ever met in her city life.

'Do you live round here?' she managed and he nodded.

'Over the rise.'

'Then... I guess that means at least you can go home and have a shower. Look, I really am sorry...'

'So what will you do?'

'Go on until I reach the next creek,' she said in a small voice. 'Samson and I can sleep in the car if the water doesn't go down before nightfall. We'll go on tomorrow.'

'Tomorrow...'

'I start work on Tuesday. I guess it's just lucky I left myself a day's leeway.'

Something seemed to be happening on her rescuer's face. There was a tic right next to his jaw. It was sort of... twitching.

Laughter? No. Exasperation?

Maybe.

'You'd better follow me,' he said at last and she blinked.

'Why? I'm sorry; that doesn't sound gracious but you've done enough. Samson and I will be fine.'

'For a fortnight?'

'A fortnight?'

'That's how long they're saying before the floodwaters subside.' He sighed. 'There's been rain all over central New South Wales. It's been dry here, which is why you've been lulled into thinking it's safe to drive, but it's been raining up north like it hasn't for years. The water's pouring into the Murray catchment and all that water's making its way downstream. Creeks that haven't seen water for years are starting to fill. If you'd followed the main road you might have made it...'

'The satnav lady said this way was much shorter,' she said in a small voice.

'Then the satnav lady's a moron,' he said bluntly. 'There's no way you'll get this little car through to Malley's Corner and there's no way you can get back. You're stuck right here and you're stuck for a while.'

She stood and stared at him and he gazed right back.

He was looking at her as if she were some sort of strange species.

An idiot.

All her careful plans. All her defiance…

This was just what her father expected—Penelope being stupid once again.

She thought of the last appalling tabloid article she'd read before she'd packed and left—her father explaining to the media why the man who'd intended to marry Penny was now marrying Penny's older half-sister, the gorgeous, clever, talented Felicity.

'They're a much more suitable match,' George had told the journalist. *'Brett is one in a million. He's an employee who's going places and he needs a woman of class to support that. My younger daughter means well, but she's much more interested in her cakes than in taking care of her man. I'm not sure why we all didn't see this was a more sensible match to begin with.'*

Sensible. Right.

She shook herself, shoving painful memories harshly behind her. No, she wouldn't be calling her father for help.

'Is there somewhere I can stay?' she asked in a small voice.

'You're on my land,' he told her. 'From here until the next two creek crossings there's nowhere but Jindalee.'

'Jindalee?'

'My home.'

'Oh.'

She looked at his horse and her mind was twisting so much she even thought of offering to buy the thing and ride off into the sunset. Fording rivers on horseback with Samson riding up front.

Um…not. Even if she could ride a horse. Even if she was game to go near it.

'Do you...do you have a four-wheel drive?' she asked. 'Is it possible that a truck or something could get through?'

'It might,' he said grudgingly.

She'd been trying to figure a way out, but she thought she saw one. 'Could you take me on to Malley's? If you have a truck that can get through we could make it. I could leave my car here and get someone to bring me back to collect it when the water goes down.'

And this is my last chance, she thought desperately, looking into his impassive face. *Please.*

He gazed at her and she forced herself to meet his gaze calmly, as if her request was totally reasonable—as if asking him to drive for at least four hours over flooded creeks was as minor as hiring a cab.

'I can pay,' she added. 'I mean... I can pay well. Like a good day's wages...'

'You have no idea,' he said and then there was even more silence. Was he considering it?

But finally he shook his head.

'It's impossible,' he told her. 'I can't leave the property. I have a team ready to start shearing at dawn and two thousand sheep to be shorn. Nothing's messing with that.'

'You could...maybe come back tonight?'

'In your dreams. The water's coming up. I could end up trapped at Malley's Corner with you. I can't risk sending a couple of my men because I need everyone. So I don't seem to have a choice and neither do you.' He sighed. 'We might as well make the best of it. I'm inviting you home. You and your dog. As long as you don't get in the way of my shearing team, you're welcome to stay at Jindalee for as long as the floodwater takes to recede.'

CHAPTER TWO

PENNY DROVE, slowly and carefully, along the rutted track. He followed behind on his horse, his dogs trotting beside him, and she was aware of him every inch of the way.

He could be an axe murderer. He was sodden and filthy. His jet-black hair was still dripping and his dark face looked grim.

He'd laughed when he first saw her but now he looked as if he'd just been handed a problem and he didn't like it.

She didn't even know his name.

He didn't know hers, she reminded herself. He was opening his house to her, and all he knew about her was that she was dumb enough to get herself stranded in the middle of nowhere. She could be the axe murderer.

She had knives. She thought fleetingly of her precious set, wrapped carefully in one of her crates. They were always super sharp.

What sort of knives did axe murderers use?

'They use axes, idiot,' she said aloud and that was a mistake. The guy on the horse swivelled and stared.

'Axes?' he said cautiously, and she thought, *He'll be thinking he has a real fruitcake here.*

That was what she felt like. A fruitcake.

'Sorry. Um…just thinking of what I'd need if… I mean, if I was stuck camping and needed something like wood to light a fire. I'd need an axe.'

'Right,' he said, still more cautiously. 'But you don't have one?'

'No.'

'You seem to have everything else.'

'I'm going to Malley's to work. I need stuff.'

'You're working at Malley's?' He sounded incredulous. 'That place is a dump.'

'The owner has plans,' she said with as much dignity as she could muster. 'I'm employed to help.'

'It could use a bit of interior decorating,' he agreed. 'From the ground up.' His lips suddenly twitched again. 'And you always carry a teapot?'

'They might only use tea bags.'

'You don't like tea bags?'

'I drink lapsang souchong and it doesn't work in tea bags. I love its smoky flavour. Don't you?'

'Doesn't everyone?' he asked and suddenly he grinned. 'I'm Matt,' he told her. 'Matt Fraser. I'm the owner of Jindalee but I hope you brought your own lapsang souchong with you. Sadly I seem to be short on essentials.'

'I have a year's supply,' she told him and his grin widened.

'Of course you do. And you are?'

'Penelope Hindmarsh-Firth.' He was laughing at her but she could take it, she decided. She should be used to people laughing at her by now. 'And I'm the owner of one pink car and one white poodle.'

'And a teapot,' he reminded her.

'Thank you. Yes.' She concentrated on negotiating an extra deep rut in the road.

'Penelope...' Matt said as the road levelled again.

'Penny.'

'Penny,' he repeated. 'Did you say Hindmarsh-Firth?'

And her heart sank. He knows, she thought, but there was no sense denying it.

'Yes.'

'Of the Hindmarsh-Firth Corporation?'

'I don't work for them.' Not any more. She said it almost defiantly.

'But you're connected.'

'I might be.'

'The way I heard it,' he said slowly, seemingly thinking as he spoke, 'is that George Hindmarsh, up-and-coming investment banker, married Louise Firth, only daughter of a mining magnate worth billions. Hindmarsh-Firth is now a financial empire that has tentacles worldwide. You're part of that Hindmarsh-Firth family?'

'They could be my parents,' she muttered. 'But I'm still not part of it.'

'I see.'

He didn't, she thought. He couldn't. He'd have no idea of what it was like growing up in that goldfish bowl, with her father's ego. He'd have no idea why she'd finally had to run.

'So if I rang up the newspapers now and said I've just pulled a woman called Penelope Hindmarsh-Firth out of a creek, they wouldn't be interested?'

No! 'Please don't,' she whispered and then repeated it, louder, so she was sure he could hear. She was suddenly very close to tears.

'I won't,' he told her, his voice suddenly softening. 'Believe me, I have no wish for media choppers to be circling. Though…'

'Though what?'

'There's someone I need to get here,' he told her. 'It'd almost be worth it—I could tell them they could find you here as long as they brought Pete with them.'

'Pete?'

She hit a bump. The car jolted and the teapot bounced and clanged against the pots underneath it.

'It doesn't matter,' he said roughly. 'I won't do it. I can understand your situation might well cause humiliation. I assume you're heading to Malley's to get out of the spot-light?'

'Yes,' she said and could have wept with gratitude.

'Then you've come to the right place,' he told her. 'And this is a lot cleaner than Malley's. Jindalee has plenty of spare bedrooms, though most are in desperate need of a good dust. As long as you and Samson keep out of my way, you're welcome to hunker down for as long as the flood lasts.'

And then they topped the last rise before the house and Penny was so astounded she stalled the car.

The rain clouds up north must have visited here a while back because the pastures were lush and green. The property was vast and undulating. There were low hills roll-ing away as far as the eye could see. The land was dotted with stands of magnificent gums. She could see the occa-sional flock of sheep in the distance, white against green.

But the house… It took her breath away.

It was a real homestead, built a hundred or more years ago. It sat on a slight rise, huge, long and low, built of whitewashed stone. French windows opened to the vast verandas and soft white curtains fluttered out into the warm afternoon breeze. Grapevines massed under the ve-randa and massive old settees sat under their shade. An ancient dog lay on the top step by the front door as if he was guarding the garden.

And what a garden. It looked almost like an oasis in the middle of this vast grazing property. Even from here she could see the work, the care…

Wisteria hung from massive beamed walkways. She could see rockwork, the same sandstone that lined the creeks, used to merge levels into each other. Bougainvil-lea, salvia, honeysuckle… Massive trees that looked hun-dreds of years old. A rock pool with a waterfall that looked almost natural. Roses, roses and more roses.

And birds. As they approached the house a flock of crimson rosellas rose screeching from the gums, wheeling above their heads as if to get a better look, and then settled again.

For why wouldn't they settle? This place looked like paradise.

'Oh, my…' She slowed to a halt. She needed to stop and take it all in.

And Matt pulled his horse to a halt as well. He sat watching her.

'This is… Oh…' She could hardly speak.

'Home,' Matt said and she could feel the love in his voice. And suddenly every doubt about staying here went out of the window.

He loved this place. He loved this garden and surely no one who loved as much as this could be an axe murderer?

'Who does this?' she stammered. She'd tried gardening in the past. It had been a thankless task as her parents moved from prestige property to prestige property, but she knew enough to know that such a seemingly casual, natural garden represented more hard work than she could imagine. 'Your wife?' she asked. 'Or…'

'I don't have a wife,' he said, suddenly curt, and she thought instinctively that there was a story there. 'But I do have someone helping me in the garden. Donald loves it as much as I do. He's in his eighties now but he won't slow down.'

'Your dad? Grandpa?'

'No.' Once more his reply was curt and she knew suddenly that she needed to back off. This guy wasn't into personal interrogation. 'Donald owned this place before I bought it. He's stayed on because of the garden.'

'That's lovely,' she breathed.

'It is,' he said and he wasn't talking of Donald. His eyes

skimmed the house, the garden, the country around them and she saw his face soften. 'There's nowhere I'd rather be.'

She gazed around her, at the low lying hills, at the rich pasture, at the massive gum trees, at the sheer age and beauty of the homestead which seemed to nestle into its surroundings as if it had grown there. 'How much of this do you own?' she breathed.

'As far as you can see and more.' It was impossible for him to hide the pride in his voice.

'Oh, wow!' The property must be vast. She sat and soaked it in, and something in her settled. Who could be fearful or even heartbroken in a place like this?

Okay, she was still heartbroken but maybe she could put it aside.

'What's the building over there?' A low shed built of ancient handmade bricks sat under the gum trees in the distance. It looked so old it practically disappeared into the landscape.

'That's the shearing shed. The shearers' quarters are behind that.'

And suddenly she was diverted from the farm's beauty.

'There's a dozen trucks. At least.'

'They belong to the shearing team. We start at dawn. You'll need to keep out of the way.'

'Oh, but…' Surely with so many…

'No,' he said, seeing where she was heading and cutting her off before she got started. 'No one's driving you anywhere. You'll find an empty garage around the back. I need to take care of Nugget and talk to the men before I come in for the night, but the back door's open. Put the kettle on and make yourself a cup of…what was it? Lapsang souchong. I'll see you in an hour or so. Meanwhile, welcome to Jindalee, Miss Hindmarsh-Firth. Welcome to my home.'

* * *

Matt led Nugget into the stables, unstrapped his gear and started brushing. Nugget looked vaguely surprised. Knowing shearing was about to start, knowing life was about to get crazy, he'd given him a decent brush this morning. But two brushes in one day wouldn't hurt and it might help get his head together.

In one sense the worsening flood was a blessing. The shearing team hadn't listened to the weather forecast. They'd come straight from a property south of here this morning, and there'd been no hint of the flooding to come. That meant when they woke tomorrow and found he had no shearers' cook they couldn't leave in disgust. At least his sheep would be shorn.

But he was facing two weeks of disgruntled shearers. Plus two weeks of a society princess who asked questions.

Penelope Hindmarsh-Firth...

He took his phone from the waterproof protector he always used—thank heaven he'd had it today—and hit the Internet. Thank heaven for satellites too, he thought, glancing at the dish on the top of the house. If he'd used the Internet to good effect he could have tracked the speed of the flooding. He could have let the shearers know not to come, but he'd gambled. He'd known the water was on its way but he'd thought they'd be able to get through this morning. They had. He had two weeks' work for them and a decent amount of supplies.

He'd also thought his cook could get through, but he'd been coming from another property in a different direction. And that had spelled disaster.

First World problem—shearers having to cook their own tucker? Maybe it was, but from time immemorial shearers had counted the quality of food and accommodation as a major enticement. This was a crack team and they expected the best. They couldn't blame him but it would be a sullen two weeks.

'So what are the odds of Miss Hindmarsh-Firth being able to cook?' he asked Nugget and thought of the teapot and grimaced. He needed to know more about the blonde and her white poodle. He leaned back on his horse's hindquarters and Nugget nibbled his ear while he searched *Penelope Hindmarsh-Firth* in his Internet browser.

And what sprang up were gossip columns—a list of them, longer than his screen. Current gossip.

'*Is one Hindmarsh-Firth as good as another?*' '*Sister Swap!*' '*Taggart's gamble pays off...*'

Bemused, he hit the first and read.

Brett Taggart, chief accountant to investment banker George Hindmarsh and heiress Louise Firth, has played a risky hand and won. He wooed the pair's daughter, company PR assistant Penelope, with what we hope were honourable intentions... Familiarity, however, meant a change of direction for our dubiously intentioned Brett. As he was welcomed into the golden world of the Hindmarsh-Firth family, his attention was obviously caught by his fiancée's older half-sister, glamorous social butterfly Felicity. Never let a promise get in the way of a good time, seems to be Brett's philosophy, and rumour has it that he and Felicity might be expecting a Happy Event in the next few months.

Such a ruckus in the family might have some parents casting children out. 'Never darken our door again!' would have been this columnist's reaction to such a back-stabbing sibling, but George and Louise seem to have taken the situation in their stride. In a recent tabloid interview George even insinuated he understands why Brett would choose the gorgeous

Felicity over her dumpy, media-shy sister, and Louise refuses to comment. So one wedding has been swapped for another.

Ugh, Matt thought, feeling a wave of sympathy for the 'dumpy, media-shy' Penny.

And then he thought…*dumpy?* What a description for those curves.

Um…let's not go there. He didn't need distraction.

He did not need anyone—except a shearer's cook.

'At least she can make her own tea,' he muttered to Nugget. 'There's a bonus. I wonder if she can make her own toast?'

Penny ventured in through the back door and was met by silence. Samson sniffed forward so she cautiously opened a few doors. The house was a beautiful…mausoleum?

It looked like a magnificent homestead built for a family of a dozen or so, with entertaining on a lavish scale. But it also looked like it hadn't been used for years. The massive sitting room off the main entrance was covered in dust sheets, as were the two other rooms she ventured into. She peeked under the dust sheets and saw furniture that'd look at home in an antique store. An expensive antique store.

There was a small sun-drenched den that looked well used. It was crammed with farming journals, books, a computer, dog beds. Matt's study? A wide passage led to what must be the bedroom wing but she wasn't game to go there.

Feeling more and more like an intruder, she retreated to the kitchen.

Which was…spectacular.

Windows opened to the veranda, to the shearing shed in the distance and to the hills beyond. Sunbeams were dancing on the floor, the ancient timbers worn by years of use. A battered wooden table ran almost the full length of the room, with scattered mismatched chairs that looked incredibly inviting. A small, slow combustion stove stood to one side of an old hearth, as if a far bigger wood stove had been removed. Beside it was a vast industrial oven and cooktop. It looked as if it could feed a small army.

How many people lived here? Hardly anyone by the look of the closed-up rooms, but these ovens... *Wow!*

She glanced again at the firestove. It was lit and emitting a gentle warmth. She'd never used one. Could she make bread?

What was she thinking of? Baking?

This situation was a mess. She didn't want to be here and Matt Fraser didn't want her here. Her job at Malley's Corner was in doubt. She'd ring them now but would they still want her when she arrived two weeks late?

She was stuck here for two weeks, with a man she didn't know.

But she was suddenly thinking: did he have decent flour?

There was a door to the side which looked like it could lead to a pantry. She shouldn't pry. The very stillness of the house was making her nervous, but he'd said she could make herself a cup of tea.

She did have tea but it was packed at the bottom of one of her crates. So she needed to check the pantry...

She opened the pantry door and gasped.

This pantry was huge, and it was stocked as if Matt was expecting to feed an army.

There were flour bins, big ones, topped to overflowing. There were bins of rice, of sugar. There were mountains of cans, stacks of packs of pasta. There was every dried herb and sauce she could imagine.

There were two vast refrigerators and freezers, and another door led to a coolroom. She saw vegetables, fruit, every perishable a cook could need. There were whole sides of beef and lamb. Who could eat this much meat?

The shearing team? She'd read descriptions of life on the big sheep stations. Gun shearers, working twelve-hour days, pushing themselves to the limits, while the farmer's wife pushed herself to the limit feeding them.

Matt had no wife. There was no evidence of a house-keeper.

Was he planning to cook, or did one of those trucks out there belong to a cook?

She closed the lid of the freezer and saw an enormous list pinned to the wall. It was an inventory of everything she'd just seen.

It was printed out as an email. She flicked through to the end.

Can you get all this in stock and have it waiting? I'll be there on the seventh by mid-afternoon, but my first cook will be smoko on the eighth. See you then.

So he did have a cook. He'd probably be over with the men now, she thought. Maybe Matt was there too. Maybe they were sitting round drinking beer while Matt told them about the dopey blonde he'd pulled out of the water.

And suddenly all the fears of the past few weeks crowded back.

She was stuck in the middle of nowhere, where no one wanted her. She was stuck for two weeks.

A shearer's cook would be taking over this kitchen from tomorrow morning. Maybe she could help, she thought, but she'd worked in enough kitchens to know how posses-sive cooks could be.

'I might be allowed to wash dishes,' she told Samson morosely.

She found a tea bag—actually, she found about a thousand tea bags. They weren't generic, but they weren't lapsang souchong either.

'We'll have to slum it,' she told her dog, and made her tea and headed out to the veranda.

The big, old collie she'd seen earlier was still snoozing on the step. He raised his head and gave his tail a faint wag, then settled back down to the serious business of sleeping.

An old man was dead-heading roses. He was stooped and weathered with age, almost a part of the land around him. He glanced up from his roses as she emerged from the back door, and startled as if he'd just seen a ghost.

'Hi,' Penny called. 'I'm Penny.'

He didn't answer. Instead he dropped the canvas bag he'd been carrying and backed away. Ghosts, it seemed, were scary.

Penny sighed. She plonked herself down on the edge of the veranda and gazed out over the garden to the rolling plains beyond. Samson eyed the old dog warily, and then plonked down beside her.

'This is a beautiful view,' she told Samson. 'But I might just get sick of it after two weeks.'

Samson put his nose into the crook of her arm and whined. Samson, it seemed, was in complete agreement.

To say the men were unhappy would be an understatement.

'So who's going to cook?' Bert, self-proclaimed shearers' foreman, sounded incredulous.

'Me,' Matt told him. 'It means I can't spend much time in the shed, but Ron and Harv will have things under control.' Ron was his right-hand man, Harv his jackeroo. They were both capable sheep men.

Leaving the shed in their hands was still a risk. Half the trick of a smooth shear was the owner being hands-on. Men worked at full capacity, day after day, pushing themselves to the limit because the sooner they finished the sooner they'd be paid, and that was a recipe for problems. Tensions escalated fast. Ron and Harv were both men who disliked conflict and backed away from it—there was a reason they both worked on such an isolated property. Matt didn't like conflict either, but he could deal. He had the authority to dock wages, to kick a drunk shearer off the team or, worse, to recommend to other station owners which teams not to employ.

But Ron and Harv couldn't cook to save their lives. They lived on a diet of corned beef, beer and the occasional apple to prevent scurvy. At least Matt could do a decent spag. bol.

He had no choice. The kitchen was his.

'So we'll be eating pasta and boiled beef for two weeks?' Bert demanded and Matt shrugged.

'I'll do my best. Sorry, guys. I'm as unhappy about this as you are.'

'So what about the sheila we just saw you drive in with?' Bert demanded. 'Have you replaced Pete with a bit of fluff?'

'I haven't. She was stuck in the creek and I pulled her out. She's stuck here too and, before you ask, I suspect she might be able to brew a decent tea but not much else.'

'Great,' Bert growled. 'That's just great.'

'Sorry,' Matt told him. 'But that's the situation and we're stuck with it.'

And also a cute blonde with curves?

Do not go there. What was wrong with him? That was the second time he'd thought it.

Two weeks...

Stay well clear, he told himself. The last thing he needed was yet another woman complicating his life.

CHAPTER THREE

MATT RETURNED TO FIND Penny on the veranda, trying to make friends with Donald's dog. He greeted her curtly. There was a lot to be done before he could sleep. If she was expecting to be entertained he might as well make things clear now.

He showed her which bedroom she could use. It was big, it overlooked the garden and it had the extra advantage of being as far away from his as possible. Plus it had its own bathroom. For a Hindmarsh-Firth it might still be slumming it, he thought, but it'd be a thousand times better than the accommodation she'd get at Malley's Corner.

What on earth was she intending to do at Malley's? He'd ask some time, he thought, but he had to be up before dawn to make sure the first mob was ready to go, he had to check the sheep again tonight and he needed to eat.

But he should offer to feed her, he decided. From tomorrow he was faced with feeding the multitude. He might as well start now.

'Dinner's in half an hour,' he told her as he dumped her gear in her bedroom—how much stuff could one woman use? 'At seven.'

'I can help.' She hesitated. 'I'd like to.'

'I'll do it.' He wanted to eat and run, not sit while she fussed over something fancy. 'Thirty minutes. Kitchen. Oh, and there's dog food...'

'Samson has his own dog food.'

'Of course he does,' he said shortly and left her to her unpacking.

Showered, clean of the river sand, he felt better but not much. He tossed bacon and tomatoes into a frying pan, put bread in the toaster and set plates on the table.

Right on seven she walked in the door. She'd changed too. She'd obviously showered as well, for her curls were still damp. She was wearing jeans and a T-shirt and she'd caught her curls back in a ponytail.

He glanced around as she came into the room and had to force himself to turn back to the frying pan.

She looked fresh and clean and…cute? More than cute.

Curvy? Bouncy?

Sexy.

Cut it out, he told himself and concentrated on the bacon.

'The house is lovely,' she told him. 'Thank you for taking me in.'

'It's not like I had a choice.' He thought about that for a moment and decided he sounded a bore. 'Sorry. You're welcome. And yes, it's lovely. Eggs?' Then he figured as a conversational gambit it needed a little extra. 'How many?'

'Two, please.' Her feet were bare. She padded over to the bench beside the firestove and hauled herself up so her legs were swinging. 'You can fry on this? I've never used a slow combustion stove.'

'It's a skill,' he said, deciding to sound modest.

'What else can you do on it?'

Uh oh. She'd called him out. He grinned and cracked an egg into the pan. 'Sausages,' he told her. 'And I can boil stuff.'

'So you use the big oven?'

'Not usually. The firestove suits me. If it's a cold morning I put my boots in the oven. Oh, and the occasional live lamb.'

'You put lambs in the oven?'

'It's the best place for a lamb that's been caught in the frost,' he told her. 'I can fit a lamb and boots in there all at once. Lamb and boots come out warm and ready to go. It's a win-win for everyone. Who needs an oven for baking?'

'But you can still bake in it?'

'I could try,' he told her. 'But anything I put in there might come out smelling of wet wool and boot leather.'

'Yum,' she said and then looked down at his frying eggs. 'Don't let them get hard.'

'What?' He stared down at the five eggs he'd cracked. He picked up the egg slice to flip them but Penny put her hand out and held his. Stopping him mid-flip.

'You want runny yolks?'

'I don't mind.'

'Runny's nicer.'

'Yeah, but...'

'Just spoon a little hot fat over them. It's much less likely to burst the yolks.'

'I don't have time for nice.'

'Then let me,' she told him and jumped down, grabbed a spoon and edged him out of the way.

Her body hit his and all of a sudden they were close. Too close.

He felt... He didn't know what he felt. How long since he'd stood beside a woman in a kitchen?

This was not a sensation he needed to be feeling tonight.

He edged away fast, and stood and watched while she carefully spooned hot fat over the yolks.

'Done,' she said.

She flicked bacon and tomatoes he'd fried earlier onto the toast and then carefully slid the eggs on top.

How had she done that? It was weird but somehow she'd made it look...sort of gourmet? When he piled eggs and bacon onto a plate they looked like eggs and bacon. She'd sort of set the tomatoes at one side and then made a round of bacon. The eggs slid on top and it looked…great.

He'd been hungry. Now he was even hungrier.

And so, it seemed, was she. She sat down and tackled her eggs and bacon as if she hadn't seen food in a week. She was enjoying every mouthful of this very plain meal.

He thought of the few women he knew and the way they ate. Not like this. This was almost sensual.

'Wow,' she breathed as she finished her first egg and tackled her bacon. 'Yum!'

'It's all in the cooking,' he said and she grinned. It was a great grin, he decided. Kind of endearing.

'Yeah, great fat scooping.' She shook her head. 'Nope. These eggs… This bacon…'

'Home grown,' he told her. 'They're Donald's projects.'

'Donald?'

'I told you about him. He used to own this property. He got too old to run it; he sold it but the thought of leaving broke his heart. I offered him one of the shearers' cottages in return for keeping up the garden. He's been with me for ten years now, running a few of his precious pigs, caring for his hens and keeping my garden magnificent. Win-win for everyone.'

'Are the eggs free range too?' she asked.

'We lock 'em up at night. Which reminds me…' He headed for the sink, dumping his dishes. 'I need to go. Sleep well. Anything you need in the morning, help yourself. I'll be gone before dawn.'

'You start shearing before dawn?'

'The pens are already full for the dawn start but I'll run the south mob into the home paddock to refill the pens as the men work. But I'll be back here by about nine to make sandwiches.'

'*You're* making sandwiches?'

'Yeah.' He grimaced. 'That's all they're getting. But it

doesn't affect you. Just stay away from the sheds, that's all I ask. I don't like distractions.'

'I'm a distraction?'

He turned and looked at her. *Cute*, he thought again. *Definitely cute.*

Her poodle was at her feet. Most of the shearers had dogs.

Penny and Samson in the shearers' shed? No and no and no.

'Definitely a distraction. Stay away,' he growled, possibly more gruffly than he intended.

But she looked distracted now. She was frowning. 'You're making sandwiches?' she said again.

'Yes.'

'And you just said all you can do is sausages and boiling stuff.'

'I'll boil a couple of slabs of beef for lunch.'

The thought of it was almost overwhelming but who else would do it? Ron and Harv could be depended on to keep the sheep coming in and clear the pens but their cooking skills were zero. Donald was eighty-seven. That was his pool of workers.

He could imagine the reaction of the shearers if he went over there now and said: *Hey, do any of you cook? Care to swap jobs?*

But he was eyeing the woman at the table with caution. She'd known how to cook an egg. That was about twenty per cent of his cooking skill. Maybe...

But she drove a pink car. She had a poodle. She came from one of the richest families in Australia.

Ask.

'I employ a shearers' cook,' he told her. 'The best. Pete sent me lists. I have everything I need—except Pete. He's stuck on the far side of the floodwater.' He hesitated. 'So I'm stuck with cooking. But any help you could give me...'

'I'll cook.'

Silence.

I'll cook.

Two magic words.

'You can cook?'

'Don't sound so shocked. Why do you think I was heading for Malley's Corner?'

'You were going to Malley's to *cook*?' He couldn't keep the incredulity from his voice.

'What's wrong with that?' She glared. 'Just because my family's...'

'The richest family in Australia?'

'We're not. There are mining magnates richer than us.'

'Of course there are.'

'Don't be sarcastic. Besides, this has nothing to do with money. Though...' she considered '... I'm stuck here so I might as well make myself useful. Consider it payment for board.'

'Do you have any idea how hard it is to cook for a shearers' team?'

'You were going to do it.'

'Now you sound sarcastic.'

And she grinned. 'I do,' she conceded. 'But I can do better than sandwiches.'

'We have a team of twenty shearers, classers and roustabouts. Do you have any idea how much they eat?'

'I've cooked for hundreds.'

'*You*...'

'You say that like I'm some sort of amoebic slug,' she said carefully. 'Why shouldn't I cook? Why do you think Malley hired me?'

'Malley would employ anyone with a pulse. Come to think of it, rumour was that his last cook didn't have one.'

'Then he's about to be surprised. I even have qualifications.'

'You're kidding.'

'Only a basic apprenticeship,' she admitted. 'But I've done lots of cooking classes in amazing places. Mum and Dad approved of those.'

'I just read an article online,' he told her. A man had to be careful but he might as well say it. Not that he had a recruitment pool of hundreds but he needed to know what he was getting into. 'It described you as a PR assistant in your family corporation. It also said you were nursing a bruised ego and a broken heart.'

She froze. 'You checked up on me.'

'I did. About the broken heart bit. Your sister... I'm sorry...'

And all of a sudden the apologetic, polite blonde was transformed by temper.

'Don't you dare go there,' she snapped. 'I don't want sorry. Every one of my so-called friends are sorry, but not sorry enough to refuse an invitation to the massive wedding my parents are organizing right now. My father says a big function's important to show there's no family rift. So there's no family rift. Business as usual.'

He winced. 'That must hurt. Every major tabloid...'

'Is enjoying it very much.' She cut him off bitterly. 'But that's important how? Right now I'm offering to cook for you. Isn't there a Discrimination Act somewhere that says asking employees about their past appalling taste in men is illegal?'

'Are you applying for a job?'

'I might be,' she snapped. 'As long as you don't rake up my family. I've left them in Sydney and that's where they're staying. I like the fact that half of Australia is flooding between here and there. Do you like the fact that I can cook?'

There was no arguing with that. 'Yes.'

'So let's move on. Your shearers like sandwiches? Are you any better at making them than frying eggs?'

'Mine would be pretty basic sandwiches,' he admitted.

The grandfather clock in the hallway chimed eight. He should be gone, he thought. There was so much to do before dark.

But he had the offer of a cook.

She intrigued him. She was half perky, half defensive.

It sounded as if her family had cut her a raw deal and he'd seen enough of the tabloids to realize how widely her humiliation must have spread. She must be hurting a lot under her pink bravado.

What he wanted was to probe deeper into what was behind her blind run to Malley's. But then…this was personal and hadn't he learned a long time ago not to get personal with women? The last thing he needed was a wealthy blonde socialite sobbing on his chest while she spilt all.

And she was right. Her past had no bearing on her ability to cook.

She could probably only do fancy, he thought. Soufflés and caviar and truffles. But she *had* cooked a mean egg, which was more than he could do. And how could her cooking be worse than his efforts?

'If you really could…'

'I could try,' she told him, her glare fading. She looked as if she was sensing his train of thought. 'You can sack me if it doesn't work.' She smiled suddenly, and he thought she had a great smile. It lit her face.

It lit the room.

'Tell me what you need,' she said and he had to force himself to focus on something that wasn't that smile.

'Morning smoko, dinner and arvo tea. The shearers make their own breakfast and evening meal, but our dinner's midday, when we need a full, hot meal to keep going.

You have no idea how many calories a gun shearer burns. Are you really serious about helping?'

'I'm serious.'

'Okay.' He took a deep breath, seeing clear air where from the time he'd had the call from Pete he'd only seen fog. 'At ten you'd provide smoko—morning tea. You'd bring the food over to the shed. I'll come and help you carry it. Then at twelve-thirty they all come here for a buffet dinner and take it onto the veranda to eat. At three it's time for arvo tea and you take that to the shed as well. It saves time. You'd be expected to cook a couple of extra roasts and leave them in the shearer's quarters so they can use that as a base for their evening meal.'

'Wow,' she said and looked at the big stove. 'No wonder you have three ovens. Is there an instruction manual?'

'On the Internet.'

'You have Internet?'

'Yep. Satellite. I'll give you the password.'

She stood up and her smile widened until the defensiveness of moments ago disappeared entirely.

'You have no idea how good that makes me feel,' she told him. 'Half an hour ago I was trapped in the middle of nowhere feeling useless. Now I have a job and Internet and there's nothing more I need in the world. Right. You'd better put those chooks to bed and gather those sheep or whatever you have to do. Leave me be, Matt. I'm about to get busy.'

He'd been dismissed.

She was needed! She stood in the great kitchen and, for the first time since that appalling night when Brett and Felicity had appeared at the family dinner table hand in hand and smugly announced the new order of things, she felt as if she was standing on firm ground again.

A shearing team of twenty. Two weeks' hard work, she

thought with satisfaction. Two weeks when she could put her head down and forget that every tabloid in the country was running articles pitying her.

She'd be working for Matt.

Matt...

And suddenly her thoughts went off at a tangent. Matt. The way he'd said he was sorry. He'd said it...as if he understood. How was that possible? It had been a throwaway line, a platitude, something that had been said to her over and over before her family and her friends had moved on to the new normal.

But his eyes were kind.

And the rest of him...

Wow.

And that was enough to make her give herself a fast mental slap to the side of the head. What was she thinking? He was her new boss. He was the owner of this place, a guy who lived and breathed the land, a guy who'd practically lifted her car and heaved it out of the water.

She'd been brought up with suits. She'd never met anyone even vaguely like Matt.

He made her feel...breathless.

Oh, for heaven's sake. It had been less than a month since she'd been unceremoniously dumped by Brett. She'd thought she was in love, and look how that had turned out.

'I have no sense at all,' she told Samson. 'Okay, he might be good-looking enough to make my toes curl but my toes are not a good indicator. My father thinks I'm an idiot, and where men are concerned I've just proved him spectacularly right. I need to ignore Matt Fraser and get on with my job.'

She opened the pantry again and gazed at the contents in delight.

This place was like a miniature supermarket. Filled with hope, she headed out the back. A vegetable garden! Herbs!

Her head was spinning in all directions. What first?

She could make cupcakes for morning tea. No. She pulled herself up short. Cupcakes might seem girly and the last thing she needed was guys thinking her food was girly. Okay, lamingtons. Better. She could whip up a couple of sponges now and coat them first thing in the morning. Then maybe a couple of big frittatas for lunch, with salads from the gorgeous stuff in the garden and fresh crusty bread. She had an overnight bread recipe. She could start it now so it'd rise magnificently overnight.

She looked at the sacks of flour and realized that Matt had supplies for an army. This must be provisioning for the rest of the year.

She wasn't complaining.

Next? What had Matt called it…arvo tea? If they'd eaten a big lunch they wouldn't want much. Chocolate brownies?

'Let's go,' she told Samson and he wiggled his tail at the joy in her voice.

There hadn't been much joy lately but she was feeling it now.

And she had to ask herself—was it just a little bit because a guy called Matt Fraser would be sharing a house with her for the next two weeks?

Was it just a little bit because a guy called Matt Fraser had caused a tingle of something she couldn't put a name to?

'It has nothing to do with Matt,' she told Samson severely. 'It's only the fact that I'm a world away from ghastly Brett and smug Felicity, and I'm needed.'

And the fact that Matt was sexy as…

Surely that had nothing to do with anything at all?

He'd met her only hours before. She was a society princess in a pink car and she had nothing to do with his world.

So why was he still feeling her hand on his, the way her

body had seemed to melt into his as she'd edged him aside to stop him doing the unthinkable—flipping his eggs!

Why did it suddenly feel as if his world was tilting?

There was no reason at all, he told himself and headed out to make sure the hens were locked up for the night.

'Who is she?' It was Donald—caring for the chooks was his job. But increasingly Donald forgot. Age was beginning to fuddle him, but he didn't seem to notice that Matt double-checked on most things he did.

Donald had run this property alone for fifty years. He was a confirmed bachelor and to say he treated women as aliens would be an understatement. Penny's presence, it seemed, had shocked him to the core.

'I pulled her out of the creek,' Matt told him. 'She was taking a dumb shortcut. She's stuck here until the water goes down.'

'Stuck. Here.' Donald said the two words as if they might explode and Matt almost laughed. He thought of the ditzy little blonde in his kitchen and wondered if there was anything less scary.

Although there were scary elements. Like the way his body reacted to her.

Um...let's not go there.

'She can cook,' he told Donald as he shooed the last hen into the pen and started collecting the eggs. 'The shearers' cook is stuck on the far side of the floodwater. If she can keep the team happy...'

'She can cook!' Donald's mother had run off with a wool-buyer when Donald was seven. His opinion of women had been set in stone since.

He grinned. 'I hear some women can.'

Donald thought about it. 'Rufus seems to like her,' he conceded at last. 'I watched her scratch his ear so she can't be all bad. What's that bit of fluff she's got with her?'

'A poodle.'

'A poodle at Jindalee! What next?'

'I'm thinking of getting him to help drafting the mobs in the morning,' Matt said and Donald gave a crack of laughter.

'He might end up getting shorn himself. I wonder what the classer'd make of that fleece?' He grinned. 'So you've got a woman and a poodle in the homestead. Want to kip in my place for the duration?'

'That'd be a bit of overkill. I've put her in your old bedroom and you know I sleep at the other end of the house. I think we can manage.'

'Women reel you in.'

'That's eighty years of experience speaking?'

'Eighty years of keeping out of their way. Mark my words, boy, it's like a disease.'

'I've been married, had a kid and have the scars to prove it,' Matt said, his grin fading. 'I'm immune.'

'No one's immune.' Donald shook his head and gestured to the house with a grimy thumb. 'Don't you go in till she's safely in bed and leave before she wakes up. Have your cornflakes at my place.'

'I'll be careful,' Matt promised him and smiled, although suddenly for some reason he didn't feel like smiling.

He thought of Penny—maybe Donald's advice was wise.

Lifting eggs from the nesting boxes, he enjoyed, as he always did, the warmth, the miracle of their production. He'd never quite got over the miracle of owning this place. Of never being told to move on.

He found himself thinking of his mother, going from one disastrous love affair to another, dragging her son with her. He'd learned early that when his mother fell in love it meant disaster.

She'd left and finally he'd figured he didn't need her.

After that…his first farm, financial security, finally feeling he could look forward.

And then deciding he could love.

Darrilyn.

And there it was again—disaster. Because Darrilyn didn't want him. She wanted the things his money represented. Two minutes after they were married she was pushing him to leave the farm he loved, and when he didn't…

Yeah, well, that was old history now. He didn't need Darrilyn. He didn't need anyone. But Donald was right.

He needed to be careful.

CHAPTER FOUR

THEY LOOKED BEAUTIFUL.

Penny gazed at the table in satisfaction. She had two plates of lamingtons ready to go. She'd rolled her cakes in rich chocolate sauce, coated them in coconut and filled them with cream. She'd thought of the difficulties of plates and spoons over in the yard so she'd gone small, but she'd made two each to compensate.

She'd piled them in beautifully stacked pyramids. They looked exquisite.

But this wasn't a social event, she reminded herself. Two lamingtons might not be enough, so she made a few rounds of club sandwiches, bite-sized beauties. She cut them into four-point serves and set them on a plate in the lamingtons' midst. They looked great.

She glanced at the clock and felt a little swell of pride. She had the ovens hot for the frittatas for lunch. They were almost ready to pop in. She had fifteen minutes before smoko and she was totally in control.

Matt would walk in any minute.

And here he was. He looked filthy, his pants and open neck shirt coated in dust, his boots caked in…whatever, she didn't want to think about it. His face was smeared with dust and his hair plastered down with sweat. 'Hey. Nearly ready?'

She lifted her lamingtons for inspection. 'We can take them over now if you like.'

He glanced at the table and his gaze moved on. 'Where's the rest?'

'The rest?'

There was a pregnant pause. And then... 'This is all there is?'

'Two lamingtons, two points of sandwiches each. How much more...'

He swore and headed for the pantry, leaving a trail of filthy footsteps over her nice, clean kitchen floor.

Her kitchen. That was how she felt when she worked. This was her domain.

Um...not. Matt had flung open the pantry door and was foraging behind the flour sacks. He emerged with three boxes.

Charity sale Christmas cakes. Big ones.

'They hate them but they'll have to do,' he snapped. 'Help me chop them up. They'll stop work in half an hour and if this is all you have...'

'But there's plenty,' she stammered and he gave her a look that resembled—eerily—the one her father gave her all the time. Like: *You've been an idiot but what else could I expect?*

'This isn't your society morning tea,' he snapped, ripping cartons open. 'It's fuel. Grab a knife and help me.'

She was having trouble moving. This was supposed to be her domain, the kitchen, her food—and he was treating her like an idiot. She felt sick.

A memory came flooding back of the dinner a month ago. She and her parents in the family home, the mansion overlooking Sydney Harbour. It had been her birthday. She'd like a family dinner, she'd told them. Just her parents, her half-sister and her fiancé.

And she'd cooked, because that was what she loved to do. She'd cooked what Brett loved to eat—stylish, with expensive ingredients, the sort of meal her father would enjoy paying a lot of money for in a society restaurant. She'd worked hard but she thought she'd got it right.

She'd even made time to get her hair done and she was wearing a new dress. Flushed with success, she'd only been a little disconcerted when Brett was late. And Felicity... Well, her sister was always late.

And then they'd walked in, hand in hand. *'We're so sorry, Penny, but we have something to tell you...'*

Matt was already slicing the first cake but at her silence he glanced up. Maybe the colour had drained from her face. Maybe she looked how she felt—as if she was about to be sick. For whatever reason, he put the knife down.

'What?'

'I...'

'It's okay,' he told her, obviously making an effort to sound calm. 'They're very nice lamingtons but this isn't a society fund-raiser where everyone's spent the last three hours thinking about what to wear. Some of these guys have shorn forty sheep since they last ate, and they intend to do forty more before their next meal. Calories first, niceties second. Help me, Penny.' And then, as she still didn't move, he added, 'Please.'

And finally her stunned brain shifted back into gear. She shoved away the sour taste of failure that followed her everywhere.

Fuel. Hungry workers who'd been head down since dawn.

Cute little lamingtons? She must have been nuts.

What then? Hot. Filling. Fast.

She had it.

'Ramp the ovens up,' she snapped and headed for the freezer. 'All of them. High as you can go. And then wash your hands. I need help and you're not touching my food with those hands.'

'We don't have time...'

'We'll be ten minutes late. They have a choice of a late smoko or eating your disgusting cake. You choose.'

He could order her aside and chop up the fruitcake the team despised—or he could trust her.

He went for the second. He cranked up the ovens and headed for the wash house. Two minutes later he was back, clean at least to the elbows.

By the time he returned, Penny had hauled sheets of frozen pastry from the freezer and was separating them onto baking trays.

'Three ovens, six trays,' she muttered. 'Surely that'll feed them.' She indicated jars of pasta sauce on the bench. 'Open them and start spreading,' she told him. 'Not too thick. Go.'

Hang on. He was the boss. This was his house, his kitchen, his shearing team waiting to be fed. The sensible thing was to keep chopping fruitcake but Penny had suddenly transformed from a cute little blonde into a cook with power. With Matt as an underling.

Fascinated, he snagged the first jar and started spreading.

Penny was diving into the coolroom, hauling out mushrooms, salami, mozzarella. She didn't so much as glance at him. She headed to the sink, dumped the mushrooms under the tap and then started ripping open the salami.

'Aren't you supposed to wipe mushrooms?' he managed. To say he was bemused would be an understatement.

'In what universe do we have time to wipe mushrooms?' She hauled out a vast chopping board and, while the tap washed the mushrooms for her, she started on the salami. Her hands were moving so fast the knife was a blur. 'I could leave them unwashed but I have an aversion to dirt.' She gave herself half a second to glance with disgust at his boots. 'Even if you don't. You finished?'

'Almost.' He poured the last jar over the pastry and spread it to the edges. 'Done.'

'Then I want this salami all over them. Rough and thick—we have no time for thin and fancy.' She hauled the mushrooms out of the sink and dumped them on a couple of tea towels, flipping them over with the fabric to get most of the water out. World's fastest wash. 'Back in two seconds. I'm getting herbs.'

And she was gone, only to appear a moment later with a vast bunch of basil. 'Great garden,' she told him, grabbing another chopping board.

He was too stunned to answer.

They chopped side by side. There was no time, no need to talk.

And suddenly Matt found himself thinking this was just like the shearing shed. When things worked, it was like a well-oiled machine. There was a common purpose. There was urgency.

His knife skills weren't up to hers. In fact they were about ten per cent of hers. He didn't mind. This woman had skills he hadn't even begun to appreciate.

Wow, she was fast.

It was the strangest feeling. To have a woman in his kitchen. To have *this* woman in his kitchen.

She was a society princess with a pink car and a poodle and knife skills that'd do any master chef proud.

Her body brushed his as she turned to fetch more mushrooms and he felt...

Concentrate on salami, he told himself and it was a hard ask.

But three minutes later they had six trays of 'pizza' in the oven.

'The herbs go on when it comes out,' she told him.

'We won't have time to garnish...'

'Nothing goes out of my kitchen unless it's perfect,' she

snapped. She glanced at the clock. 'Right, it's nine minutes before ten. This'll take fifteen minutes to cook so I'll be exactly ten minutes late. I hope that's acceptable. Come back at eight minutes past and help me carry it over.'

He almost grinned. He thought of his shearing team. Craig was the expert there, and Matt was wise enough to follow orders. Did he have just such an expert in his kitchen?

'How can it be ready by then?' He must have sounded incredulous because she smiled.

'Are you kidding? I might even have time to powder my nose before I help you take it out there.'

Taking the food over to the shed was an eye-opener.

A campfire had been lit on the side of the shed. There were a couple of trestle tables and a heap of logs serving as seats. Three billies hung from a rod across the fire.

The fire was surrounded by men and women who looked as filthy as Matt—or worse.

One of the men looked up as Penny and Matt approached and gave a shrill, two-fingers-in-the-mouth whistle. 'Ducks on the pond,' he called and everyone stopped what they were doing and stared.

'Hey.' It was hard to tell the women from the men but it was a female voice. 'You idiot, Harry. Ducks on the pond's a stupid way of saying women are near the shed. What about Marg and me?'

'You don't count,' one of the shearers retorted. 'You gotta have t… I mean you gotta have boobs and legs to count. You and Margie might have 'em but they're hidden under sheep dung. Put you in a bikini, we'll give you the respect you deserve.'

'Yeah, classifying us as ducks. Very respectful.' One of the women came forward and took plates from Penny. 'Take no notice of them, sweetheart. I'm Greta, this is

Margie and the rest of this lot don't matter. If they had one
more neuron between them, it'd be lonely.' She glanced
down at the steaming piles of pizza. 'Wow! Great tucker.'

And then there was no more talk at all.

The food disappeared in moments. Penny stood and
watched and thought of the two frittatas she had ready to
go in the oven.

How long before the next meal?

But Matt had guessed her thoughts. He'd obviously seen
the pathetically small frittatas.

'There are a couple of massive hams in the cool room,'
he told her. 'We can use your pretty pies as a side dish for
cold ham and peas and potatoes. Penny, you saved my butt
and I'm grateful, but from now on it doesn't matter if it's
not pretty. At this stage we're in survival mode.'

And she glanced up at him and saw…sympathy!

The team had demolished the food and were heading
back to the shed. Matt was clearly needing to head back
too, but he'd stopped because he needed to reassure her.

He wanted to tell her it was okay to serve cold ham and
peas and potatoes.

She thought again of that dinner with her parents, the
joy, the certainty that all was right with her world, and
then the crashing deflation.

This morning's pizza had been a massive effort. To
serve quality food for every single meal would see her
exhausted beyond belief.

She *could* serve his horrid cold ham, she thought, but
that would be the equivalent of running away, as she'd run
away from Sydney. But there was nowhere to run now.

She braced her shoulders and took a deep breath, hauling herself up to her whole five feet three. Where were
stilettoes when a girl needed them?

'I'll have lun…dinner ready for you at twelve-thirty,'
she told him. 'And there won't be a bit of cold ham in sight.'

* * *

He should be back in the shed. These guys were fast—they didn't have the reputation of being the best shearing team in South Australia for nothing. The mob of sheep waiting in the pens outside was being thinned by the minute. He needed to get more in.

Instead he took a moment to watch her go.

She was stalking back to the house. He could sense indignation in the very way she held her shoulders.

And humiliation.

She'd been proud of her lamingtons.

They were great lamingtons, he conceded. He'd only just managed to snaffle one before they were gone. There was no doubt she could cook.

She'd pulled out a miracle.

He watched as she stopped to greet Donald's dog. She bent and fondled his ears and said something, and for some reason he wanted badly to know what it was.

She was wearing shorts and a T-shirt. Her bouncy curls were caught in a ponytail. The media thing he'd read yesterday said she was twenty-seven but she looked about seventeen.

'Hey, Matt...' It was Harv, yelling from the shed. 'You want to get the next mob in or will I?'

He shook himself. It didn't matter what Penny did or didn't look like. He needed to get to work. He'd have to knock off early to go and make sure she'd sliced enough ham. Could she guess how many spuds she had to cook?

He glanced at her again. She was heading up the veranda. She looked great in those shorts. Totally inappropriate for this setting but great. She'd squared her shoulders and she was walking with a bounce again. Rufus was following and for a weird moment he wouldn't mind doing the same.

* * *

Food. Fast. Right.

She stared at her two quiches and three sticks of bread dough doing their final rise in a sunbeam on the window ledge—an entrée for that mob, she thought. A snack.

The reason that pantry was packed... Yeah, she got it.

There were sides of lamb, pork and beef hung on great hooks in the coolroom. Whole sides.

She usually bought lamb boned out and butterflied, pork belly trimmed to perfection.

But she had done a butchering course. Once upon a time a two star chef who'd agreed to have her help in his kitchen had yelled it at her. 'You want to understand meat, you need to understand the basics.' He hadn't made her kill her own cow but she had handled slabs of meat almost as big as this.

But to cut it into roasts, marinade it, get it into an oven she didn't know...

'Not going to happen,' she muttered. 'But I reckon I could get chops cut and cooked in time. First, let's get the bread divided and pies baked, and then I'm going to tackle me a sheep.'

Matt didn't leave the shed until ten minutes before the team was due to head to the kitchen.

He was running late. With Penny's knife skills though, and now she knew how much they ate, surely she'd have plated enough?

He opened the kitchen door—and the smell literally stopped him in his tracks. He could smell cooked lamb, rich sauces, apple pies redolent with cinnamon and cloves. Fried onions, fried chicken? His senses couldn't take it all in.

He gazed around the kitchen in stupefaction. The warming plate and the top of the damped-down firestove were piled high with loaded dishes, keeping warm. There were rounds of crumbed lamb cutlets, fried chicken, slices of some sort of vegetable quiche that looked amazing. Jugs of steaming sauces. Plates of crusty rolls. A vast bowl of tiny potatoes with butter and parsley. Two—no, make that three—casseroles full of mixed vegetables. Was that a ratatouille?

And to the side there were steaming fruit pies, with great bowls of whipped cream.

'Do you think we still need the ham?' Penny asked demurely and he blinked.

This wasn't the same clean Penny. She was almost as filthy as he was, but in a different way. Flour seemed to be smudged everywhere. A great apricot-coloured smear was splashed down her front. The curls from her ponytail had wisped out of their band and were clinging to her face.

And once again came that thought... She looked adorable.

'I'm a mess,' she told him when he couldn't find the words to speak. 'The team'll be here in five minutes, right? If you want me to serve, I'll go get changed. Everything's ready.'

And it was. The team would think they'd died and gone to heaven.

'Or do you want me to disappear?' Penny added. 'Ducks on the pond, hey?'

'Ducks is a sexist label,' he told her. 'Harry's old school—Margie and Greta have spent the last couple of hours lecturing him on respect.' He grinned. 'But, speaking of respect... You, Penelope Hindmarsh-Firth, are a proper shearer's cook and there's no greater accolade. Don't get changed. What you're wearing is the uniform of hard work and the team will love you just the way you are.'

CHAPTER FIVE

THE TEAM KNOCKED off at five but Matt didn't. Matt owned the place. No one gave him a knock-off time. He and Nugget headed out round the paddocks, making sure all was well. Thankfully, the night was warm and still, so even the just-shorn sheep seemed settled. He returned to the homestead, checked the sheep in the pens for the morning and headed for the house.

Then he remembered the chooks; Donald hadn't fed them for a week now. He went round the back of the house and almost walked into Penny.

'All present and correct,' she told him. 'At least I think so. Fourteen girls, all safely roosted.'

'How did you know?'

'I saw you do it last night. I took a plate of leftovers down to Donald and saw they were still out. I don't know how you're coping with everything. You must be exhausted.'

'It's shearing time,' he told her simply. 'Every sheep farmer in the country feels like this. It only lasts two weeks.'

She eyed him sideways in the fading light. He waited for a comment but none came.

She'd changed again, into jeans and a windcheater. She looked extraordinarily young. Vulnerable.

Kind of like she needed protecting?

'Thank you for thinking of Donald.'

'He wouldn't come in with the shearers so I saved some

for him. I think he was embarrassed but he took it.' She hesitated a moment but then decided to forge on. 'Matt... he told me he had to put Jindalee on the market but it broke his heart. And then you came. You renovated the cottage for him, even extending it so he could fit in everything he loved. And he can stay here for ever. I think that's lovely, Matt Fraser.'

'It's a two-way deal,' Matt growled, embarrassed. 'Don knows every inch of this land. I'm still learning from him. And I bet he appreciated the food. How you had the time to make those slices...'

'For arvo tea?' She grinned. 'I even have the jargon right. There'll be cakes tomorrow, now I'm more organized.'

'I'll pay you.'

'I don't need...'

'I'd have paid Pete. A lot. You'll get what he was contracted for.'

'You're giving me board and lodging.'

'And you're feeding a small army. I know it's a mere speck in the ocean compared to the money your family has, but I need to pay you.'

'Why?'

'So I can yell at you?' He grinned. 'I haven't yet but you should hear the language in the sheds.'

'Margie and Greta don't mind?'

'They use it themselves. As an official shearers' cook, you're entitled as well.'

'Thank you. I think.'

He chuckled and they walked back to the house together. The night seemed to close in on them.

The moon was rising in the east. An owl was starting its plaintive call in the gums above their heads.

She was so close...

'There's a plate of food in the warming oven,' she said

prosaically and he gave himself a mental shake and tried to be prosaic back.

'There's no need. I could have cooked myself...'

'An egg?' She gave him a cheeky grin. 'After my lesson last night you might do better, but if you're hungry check what's in the oven first.'

'You're going to bed now?'

'If it's okay with you, I might sit on the veranda and soak up the night until I settle. It's been a crazy day and here's pretty nice,' she said diffidently.

'It is, isn't it?' He hesitated and then decided: *Why not?* 'Mind if I join you?'

'It's your house.'

'That's not what I asked.'

She stopped and looked up at him. Her gaze was suddenly serious. There was a long pause.

'No,' she said at last. 'I don't mind if you join me. I don't mind at all.'

She should go to bed. She shouldn't be sitting on the edge of the veranda listening to the owls—waiting for Matt.

Why did it seem dangerous?

It wasn't dangerous. He was her employer. Today had been a baptism of fire into the world of cooking for shearers and she needed downtime. He'd asked to join her—it was his veranda so how could she have said no?

She could change her mind even now and disappear.

So why wasn't she?

'Because I'm an idiot with men. The only guys I've ever dated have turned out to be focused on my family's money.' She said it out loud and Samson, curled up by her side, whined and looked up at her.

'But I do a great line in choosing dogs,' she told him, and tucked him onto her knee and fondled his ears. 'That's my forte. Dogs and cooking.'

He still looked worried—and, strangely, so was she. Because Matt Fraser was coming to join her on the veranda?

'He's my employer,' she told Samson. 'Nothing else. He could be a seventy-year-old grandpa with grandchildren at heel for all the difference it makes. I'm over men. Matt's my boss, and that's all.'

So why were warning signals flashing neon in her brain?

Leftovers? He stared at the plate incredulously. These were some leftovers!

The midday meal had been crazy. For the shearers it was a break, a time where they stopped and had a decent rest. They'd come in and seen Penny's food and basically fallen on it like ravenous wolves. Then they'd settled on the veranda to enjoy it.

Meanwhile, Matt had grabbed a couple of rolls and headed back to the shed. The shearers' break was his only chance to clear the place and get it ready for the next hard session.

Shearing was exhausting. He'd been supervising it since he was a teenager and he'd never become used to it. Even when Pete was here, the best shearers' cook in the district, Matt usually ended up kilos lighter by the end of the shear. He'd come in after dark and eat what he could find, which generally wasn't much. Shearers didn't leave much.

But Penny must have noticed, for in the warming drawer was a plate with all the best food from midday.

It hadn't been sitting in the oven all afternoon either. She must have guessed he'd come in at dark, or maybe she'd asked one of the men.

He poured himself a beer, grabbed his plate and headed out to the veranda. He settled himself on one of the big cane settees. Penny was in front of him, on the edge of the veranda, her legs swinging over the garden bed below.

'Thank you,' he said simply.

'You're welcome.'

Silence. It wasn't an uncomfortable silence though. Matt was concentrating on the truly excellent food and Penny seemed content just to sit and listen to the owl and swing her legs. She was idly petting her dog but Samson seemed deeply asleep.

Samson had spent the day investigating chooks, making friends with the farm dogs and checking out the myriad smells of the place. This afternoon he'd even attempted a bit of herding but some things were never going to work. Matt had plucked him from the mob, hosed him down and locked him in the kitchen with Penny.

There'd be worse places to be locked, Matt thought idly, and then thought *whoa*, Penny was his shearers' cook. It was appropriate to think of her only as that.

'So where did you learn to cook?' he asked as he finally, regretfully finished his last spoonful of pie.

'Not at my mother's knee,' she said and he thought about stopping there, not probing further. But there was something about the night, about this woman...

'I'd have guessed that,' he told her. 'The article I read... It doesn't suggest happy families.'

'You got it.'

'So...cooking?'

She sighed. 'My family's not exactly functional,' she told him. 'You read about Felicity? She's my half-sister. Her mother's an ex-supermodel, floating in and out of Felicity's life at whim. My mother was Dad's reaction to a messy divorce—and, I suspect, to his need for capital. Mum was an heiress, but she's a doormat and the marriage has been...troubled. To be honest, I don't think Dad even likes Mum any more but she won't leave him. And my sister... Even though Mum's been nothing but kind to Felicity, Felicity barely tolerates Mum, and she hates me.

My life's been overlaid with my mother's mantras—avoid Felicity's venom and keep my father happy at all costs. So my childhood wasn't exactly happy. The kitchen staff were my friends.'

'So cooking became your career?'

'It wasn't my first choice,' she admitted. 'I wanted to be a palaeontologist. How cool would that have been?'

'A…what?'

'Studier of dinosaurs. But of course my father didn't see a future in it.'

'I wonder why not?'

'Don't you laugh,' she said sharply. 'That's what he did. I was the dumpy one, the one who hated my mother's hairdresser spending an hour giving me ringlets, the one who'd rather be climbing trees than sitting in the drawing room being admired by my parents' friends. And then, of course, I was expelled from school…'

'Expelled?' He'd been feeling sleepy, lulled by the night, the great food, the fatigue—and this woman's presence. Now his eyes widened. 'Why?'

'Quite easy in the end,' she told him. 'I don't understand why I didn't think of it earlier. I didn't mind being expelled in the least. It was boarding school—of course— the most elite girls' school my father could find. But I wasn't very…elite.'

She kicked her legs up and wiggled her bare toes in front of her and he could see how she might not be described as elite.

She wasn't elite. She was fascinating.

'I hated it,' she told him bluntly. 'I was there to be turned into a young lady. We had a whole afternoon every week of deportment, for heaven's sake. We learned to climb in and out of a car so no one can catch a sight of knickers.'

'Really?'

'It sounds funny,' she told him. 'It wasn't. I learned to

wrangle a purse, a cocktail and an oyster at the same time, but it's a skill that's overrated.'

'I guess it could be.' She had him entranced. 'So...'

'So?'

'Expulsion? Explain.'

'Oh,' she said and grinned. 'That was our annual ball. Very posh. We invited the local Very Elite Boys' School. Deportment classes gave way to dancing lessons and everyone had Very Expensive new frocks. And hairstyles. It was the culmination of the school year.'

'So...'

'So you might have noticed I'm little,' she told him. 'And...well endowed?'

'I hadn't,' he told her and she choked.

'Liar. I'm a size D cup and it's the bane of my life. But my mother bought me a frock and she was so delighted by it I didn't have the heart to tell her I hated it. It was crimson and it was low-cut, with an underwire that pushed everything up.'

He had the vision now. He blinked. 'Wow.'

'My mother's willowy,' she said, with just a trace of sympathy for a woman who'd never understood her daughter's figure. 'It would have looked elegant on Mum, but on me? It just made me look like a tart, and it got attention.' She paused for breath. 'Rodney Gareth was a horrid little toad, but sadly he was also the son of Malcolm Gareth QC, who's a horrid big toad. Rodney asked me to dance. He held me so tight my boobs were crushed hard against him. He swaggered all over the dance floor with me and I could feel his...excitement. I could hear the other girls laughing. And then...'

She fell silent for a moment and he thought she was going to stop. 'And then?' It'd kill him if he didn't get any further, he thought, but she relented.

'We all had these dinky little dance programmes, with

pencils attached,' she said. 'And, before I could stop him, he pulled mine from my wrist and held it up, pretending to check for my next free dance. And then he deliberately dropped the pencil down my cleavage.'

'Uh oh,' he said.

'Uh oh is right,' she said bitterly. 'I was standing in the middle of the dance floor and suddenly he shoved his whole hand down there. And people started laughing...'

'Oh, Penny.'

'So I kneed him right where it hurt most,' she said. 'I used every bit of power I had. I still remember his scream. It was one of the more satisfying moments of my life but of course it didn't last. I felt sick and cheap and stained. I walked out of the ball, back to my dorm, ripped my stupid dress off and called a cab to take me home. And don't you dare laugh.'

'I never would.' He hesitated. 'Penny... Did your parents laugh?'

'They were appalled. Mum was horrified. She could see how upset I was. But Dad? The first thing he did was ring Rodney's parents to find out if he was okay. His father told Dad they weren't sure if I'd interfered with the Gareth family escutcheon. He said they were taking him to hospital to check—I hadn't, by the way—and they intended to sue. Then the headmistress rang and said I wasn't welcome back at the school. Dad was furious and Mum's never had the nerve to stand up to him.'

'So what happened?'

'So I was packed off to Switzerland to a finishing school. That pretty much knocked any idea of being a palaeontologist on the head but, on the other hand, they ran cooking classes because that was supposed to be seemly, and if I wanted to do five cooking classes a week that was okay by them. So we had Monsieur Fromichade who I promptly fell in love with, even though I was sixteen and he was sixty. We still exchange recipes.'

'So happy ever after?'

She grimaced. 'It worked for a while. I took every cooking course I could and that was okay. Dad approved of what he told his friends were my three star Michelin intentions. Finally I took a job as an apprentice in a London café. It was simple food, nothing epicure about it. But I loved it.'

She paused, seemingly reluctant to expose any more of her family's dirty linen, but then she shrugged and continued. 'But then things fell apart at home.' She sighed. 'My sister had been overseas for years. There were rumours circulating about her behaviour on the Riviera and somehow Dad made it all Mum's fault. He's always favoured Felicity and he blamed Mum for her leaving home. Then Grandma died and Mum…got sick. Depression. She started phoning every day, weeping, begging me to come home. Finally I caved. I came home and Mum was in such a state I was frightened. I even agreed to what my Dad wanted, for me to be a company PR assistant. I thought I'd do it for a while, just until Mum recovered.'

She shrugged again. 'And it worked for a while. With me around to stand up for her, Dad stopped being such a bully. That took the pressure off Mum and things looked better. For Mum, though, not for me. And then Brett decided to court me.'

'Brett?' He shouldn't ask but how could he help it?

'It seems every guy I've ever dated has turned out to be fascinated by my parents' money,' she said bluntly. 'So I should have known. But maybe I was vulnerable, too. Brett's yet another toad, but I was too dumb and, to be honest, I was too unhappy and caught up in family drama to see it. I hadn't realized until I got home how close to the edge Mum was, and I was scared. I was trying every way I knew to make her feel good. Brett's a financial guru, smart, savvy and he knows how to pander to Dad. He's also good-looking and oh, so charming. In those awful months Brett helped. He honestly did. You have no idea how charming he was. He made me feel…special, and when he asked me to marry him I was dumb enough to say yes.'

'So celebrations all round?'

'You think?' she said bitterly. 'You know, the moment I said yes I had my doubts but I'm my mother's daughter. Dad was happy. Mum was well. For a while it was happy families all round. But then Felicity returned and Brett realized Felicity was Dad's absolute favourite and he could be part of our family and not have to sacrifice himself with the dumpy one.'

'Humiliation piled on humiliation,' he said softly and she cast him a glance that was almost scared.

'Yeah. I was paying too big a price to keep people happy and I've realized it. I'm over it.'

'I'm sure you're not.'

And she managed a smile. 'Maybe not quite, but I will be after a year's cooking at Malley's.'

'You can't go there.'

'When the water goes down, of course I can.'

'You'll hate it. The last time Malley set a mouse trap… Well, I've never seen one. What I have seen are dead mice.'

'Ugh!'

'Everywhere. He baits them and doesn't bother to clean.

'I can clean,' she said in a small voice.

'I bet you can but you shouldn't have to. Don't Mummy and Daddy supply you with enough money to be fancy-free?'

'That's offensive.'

'True.'

'Okay,' she conceded. 'Dad holds the purse strings but a legacy from Grandma left me basically independent. Not rich, but okay. Eventually I might set up a catering company in Adelaide or in Brisbane, but for now I need time to get my head together. I need to be as far from Sydney as possible.'

'Which is why you headed into the outback in *that* car?'

Now she grinned. 'Isn't it fun? Dad probably wants it back, though. He gave it to me when Brett and I got engaged. With a huge pink ribbon on it. I was momentarily the golden girl.'

'Shall we take it back to the creek and launch it? Let it float ceremoniously a few hundred miles to the ocean?'

She stared. 'Pardon?'

'We could take pictures of it floating out of sight and send them to your father. Very symbolic.'

She choked. 'Dad'd have a stroke. To say he's careful is an understatement.'

'But not careful of his daughter,' Matt said, his voice softening.

'Don't.'

'Don't what?'

'Get sympathetic. I'm fine as long as no one minds.'

'So no one minds?'

'No,' she said fiercely. 'No one at all. That last awful dinner, when Brett and Felicity walked in hand in hand, Mr and Mrs Smug... I was too gobsmacked to yell and Mum didn't have the strength to stand up for me. But I guess that was my line in the sand. I can't help Mum and I won't keep trying to please my father. And in a way it's liberating. I've walked away. I'm free.'

Then she paused. The night stilled and he thought of what he should say next.

But she got there before him.

'So what about you?' she asked.

He'd finished his beer. He was tired beyond belief. He should pick up his dishes and head via the kitchen to bed.

'What do you mean, what about me?'

'Who minds?' she asked. 'That's what you asked me. Who cares, Matt Fraser? You live here by yourself. No girlfriend? Boyfriend? Whatever?'

'I have a…' he said slowly, and then he paused. He didn't want to talk about Lily.

But this woman had just opened herself to him. She might say she was free, she was over being hurt, but he knew vulnerable when he saw it.

She'd trusted him with her story. How mean would it be not to give the same to her?

He tried again. 'I have a daughter,' he told her. 'Lily's thirteen years old and lives in the States with my ex-wife.'

She'd been gazing out over the farmland but now she swivelled to stare at him. He hadn't turned the porch lights on, but the moonlight and the light filtering from inside the windows was enough for her to see.

Not that he wanted her to see. He wanted his face to be impassive.

Which was pretty much how he wanted to be when he thought of Lily.

'Thirteen! You must have been a baby when she was born,' she stammered and he thought: *Yep, that just about summed it up.*

'I was twenty-four.'

'Wow.' She was still staring. 'So your wife took Lily back to the States. Isn't that hard to do? I mean…did you consent?'

'Darrilyn met an investment banker, coming to investigate…a project I was working on. He was rich, he lived in New York, she was fascinated and he offered her a more exciting life than the one she had with me. She was also four months pregnant. When you leave Australia with your child, the child needs the permission of both parents. When you're pregnant no one asks.'

'Oh, Matt…'

'It's okay,' he said, even though it wasn't. 'I have the resources to see her a couple of times a year.'

'Does she look like you?'

And, for some reason, that shook him.

The guys on the farm knew he had a daughter—that was the reason he took off twice a year—but that was as far as it went. When had he ever talked about his daughter? Never.

'I guess she does,' he said slowly. 'She has my black hair. My brown eyes. There's no denying parentage, if that's what you mean.'

'I guess. I didn't mean anything,' she whispered. 'I'm just thinking how hard it would be to leave her there.' She gave herself a shake, a small physical act that said she was moving on from something that was clearly none of her business. But it seemed she did have more questions, just not about Lily.

'So you,' she said. 'I've told you all about my appalling family. Your mum and dad?'

'Just mum.' Why was he telling her this? He should excuse himself and go to bed. But he couldn't. She was like a puppy, he thought, impossible to kick.

Or was there more? The need to talk? He never talked but he did now.

'This farm,' she was saying. 'I assumed you'd inherited it.'

'Sort of.'

'So rich mum, hey?'

'The opposite.' He hated talking about it but he forced himself to go on. 'Mum had me when she was eighteen and she had no support. I was a latchkey kid from early on, but we coped.' He didn't say how they'd coped. What use describing a childhood where he'd been needed to cope with his mother's emotional messes?

'Give me a hug, sweetheart. Sorry, I can't stop crying. Can you go out and buy pies for tea? Can you go down to the welfare and say Mummy's not well, we need money for food? But say I've just got the flu... I don't want them sticking their noses in here...'

He shook himself, shoving back memories that needed to be buried. Penny was waiting for him to go on.

'When I was twelve Mum took a housekeeping job about five hundred miles inland from Perth,' he told her. 'Sam Harriday was an eighty-year-old bachelor. He'd worked his parents' farm on his own for years and was finally admitting he needed help. So off we went, to some-where Mum hoped we'd be safe.'

'Safe?'

'Sorry.' He caught himself, but now he'd said it he had to explain. A bit. 'There were parts of Mum's life that weren't safe.'

She was silent at that, and he thought she'd probe. He didn't want her to but he'd asked for it. But when she spoke again she'd moved on. Maybe she'd sensed his need for barriers. 'Good for your mum,' she told him. 'But so far inland... You were twelve? How did you go to school?'

'School of the Air.' He shrugged and smiled at the mem-ory of his not very scholastic self. 'Not that I studied much. I took one look at the farm and loved it. And Sam...' He hesitated. 'Well, Sam was a mate. He could see how hun-gry I was to learn and he taught me.'

'But—' she frowned, obviously trying to figure the whole story '—this isn't his farm?'

'It's not,' he told her. 'Cutting a long story short, when I was fifteen Mum fell for a biker who got lost and asked for a bed. She followed him to the city but Sam offered to let me stay. So I did. I kept up with School of the Air until I was seventeen but by then I was helping him with everything. And I loved it. I loved him. He died when I was twenty-two and he left me everything.' He shrugged. 'An inheritance seems great until you realize what comes with it. The death of someone you love.'

'I'm sorry...'

'It's a while back now and it was his time,' he said, but he paused, allowing a moment for the memories of the old man he'd loved. Allowing himself to remember again the pain that happened when he'd been needed so much, and suddenly there was no one.

'So the farm was mine,' he managed, shaking off memories of that time of grief. It was rough country, a farm you had to sweat to make a living from, but it did have one thing going for it that I hadn't realized. It was sitting on a whole lot of bauxite. That's the stuff used to make aluminium. Apparently geologists had approached Sam over the years but he'd always seen them off. After he died one of them got in touch with me. We tested and the rest is history.'

'You own a bauxite mine?' she said incredulously and he laughed.

'I own a great sheep property. This one. I own a couple more properties down river—economies of scale make it worthwhile—but this place is my love. I also own a decent share of a bauxite mine. That was what got me into trouble, though. It's why Darrilyn married me, though I was too dumb to see it. But I'm well over it. My current plan is to make this the best sheep station in the state, if not the country, and the fact that I seem to have hauled the best shearers' cook I can imagine out of the creek is a bonus.'

He smiled and rose, shaking off the ghosts that seemed to have descended. 'Enough. If I don't go to bed now I'll fall asleep on top of a pile of fleece tomorrow. Goodnight, Penny.'

She stood up too, but she was still frowning. 'The mine,'

she said. 'Bauxite… Sam Harriday… It's not Harriday Holdings?'

'That's the one.'

'Oh, my,' she gasped. 'Matt, my father tried to invest in that mine. He couldn't afford to.'

'The shares are tightly held.'

'By you?'

'Mostly.'

She stood back from him and she was suddenly glaring. 'That must make you a squillionaire.'

'I told you I'd pay you. Now you know I can afford to. And I doubt I'm a squillionaire.' He shrugged. 'I don't even know what one is. And, by the way, I'd appreciate it if you didn't broadcast it. The locals don't know and I have no idea why I told you.'

'Because it's our night for secrets?' She hesitated and then reached out to touch his hand. 'Matt?'

He looked down at her hand on his. It looked wrong, he thought. This was a gesture of comfort and he didn't need comfort. Or maybe she intended to ask a question that needed it.

'Yes?' That was brusque. He tried again and got it better. 'Yes?'

'Where's your mother now?'

How had she guessed? he thought incredulously. How had she seen straight through his story to the one thing that hurt the most?

'Dead.'

'I'm sorry. But something tells me…'

'Don't!'

She hesitated and then her hand came up and touched his cheek, a feather-touch, a fleeting gesture of warmth.

'I won't ask but I'm sorry,' she whispered. 'And I'm even more sorry because…you might be a squillionaire, but something tells me that all the whinging I've just done doesn't come close to the pain you're hiding. Thank you for rescuing me yesterday, Matt Fraser. I just wish I could rescue you right back.'

CHAPTER SIX

IF EVER THERE was a cure for humiliation piled on humiliation, it was ten days of cooking for shearers. Ten days of pure hard work.

'We've only two more mobs left,' Matt told her with satisfaction. 'That's four days shearing and we're done. We've had the best weather. The best food. The best shear I've ever organised. You're our good luck charm, Penny Hindmarsh-Firth. I've a good mind to keep you.'

Matt hadn't stopped for ten days, Penny thought. He'd worked until after midnight almost every night. He said he went to bed but she saw his light at the far end of the veranda.

She had his situation pretty much summed up by now. Five sheep properties. A bauxite mine worth heaven only knew how much. Responsibilities everywhere.

The drapes in his bedroom were often pulled back. She could see his shadow against the light, sitting at his desk, working into the night.

He had a massive desk in his study. He wasn't using that.

Because she was here? She knew it was, but he wasn't avoiding her.

They'd fallen into a routine. Matt left the house before dawn, she saw him only briefly at meals but at dusk she sat on the veranda and talked to the dogs and he'd finally fetch his plate of leftovers from the warming drawer and come out to join her.

He was always dead tired. She could hear it in his voice, in the slump of his shoulders. Sometimes he seemed almost too tired to talk and she respected that, but still he seemed to soak up her company. And for herself? She liked him being here too, and she didn't need to talk. She was content to sit and watch the moon rise over the horizon, to breathe in the night air and let go of her fast-paced day.

And it was fast-paced. She'd set herself a personal challenge. Each day's cooking had to be at least as good as the days' before. It was worth it. 'Great tucker,' a shearer growled as he headed back to work. Or, 'Strewth, Pen, that sponge's almost as good as my gran used to make.'

And Matt had nothing but praise. 'I'd have pulled a rhinoceros out of the creek to get cooking like this,' he'd told her after the first couple of days and she had no idea why that throwaway line had the capacity to make her feel as if her insides were glowing.

The way he ate her food at night was compliment enough. He was always past exhaustion but he sat and savoured her food as if every mouthful was gold. He was enjoying his dinner now, as she sat and watched the moon rise.

She thought about the way he'd smiled at her when she'd handed him his plate. Somehow he didn't feel like an employer. She wasn't sure what he felt like, but...

'Malley doesn't know what he's getting.' Matt's low growl from where he sat behind her made her jump. She'd been dreaming. Of a smile?

Idiot!

She didn't answer. There was nothing to say to such a compliment. There was no reason his comment should have her off balance.

Though, actually, there was.

There were four more days of shearing to go. The floodwaters were slowly going down. She could probably leave now, though it'd still be a risk. And Matt still needed her.

But in four days…

'You are still going to Malley's?' Matt asked and she tried to think of a way to say it, and couldn't.

But he guessed. Maybe her silence was answer enough. 'You've changed your mind?' Matt put his empty plate aside and came across to where she sat on the edge of the veranda. He slipped down beside her and the night seemed to close in around them, a warm and intimate space that held only them.

What was she thinking? *Intimate?* He was her boss!

He was a man and she didn't trust herself with men. Didn't they always want something? Something other than her? Even Matt. He needed her to cook. She was useful, nothing else.

So stop thinking of something else.

'Malley changed my mind,' she managed, and was disconcerted at the way her voice worked. Or didn't work. Why were emotions suddenly crowding in on her?

And it wasn't just how close Matt was sitting beside her, she thought. It was more. In four days she wouldn't be needed. Again.

Wasn't that what she wanted?

Oh, for heaven's sake, get over it, she told herself and swung her feet in an attempt at defiance.

As if sensing his mistress needed a bit of support, Samson edged sideways and crept up onto her knee. He was filthy but she didn't mind. Penny had given up on the bathing. Samson was now a farm dog.

If her mother could see her now she'd have kittens, Penny thought. She was filthy too, covered in the flour she'd used to prepare the bread dough for the morning. She was cradling a stinking poodle.

But Matt was sitting by her side and she thought, *I don't*

*care. Mum has Felicity if she wants a beautiful daughter.
I'm happy here.*

It was a strange thought—a liberating thought. She tried
to think of Brett. Or Felicity. Of the two of them hand in
hand telling her they'd betrayed her.

They can have each other, she thought, and it was the
first time she'd felt no bitterness.

Ten days of shearing had changed things. Ten days of
sitting outside every night with Matt? But there were only
four days to go.

'You going to tell me about Malley?' Matt asked. He'd
given her time. He'd sensed there were things she was coming to terms with, but now he was asking again.

What had she told him? *Malley changed my mind.*

Yeah, he had, and she'd been upset and she should still
be upset. But how hard was it to be angry when she was
sitting with this man whose empathy twisted something
inside her that she hadn't known existed.

'I phoned Malley the night I got here,' she admitted.
'He told me I was a…well, I won't say what he said but the
gist of it was that I was a fool for taking the route I did and
he was an idiot himself for thinking a citified b…a citified woman could do the job. He said he'd find someone
else. He called me a whole lot of words I'd never heard of.
I guess I was pretty upset so when he rang back and expected me to drop everything…'

And then she stopped. She hadn't meant to say any
more. What was it about this man that messed with her
head? That messed with the plan of action she knew was
sensible?

'Drop everything?' he said slowly, and she thought *uh
oh*. She went to get up but he put his hand on her arm and
held her still. 'You mean abandon this place?' He was
frowning. 'Is that what he meant?'

'He rang me back two days after I got here,' she admitted. 'But it's okay. I used a few of his words back at him. Not…not the worst ones. But maybe the ones about being an idiot for ever thinking I'd take the job.'

'But why did he ring?'

This was sort of embarrassing. She'd been dumb to say anything at all but Matt was watching her. He was frowning, obviously thinking through the words she'd let slip. She had no choice but to be honest.

'He ended up almost as trapped as we are, so finding another cook wasn't an option,' she told him. 'And it's costing him. Malley's hotel is the base for scores of stranded tourists. He has supplies but no one to cook. He's losing a fortune.'

'So?' Matt said slowly.

'So he knows one of the chopper pilots who's doing feed drops up north. I gather for two days he fumed at how useless I was and then he realized he didn't have a choice. So he bribed the chopper pilot to come and get me.'

There was a loaded silence.

'So why didn't you go?'

'You told me he had mice.'

'And you told me you could clean.'

'So I could,' she said with sudden asperity. 'But I didn't see why I should clean for someone with such a foul mouth. The tourists can cook for themselves if they need to. Why should I go?'

'But you came all the way here to take a permanent, full-time job.'

'I did.'

'And shearing finishes in four days.' He frowned. 'Why didn't you accept? I don't understand.'

And she didn't, either. Not totally. It had been a decision of the heart, not the head, but she wasn't about to tell him that.

She reverted to being practical. 'The chopper pilot was

supposed to be dropping food to stranded livestock, so what was he about, agreeing to pick me up? How could I live with myself knowing cows were hungry because of me? Besides, they couldn't fit my car into the chopper.'

'You were the one who suggested leaving your car here until after the floods.'

Drat, why did he have to have such a good memory?

'So why?' he asked again, more gently, and suddenly there seemed nothing left but the truth.

'You needed me,' she told him. 'And...'

'And?'

Her chin tilted. This was something her family never got. Her friends never got. She'd been mocked for this before but she might as well say it. 'I was having fun.'

'Fun?' He stared at her in amazement. 'You've worked harder than any shearer. You've planned, you've cooked, you've cleaned. You've gone to bed as exhausted as me every night and you've got up every morning and started all over again. You call that fun?'

'Yes.' She said it firmly. It was a stand she'd defended for years and she wasn't letting it go now. Cooking was her love, and cooking for people who appreciated it was heaven. 'But you needn't sound so amazed. Tell me why you're here. You own a bauxite mine, one of the richest in the country. You surely don't need to farm. You're working yourself into the ground too. For what?'

'Fun?' he said and she smiled.

'Gotcha.'

'Okay.' He sighed. 'I get it, though I'm imagining the work at Malley's would have been just as hard. So where do you go from here? You knocked back a permanent job to help me.'

'I knocked back a permanent job because I wanted this one. And, even without the mice, Malley sounds mean.'

'The man's an imbecile,' Matt said. 'To bad-mouth a

cook of your standard? He obviously has the brains of a newt. To lose you...'

And then he paused.

The atmosphere changed. That thing inside her twisted again. To have someone defend her...value her...

It's the cooking, she told herself. She was never valued for herself.

But suddenly his hand was covering hers, big and rough and warm. 'Thank you,' he told her and it sounded as if it came from the heart. 'Thank you indeed—and I think your wages just went up.'

Fun.

He thought of the massive amount of work she'd put in over the last ten days. He thought of the drudgery of planning, chopping, peeling, cooking and cleaning. He thought of the mounds of washing-up. How had he ever thought he could handle it himself? In the end he'd hardly had time to help her cart food across to the shed, but she hadn't complained once.

She was a pink princess, the daughter of one of the wealthiest families in Australia, yet she'd worked as hard as any shearer.

And in four days? Shearing would be over. The water was already dropping in the creeks. Cooking at Malley's was obviously out of the question. Penny's long-term plan to set up a catering company would take months. Meanwhile, what would she do?

She'd come a long way to be here, and she'd come for a reason. She'd exposed her pain to him. She'd exposed the hurt her family had heaped on her. She was here to escape humiliation—and now, because she'd decided to help him she had little choice but to head back and face that humiliation again. Even if she went to another city the media would find her. He had no doubt the media frenzy during her sister's wedding would be appalling.

'Stay for a bit,' he found himself saying. Until the words were out of his mouth he didn't know he'd intended to say them, but the words were said. He'd asked the pink princess to stay.

There was a moment's silence. Actually, it was more than a moment. It stretched on.

She was considering it from all angles, he thought, and suddenly he wondered if she was as aware as he was of the tension between them.

Tension? It was the wrong word but he didn't have one to replace it. It was simply the way she made him feel.

She was little and blonde and cute. She played Abba on her sound system while she worked and she sang along. This morning he'd come in to help her cart food over to the shed and found her spinning to *Dancing Queen* while balancing a tray of blueberry muffins. She'd had flour on her nose, her curls had escaped the piece of pink ribbon she'd used to tie them back and Samson was barking at her feet with enthusiasm.

He'd stopped at the door and watched, giving himself a moment before she realized he was there. He'd watched and listened and he'd felt...

It didn't matter how he'd felt. He didn't *do* women. His mother and then Darrilyn had taught him everything he needed to know about the pain of relationships and he wasn't going there again. Especially with an indulged society princess.

The label wasn't fair, he told himself, and he knew it was the truth. Penny had proved she was so much more. But past pain had built armour he had no desire to shed, and right now he felt his armour had to be reinforced. Yet here he was asking her to stay.

'Why would I stay?' Penny asked cautiously and he tried to think of an answer that was sensible.

'I… This place… I was thinking maybe I could open it up a bit. Get rid of a few dustcovers. There's a possibility my daughter might come and visit.' That was the truth, though he wasn't sure when. 'I wouldn't mind if it looked a bit more like a home when she came. Maybe you could help. I'd pay.'

'I don't need…'

'I know you don't need to be paid,' he said. 'But I pay for services rendered. The shearers will move on, but I'd need you for another two weeks in total—a few days' slack then getting the house in order. Of course—' he grinned suddenly '—cooking would be in there as well. Donald and Ron and Harv would kill me if I didn't say that. They've been in heaven for the last ten days.'

And then he paused and tried to think about why he shouldn't say what came next. There were reasons but they weren't strong enough to stop him. 'And so have I,' he added.

Heaven…

That was pretty much what she was feeling.

She was breathing in the scents from the garden, watching the moon rise over the distant hills, listening to the odd bleat of a sheep in the shearing pens and the sound of a bird in the gums at the garden's edge.

'What's the bird?' she asked. It was an inconsequential question, a question to give her space and time to think through what he was proposing. There was a part of her that said what he was suggesting was unwise, but she couldn't figure out why.

Or maybe she knew why; she just didn't want to admit it. The way he made her feel… The way his smile made her heart twist…

'It's a boobook owl,' Matt said, quietly now, as if there was no big question between them. 'It's a little brown owl, nocturnal. He and his mate are the reason we don't have mice and places like Malley's do. Malley's stupid enough to have cleared the trees around the hotel and he's probably even stupid enough to shoot them. They're great birds. Listen to their call. *Boobook*. Or sometimes people call them mopokes for the same reason. So there's a question for you. Do you side with mopoke or boobook?'

It was an ideal question. It gave her time to sit and listen, to settle.

'Mopoke,' she said at last. 'Definitely mopoke.'

'I'm a boobook man myself. Want to see?'

'You need to go to bed.'

'So do you, but life's too short to miss a boobook.'

'A mopoke.'

He grinned. 'That's insubordination,' he told her. 'I believe I've just offered you a job for the next two weeks. Therefore I demand you accept your boss's edict that it's a boobook.'

'I haven't agreed to take the job yet.'

'So you haven't,' he said equitably. 'But you are still employed for four more days. So it's boobook tonight.' He pushed himself to his feet and held out his hand to help her up. 'Come and see.'

She looked at his offered hand and thought… *I shouldn't.*

And then she thought: *Why not?* There were all sorts of reasons, but Matt was smiling down at her and his hand was just there.

She shouldn't take it—but she did.

What was he doing?

He was more than tired. By this stage in shearing he was operating on autopilot. He'd averaged about five hours of sleep a night for the past ten days and, apart from the tiny window of time on the veranda at night, every minute he was awake was crammed with imperatives. Most of those imperatives involved tough manual labour but he also had to be fine-tuned to the atmosphere in the shed. One flare-up could mess with a whole shear. Angry shearers usually meant sloppy shearing and the flock suffered.

So far the tension had been minimal. The shearers had worked through each run looking forward to Penny's next meal, bantering about the last. This shear was amazing and it was pretty much thanks to the woman beside him. So surely he could take a few minutes to show her a boobook?

Besides, he wanted to.

He had a torch in his pocket. It was strong but it was small, casting a narrow band of light in front of them as they walked. They needed to go into the stand of gums behind the house. The ground was thick with leaf litter and fallen twigs so it was natural—even essential—that he keep hold of her hand. After all, she was a vital cog in his business empire. He needed to take care of her.

Even though it made him feel… How did he feel?

Good. That was too small a word but his mind wasn't prepared to think of another. Her fingers were laced in his and her hand was half his size. His fingers were cal-loused and rough, too rough to be holding something as warm and…trusting?

That was what it felt like but that was dumb. He'd fig-ured enough of Penny by now to know that she could look after herself. One move that she didn't like would have her screeching the farm down, and an inkling of Penny in peril would have the entire shearing team out in force.

He grinned at the thought and Penny must have heard his smile. 'What's the joke?'

'I just thought…if I tried a bit of seduction you'd have the team out here ready to defend you. Shears at the ready. Ron was watching you go back to the house yesterday and said you had a nice rear end. Margie told him where he could put his sexist comments and suddenly we had the whole shearing shed coming down on Ron like a ton of bricks. The poor guy had to bury himself packing fleeces into the wool press for the rest of the afternoon. You have an army at your disposal, Penelope Hindmarsh-Firth.'

'Excellent,' she said and smiled and was it his imagination or did her hold on his hand tighten a little? She paused for a moment as if she was thinking of something important—or trying to find the courage to say something—and finally out it came.

'Do you think I have a nice...rear end?'

Whoa. 'You have a very nice rear end,' he admitted. Who could argue with the truth?

'Thank you,' she told him. 'Yours isn't so bad either.'

That set him back. A woman telling him he had a good butt?

'But don't let it go to your head,' she told him. 'And I'll try and swallow my conceit too. Where did you say these owls are?'

The calls had ceased. That was because they were standing right under the trees the birds were nesting in.

It took him a moment to collect himself and direct his torchlight up. She disconcerted him. She was so close. She still smelled faintly yeasty, from the bread she'd set to rise. From something citrusy in her hair. From...being Penny?

What was he here for? He was looking for owls. *Right.*

'There...' Penny breathed—she'd caught sight of the first bird before he had. Even though he was holding the torch. *Good one, Fraser,* he told himself. *Get a grip.*

'The other will be close,' he managed.

'The other?'

'This is a nesting pair. They've been using the same nest for years, very successfully. Their young populate half this valley. Look, there's the female. She's a bit bigger than the male. They're feeling a bit threatened now. See, they're sitting bolt upright, but they've seen me so often I can't imagine they think of me as a threat.'

He was concentrating on the birds rather than Penny.

'Would the shearing team leap to their defence too?' she asked mildly and he smiled.

'They might. No one likes their quarters overrun by mice. These guys do us a favour. But I don't think they'd come quite as fast as if you needed help. You've—deservedly—made some pretty fierce friends.'

'Matt?'

'Mmm?'

'Stop it with the compliments. They don't mean anything and I don't want them.'

And the way she said it made him pause. It made him stop thinking of how she smelled and, instead, think about where she'd come from.

He got it, he thought. She'd just been through one messy relationship. He didn't know this Brett guy who'd been such a toe-rag but he could imagine. Somehow, he had a pretty clear idea of her family dynamics by now. In some ways Penny was tough but in others…she was exposed, he thought, and Brett must have sensed that weakness. If he'd said great things to her she would have believed them. She'd believed them all the way to a calamitous engagement.

So now she thought compliments were a means of manipulation and he could understand why. He had to shut up. Except suddenly he couldn't.

'Right,' he told her. 'No more compliments. But there are a few truths—not compliments, truths, that I'm not taking back. Firstly, your cooking is awesome and I'm incredibly grateful. Second, I'd agree with Ron—you do have a nice rear end, even though it's an entirely inappropriate comment for a boss to make about his employee. And finally there's one more thing which I need to say and it'll make you blush because it's a ripper.'

'A ripper?' she said faintly. 'A ripper of a compliment?'

'Not a compliment,' he told her, throwing caution to the wind. He took her other hand and tugged so she was facing him. 'Just the truth. Penelope Hindmarsh-Firth, you smell of fresh baked bread and yeast and the aroma of a day spent in the kitchen, my kitchen, and if you think me telling you that you have a nice backside is an empty compliment then the world's upside down. This is a gorgeous night and I'm holding the hands of a woman who's saved my butt. She has a beautiful backside, not to mention the rest of her—and she smells and looks beautiful. Messy but beautiful. No more compliments, Penny. Just the truth. So…'

He paused then and took a deep breath and fought for the strength to say what had to be said. Because it was unwise and shouldn't be said at all but how could he not?

'So?' she whispered and somehow he found himself answering. Still telling it like it was.

'So we need to go in now because if we stay out here one moment longer I'll be forced to kiss you.'

And there it was, out in the open. This thing…

'And you don't want to?' It was a whisper, so low he thought he'd misheard. But he hadn't. Her whisper seemed to echo. Even the owls above their head seemed to pause to listen.

This was such a bad idea. This woman was his employee. She was trapped here for the next four days, or longer if she took him up on his offer to extend.

What was he doing? Standing in the dark, talking of kissing a woman? Did he want to?

'I do want to,' he said because there was nothing else to say.

'Then what's stopping you?'

'Penny...'

'Just shut up, Matt Fraser, and kiss me.'

And what could he say to that?

The night held its breath and Matt Fraser took Penny Hindmarsh-Firth into his arms and he kissed her.

Wow.

Um...

Wow?

This was wrong on so many levels. Firstly, she should still be in mourning for her broken engagement and the betrayal that went with it.

Second, this man was her boss.

Third, she was alone out here, under the gums and the starlight with a man she'd met less than two weeks ago.

The owls above their heads had decided they no longer needed to be wary and were swooping off, dark shadows against the moonlight as they continued their night's hunt.

Under her feet was a carpet of leaf litter that gave off the scent of eucalypts when she moved. But how could she move?

Matt was tugging her close. Her face was tilting up to his and his mouth met hers.

Matt hadn't shaved for a couple of days—when would he find time? His clothes were rough, heavy moleskin pants and a thick shirt open at the throat, sleeves rolled back to reveal arms of sheer brawn. His hands were scarred and weathered.

He smelled of the shearing shed. He'd washed and changed before he'd come out to the veranda but the lanolin from the fleeces seemed to have seeped into his pores. He smelled and felt what he was. He owned this land but he stood beside his men. He did the hard yards with them.

He was a man of steel.

He kissed her as if this was the first time for both of

them. As if he had all the time in the world. As if he wasn't sure what it was he'd be tasting but he wasn't about to rush it.

His hands moved to her hips but he didn't tug her into him, or if he did it wasn't hard, and maybe the fact that she was melting against him was an act of her own volition. She could back away at any time.

But oh, the feel of him. The sensation of his lips brushing hers. For now it was just brushing, almost a feather-touch, but it was the most sensual thing she'd ever felt. His hands on the small of her back… The feel of his rough hair as she tentatively lifted her hand and let herself rake it…

Oh, Matt.

Oh, wow.

But he wasn't pressing. He wasn't pushing and suddenly she saw it from his point of view.

She was in his terrain, and she was all by herself. He was a man of honour. He was kissing her on terms that said the control was hers. She could pull back.

And with that thought came the most logical next thought.

If she was in control then bring it on. How could she not? This man was gorgeous. The night was gorgeous. She was a twenty-seven-year-old woman out under the stars with a man to die for.

And then, quite deliberately, she let her thoughts dissolve. She raised her hands to his hair so she had his head and she tugged him closer. She stood on tiptoe to get closer still.

She opened her lips and she welcomed him in.

Penny was melting under his hands and there wasn't a thing he could do about it.

How could he want to do anything about it?

She'd stood on tiptoe and surrendered her mouth to him.

Her hands claimed him. Her body said she wanted this kiss as much or more than he did, and he'd better get on with it.

And so he did, and the sensation was enough to do his head in. The warmth, the heat, the fire… The night was dissolving in a mist of desire where nothing existed except this woman in his arms. This woman kissing him as fiercely as he kissed her. This woman whose body language said she wanted him as much as he wanted her.

A moment in time that was indescribable. Inevitable. World-changing?

The moment stretched on, a man and a woman in the moonlight, almost motionless, welded together by the heat from this kiss. From this need.

From this recognition that something was changing for both of them?

And with that thought…*trouble*.

It was as if his past had suddenly flown back, a cold chill of memory. Of love given and not returned. Of faith and trust blasted. Of the emptiness of loss. The grief…

He felt it almost as a physical jolt and, as if she'd felt it, she was suddenly tugging back. Maybe she'd had the same jolt of uncertainty, the same frisson that their worlds were both under threat by some new order.

And it almost killed him, but he let her go.

'W…wow,' she breathed and he thought: *Good description*. He couldn't think of a better word himself.

'You kiss good,' she managed. She looked dazed. A curl had escaped her ponytail and was coiling down across her eyes. He couldn't help himself—he lifted it and pushed it back.

But he didn't take her back into his arms.

'You're not so bad yourself,' he ventured, but the ghosts had been right to tug him back. He had no intention of getting involved with any woman. He would not face that kind of grief again.

But this wasn't any woman. This was Penny.

'We...we should be careful.' She couldn't quite disguise the quaver in her voice. 'If we go any further we'll shock the owls.'

'Probably not wise,' he managed.

'None of this is wise,' she whispered. 'But I'm not sure I care.'

It was up to him. And somehow he made the call. Somehow the ghosts prevailed.

'I need to be up before dawn,' he told her.

There was a long silence. Then, 'Of course you do.' There was still a tremble in her voice but she was fighting to get it under control.

Somehow he stayed silent. Somehow he managed not to gather her into his arms and take this to its inevitable conclusion.

It almost killed him.

But she had herself under control now. He could see her gathering herself together. This was a woman used to being rebuffed, he thought, and somehow that made it worse. But the ghosts were all around him, echoes of lessons long learned.

He didn't move.

'Then goodnight, Matt,' she whispered at last, and she reached out and touched his face in the most fleeting of farewell caresses. 'Sleep well. Sleep happy and sensible.'

And she turned and, without a torch, not even noticing the rough ground, she practically ran back to the relative sanctuary of the house.

It was done.

Sense had prevailed.

CHAPTER SEVEN

THEY WORKED SOLIDLY for the next four days. The timetable remained the same. They hardly saw each other during the day but at night Matt continued bringing his meal out to the veranda. Penny was always there, watching the moonlight, soaking up the stillness. Nothing had changed.

Except everything had.

There was a stillness between them. It was a kind of tension except it wasn't a tension. There was something happening that Matt couldn't figure.

He'd hurt her. He knew he had, he thought, as he sat on the veranda four nights later. He'd seen her face as he'd pulled away that night. She'd practically thrown herself at him. Now she was humiliated and he didn't know what to do about it.

Saying sorry wasn't going to cut it. Saying sorry would simply be saying she'd offered herself to him and he'd refused, but that wasn't how it had been. The tug between them was mutual.

But he'd had no choice. Penny had been honest enough to accept their desire was mutual, but the barriers he'd put up over the years had held. He wasn't going down that path again.

But what path? The path of grief he'd felt when his mother had left? When the old man who'd befriended him had died?

Or the path of betrayal both his mother and his wife had shown him?

He'd put Penny in the same bracket and she knew it. He'd humiliated her. He'd hurt her. He knew it but he didn't have a clue what to do about it.

And maybe Penny was used to such humiliation because she simply got on with it. She smiled at him, she used the same casual banter, she sat on the veranda now and shared the silence and it was as if nothing had happened.

Except the hurt was still there. How did he know? The sparkle of fun behind her eyes had changed, just a little. She was good at hiding hurt, he thought. If he didn't know her so well...

How did he know her so well? He didn't have a clue. He only knew that he did and he also knew that it had him retreating.

If he went one step further...

He couldn't. The next step would be a crashing down of those boundaries. A shattering of armour.

After all those years, how could he do that?

Penny rose. They'd been sitting on the veranda for only twenty minutes or so and they usually stayed an hour, but tomorrow was the last day of the shear. He had things to do and maybe she did too.

Or maybe this thing between them was too much.

'I'm making bulk choc chip cookies before I go to bed,' she told him. 'The team's heading on to McLarens' tomorrow and they're already whinging about the cooking they'll get there. I thought I'd send them with a goodbye kit.'

'They'll expect you back next year,' Matt told her and she paused and looked down at him in the dim light.

'I'll be well into organizing my catering company by then,' she said thoughtfully. 'But if you pay me enough I'll come.'

'Is that what you plan to do? Set up a catering company?'

'Yes,' she said, almost as if she was speaking to herself. 'I'll make it a success. I know it. Maybe I can find enough competent staff interested in outback experiences to let me offer catering for shearing.'

And he had to ask. 'So will you come, or will it be your competent staff?'

'Who knows?' She said it lightly but he still heard the pain.

'Penny?'

'Mmm?' She leaned down to lift his empty plate from the bench beside him but he reached out and took her wrist before she could lift it.

'Are you staying for the next two weeks?' he asked. 'You haven't said.'

She stilled. She looked down at her wrist.

He released it. No pressure.

What was he thinking, no pressure? There was pressure everywhere.

'Do you still want me to?'

And of course he should say no. He should say the thought had been a dumb one when he'd made the offer. His barricades needed reinforcing.

He'd hurt her and he had no intention of hurting her again. He needed to back off and let her go.

But the night was still and Penny didn't move. His grip on her wrist was light. She could pull away if she wanted.

She didn't.

And all at once he thought: *To hell with barricades. Let's just…see.*

'This thing between us…' he managed and she stayed silent. What happened next was obviously down to him. As it should be.

'Penny, the way I feel…it's been so long. And, to be honest…' He shook his head and finally released her wrist. 'Penny, you've been hurt. You know how it feels. But me?'

And then he stopped. How could he explain? How could he tell anyone the hurt of those long years?

But then he thought this was Penny and he'd hurt her. He couldn't let it stay like this. He needed to let down the barricades a little.

He needed to talk.

'If you don't want to tell me, you don't need to,' she said gently.

She was giving him an out. Her generosity almost took his breath away, and it tore away the last of his reservations.

She sat beside him, as if she understood he needed time. He couldn't look at her. For some reason it seemed impossible to say what had to be said when he was watching her.

But her body was touching his and the warmth of her, her closeness—her trust?—made it imperative to tell her what he'd told nobody. Ever.

And finally he did.

'Penny, my mother was a serial relationship disaster,' he said at last. 'She went from man to man to man. Every time she fell deeply, irrevocably in love, and every single relationship meant our lives were turned upside down. Romance for my mother inevitably ended in chaos and heartbreak. Moving houses, moving schools, debt collectors, sometimes even assault, hospitals, the courts. The best thing Mum ever did for me was run from a calamitous relationship and take the housekeeping job on Sam's farm. That was my salvation. If she hadn't done that, heaven knows where I'd have been. Sam's farm was my first and only taste of stability and I stayed there for ten years. Sam left me the farm and I thought I'd stay there for ever. And then I discovered the bauxite and Darrilyn discovered me.'

'More chaos?' Penny whispered. She was looking out at the moonlight too, giving him space. Giving him silence to work out what he needed to say.

'More chaos,' he said grimly. 'I was naïve, little more than an idiot kid, and I was besotted. I didn't put the discovery of bauxite and the sudden interest of the neighbouring farmer's gorgeous daughter together. I married her and when we found out she was pregnant I was over the moon. But marriage and pregnancy had been her only goals. Legally, they gave her the right to the money she wanted. She headed to the US with a guy who knew her worth and was probably in on her plan from the beginning. So that's it. I see Lily twice a year and it breaks my heart.'

'But now?' She sounded as if she was walking on eggshells. 'You said she might be coming home.'

'Home?' He gave a hollow laugh. 'Does she have such a thing? Her mother's relationships have broken down again and again. Lily's been given the same raw deal as me, but there's nothing I can do about it. Her mother's always refused to let her come to Australia. I leave the farm with the boys twice a year and spend as much time with her as I can, and every time I leave it rips me in two. But even if I moved there Darrilyn wouldn't give me more access. So that's it, Penny. That's where I've been with relationships. Burned. I don't need them.'

'So…' Penny took a deep breath '… Matt, what's that got to do with me?'

'I don't know.' And it was an honest answer. How could he explain what he didn't understand himself? 'Penny, how I feel…'

'Must be like I feel,' she ventured when he couldn't go on. 'Like I've been an idiot and how can I trust myself to try again? Only your ghosts must be harder on you than mine. My parents have their faults but they've given me stability.' Her gaze raked the moonlit landscape. 'You know, this is the most settled place I've ever been in. I'm imagining how you must have felt as a child when you finally made it to Sam's farm. And now. Here's your home and life is good. You wouldn't want to mess with that for anything.'

'You mean I wouldn't want to mess with that for you?'

'I'm not putting words into your mouth,' she said with sudden asperity. She rose, breaking the moment, and a tinge of anger entered her voice. 'I can't help you, Matt. I have my own demons to deal with and, believe me, the fact that I've been monumentally dumb is a huge thing to accept. I don't need a relationship either.' She took a deep breath as if she was having trouble forcing the words out, but finally she managed it.

'But you know what? Regardless of relationships, I'm moving on. Being here has kept my demons at bay, regardless of...of what's happening between us. And I still have the same problem—media interest in my appalling sister and her equally appalling fiancé. I like working here,' she confessed. 'It feels good and I suspect if I made a pile of meals and stocked the freezer, you guys would be grateful.'

'We would.' He definitely would.

'There you go, then. Maybe that's my bottom line. There's cooking to be done and organization in the house. I can put my head down and go for it.'

'I don't want you to work...'

'I'm staying to work, Matt,' she said, still with that trace of astringency. 'Anything else...who knows? As I said, we each have our own demons. But should they affect the next two weeks? Maybe not. So let's make this an employment contract only. Two more weeks of work—at shearers' cook rates.'

'Hey! You're not cooking for a team. Shearers' cook rates?' But he felt himself starting to smile.

She arched her brows and met his gaze head-on. 'I'm filling the freezer and that'll be like cooking for a team. Shearers' cook rates or nothing. That's my offer, Matt Fra-

ser, and it's final. So…do you still want me to stay or do
you not?'

She was looking up at him, resolute, courageous, firm.

When he'd first met her he'd thought she was ditzy. She
wasn't. She had intelligence to spare.

She was beautiful.

Suddenly he wondered—was this the courage to try
again?

And then there was no choice. The night righted itself.
He rose and took her hands.

'Penny, I want you to stay.'

'Really?'

'Really.'

'Then I accept. I'm on a great wage. You have big freezers and I like a challenge. What's not to love?'

What's not to love?

It was all he could do not to kiss her. And then he
thought: *Why not?*

So he did and, amazingly, wonderfully, she didn't object. She responded.

But this wasn't the kiss of passion they'd shared on the
night of the owls. It was tentative—a question—and when
they pulled apart the question was still in their eyes.

'You know, when you're around I have trouble being
interested in how empty my freezers are,' he confessed.

'Well, you should be.' She was smiling as she stepped
back. She seemed suddenly a woman in charge of her
world, ready to move on. 'Because you're paying me
heaps.' She tugged her hands back and he let her go. 'For
the rest, let's just see. But for now… Matt, I need to go
bake some cookies. Freezers, here I come.'

He headed out to check on the last pens of sheep, the last
runs before the end of shearing.

Penny headed for the kitchen.

She'd promised the shearing team takeaway choc chip cookies. Right. She could do that.

Samson snoozed by the fire. The kitchen felt like a refuge.

She mixed her two flours and then stared at the mixture and stared at the flour sacks and wondered—had she just used half self-raising flour, half plain, or had she put in two lots of plain?

Uh oh.

She started again, this time trusting herself so little that she made a list of ingredients that were usually in her head and ticked them as she put them in.

But how could she think of ingredients?

Matt had kissed her. Twice. Matt wanted her to stay.

And she understood him. From that first day when she'd seen him on his gorgeous black horse she'd thought of him as a man in charge of his world, and little had happened to change that. The shearers looked up to him and it wasn't because he owned the place. She'd learned enough of human nature now to know bosses earned respect; they didn't buy it.

So Matt was a man of strength, intelligence and honour, but she'd just been allowed a glimpse of the building blocks that had made him. It felt like an enormous privilege.

She put both her hands in the bowl and started mixing. The feel of the cookie dough under her hands was a comfort. It was a task she'd loved doing for years.

The family cook had taught her to do this. Her parents hadn't been around much but they'd been in the background.

Who'd baked choc chip cookies for Matt?

No one. She knew it as surely as she knew what he'd told her was scarcely the tip of the iceberg that was the nightmare of his childhood.

'Bless you, Sam,' she told the old farmer who'd finally

taken the young Matt under his wing. 'I wish I could make you choc chip cookies.'

And suddenly her eyes filled with tears. Why? It hardly made sense. She sniffed and told herself she was a dope but the tears kept coming.

'So we're adding a little salty water into the mix,' she said out loud. 'My secret ingredient.'

Two weeks to cure a lifetime of hurt?

That wasn't the way it worked. Matt didn't see himself as someone who needed curing, and she was hardly qualified to help.

'But he might kiss me again...'

The tears disappeared. Hope was suddenly all around her, a bright, perky little voice that bounced with delight. Enough with the past. She had freezers to fill.

And demons to scatter?

'I hope he likes choc chip cookies,' she told the sleeping Samson. 'Because I'm about to fill his freezers with a ton.'

He'd hired her for two more weeks. He'd told her his past.

Was he nuts?

He checked the pens and then walked down the paddocks to check the newly shorn sheep. The weather was brilliant, as it had been for the whole shear. The starkly white sheep didn't even appear to notice that they'd lost their coats. They were relaxed, hardly edging away as he walked the boundaries of the holding paddocks. There were no problems with the flock that he could see. No problems on the horizon either.

He opened the gates of the house paddocks to the pastures beyond. To all intents and purposes, the sheep were free.

Like he intended to be.

Freedom. That was what he'd craved when he'd somehow hauled himself together after Darrilyn walked out.

His mother had moved from one hysterical mess to another. He'd spent his childhood dealing with her tears, her drama, her hopelessness, and his one foray into marriage had been more of the same.

Freedom had looked good. This place was his solace, his refuge, his love.

But now? Not only had he just opened himself up to Penny, exposing pain he'd never thought he'd reveal, but he'd pushed her to stay for two weeks.

And a question was starting to niggle.

Did he have the courage to try again? With a pink princess with a past almost as troubled as his?

He walked on. In the distance he could still see the house. The lights were on at the south end, which meant the kitchen was still in use. Penny would be cooking.

He could go and join her. He could sit at the kitchen table and watch her hands create food to die for. He could watch the flour accumulate on her nose—she always seemed to have flour on her nose.

Maybe he could offer to help—he could wash while she wiped.

There was a romantic thought.

He stopped and closed his eyes. The silence was almost absolute. Even the owls were silent and he thought suddenly: *It's as if something momentous is about to happen.*

Momentous? Like Matt Fraser breaks his own rule and lets his guard down with a woman?

How insulting was that? he thought, and swore silently to himself. What was he expecting, that Penny jump him? That he'd have to fight her off?

It was a dumb thought, but it had its merits. He found himself smiling as he walked on. He wouldn't mind.

He wouldn't fight her off.

'I won't hurt her.' There was another thought, almost a vow.

How serious was he getting, and how fast?

'Not serious at all,' he told himself as he finally turned for home. Surely she'd finished cooking by now? The house would be in darkness and he could slip in without seeing her.

Was that what he wanted? To avoid her for two weeks?

'You know it's not or you wouldn't have invited her,' he told himself and he found himself wishing his dogs were with him. His own company wasn't cutting it. But the dogs were exhausted after a full day in the yards.

So was he. He needed to go to sleep and stop worrying about what lay ahead.

And stop fancying what else might happen.

'When are you coming home?'

Penny's mother hadn't phoned her for two weeks. When she didn't phone, Penny knew she was in trouble. Depression dogged her mother, and silence was a symptom. But Louise's silence while Brett and Felicity outlined their marriage plans had made Penny decide enough was enough.

Penny's father was a bully and her half-sister was a self-serving shrew, but Louise didn't have the courage to stand up to either of them.

Tonight her mother's voice sounded thick with tears. Penny was willing herself not to care.

It didn't work. How could she stop caring?

'I told you, Mum, I'm working out here. It doesn't matter when I get home.'

'Where exactly are you working?'

'South Australia. Murray River country. I'm working as a cook, Mum. I'm safe, I'm doing a good job and I'm keeping…' She paused, but why not say it like it was? 'I'm keeping myself occupied so I don't need to think about Felicity and Brett.'

'They're both unhappy about hurting you.'

'You know, I'm very sure they're not.'

'No, they are.' And here she went again, Penny thought. Her mother spent her life pretending they were happy families. 'I'm sure Felicity would like you to be her bridesmaid.'

'I'm sure she'd hate it.'

'Well, she *should* have you.' The tears were unmistakable now. 'I don't like you unhappy. I want you to be her bridesmaid and I told her that.'

'It's not going to happen,' Penny said gently. 'I wish Felicity all the best but I'm not coming home for the wedding.'

'Not even coming?' Her mother sounded appalled.

'Mum, how can I?'

'Sweetheart, you must.' Her mother hiccupped on a sob. 'It's in three weeks. St Barnabas Chapel followed by a grand reception on the Harbour. For you not to be there...' Another sob. 'Felicity's mother will lord it over me. Your father won't care. Penny, I can't do it without you.'

How impossible was it to harden your heart? She tried. 'Mum, I'm happy here.'

There was a moment's pause. Maybe something in Penny's voice had got through. 'Really?'

'I am,' she told her. 'And Samson's turning into a sheepdog. You should see him.'

'I thought you were working at a hotel.'

'This is sheep country.'

'So you're meeting the locals?'

'I...some of them. But Mum, I can't come to the wedding. I'm so busy I'm even starting to forget what Felicity and Brett did to me.' She took a deep breath and decided to say it like it was. 'To be honest, I'm even starting to feel sorry for Felicity. And worried. You should tell Felicity there are a lot nicer men than Brett.'

'You wanted to marry him.'

'That was before I knew what a toerag he was. There are still some honourable men in the world.'

She shouldn't have said it. If there was one thing Louise was good at, it was sussing out gossip and, despite her distress, she could almost feel her mother's antennae quiver. '"Honourable men",' she said slowly. There was a loaded pause and then, 'Penny, have you met one?'

Shut up, Penny, she told herself. Get off the phone fast.

But she wouldn't lie. Had she met an honourable man? Yes, she had, and the thought was a good one.

'That's for me to know and you to guess,' she told her mother, forcing herself to sound breezy. 'Goodnight, Mum.'

'Penny, please come.'

'I can't.'

But she lay in bed that night and thought of her mother's tears. She thought of her mother, isolated at the wedding by her appalling husband and her even more appalling stepdaughter.

How did you rid yourself of the ties of loving?

She should ask Matt.

CHAPTER EIGHT

IN THE NEXT few days, while Matt coped with the tasks that had to be done before the wool was sent for sale, Penny attacked the house.

If anyone had ever told her she'd find joy in a mop and bucket, she'd have told them they were crazy. But cleaning took her mind off her mother's increasingly distressed phone calls, and this was a challenge worth tackling.

Ever since she'd walked into the house she'd thought of it as something out of a Charles Dickens novel. 'I feel like I might find Miss Havisham under one of these dust sheets,' she told Matt as they sat on the veranda that night. 'How long have they been here?'

'Donald's mother was a socialite,' Matt told her. 'She ran away when Donald was seven and his dad pretty much closed the house. When Donald sold me the house and contents I left it as it was. I use my bedroom, the den and the kitchen. I've no need for anything else.'

'You're two male versions of Miss Havisham,' she told him. 'Not that I mind. You can gloat over your wool clip while I clean. I'll even enjoy it.'

'I would be grateful,' Matt admitted. 'If Lily comes…'

'Is that likely to happen?'

'Maybe,' he said slowly. 'She's not getting on with Darrilyn's new partner. Darrilyn's talking about sending her to school in Australia so it's not impossible.' But he sounded like a man who was scarcely allowing himself to hope.

'Does she know anyone in Australia?'

'No, and that's why I'm telling Darrilyn she'd need to come here first. So she knows some sort of base.'

'Poor kid,' Penny said, and meant it. She knew all about being a teenage thorn in her socialite parents' lives and the thought of the unknown Lily was part of her driving force.

'The sofa in the main sitting room's so hard it feels like sitting on bricks,' she told him. 'Why not replace it with something squishy? Now the flood's receded you can get it delivered and, with the fire lit, that room would be lovely. It needs a big telly, though, and all the things that go with it. If Lily comes she won't feel welcome if she has to sit on a horsehair brick. And her bedroom… I'd suggest buying a four-poster bed. Not pink, unless you see her as a pink girl.'

'I don't,' he said faintly. 'Penny, she probably won't come.'

'You know,' she said diffidently, 'if I was thirteen and there was conflict at home, my dad sending pictures of the bedroom he'd prepared for me might well make me feel a whole lot better about myself, whether I was allowed to come or not.'

'Even if they're never used?'

'You can afford it,' she told him bluntly. 'And Lily sounds like she needs it.'

'How do you know?'

'I don't. I'm guessing. You want to go with my guess or with yours?'

He looked at her for a long moment and then raked his hair. 'You probably do know more about thirteen-year-old girls than I do.'

'Hey, I was one once,' she said cheerfully. 'If you agree, I'd suggest we go with a theme of antique white. The rooms are so old-fashioned, why don't we…'

'We?'

'Me then,' she said and grinned. 'Why don't I go for white on white? Broderie anglaise, heritage quilting, a deep rug on the floor, some old-fashioned sampler type pictures on the wall...'

'How do you know what she'd like?'

'I know what I'd like,' she told him. 'If my parents had done something like this for me...'

And then her voice cracked. She heard it but there wasn't a thing she could do about it.

'Still hurting, huh?' Matt said. They were sitting on the edge of the veranda and he reached out and touched her face. It was a fleeting gesture, but it said, in some deep way, that he understood the distress she still felt whenever she thought of her mother's pleas. The knowledge was enough to make her toes curl.

She concentrated fiercely on getting them uncurled.

'I can forget about it here,' she managed.

'But you can't stay here for ever?'

'No. And Malley's isn't an option any more. But neither is staying away, I guess. My sister's getting married on the seventeenth and Mum's organising a family dinner on the twelfth. On Dad's orders. To heal differences, he says, and he expects me to be there. He'll blame Mum if I'm not.'

'Surely you won't go?' He sounded appalled. That was how she felt but what choice did she have?

'You see, I love Mum,' she said simply.

She loved, therefore she did what was expected.

Matt was silent for a while. The night was closing in on them and somehow it felt...almost threatening? Why did this man make her feel so exposed?

'I guess that's why I don't love,' Matt said at last. 'I won't let myself need people and I won't be needed.'

'No?' She gave a hollow laugh. 'What about Lily?'

'Lily's different. She's my kid.'

'And this is my mum.'

'And your mum should be protecting you, as I'd protect Lily. Penny, your mum's an adult. She's had a lifetime to form her own armour and maybe that's what you need to do.'

'That's cruel.'

'It is,' he said gently. 'But your mother's made her own choices and maybe it's time for you to do the same. You only have one life. Will you spend it trying to please your family? Being a doormat?'

'What's the alternative? Carrying a bucketload of guilt for the rest of my life?' She tried to say it lightly but failed.

'So you'll go back to your mum.'

'I might.' But she knew she would.

'Maybe your mum could come to you?'

'What, here?'

'Maybe not. It'd be a bit of a culture shock—from Sydney to Jindalee.' She heard Matt's smile rather than saw it. They hadn't turned on the veranda lights and the darkness had crept up on their silence. 'But Penny, if you make yourself a life, set up your catering company, do what you want to do... If your mum wants, then maybe she could choose to help you? Maybe she could live near you, on her own rather than in an unhappy marriage? You could help her on your terms rather than hers.'

'She'll never leave.'

'Then that's her choice,' he said gently. 'But it doesn't have to be your choice. Attending the wedding should be your line in the sand. Maybe you should do something for yourself instead. Have a weekend in a fabulous resort. I'll arrange it for you if you like, as a thank you for getting me out of such trouble at shearing. But, no matter what, just say no.'

'Oh, Matt...'

'You can do it,' he growled and he rose and leant down and ran a finger lightly through her curls. The touch made her shiver. 'If you can keep a mob of shearers happy, you can do anything. I believe in you, Penny Hindmarsh-Firth, so maybe it's time for you to believe in yourself.'

And then there was another of those silences which fell between them so often. Mostly they felt natural. Mostly they felt good. But this one...

This one seemed loaded.

You can do it. That was what Matt had said.

Do what? What she really wanted?

If she really believed in herself, Penny thought, she'd get up from where she was sitting and she'd kiss this guy senseless. She might even demand he let go of his own ghosts and come to this luxury resort with her.

But she was Penny. Asking for love? She never had. She'd loved and loved and where had that got her?

You can do it.

Yeah, right. Not in a million years.

'Goodnight, Penny,' Matt said heavily then, as if he too acknowledged the impossibility of moving on.

'Goodnight,' she whispered.

She felt sad. No, she felt desolate, but still she went inside and rang her mother. She said no and she meant it—and, despite the weird feeling of desolation, it felt like a beginning.

Two days later, the year's wool clip was finally loaded for market. She saw the slump of Matt's shoulders as he watched the line of trucks roll off the property. She thought of the work he'd put in, the late nights he'd pulled, the light on in his study until almost dawn.

And suddenly she thought...picnic?

She walked out to meet him in the driveway.

'Well done,' she told him.

'The fleece is great. It feels a whole lot better than taking money from a bauxite mine.'

'I'll bet it does,' she said and then added diffidently, 'Want to come on a picnic?'

'What?' It was as if he hadn't heard the word before.

'You haven't stopped for weeks,' she told him. 'Ron and Harv are rested. They can take over anything that needs to be done. Is there anywhere we can go? Somewhere you can't see a single sheep? Honest, Matt, you must be seeing them in your sleep.'

'If I fell asleep every time I counted them I'd be in trouble,' he agreed, smiling faintly. 'But now I need to get onto drenching.'

'Matt. One day. Holiday. Picnic.'

And he turned and looked at her. 'You must be exhausted too.'

'If it'll make you agree to a picnic, yes, I am.'

She met his gaze, tilted her chin, almost daring him to refuse.

Finally he seemed to relent. 'There is somewhere...' he said doubtfully. 'But we'd have to take horses. The ground's undermined by rabbit warrens and the four-wheel drive won't get in there without damaging the ferns.'

'And we don't want that,' she said, not having a clue what he was talking about but prepared to encourage him. And then she thought about it a bit more and said, less enthusiastically, 'Horses?'

'Do you ride?'

'My mother bought me a pony when I was seven,' she said, feeling more and more dubious. 'It was fat and it didn't go any more than a dozen steps before it needed a nap. So I know which side to get on and I'm not too bad at sitting. Anything else is beyond me. Is there anywhere else we can go?'

'I have a horse who'll fit the bill,' he said cheerfully and her heart sank.

'Really?'

'Maisie's thirty. Sam bought her for me when I was

twelve, and I loved her. She and I ruled the land but she has become rather fat. And lazy. But she'll follow Nugget to the ends of the earth. It'll be like sitting on a rocking chair.'

But she'd been distracted from the horse.

'Why do I keep loving your Sam more and more?' she whispered. 'He bought the son of his housekeeper a horse?'

'Yeah, he did,' Matt told her and his voice softened too. 'He changed my life.'

'Would he tell you to go on a picnic?'

'I guess…maybe.'

'Then let's do it,' she told him. 'As long as I can borrow one of the living room cushions. How far is it?'

'It'll take about an hour.'

'Two hours there and back?' She took a deep breath and then looked up at Matt and thought…

'I'll take two cushions,' she told him. 'Let's do it.'

Maisie was a fat old mare, used to spending her days snoozing in the sun and her nights nestled on the straw in Matt's impressive stables. But she perked right up when Matt put the saddle on her, and when Penny tentatively— very tentatively—clambered aboard, she trotted out into the sunshine and sniffed the wind as if she was looking forward to the day as much as Penny.

Matt's two dogs raced furiously ahead, wild with excitement, as if they knew the day would be special. Samson, however, had been racing with them since dawn. He was one tired poodle and he now sat in front of Matt, like the figurehead on the bow of an ancient warship. He looked supremely content and, fifteen minutes into the ride, Penny decided she was too.

The old horse was steady and placid. The day was perfect. Matt rode ahead, looking splendid on his beautiful Nugget. There was little for Penny to think about, or do, for Maisie seemed totally content to follow Nugget. And Matt.

As was Penny. 'I'm with you,' she muttered to Maisie. 'Talk about eye candy. Wow…'

'Sorry?' Matt turned and waited for her to catch up. 'I didn't hear that.'

'You weren't meant to. Maisie and I were communing. I think we're twin souls.'

'I can see that,' he said and grinned and the eye candy meter zipped up into the stratosphere. Matt was wearing jeans and riding boots, and an ancient khaki shirt, open at the throat, sleeves rolled above the elbows. He'd raked his hair too often during shearing and the lanolin from the fleeces had made it look more controlled, coarser. Now, though, the last of the lanolin had been washed away. His hair was ruffled in the warm wind. His face looked relaxed. His deep-set eyes were permanently creased against the sun, but they were smiling. He looked a man at ease.

His horse was magnificent. He looked magnificent.

If I were a Regency heroine I'd be reaching for my smelling salts right now, she thought, and she wanted to tell Maisie because Maisie was watching Nugget with exactly the same look of adoration.

Wait, was she looking at Matt with adoration? She pulled herself up with a jolt.

'You be careful of those saddlebags,' she said, fighting for something prosaic to say. 'I don't want squashed cream puffs.'

'You packed cream puffs?' He'd loaded the cartons of food into his saddlebags without question.

'Why wouldn't I?' she asked with insouciance.

'Why indeed? I thought picnics were sandwiches and apples.'

'Not in my world. Where are we going?'

'We're heading for the hills,' he told her. 'After this rain I'm betting the place we're going will be amazing. I hope I'm right.'

* * *

This was his favourite place on the entire property. He'd seen it first the day he'd come to inspect the land. Donald had driven him over the paddocks, shown him the house, the shearing sheds, the outbuildings. He'd shown him the sheep and then he'd driven him here. Donald couldn't make it down the last steep climb. He'd driven him to the top and said, 'There's something down there that's worth a look, boy, if you have the energy to walk down.'

When he did, he'd known that not only would he buy Jindalee, but Jindalee would be his home.

This was his refuge. His quiet place. His place for just… being. Over the years, he and Nugget had forged a track through the undergrowth that was secure enough to get right down to the bottom. He led the way now, slowly and surely, with Maisie plodding behind. He glanced back to tell Penny to hold on tight but he didn't need to. Penny's knees were tight to the saddle. Her hands gripped the knee-pads even though her fingers were still light on the reins. She wouldn't take her fear out on Maisie. And now…fear or not, her face reflected pure awe.

The country on this section of the river was so rough, so undermined by underground waterways that no farmer had ever tried to clear it. Now the massive gum trees towered over their heads. The vast, shading canopy meant the understory was an undulating carpet of ferns, a wondrous mat of green that flowed down to the water.

They weren't going all the way to the river. The Murray here was wide and wild, a vast expanse of water where the banks would still be covered with debris from the recent floods. This place was better.

He remembered Donald describing it to him all those years ago.

'There's a place, boy, where one of the creeks flowing underground sneaks up and burbles up over the rocks,'

Donald had told him. 'Then it falls and forms a pool bigger'n most swimming pools. You can swim there if you can cope with a bit of cold. It's the cleanest water on God's earth, I swear. And then it slithers through a bed of tumbled rocks and disappears back underground. The ground around is covered with moss. A man can lie on that moss and look up through the gums and see the sky. It's like a slice of heaven.'

Matt had come and seen and fallen in love, and now, as their horses turned into the final clearing, he saw Penny's face and knew she saw it exactly the same way.

'Oh,' she breathed and then fell silent. Awed.

'Not bad, huh?' he said, trying to bite back pride and then he thought: *Why not say it like it is?* 'Best place in the world.'

'Oh, Matt.' She slipped off Maisie and the horse turned to nibble her ear. Her hand automatically went to scratch Maisie's nose. She was a natural horsewoman, Matt thought. He could buy another horse and...

What was he thinking?

The dogs were heading into the ferns, wild with excitement at the smell of rabbits, of something other than sheep, maybe simply at the day itself.

Matt pretty much felt the same—although he surely wasn't thinking of rabbits.

'Can we swim?' she breathed.

'It's icy.'

'But there aren't any... I don't know...crocodiles?'

He grinned. 'No crocodiles.'

'Then I'm in.'

'Did you bring your swimmers?'

'No,' she said and suddenly she was glaring. 'I did not because no one told me that swimming was an option.' She looked again at the waterhole and he saw the moment she made a decision. 'Well,' she said, 'you didn't tell me so you need to face the consequences. My knickers and bra are respectable. You're sure there isn't a posse of photographers behind these trees?'

What sort of world did she live in? 'I'm sure.'

'Don't sound so cocky. They'd be onto you if you didn't have such an ordinary name. You must have kept deliberately under the radar. Matt Fraser? No headlines and I bet you've fought hard to keep it that way. As squillionaire owner of Harriday Holdings, you'd be every women's magazine's Bachelor of the Year, no sweat.'

'So you didn't fight?' he said curiously. 'To keep under the radar?'

'With my father? I was in front of a camera practically before they cut the cord. And with a name like Hindmarsh-Firth it's impossible to duck.'

'So change it.'

'Right,' she said grimly. 'By deed poll? I don't think so. I'd be splashed all over the dailies with *Family Feud* as the headline.' She shrugged. 'No matter. It's all a long way from here and this place is magic. Can I swim?'

'The water's coming straight up from underground. Cold doesn't begin to describe it.'

'You swim here?'

'Yes.'

'But you never bother to pack your bathers when you come here?' Her smile returned. 'I get it. Every respectable squillionaire has his own private swimming pool and this is yours. Can I share?'

'If you dare.'

And she chuckled and tugged her T-shirt off, revealing a sliver of a pink lace bra. 'Of course I dare,' she told him. 'But I'm not doing your naked thing. I happen to be wearing matching knickers and panties—isn't that lucky? Will you join me?'

'I...yes.'

'Then are your boxers respectable, because we Hind-marsh-Firths have our standards?'

He grinned. 'I believe they are—although they're not pink and they're not lace.'

'I don't know what squillionaires are coming to,' she said, mock serious. 'But I can slum it. Swimming with a guy in cotton boxers? If I must.'

And she turned her back on him, kicked off her shoes, tugged off her jeans—to reveal a pair of knickers that were just as scanty as her bra—and dived straight in.

He'd said it was cold, but this wasn't just cold. This was half a degree above ice. She reached for the rock ledge and gasped and gasped.

And Matt was beside her.

He must have dived in almost as soon as she had. She hadn't noticed him shedding his clothes. She'd been more than a bit embarrassed about the panty-bra thing and had turned her back but now he was beside her.

His arm came out to support her. Maybe he thought her heart might stop.

It felt as if it might stop.

'I told you it was cold,' he said, a trifle smugly, and the iciness of the water and the sudden sensation of his arm around the bare skin of her waist and the smugness in his tone made her want to retort—but how could a girl retort when she was gasping like a fish out of water?

'Oh… Oh…'

'You get used to it if you swim,' he told her. Dammit, his voice wasn't even quavering. Was the man immune?

'This is like those winter plunge ceremonies in the Antarctic,' she stammered and tried to tug herself up to the ledge.

'Penny?'

'Mmm?' She couldn't get a handhold.

'There's a ledge over there that makes it easy to get out, but if you can bear it then try swimming. The cold eases and there's something I want to show you.'

Every nerve ending in her body was screaming for her to get out. But something else was cutting in, overriding the cold of the water.

Matt's arm was around her waist. He'd stripped to his boxers. His body was big and tanned and strong and he was holding her against him.

Was it her imagination or was she warm where she was touching him?

The initial shock was wearing off now—a little. She could breathe again, enough to take in her surroundings.

The pool was magnificent. At one end was a waterfall, not high, maybe head height, but enough to send white water tumbling down over rocks to the pool below. The pool itself was clear and deep, but not so deep that she couldn't see the sandy bottom. Now that she had her breath back she could see tiny slivers of darting fish.

The canopy of trees had parted a little over the pool, so dappled sunlight was playing on the water. Moss covered the surrounding rocks, and beyond the moss the horses had started grazing. They were obviously appreciating the lush grass in the slice of land where the moss ended and the ferns began.

The scene was idyllic. Enough to make her forget the ice?

Or maybe that was because Matt was beside her. Holding her.

What was a little ice compared to Matt?

'Sh...show me,' she managed through chattering teeth and he grinned.

'Swim first,' he told her. 'Half a dozen fast laps to warm up. Can you do that?'

'Of course. Bossy.'

'I'm not bossy, I'm wise,' he told her. 'Swim or you'll have to get out. Believe me.'

So she swam. The pool was the length of the pool her parents had in their current mansion. She'd spent a lot of time in that pool since the night Brett and Felicity had made their announcement. Swimming was a way she could block out the world.

But she had no intention of blocking the world now, for Matt swam beside her, matching her stroke for stroke. Maybe he wasn't too sure of her ability, she thought. Maybe he thought she might drown if he didn't stick close enough to save her.

Saved by Matt... It was a silly thought but it did something to her insides. The water was still icy but she was warming up, and half of that warming process was Matt. Matt's body inches from hers. Matt's presence. Matt...

They turned in unison and then turned again. Four lengths, five...and then six. She reached the end and grasped the ledge. Matt's arm came around her and held again.

He couldn't think she was drowning now. He was holding her because...?

'Game for the next bit?' he asked and she thought: *With your arm around me I'm game for anything.*

'I...yes.' Her teeth weren't chattering any more. She couldn't say she was warm but the iciness had dropped a notch. The water felt amazing. You could drink this water, she thought, and took a tentative mouthful and it tasted wonderful.

'If the bauxite mine ever fails I can put a bottling factory here and make a mint,' Matt said smugly.

'Don't you dare.'

'Don't worry, I won't,' he told her and he smiled at her again. That smile... It was a caress all by itself.

But he was a man on a mission. He had something to show her.

'The waterfall,' he told her. 'We're going behind it.'

'We are?'

'You can't see anything from out here,' he told her. 'But if you aim to the left of centre, put your head down, hold your breath for thirty seconds and swim right through, you'll find there's a cave.'

'Really?' She stared at the innocent-looking waterfall. 'There's no way I can be trapped?'

He grinned at her note of suspicion. 'You guessed it. You'll find forty-seven skeletons in there, the remains of every single maiden I've ever enticed into my secret lair.'

And she thought suddenly: *How do I know he's not telling the truth?* She'd known him for less than three weeks.

She'd been a fool for Brett. How could she trust her judgement now?

Except this was Matt. And Matt was smiling just a little, teasing.

'I know you're lying,' she told him and he raised a quizzical brow.

'How?'

'Because you couldn't possibly have persuaded forty-seven maidens to jump into this ice.' And she turned towards the waterfall and swam.

It was a weird feeling, to think of swimming through the wall. Instinct told her to reach the tumbling water and stop. She did for a moment, pausing to tread water, feeling the spray of the falls splash on her face.

But Matt was beside her. She could scarcely see him through the mist but he touched her shoulder. 'Here,' he said. 'Straight ahead. Put your head down and swim. It's narrow—you'll feel rocks on either side—but you'll be through in seconds.'

'I...is it dark in there?'

'I promise it's not,' he told her. 'It's safe as houses.'

'Really?'

'Well, not a centrally heated house,' he admitted. 'But it's worth it. Penny, trust me?'

Did she trust him? She stared at him for a long moment. His face was blurred behind the mist of the waterfall but she could still see him. He'd ceased smiling. He was waiting for her to come to a decision—and suddenly it was about more than the trust required to swim through a waterfall.

It was about total trust.

It was about taking a step that felt momentous.

He put out a hand and touched her face, making the rivulets of water stream across his hand rather than across her eyes. Her vision cleared and she saw him as he was.

A loner. A man of strength and courage. Matt.

And something shifted inside her. Something she couldn't name. Something that had never been touched before.

She put out her hand and touched his face back.

'I trust you,' she whispered and he smiled but it was a different kind of smile. It was a smile that said he was in the same unchartered territory as she was.

'Then let's go,' he told her. 'Come on, Penelope Hindmarsh-Firth. Let's do it.'

And he put his hands on her shoulders and twisted her around so she was facing the waterfall and gave her a slight push forward.

'Through you go,' he told her. 'And know that I'm with you all the way.'

Okay, it was scary. The first bit did involve trust. The wash of tumbling water as she swam through was almost enough to push her under, and then she felt the rocks on either side.

Matt had said to swim through. Just keep on going.

She wasn't completely enclosed. She could still surface and breathe if she needed to, though the mist from the falls made that hard. It was a narrow channel through the rocks, and it was getting narrower.

But Matt was behind her. She held her breath and dived like a porpoise.

The rocks on both sides touched her shoulders. She used them to pull herself the last little way.

And emerged...to magic.

It was an underground pool that must feed out somehow into the pool they'd just been in, but at the same level. She could hear the rush of water over her head. The creek must branch, above and below. This pool was roofed, and yet not. There were fissures where the sunlight glimmered through, shafts of golden light making the surface of the underground water glimmer in light and shade.

She could see the canopy of the trees through the fissures, but only glimpses. In a couple of places the water course above was overflowing and spilling down, so rivulets of water splashed the surface of the water in the cavern. Some sort of tiny, pale green creeper was trailing downward, tendril after tendril of soft, lush vine.

And at the edges were flat rock ledges. It was, as Matt had said, totally safe.

It took her breath away.

She trod water and turned and Matt was right behind her. Watching her. And the expression on his face... He loved this place, she thought.

'Oh, Matt, it's beautiful,' she breathed, and he smiled, an odd little smile she'd never seen before.

'Beautiful,' he agreed, and the way he said it... It took her breath away all over again.

'I...do you come here often?' She sounded nervous, she thought, and maybe she was, but in a weird way. It was as if the world was holding its breath. Something seemed about to happen and she wasn't sure what.

'Just when I need to,' he told her. 'Even Donald doesn't know about this secret place. Isn't it great?'

'It is,' she breathed. 'So…your forty-seven maidens?'

'Okay, I made 'em up.' They were treading water. If they swam a couple of yards further on they could stand, but for some reason that seemed dangerous. 'The water above doesn't run except in times of flooding, so the waterfall's a rare thing. But this underground cavern's always here. You're the first person I've ever brought here.'

'That sounds…momentous.'

'I think it is,' he said seriously. 'Penny?'

'Mmm?' What else was a woman to say?

'I'd like to kiss you.'

And suddenly she wasn't cold at all. She was exceedingly warm.

Apart from her body.

'I'm all for it,' she told him. 'Except that I can't feel my toes and if I kiss you I might forget about them and I'll get frostbite from the toes up.'

'Ever the practical…'

'Someone has to be,' she told him and only she knew what a struggle it was to say it. 'But I have a suggestion.'

'Which is?'

'That we swim back through that waterfall, we get ourselves dry and then we think about kissing.'

There was a moment's pause. 'You mean we have an agenda?'

'I think it's more than an agenda,' she told him, and smiled and smiled. 'Agendas can be changed. The time for agendas is past. Consider the kiss a promise.'

'Then one for the road,' he told her and he tugged her forward and kissed her, as long and as deeply as two people treading ice-cold water could manage.

And then they turned to the sheen of white water that marked the entrance to their tiny piece of paradise and swam right through.

Back to where the horses were waiting. Back to where their picnic was waiting.

Back to the promise of a kiss and so much more.

Matt produced a towel and insisted on drying her. He rubbed her body until she could feel her toes again, until her body was glowing pink, until the feel of his hands rubbing her dry started sending messages to her brain she had no hope of fighting.

Who'd want to fight?

Then he gathered her to him and he kissed her as she'd never been kissed before.

His skin was still damp, but out of the water the sun did the drying for him. And who was worried about a little damp? He felt almost naked and her tiny wisps of lace hardly seemed to exist.

She melted into him. His mouth claimed hers, her body moulded to his and the kiss lasted an eternity.

But of course it couldn't.

'Dammit, I should have...' he said at last, putting her away from him with what seemed an almost superhuman effort.

'So should I,' she told him, knowing exactly what he was talking about. 'I packed sandwiches, cream puffs, wine, chocolate. I can't believe I forgot the After-Picnic essentials.'

'It wouldn't have been After-Picnic,' he told her and tugged her forward again. This kiss was even better. Longer. Deeper.

This was a kiss that had a language all its own. It was a kiss that promised a future.

It was a kiss that sent her senses into some sort of orbit.

But finally sense prevailed—as did hunger. They attacked the picnic basket as if there was no tomorrow—indeed, for now it seemed as if tomorrow wasn't on the horizon. And then they lay back on the moss and gazed up through the canopy at the sky above.

We might just as well have made love, Penny thought dreamily. She was held close in the crook of Matt's arm. They hadn't bothered dressing—with the warmth of the sun there was no need, and to put any barrier at all between them seemed wrong. She was warm, she was sated, the ride and the swim had made her sleepy...

'Penny?'

'Mmm?' It was hard to get her voice to work.

'How heartbroken are you about Brett?'

Brett. He seemed a million miles away. Part of another life.

If it hadn't been for Felicity, she'd be married by now, she thought, and it was enough to wake her up completely. She shuddered.

Matt tugged her tighter. The warmth of him was insulation against pain, but then she thought: *There's no pain.*

Humiliation, though, that was a different matter.

'There's no need to be jealous,' she told him.

'Hey, I'm not jealous.' She could hear the smile in his voice. 'I've got the girl. Whoever Brett's holding now, he's welcome. No one can match the woman I have in my arms.'

It took her breath away, even more than the icy water had. The statement was so immense...

And it was the truth. She heard it in his voice and part of her wanted to weep. Or sing. Or both.

Instead, she twisted herself up so she could kiss him again. He kissed her back but then tugged her close, held her tight and said again, 'Talk about Brett.'

'Why do you want to know?'

'Because he's important,' he told her. 'Because he made

you run. Because your family's important to you and I figure if they're important to you then maybe I need to know about them. So Brett seems a way in.'

And there was a statement to take her breath away all over again. He wanted… No, he hadn't said wanted… He needed to know about them.

He was talking of the future?

So tell him.

'It was dumb,' she told him. 'I was dumb. I'm a people pleaser. My family's nothing if not volatile and my father's a bully. My half-sister's an airhead but she also has a temper. My mum…' She hesitated. 'She might seem like an airhead too, but she's not. Maybe underneath she's like me. She tries to keep us all happy. But she won't stand up to Dad. She never has. She just tries to smooth things over, to present the perfect appearance to the outside world. And somewhere along the line I learned to go along with her. Keep the peace. Make them happy.'

'So… Brett?'

'I was cooking in London,' she told him. 'I seldom went home—to be honest, as little as possible because Dad hates what I do and he gives me a hard time. But Mum rang me every night. Things seemed okay. But then Grandma died—Mum's mother—and I hadn't realized how much Mum needed her. Like she needs me. It's weird but being needed seems to be hardwired into us. Grandma supported Mum any way she could, which gave Mum the strength to stay in an awful marriage. When Grandma died she fell apart.' Penny sighed.

'Anyway, I came home and Dad pushed and pushed me into the PR job and I was so scared for Mum that finally I said yes. And what a disaster. I must have been depressed too, or at least my radar for slimeballs was depressed because Brett found me easy pickings. I was the daughter of the man he wanted to schmooze. Only, of course, he misjudged. He hadn't figured the family dynamics until it was too late—that Felicity is Dad's favourite. But then Felicity came home and he figured it out and the rest is history.'

'He's an idiot.'

She thought about that for a while. It was odd, but lying here on the moss, held hard against such a man as Matt… her perspective changed. Somehow the fog of humiliation that had been with her since that appalling dinner suddenly cleared, vaporising into the filtered sunlight and the shadows of the gums above her head.

'He's not an idiot,' she said softly. 'He's a lying, scheming toad who thinks he can get near Dad's fortune by marrying into the family. And maybe he can, and yes, he now has the beautiful daughter, but what he hasn't reckoned on is Felicity's temper. Felicity's hysterics. He doesn't know what it's like to live with Felicity. I wish him joy.'

'Punishment enough?'

'You said it,' she said softly. 'And now… I'm here with you. I still worry about Mum but, as you said, there's no way I can fix her problems for her.'

'Not when there're cream puffs and waterholes and sheep…'

And there it was again. That suggestion of a future.

'No indeed,' she said and smiled, because how could she not? She kissed him again because there was no choice in that either. 'Brett and Felicity are no longer in my world. I think, right now, I could even face their wedding. But you're right, I won't.'

And then Samson, who'd been sleeping on the edge of the clearing in between Matt's two dogs, suddenly decided he needed a little of his mistress's attention. He edged forward to wiggle between them, and suddenly they were both laughing.

'Right now my world seems to smell of sheep,' she said happily, even joyfully. 'And eau de rabbit burrow and damp dog. And is there horse dung in the mixture as well? And you know what? I love it. Just for now, Matt Fraser, I am a very happy woman. Brett and Felicity can have my old world. For now I'm happy in this one.'

CHAPTER NINE

THE NEXT WEEK passed in a blur of hard work and happiness. Matt was pressuring her to slow down, to give herself a break after the exertion of shearing, but why would she?

She made the house pristine. The orders for the new furniture were coming in, to be admired, placed, enjoyed. She was still cooking but there were only four men to cook for. She could do it with her hands tied.

Matt was outside working, so she was too.

She was getting pretty good at riding Maisie now. She could round up the mobs of sheep with him, listening to his plans for building his bloodlines, or explaining how this ewe had triplets last lambing and all of them survived, or introducing her to Roger the Ram, whose bloodlines were suspect but who'd been having his way with the ladies for so long that he didn't have it in him to get rid of him.

His pride in his land and his flock was contagious. Penny found herself starting to decipher individual differences, knowing what to look for in the best breeding stock, looking at the signs of capeweed in the top paddock and frowning because Matt had told her the effort it was to keep the pasture lush and healthy.

Then they started drenching, and working in the house disappeared from her agenda. They lived on soup and sandwiches because Penny was out there, learning how to deal with a drenching gun to make sure the sheep would be pest-free, learning how to encourage the dogs and herd a mob of sheep into the yards, how to be a useful farmhand.

She came in at night tired and filthy—she smelled the same as Samson—and every night she fell into bed exhausted.

She fell into bed with Matt.

On the night of the picnic he'd taken her to his bed and she'd melted into his arms with joy. It felt right. It felt like home.

It was as if she hadn't lived until now. He smiled and her heart sang. He touched her and her body melted into his.

This wasn't forever. She was sensible enough to know those demons were still out there. She was still Matt's housekeeper, being paid the exorbitant wage she'd demanded. He was still her boss.

But he wasn't her boss at night and the nights were theirs. Their nights were a time for no promises, no thought of the future and no looking back on the past.

Here, in Matt's arms, she could pretend the rest of the world didn't exist. She could forget her father's scorn, Brett's betrayal, her mother's needs.

Here she could pretend she was loved and, for the moment, it was all she asked.

And as for Matt's demons? She wasn't asking questions and neither was he. For both of them the future seemed too far away, too hard. There was just the oasis of now.

Old resolutions were put aside. She knew they were still there—for both of them—but for now why ask questions? Right now was perfect.

If this was all there was, she'd take it.

So would Matt, but in the dawn light he was awake, staring at the ceiling, seeing trouble.

There'd been a couple of phone calls from Darrilyn, hysterical ones—calls that reminded him of times past.

'She's impossible!' Darrilyn had practically screeched it down the phone. 'She's a thirteen-year-old witch. Ray's starting to say he won't have her in the house. All she does is sulk and listen to her appalling music and throw insults at Ray. If it gets any worse... You'll have to cope.'

You'll have to cope.

His mother had used that line. He remembered her getting ready to go out for an evening with her latest boyfriend. He must have been about seven.

'You're a big boy now, Matt. There are cold sausages in the fridge and cola. If I'm not back by morning you know where your school uniform is. Make sure you brush your hair before you walk to school. And make sure you're not late or I'll have teachers asking questions.'

'I don't like being by myself.' He could still hear his childish plea.

'Nonsense,' she'd said. 'Don't be stupid, Matt. I'm entitled to have fun. You'll just have to cope.'

He did have to cope. Somehow.

But this woman in his arms? This woman who trusted absolutely? Penny, who wore her heart on her sleeve...

She was the best thing to happen to him, he thought. She was someone he'd never thought he could meet.

He was a loner. He'd learned not to need anyone. But he lay with her in his arms and he thought it'd be okay. He could love her.

His life was changing. His life right now was better than okay.

But Penny looked at him with love and a voice inside his head was telling him that love came with strings.

If she needed him... If he admitted he needed her...

What was wrong with that?

Nothing, he told himself as she woke and he held her close. As her body melted into his, as the dawn dissolved in a mist of love and desire, the problems of the past seemed far away.

What was wrong with needing this woman?

Nothing at all?

* * *

They were at the end of drenching—squirting stuff on the sheep's backs that'd protect them from internal parasites. Penny was having more fun than she'd ever had in her life.

There'd been a mishap. A tree had fallen over a fence. It meant one mob of sheep already drenched had surged through and mingled with the final mob. So Penny was now in charge of drafting.

The sheep were being herded into the yards by the dogs—with Samson helping a lot! Penny stood at the gate separating the runs.

She had to hold the gate, check the markings and direct the sheep either way by opening and shutting the gate.

Ron and Harv stood beyond her in the drenching run, and Matt stood beyond that, doing a fast visual check of each animal. It meant that not only were they drenched but any problems left from the shear, nicks and cuts that hadn't been picked up and hadn't healed, were picked up there and then.

She was part of a team. The sun was warm on her face. Samson was having the time of his life, and so was she.

In an hour or so the final drenching would be done. She and Matt would head to the house and clean up, and the evening would be theirs.

She felt like singing—though maybe not, she thought. Her nice, calm sheep might decide not to be so calm.

'What's funny?' Matt asked and she glanced along the run and saw him watching her. She smiled at him and he smiled back, and Harv groaned.

'Leave it off, you two. You're enough to curdle milk.' But he was grinning as he said it.

Matt and Penny. The men were starting to treat them like a couple.

It felt…okay.

'I was just considering a little singing to work by,'

Penny said with as much dignity as she could muster. 'Like sea shanties. Heave, ho, blow the sheep down.'

'You'd have the sheep scattering into the middle of next week,' Ron told her but he was grinning too, and Penny felt so happy that even a sea shanty wasn't going to cut it.

In deference to the sheep she was singing inside herself, but still she was singing.

She glanced back at Matt again and saw his smile which was a mixture of laughter and pride and something else.

Something that took her breath away.

And then his phone rang. The moment was broken.

Interruptions happened often enough to be mundane. The line slowed. Harv continued with the drenching and Ron moved to do the checking. Penny slowed letting the sheep through. The team worked on, but Matt disappeared behind the shed to talk in private.

And when he returned...he didn't say anything. Work continued, but Penny saw his face and knew that things had changed.

With the drenching finished, Matt excused himself and took Nugget up to the top paddocks to check the flocks. He did it every night, but tonight he took longer and went alone. 'I need some time to think,' he told Penny and she headed inside feeling worried.

She showered and changed, made dinner, waited and eventually ate hers and put Matt's in the warming drawer.

She sat on the veranda as she always did, but tonight she sat with a sense of foreboding.

She'd seen Matt's face when he'd returned from the call. She knew trouble when she saw it.

She knew this man by now.

Finally he came. He snagged himself a beer, brought his plate from the warming drawer and came out to join her.

'All's well,' he said briefly.

She didn't comment. She knew a lie when she heard one.

She hugged Samson while he ate. She'd washed him while she was waiting and he was fluffy and clean on her knee. He looked almost normal, a little white poodle instead of a sheepdog.

And with that word *normal* came another thought. What was normal?

Her life before, where Samson was clean all the time?

Life before Matt.

'That was great,' Matt said, and Penny looked at his empty plate and knew something was seriously wrong.

'Sausages and chips that have been in the warming drawer for over an hour? I don't think so.'

'Your cooking's always great.' He shrugged and tried to smile. 'You're great.'

'What's wrong?'

He didn't answer. He hadn't come to the edge of the veranda to join her as he usually did. He was sitting on the cane sofa, back in the shadows.

The silence stretched. It felt as if something was hovering above their heads, Penny thought.

Something fearful?

'Matt?' she said again, and it was a question.

He rose and walked to the edge of the veranda. For a couple of moments he stayed silent, staring out into the night. Finally he spoke.

'Penny, Lily's coming.'

Lily? His daughter.

'That's good? Isn't it?'

'The timing's appalling, but it is.'

'Why is the timing appalling?'

'I never thought she'd come so soon.' He hesitated. 'To be honest, I never thought she'd come at all.'

'So why now?'

'The phone call this afternoon was from Darrilyn. It

seems there was a fight last night between Lily and Darri-lyn's boyfriend. Apparently Ray's a hunter. He has trophies all over the house. He's just been to Africa and brought home stuffed heads from his latest kill, and it seems Lily hit the roof. According to Darrilyn, she said some unfor-givable things and Ray hit her. They went out and left Lily at home, and Lily took scissors and Ray's razor and shaved every single stuffed head in the house.'

'Oh…' Penny almost laughed. So the kid had spunk. 'Oh, my…'

'So Ray wants her gone, now. She's been in boarding school, but it's vacation and Ray says she's not even stay-ing with him until school starts. And Darrilyn… To be honest, I don't think she ever really wanted her. Having Lily's simply been a way of accessing my money and now it's all too hard. So Darrilyn's organizing a school here but, until she can start, she's sending her to me. She's putting her on a plane as we speak. I'll pick her up in Adelaide and bring her here. Not for long, though. Darrilyn's currently researching schools, probably finding the most expensive one she can make me pay for.'

'I…see.' She felt vaguely ill for the unknown and un-wanted Lily. Maybe she could help, she thought.

And then she thought: *No—really no.*

Because suddenly she saw exactly what the problem was and, looking at Matt's shadowed face, she knew that he'd got there too. She understood the heaviness.

She was suddenly imagining the thoughts of the un-known Lily. The kid was being thrown out of the only home she knew and was heading halfway across the world to meet a father she saw twice a year.

She'd be terrified.

But Matt would have told his daughter about this farm. All her life she'd have heard stories of Jindalee, of Ron and Harv and Donald, and the dogs and the sheep. Maybe she

knew about Maisie as well. Being here… Riding Maisie…
Exploring the farm with her father…finally they might
bond.

But, to do that, to have any chance at all, they couldn't
have an outsider, a pink princess tagging along with them.

She saw the whole situation now, and it made her feel…
hollow? Lily would arrive traumatised—Penny knew
enough of troubled teenagers to realise that. She'd need
all Matt's attention and more.

But, as for Penny? As for Penny and Matt? Well, that
was never going to work out.

Relationships and Penny? *Ha.*

And reality flooded back. For these last few nights,
lying with Matt's body curved protectively against hers,
she'd allowed herself to dream, but that was all it was. A
dream. Matt had needed her over shearing, and he'd enjoyed her in his bed. But now he no longer needed her and
it was time to move on.

Matt knew it. They both did. So say it.

'I need to go.'

'No.' Matt's response was a savage growl, but she met
his gaze and she knew he saw the situation as clearly as
she did.

He should be joyful that his daughter was finally arriving. Instead he was heavy-hearted because an embryonic
relationship was getting in the way of what had to happen.

Matt Fraser was a good man. An honourable man. She
knew he'd do the right thing, but for now the right thing
was to put his daughter first.

So if he couldn't—maybe she had to be cruel for him.

'It's been fun,' she managed and she set Samson down
and pulled herself to her feet. 'But you don't need me here
when Lily arrives. She'll need your sole attention.'

'I want you to stay.'

'Do you really?' She put her hands on her hips, feeling a surge of anger. She'd faced enough harsh reality in relationships to be used to confronting the truth, and he needed to see it, too. Coating it with sugar, with regrets, with apologies, didn't help at all. 'Matt, I came uninvited. I've had a wonderful time and, what's more, you've paid me brilliantly. It's been the job of a lifetime and you and I have had fun. But it's time for Samson and me to move on.'

'Penny, I need you to stay.'

But the anger was still with her. She knew impossibility when she saw it.

'Why?'

'Because I think I might love you.'

And the night stopped, just like that.

Love.

It was a tiny word. It was a word that was terrifying.

Normal people understood the love thing, she thought bleakly. Normal parents picked their kids up when they fell over, kissed scraped knees, told them they were loved and set them down to toddle off to the next scrape.

For Penny, though... *'Penny, how can you expect us to love you if you look a disgrace? Why aren't you more like your sister? For heaven's sake, lose a few pounds—that a daughter of mine looks pudgy... If you love us, girl, you'll do what I tell you...'*

It was always her father's voice, with her mother in the background, looking distressed but saying nothing.

And then Brett... *'Penny, I love you and all I want is to make you happy.'*

Love. It should make her heart sing and yet all it did was make her mistrust.

'No,' she said, more harshly than she intended. She hauled her dignity around her like a cloak, and maybe only she could see how tattered that cloak was. 'Love. It doesn't mean anything. We've known each other for how long? To talk of love is crazy. We need to face reality. These last weeks have been great but you don't need me any more. If and when Lily settles into school and you'd like to catch up then maybe we can meet, but let's leave it with no promises. Don't make your life any more complicated than it already is. Samson and I will leave in the morning.'

'What will you do?' And he'd accepted it, she thought. He knew there was no choice.

He really did love his daughter and he was an honourable man.

'I'll go back to Sydney,' she told him. 'I'll get myself together and decide on a serious career path rather than head back to the outback on a whim. I might even help my mother face this wedding down.'

'Penny, don't!'

'I think I must,' she said, striving for lightness. 'Because I love my mum. Like you love Lily. We shouldn't fight these things even if we want to. You know your first commitment needs to be to Lily?'

'Yes,' he growled. 'But I don't have to like it.'

But she smiled and shook her head. 'This is your daughter and I'm very sure you do. Love between you and me? Well, that's something we can control. It's something we can back away from because we both know it won't work. But the way you love Lily, and the way I love my mum, well, that's non-negotiable.'

And then she couldn't help herself. She stood on tiptoe and kissed him lightly on the lips, but retreated before he had the chance to respond.

'You're a wonderful man, Matt Fraser,' she told him. 'I've had an amazing time. You've rescued me really well, but now it's time for your rescued maiden to move on.'

Matt stayed on the veranda for a long time.

She was desperately hurt. He could see it in the way her face had closed, in the way she'd tucked herself into herself, in the dignity she'd summoned as she'd said good-night.

All he wanted to do was follow her, fold her into his arms and tell her how loved she was. How she was the best thing to happen to him…ever? Love was something they could control? *Ha!*

But he'd known her for less than a month. Maybe she had it right.

He thought of his mother, bursting in the door after a night out. *'Darling, I've met the most wonderful man.'* Then there'd be weeks, even months, of glowing happiness while she ignored everything else but the new love in her life. In the end Matt had learned to ignore it, put his head down, battle through as best he could until his mother finally surfaced. Even when he was tiny, she'd wanted him to pick up the pieces.

'Oh, darling, give your mummy a hug. Hug her until she feels better. Is there anything in the fridge? Oh, sweetheart, is that all? You need to come with me to the Welfare. They'll give me more if I take you with me.'

This wasn't anything like that, he thought savagely. It didn't come close.

But his daughter? Lily had been brought up with Darrilyn's version of the same scenario. Darrilyn had moved from one disastrous situation to another as she'd searched for the next socially desirable catch. If he'd thought there was any way he could help he'd have moved to the States, but Darrilyn had sole custody, granted by the US courts. His visits had been formally arranged and necessarily brief. But now, finally, Lily was coming home.

He'd always told her she was welcome here. 'If ever your mother agrees, you have a home in Australia,' he'd told her. 'A farm, your own horse, stability. And a dad who loves you and only you.'

Okay, it had been a promise that in retrospect was

stupid, but he'd never believed he could fall for another woman.

He had fallen, but what he had with Penny was only weeks old. Even his mother's relationships had looked rosy after less than a month.

'Leave it,' he told himself heavily and he knew he couldn't do anything else. He'd try and talk to Penny again at breakfast. Try and explain.

Except she understood. He knew she did.

She got it.

She was one amazing woman. When Lily was settled, he could find her...

'Yeah? You think she'll hang around and wait?'

There was no answer. She'd gone to bed. Even the dogs had gone to bed.

He was alone, as he'd promised his daughter he would be.

'And that's the way it has to be.' He knew it but he didn't have to like it.

He'd hurt Penny but how could he fix it?

'Maybe in time...'

Or not. *Leave it,* he told himself. For now he had this one chance with his daughter and he couldn't blow it.

Even if the hurt in Penny's eyes was like a stab to his own heart.

CHAPTER TEN

MALLEY'S DIDN'T WANT HER, or if they did she didn't stick around to find out. Malley's was too close to Jindalee. Too close to Matt.

She headed back to Sydney because her mother's pleas were still ringing in her ears. She no longer had an excuse not to attend her sister's wedding and, for some strange reason, she now felt she had the strength to be there.

She wasn't sure where it had come from but this new strength was with her. The new, improved Penny… She could have cried all the way home, but she refused. Instead she lowered the sunroof, put every powerful woman singer she knew on her sound system and let them rip. *I am woman*… She surely was. She arrived back in Sydney sunburned and with no voice but she didn't care.

Anger helped. And a new-found determination.

She'd put her career aside once because she loved her mother. What a disaster. Then she'd thought she'd loved Brett and where had that got her?

Now…she'd exposed her heart even more, and all she felt was pain.

'So no one needs me and I refuse to need anyone,' she told Samson. 'Who needs love?' It didn't quite work but it was worth a try.

Her mother was overjoyed to see her but Penny didn't stay at home except to sleep. She had things to do. Moping gave her time to think and the last thing she wanted was thinking time.

In some strange way things had changed inside her. She thought of the times she'd pleaded with her father to do what she wanted, and had passively accepted dismissal and scorn. But this time...

'I'm setting up my own catering company,' she told her parents. 'My plan is to do proper meals—family meals. If a young mum has a baby, I'll come in with a full week's worth of nutritious comfort food. If someone's ill, I'll supply what the family needs. I'll start small, but I'm thinking in the end I'll have staff and a fleet of delivery vans and caterers who can move into people's homes. And I'll be hands-on. Any time there's a need for a good feed, I'm your girl.'

'I won't have the media saying my daughter's a servant,' her father snapped but she'd had enough.

'I'm not a servant, and the only time I've ever felt like one was when I tried to please you. Look where that got me. So this time I'm pleasing myself and don't you dare put pressure on Mum to make me change my mind. And I won't be staying in Sydney. I'll be moving to Adelaide or Melbourne. It depends where I can get decent premises and that'll take time but I'll do it right. And Mum, I won't let Dad blackmail me into doing what he wants by using your sadness, so you might as well get used to the new order.'

She left them speechless. To say her father was unused to the women in his family standing up to him would be an understatement but she'd done it. She'd stay for a few weeks. She'd get her mother through this wedding, she'd get her own head together and then move on.

Matt would be proud, she thought, but that was a concept that hurt. So, instead of thinking about Matt, she forced herself to focus on work.

She put out feelers for long-term premises in Melbourne and Adelaide but she was sensible enough to accept that long-term plans should be put on hold until she was emotionally level-headed again.

She found a decent commercial kitchen and took a short-term lease, then contacted a local refuge for the homeless. The homeless were delighted, and cooking was a balm.

She needed someone to help her if she was going to do the deliveries as well so she advertised for an assistant. A young woman applied who was from Adelaide. Was that a sign? Maybe her new life could be in Adelaide.

It was too soon to decide. For now she was busy. She was doing what she wanted.

So why did she feel so empty?

At least Matt had banished the humiliation Felicity and Brett had caused, she conceded. That was the one good thing, so when her mother asked again—very tentatively—about the family pre-wedding dinner, she agreed.

Do it and move on, she told herself. *I am woman...*

'That's lovely, dear,' Louise said. 'It'll be just the five of us.'

Just like last time, Penny thought, and was proud of herself for not saying it.

So, two weeks after she'd left Jindalee, five days before her sister's wedding, she found herself dressing up and heading downstairs for a formal pre-wedding dinner.

Not a dinner cooked by her, though. Her parents had hired a trendy caterer for the occasion.

'It'll be something with kale in it,' she muttered to herself. 'With accents of Japanese on the side. Seaweed maybe.'

She thought suddenly of her shearers being given kale and seaweed and found herself grinning.

'Hold that thought,' she muttered and headed for the dining room. She was halfway down the grand staircase when the doorbell rang.

Felicity and Brett had arrived together ten minutes earlier. She could hear Brett pontificating with her father in the dining room. They weren't expecting anyone else.

Her parents' butler swung the door wide. The porch was well lit.

It was Matt.

She was halfway down the stairs and she was dressed as he'd never seen her—in a sky-blue cocktail dress that accentuated her curves to perfection. It had a mandarin collar, slit deep to reveal the beautiful curves of her breasts. It had tiny capped sleeves, a cinched waist and a skirt that swirled softly to below her knees. She was wearing high silver stilettoes and loopy silver earrings. Her hair was caught up in a soft knot of tumbled curls.

She looked elegant and poised and about a million miles from the Penny he knew. She looked as if she belonged here.

What was he doing? He felt like he should cut and run.

But it had cost him considerable trouble to get this far. There were security gates at the start of the mansion's long drive but by coincidence they'd been left open. That coincidence had taken research, an extensive phone call to the family butler, an explanation he was hardly ready to give and an eye-watering bank transfer.

So now he was where he needed to be, but did Penny want him? This house was all marble stucco, Grecian columns—grand, grand and more grand. And Penny looked… amazing.

Was this the Penny he knew?

He'd spent the last two weeks fighting an internal battle, which he'd lost. He was in Sydney, Penny was close and he knew her appalling family dinner was tonight. Letting her face it by herself seemed the act of a coward.

That was what he'd told himself, but he knew it was more than that. He'd spent two weeks without her and those two weeks had left him feeling gutted.

It was too late to back out now. Penny had seen him. She paused on the stairway, looking stunned. 'Matt,' she breathed and he felt his world settle a little. Just to hear her voice made him feel better.

'Hi.' He smiled, but the butler moved imperceptibly, blocking the path between them. Refusing him entry.

Fair enough. The man had agreed to let him as far as the door. He now had to resume his role.

'I had no right to come,' he managed, talking up towards Penny. 'But I don't have your phone details. I've brought Lily to Sydney to her new school and I wanted...well, I hoped for your advice.' He took a deep breath and looked again at the vision in blue. *Wow.*

'I'd hoped to talk to you,' he managed. 'But if it's a bad time...'

'What's happening?'

A woman emerged from double doors leading from the hall. She was slim and elegant, immaculately groomed, looking worried. Penny's mother?

'Brian, who is it?' she demanded of the butler. 'You know George said no interruptions. Felicity says Brett must have failed to hit the remote and left the gate open. George is already angry.'

Matt glanced again at Penny. Penny's initial smile had faded. She was standing like stone.

Okay, back to the plan. He turned to her mother. 'I'm sorry to interrupt,' he said. 'I met Penny when she was working in South Australia. I've brought my daughter to school in Sydney but I didn't have Penny's contact details. Your number's not listed but I knew where you live. I'd like to talk to her for a moment, but if I'm intruding ...'

'Are you her friend?' The woman's gaze flashed to her daughter, interest quickening. 'I *knew* she'd met someone.'

'Mum, no…'

But welcoming good-looking men into her orbit was one of Louise's principal skills, coming to the fore no matter what personal turmoil surrounded her. 'Come in. Brian, let the man in. Penny, introduce us.'

'This…this is Matt,' Penny stammered. 'He's a farmer… from where I worked. Matt, this is my mother, Louise.'

'A farmer?' Louise's smile hit high beam. 'How lovely. Come and have dinner with us.'

And this was exactly what he'd hoped for. Plan B was to sweep her up and take her out to dinner somewhere else. Or leave.

But a third option seemed most likely. 'He can't stay,' Penny said in a haunted voice and her mother looked at her again. Harder.

'Really? You don't want him to?'

He'd accept it. His plan had been simply to give her an escape route, or support, or both, but only if she wanted it. If she didn't then he'd walk away.

But Louise was looking exasperated. She turned back to him. 'Dear, if you know Penny then you'll know this is an awkward night for her,' she confided. 'She's agreed to have dinner with her sister and her ex-fiancé. Has she told you about it?'

'I…yes.'

'Then what we want,' she said with asperity, 'is a stranger to leaven the occasion.' She eyed him up and down. It'd have been too obvious to arrive dressed for a dinner party, but he was wearing new chinos, a decent shirt and a tie. His jacket was aged leather but it was decent quality. He could see Louise assessing and deciding to approve.

'Please, come on in,' she told him. 'Penny, you want him to stay? Don't you?'

* * *

Did she want him to stay?

Yes! part of her was yelling, but this was a new Penny. Okay, she'd only had two weeks of wearing her new skin but it had been a long drive back to Sydney and she'd had that radio up loud.

I am woman...

She was not her mother. She was not a doormat.

Did Matt want something? Didn't they all? She was suddenly feeling unbearably tired.

But her mother was letting her guard slip. Her social façade had disappeared and she was addressing her daughter with a degree of desperation. 'Penny, agree,' she told her. 'What your father is asking of you is impossible.' She turned back to Matt. 'Penny's ex-fiancé and her pregnant sister are here, and her father's expecting her to act as if everything's normal. I know she can do it—my daughter can do anything—but your presence...' She turned back to Penny again. 'Sweetheart, it would help. You know it would.'

It was the first time her mother had acknowledged her pain, and her words pierced a chink into the armour she'd so carefully built.

And then Matt looked up and met her gaze. He didn't smile. His gaze was serious, steady—loving?

And the chink grew wider.

'I won't be where I'm not wanted,' he said simply. 'Penny, if you'd like me to stay, then of course I will. You helped me and of course I'd like to help you. But I didn't come to intrude.'

Of course I'd like to help you. How could she believe that?

And then she thought: *I told him the date of this dinner.* Was it possible he'd planned this?

The thought that he'd do that for her... It was like a lightning bolt.

He'd come...for her.

'Stay.' She couldn't believe she'd said it, but it was out there.

His gaze didn't leave hers.

'You're sure?'

'Yes.' And she was sure. He'd planned it. It would be too big a coincidence. She gazed at Brian, who was looking blandly at nothing. Matt. Brian.

This was a plot!

For her.

'Then thank you, I will,' he said but still he didn't smile.

Her mother did, though. This was what she was all about—trying to please everyone, keeping her family happy. And Penny had a man! Penny could almost hear her think it, and the fact that he looked...well, he looked a hunk, did him no disservice in her mother's eyes.

Her father, though... And Brett and Felicity? A complicated night had suddenly become a whole lot more complicated.

But he'd planned it. For her.

Introductions all around.

George was urbane enough to be polite, even though he clearly didn't like his family dinner being gate-crashed.

'Sherry?' he asked Matt. 'It's a magnificent one my people have sourced from Almacenista. Or would you prefer a red? We have an aged...'

'I'd like a beer, if you have one,' Matt told him. 'Otherwise, water's fine.'

'As you wish,' George said stiffly, glancing at Penny as if she was responsible for allowing the cat to drag something in. And, as Brian poured a designer beer, he homed right in. 'So... Matthew, is it? What do you do?'

'I run sheep on the Murray,' Matt told him.

'You're a farmer?'

'Yes, sir.'

'That's where my daughter met you?'

'It is.'

'Her mother tells me it's flood country. How long have you been there?'

'Ten years.'

'It's a family farm?'

'No, sir, I bought it.'

'Well, that's a risk I wouldn't have taken. Small holdings take a lot to make them pay and if they're on flood plains…' Matt had clearly been pigeonholed and dismissed. 'I wish you well making a success of it.'

'Thank you,' Matt said. He took a swig of his beer and Penny almost smiled. Matt was drinking from the finest crystal but he drank like he was swigging from a can. She saw the exact moment when he stopped holding himself erect, when his voice took on the country drawl he used among the men—when he decided that if George had him down as a small time farmer then that was what he'd be.

And he'd also decided to be jovial.

'So Brett,' Matt said to Penny's ex-fiancé as he finished his beer and Brian poured him another. 'What do you do?'

'I'm a financial controller for the Hindmarsh-Firth Corporation,' Brett told him. 'If you understand what that is. Imagine the day-to-day cash flow problems you have on the farm and multiply them by thousands. Possibly millions.' Brett was smirking a little. He hadn't realised yet, Penny thought, that Matt's arrival had made him look small.

And then she thought, why hadn't *she* realised how small Brett was? Or maybe the word shouldn't be small. Maybe the word should be *insignificant*.

'Well, that must be fascinating,' Matt was saying, his

voice full of awareness of the huge responsibility Brett faced. 'All that adding up. So…you work for your fiancée's father?'

'He works *with* my father,' Felicity snapped.

'Of course. And you, Felicity?' His attention was suddenly switched to high beam on Penny's half-sister. 'Penny tells me you've been overseas. Working or pleasure?'

Felicity was not in a great mood. She was twelve weeks pregnant and she was nauseous. She was drinking soda, which she hated. What was worse, the new dress she'd bought specifically for this event only ten days ago would no longer fit, but she wasn't pregnant enough for the sexy maternity clothes she'd been admiring when she'd decided to try for a baby. She'd had to revert to last year's fashion.

And now her half-sister was sitting opposite her with a guy who might well be a small time farmer but wow…

'It's nice that Penny's found herself a friend,' Felicity said waspishly, ignoring Matt's question. 'Even if she had to go halfway across Australia to do it.'

'And wasn't I lucky that she did?' Matt said, and he smiled at Penny, and that smile…it even made her mother gasp. 'I hear you found your man much closer to home. Not that I'd describe myself as Penny's man, but I hope I'm her friend. That's such a privilege I can't begin to tell you.' He glanced at Brett. 'The local men obviously don't know what they're missing. Penny's one in a million.'

And suddenly, despite her discomfiture, Penny started enjoying herself. Matt could hold his own. Her mother was beaming. But the rest…

Her father and Brett were reacting like two roosters with a much larger and more impressive rooster invading their patch. Both were assured of their own superiority but Matt's calm acceptance of snide criticism had unnerved them.

And Felicity was jealous. Again.

Penny watched Matt smile at something her mother said. She witnessed his skill in deflecting Brett's barbs, and she watched him flirt mildly with the bristling Felicity. He was placating her with compliments. He was also exposing her shallowness and making Brett angry, but she knew instinctively that he was doing it only because he was angry on her behalf.

He'd come tonight, to this dinner, because he'd thought she needed him. She did need him.

No! Had she learned nothing? She did not need him! *I am woman...*

I'm no longer the poor relation at this table, she thought. She had her embryo catering company. She'd stood up to her father. She'd baked—successfully—for a full mob of shearers, and she had a friend. And such a friend.

She looked across the table at Matt and found him watching her, and suddenly she was smiling and smiling.

'How long are you in Sydney?'

'I've been here for a week and I may stay longer,' he told her. 'I need to wait until I'm sure Lily's settled.'

'What school's she going to?'

Matt told her—and that pretty much brought the conversation to a standstill.

'Why...that's the one Penelope and Felicity attended,' Louise gasped.

'How can you afford that?' George demanded and Penny thought a lesser man might have got up and punched her father's lights out for the offensiveness in the way he'd barked it.

But Matt merely shrugged. 'I'm divorced,' he said neutrally. 'My ex-wife has money.'

'Lucky for some,' Brett sneered but Penny wasn't listening. She was side-tracked.

'Matt, I hated that school.'

'It's the one Darrilyn's chosen.'

'Then un-choose it.'

'I'd like to talk to you about it, if I could,' he confessed. 'But now's not the time.'

And then the main course arrived, with all the theatre the hired, trendy catering staff could muster. Penny fell silent.

The choice of Matt's daughter's school was nothing to do with her, she told herself. It was none of her business.

But Matt wanted her advice.

He wanted her to be his friend.

He'd come tonight to help her.

The talk went on around her. She was aware that Matt was watching her but she wouldn't meet his gaze.

He chatted on easily, ignoring the undercurrents, making the gathering seem almost civil, but Penny's mother also fell silent. She looked as if cogs were whirring unseen. Comments to Louise went unanswered, and then, halfway through the dessert, she looked up from her peach flambé and beamed.

Penny knew that beam. *Uh oh.*

'Matthew?' Louise asked and Penny thought *uh oh, uh, oh, uh oh.*

'Ma'am?'

'What are you doing on Saturday?'

'I'm not sure,' he told her, glancing at a bemused Penny. 'It depends on my daughter.'

'Bring her to Felicity and Brett's wedding,' Louise said, with what was, for her, a defiant look at her husband. 'We seem to have invited half of Australian's *Who's Who* to this wedding so two more won't make a spot of difference. Do you have a suit?'

'I do,' he said gravely.

'Then I'd like to invite you. Please,' she added. 'If you're a friend of Penny's then you'll know that there are things about this wedding that make her...uncomfortable. You'll be doing us all a favour if you come. We'd love it if you could bring your daughter, but for the night…' She cast an uncertain glance at Penny but decided to forge right on. 'Come as Penny's partner. Like a little family. It'll take the media attention off Penny and I'm sure we'd all be very grateful.'

There was a deathly silence.

George and Brett and Felicity all looked as if Matt would be doing them the very opposite of a favour.

Louise smiled defiantly on.

And Matt looked at Penny.

'Penny?'

Matt, as her partner, at a wedding she didn't wish to go near?

But this was her half-sister's wedding and, hate it as she did, she'd made the decision to support her mother. The media fuss if she didn't go would be worse than if she did.

And, besides, there were parts of tonight's dinner she'd actually enjoyed.

Matt.

In a suit.

With his daughter?

His daughter was being sent to a school she'd surely hate.

Okay, she didn't want to be involved but she was. Like it or not. But she wouldn't be a doormat.

'I'm setting up a catering company,' she told him. 'I have temporary premises in Darling Harbour and I'll be there all day tomorrow. If you'd like to come around we can discuss it then.' And she could tell him exactly what she thought of his choice of school.

'I'd appreciate that,' he said gravely.

'So you will come to the wedding?' Louise demanded.

'Only if Penny wants me to,' Matt told her. 'I'd never pressure her.'

But it was too much for Felicity. She'd been growing angrier and angrier.

'Penny doesn't choose the guests,' she said in a voice that dripped ice. 'This is my wedding. I decide.'

'It's my wedding too,' Brett corrected her. '*Our* wedding, sweetheart. But he's certainly not on my list.'

But Felicity didn't take rebukes well. From anyone. She cast her fiancé a look loaded with such acid it could have cleaned warts off toads, and of course she changed her mind. 'Oh, for heaven's sake,' she muttered. 'If it'll make Penny feel better then of course she can bring a friend.' And she sent Penny such a condescending smile that she thought she might throw up.

'I don't need your sympathy,' she managed.

'But you have it,' Felicity said and smirked. 'Brett's in love with me.'

'Of course he is.' But then Penny hesitated. She cast a look at Matt. He was just…here. Big and strong and solid. She had backup, she thought. He'd come to support her—why not use it? Why not say what she'd been wanting to say to a big sister she'd once looked up to? 'But Felicity, have you any idea what you're getting into?' she asked gently. 'Brett went behind my back to get you pregnant. Do you think he'll stay loyal to you? You'll have family support, no matter what you do. It's not too late to pull out of a wedding you're not committed to.'

And that was too much for her father.

'Keep out of what's not your business,' George snarled. 'The wedding's happening in five days.'

'And this man's not coming,' Brett snapped.

'I agree,' George snapped back. 'My wife's in charge of the invitation list for this side of the family, and this man's not on it.'

So that was it.

Except Matt was looking at Louise.

Just looking.

And suddenly Penny wasn't sure what was happening.

Matt had charisma. Or something? She wasn't sure what. She only knew that Matt was looking directly at her mother and whatever was passing between them had the power to make the rest of the table shut up.

Even her father seemed momentarily baffled. Stymied by silence.

When finally Matt spoke his voice was low, reasonable and total mesmerizing.

'It seems to me,' he said softly, speaking directly to Louise and no one else, 'that Penny's been treated appallingly by those who love her. It seems to me that no one's spoken up for her. She's attending her sister's wedding—to support you, I suspect—and in the circumstances that leaves me stunned. If she needs me to lend her even more dignity and honour—two virtues that Penny already has in spades—then it would be my very real pleasure to be there for her. But, ma'am, I suspect that decision is up to you. And maybe it's time we all showed Penny how much she means to us. Especially, maybe, it's time her mother did.'

And he smiled at Louise, a smile that took Penny's breath away. A smile she'd never seen before.

'Maybe it's the right time now,' he said gently. 'To show Penny how much she's loved by us all.'

Silence. Deathly silence.

George was staring at Matt as if he were something from another planet.

Felicity and Brett were sitting with their mouths open, obviously struggling to find the words to retaliate.

But Penny's mother stared at Matt and he kept smiling at her. She stared…and then she turned to Penny.

'Penny,' she whispered and Penny gave her a wobbly smile.

'It's okay, Mum.'

'But it's not,' Louise whispered and she looked again at Matt.

And then, suddenly, Louise was standing. Her eyes were over-bright. She'd had one, possibly two more wines than was wise, but her speech was clear. 'Matt's right,' she quavered, speaking to Felicity. 'I've done every scrap of organization for this wedding, and you and your father haven't lifted a finger. And after the way you've treated *my* daughter... I could make one phone call to the caterers tomorrow, and with the demand for their services you'd find yourself without a wedding. Even if you did manage to salvage it, the ensuing media fuss would cause a riot.'

'You wouldn't,' George barked. 'Felicity's your daughter. We agreed when we married that you'd...'

'Look after her as if she were my own? Yes, I did.' She glanced again at Matt and what she saw there seemed to give her courage. 'I've loved Felicity even though she has a perfectly good mother of her own. But I've had enough. Felicity's not acting like my daughter. She and Brett have hurt Penny deeply, so deeply that all deals are off.'

And she turned again and looked at Matt.

Penny thought, *It's as if Matt's giving her strength.* She'd never known her mother to stand up for herself. Or stand up for her.

What was it about Matt?

'I've shut up for years,' Louise went on, enunciating every syllable with care. 'But now... Felicity, Penny's right to question what you're doing. You took Brett because Penny was marrying him and you were jealous of the attention. Amazing bridal gowns and maternity clothes are the latest fashion. Penny was getting what you don't have, and you've always thought like that. So now you're having your wedding and you're having your baby and you have Brett. And if you don't let Penny have Matt...'

'I don't want Matt,' Penny managed and the look Louise cast her was wild.

'It doesn't matter,' she told her. 'He's lovely—even I can see that. But it's *your* choice. Matt said it himself.'

'It is your choice,' Matt said. The corners of his mouth were twitching. The table seemed in total shock. 'But Penny, we're talking about a partner for a wedding, not a choice of life partner. Louise, thank you for your kind invitation. I may well take you up on it, if Penny thinks it's appropriate.' He smiled at Penny, a reassuring smile that held warmth and strength and promise but then he rose. 'I need to go,' he told her apologetically. 'I'm expecting a call from New York in half an hour. But are you okay by yourself here?' He cast a glance at the almost apoplectic George. 'There's room at the Caledonian. You can come back with me if you like.' And then he looked at Louise. 'Your mum too, if she'd like.'

If she'd like, Penny thought wildly. To get up from this table and run...

No.

I am woman?

Her world was quaking, but running away wasn't an answer. And running to Matt? For protection? For sympathy?

She had no need of either, she thought, and she looked at her father.

How had he grown to be such an ogre when he was just a puffed-up bully?

She looked at her mum and she grinned.

'We can look after ourselves, can't we, Mum?'

Louise was wavering a little on her feet—she really had had too much wine—but once again she looked at Matt and what she saw there seemed to reassure her.

'I...yes. I believe we can.'

'Excellent,' Penny said. She smiled at Matt and only she knew how much of an effort it cost her to stay perky.

'We're fine,' she told Matt. 'Obviously, I'm not sure about the wedding—for all sorts of reasons. But I'll tell you where my catering premises are and if you're still interested then we'll talk about it tomorrow.'

'Tomorrow,' Matt said and smiled at her and her heart twisted in such a way...

Tomorrow.

It was enough.

CHAPTER ELEVEN

PENNY'S NEW ASSISTANT arrived at ten the next morning. Noreen was a shy nineteen-year-old who was practically shaking in her boots. During the phone interview she'd seemed confident and perky, but it had obviously been an act. The only way to settle her and see what she could do was to cook.

And the promise from the interview was more than fulfilled. By late afternoon the kitchen was filled with the smells of tantalizing food.

Penny was covered in flour, elbows deep in baking, trying to focus on what Noreen was doing—and trying very hard not to wonder why Matt hadn't come.

If Noreen hadn't been here she might have gone crazy, she thought, but then she thought she was going a little crazy anyway.

And then the outside bell rang and her heart seemed to stop.

'Do those pies need to come out of the oven?' Noreen asked and her world settled a little. Pies. Cooking. That was the important stuff.

Not Matt?

She wiped her hands on her apron, which made no difference to her general level of messiness. She ran a floury hand through her curls—*gee, that helped*—and then she tugged the door open.

Matt was right in front of her—and so was his daughter. He was holding her hand.

She looked young for thirteen, but there was no mistaking who she was. She was thin and dark like her father. Too thin. Her hair was shaped into an elfin cut. Her eyes looked too big for her face, and they were shadowed.

She looked like a nervous colt, needing to escape but not sure where to run.

She was wearing the school uniform Penny had loathed and she looked so scared it was all Penny could do not to gather her into her arms. But she'd been thirteen once, and she knew such a thing was unthinkable.

She stood back and smiled a welcome. 'Hi,' she managed. 'I'd started to think you weren't coming.'

'I've been at Lily's school.' He looked almost as nervous as his daughter. 'Penny, this is my daughter, Lily. You don't mind that we came together?'

'Of course not.' She stepped back to let them in. 'Noreen and I are in the middle of baking. We have fifty homeless men to feed tonight. We've just finished apple pies. We're now making gingerbread men, as a post dinner snack.'

'Gingerbread men?' Matt said faintly and Penny fixed him with a look.

'Shearers need calories and so do the homeless, but the homeless have more time than shearers. So we'll feed them calories and then have fun. We thought we'd ice them with little backpacks and swags. Our aim is to make everyone smile.'

She cast a glance at Lily and saw her gaze around the messy, warm kitchen. She had the same starved look she remembered from her own childhood, when the kitchen was a refuge.

She thought of Matt's story, of this girl standing up to her stepfather, with his appalling stuffed animals, and the chord of recognition grew louder. 'Do you like cooking?'

'I haven't done much,' Lily whispered. She gazed at the

bowls of coloured icing and piping bags. 'It looks fun but I wouldn't know what to do.'

But Noreen, herself a gangly adolescent, saw a kindred spirit and beamed.

'It's easy,' she scoffed. 'I'll show you.' So, two minutes later, Noreen and Lily were piping multicoloured skirts on gingerbread ladies and Penny and Matt were free to talk.

Matt couldn't believe the transformation in his daughter. Lily was intent on her piping. Noreen said something to her and she giggled.

Matt felt as if he might cry.

He felt the strain lift from his face as his daughter relaxed.

'So what's happening?' Penny asked him. 'I can't tell you how grateful I am for last night, but now... You look more tired than when you were facing thousands of sheep and no cook.'

He gave a tired smile. 'Maybe I am,' he said. 'I've had one heck of a day.'

'Want to tell me about it?'

She led him over to the table at the end of the room. Sun was streaming in through the clerestory windows overhead. The room was full of the smells of new baking.

It felt like home, Matt thought, and then he realized he didn't really know what home was. And neither did Lily.

Suddenly there was a mug of tea in front of him and Penny was sitting opposite him. Waiting.

The last thing he wanted was to offload his problems onto her. The last thing he wanted was to need her.

'Tell me,' she said simply.

Penny had driven away from him because he'd put his daughter first. How could he do it again? But he glanced across at Lily and he knew that once again there was no choice.

'I knew there'd be settling in problems with a new school,' he started. 'But I hoped it'd work. But this morning she rang and she couldn't stop crying.'

'Because?'

His gaze was still on Lily. She seemed so young. Thirteen… He'd hoped she'd be old enough to fend for herself.

She wasn't.

'She's been there for a week,' he told her. 'And she's been put into a shared dorm with three other girls. But it seems they had to give up a settee so they could fit her bed into the room and they resent it. They complained to the school and to their parents, and then they stopped speaking to her. But they still didn't get what they wanted. Lily had to stay. Finally this morning they woke her with iced water tossed in her face. And they gave her a note.'

'A note?'

'It seems they're the school bullies,' he told her. 'Girls with rich families, used to getting their own way. The note told her that she should leave. It said no girl in the school will talk to her and if they do then they'll get the same treatment she does.'

'Oh, Matt…'

'So of course I fronted the headmistress,' he told her. 'I showed her the note and was expecting horror. But instead I heard pretty much what Lily did. "Friendships have been formed, Mr Fraser," she said. "It's difficult to make the girls accept an outsider, especially when she's arriving mid-term."

'Then I asked if Lily could be moved into a friendlier dorm and I had my head bitten off. She can't be bothered with what she terms "childish squabbles". She says if that dorm's unsuitable then the school's unsuitable.'

'So?'

'So we grabbed Lily's gear and moved out,' Matt told her. 'Oh, Matt.' And then she smiled. 'Good for you.'

'Yeah,' he said morosely, still watching his daughter. 'But now… Darrilyn's decreed that's the school she'll attend, and I don't want her taking her back to the States.'

'Does Darrilyn want her?'

He raked his hair. 'I don't know. No, I suppose not.'

'You could always call her bluff,' Penny told him. 'Choosing another school is hardly cause for her to change her mind.'

Matt fell into silence, feeling the weight of the world on his shoulders. How to cope with a kid he hardly knew—but a kid he loved.

The silence stretched on. Penny watched Lily. The girl was carefully piping, laughing shyly at something Noreen said. She was gangly, awkward, tentative. Even her smile was scared.

She looked like Matt.

She knew how Lily felt. She'd been given everything money could buy but no foundations.

'You can't keep her on the farm with you?'

'She's great there,' Matt told her. 'She was only there for a week, but already she loves the animals and I think she feels safe.' He hesitated. 'Penny, I'm sorry, but it was the right call…that you left. Thank you,' he said simply and her heart gave that twist again. The twist that was all about Matt.

He'd come last night because she needed him.

'Moving on,' she managed hurriedly, because emotions were threatening to derail her. 'There's no school she can attend as a day kid?'

'Are you kidding? You know how isolated Jindalee is. I'd need to move back to the city.'

'Yeah, and you'd hate that. Making one person happy at the expense of another sucks.' She stared into the dregs of her mug and then looked again at the two girls, who were now giggling over designs for clothes for their homeless gingerbread. Lily... Matt's daughter...

And suddenly—where it came from she could never afterwards figure—she had such a surge of bonding that she couldn't explain.

Maybe she could help.

'Adelaide's a lot closer to Jindalee than Sydney,' she said slowly. 'And Noreen's from Adelaide. She came to Sydney following a boy. It didn't work out.'

'Yeah?' He obviously wasn't following.

'There's nothing holding me here either,' she said.

He'd been watching the girls. Now he turned and stared. 'Penny, what are you suggesting?'

'I know a good boarding school in Adelaide. One of the Aussie girls at finishing school in Switzerland told me about it. They run a decent academic programme but they also have their own farm. There's an emphasis on things other than academia. Lots of camping, hands-on stuff, fun. Alice told me it was the only time in her life she'd felt she belonged.'

'I need the details.'

'Yeah, but it won't be enough,' she told him. 'Lily needs a base in Adelaide. She'll know no one outside school.'

'I can get an apartment and be there whenever I'm needed. Or I'll stay if I must.'

'And leave the farm completely? That'd suck.'

'I'll do it if I need to.'

Of course he would, because this was Matt.

But maybe... Maybe she could help. *I am woman.*

Matt was a friend. Women helped their friends. And didn't this fit into her plans anyway?

'It's early days yet, but if she likes the school... Matt, if you think it might work, maybe I could set myself up in Adelaide?' And then, as his face creased into a frown, she rushed on.

'I've decided not to stay in Sydney,' she told him. 'This place is temporary while I sort things out, apply for finance, put a business plan together. My hope is to set up a catering company in a city other than this one. Noreen would love to go home to Adelaide with her pride intact and I'm thinking we could search for premises near Lily's school. It would mean she doesn't feel so alone. With your permission, she could drop in after classes. She'd have you coming back and forth, and my place as a backup when you're not there.'

'Why would you do that?' he asked at last. 'Penny, what are you offering?'

'Not much,' she said diffidently. 'Lily might not need or want me but it doesn't matter. And it might end up working for us both.'

'To move your whole life…'

'Hey, it's better than cooking at Malley's,' she said and grinned. 'And I need to move somewhere.' She took a deep breath. 'Where Mum got the courage from I don't know, but we've talked and she's decided to leave Dad. She should have done it years ago. Dad's had mistress after mistress but she's tried to keep everyone happy. It'll take decent lawyers to extricate her money from Dad's clutches, but now… You saw the way she pulled you into dinner last night. She's a born hostess. I see her as the front man for my company.'

'But… Adelaide? For Lily?'

She hesitated, still watching Lily. It was a good way not to look at Matt.

'Matt, this isn't a sacrifice,' she told him. 'Who knows if Lily will even need somewhere like my kitchen after she's settled? Who knows whether my mum will like Adelaide, and who knows if Adelaide likes my kind of catering?'

'But you'll do it for Lily.'

'Lily could be a deciding factor,' she confessed. 'But

it's no big deal. Helping your daughter seems right. We are friends, are we not?'

'No,' he said forcibly, and he said it so loudly that Lily and Noreen stopped what they were doing and turned and stared.

'No, Penny, we're not friends. Or not *just* friends. Penny Hindmarsh-Firth, I said it before and I hardly believed that I'd said it. But I believe it now. I believe that I love you.'

In a romance movie she might have fallen into his arms right then. Hero declares his love. Heroine swoons with joy.

She wasn't having a bar of it.

I am woman...

In an hour a van would arrive from the homeless refuge and she'd promised a meal for fifty. She didn't have time to sit around and listen to declarations of love.

Because she had qualms and she wasn't falling for a line she'd heard before.

She'd been nice to his daughter and he'd told her he loved her. But she had no intention of being loved because she was needed. Of being loved because she'd done the right thing.

Not any more.

There was a part of her that would have allowed Matt to sweep her up in his arms and carry her off into the sunset with violins playing in the background.

She wanted him—but not on those terms.

So... *Get thee back*, she told the insidious voice in her head that would have welcomed being carried off on whatever terms Matt offered. But she'd been burned too often. She'd spent her life trying to please her father, learning from her mother that love meant sacrifice. Heaven, she'd almost married the despicable Brett because of it.

And then she'd fallen heart over head in love with Matt and broken her heart when she'd had to leave. And yes, leaving had made sense on all sorts of levels, but Matt had let her go. Two weeks ago she'd stood on his veranda and part of her had felt like dying.

She'd been burned too often. How could she believe?

'Why don't you kiss him?' Noreen asked. Both girls were watching, fascinated, but Penny turned away from Matt with a disbelieving snort and headed back to her pies.

'Because it's cupboard love,' she said, fighting to keep her voice light. To keep the whole thing light. 'It's like giving a kid a cookie. Will you love me if I give you this cookie?'

'Hey, Dad.' Lily picked up one of her luridly dressed gingerbread ladies. 'Will you love me if I give you this cookie?'

And Matt looked at Penny for a long, long moment while emotion went zinging back and forth between them. But finally he nodded gravely, as if acceding to an unspoken request.

He turned to his daughter.

'I surely will,' he said and headed over to eat the proffered cookie.

Good. That was the way she wanted it—wasn't it?

How else can I have it? she thought. *How can I trust?*

And then she thought, maybe it had just been a throwaway line after all.

Penny... I love you.

Easily said.

Prove it, she whispered under her breath. But why should he prove it?

'Am I still invited to your sister's wedding?' he asked and she blinked. Felicity's wedding. Okay, life had to go on.

'My mother invited you.' She was fiddling with the oven. She didn't turn round to face him. She daren't.

'So that's a yes?'

'If it's still on. I told Felicity...'

'She won't cancel a wedding,' Matt told her. 'Besides, they suit. Will you be leaving from your parents' house?'

'I...yes. Mum and I have decided to stay until after the wedding. We don't dislike Felicity enough to cause a media furore beforehand.'

'So what time would you like me to meet you?'

She turned to face him. 'Matt...'

'Penny.' He smiled that gorgeous, heart-warming smile that had her totally befuddled. 'I still want to come. Your mum says you need me.'

'I don't want to need you.'

His smile faded. 'Really?'

'Really.'

'Even if it's a two-way deal?'

'I don't know what you're talking about,' she said shortly, breathlessly. And then, more seriously, 'Matt, I need time. I know you can hurt me and I don't like that I'm exposed. I'm trying to get myself back together. To find who I really am. Falling for you complicates things.'

'It might simplify things.'

Noreen and Lily were watching with fascination but it couldn't matter. What needed to be said was too important.

'How?' she demanded. 'Matt, I've just come from a very messy relationship. I've spent my life watching my mother ruin her life trying to please everyone. I won't do the same.'

'If I swore to spend my life making you happy...'

'Matt, don't,' she said breathlessly. The memory of that moment on the veranda was still so raw it made her cringe. It made her block her heart from what was happening. 'I can't,' she said. 'It's too soon. I can't get my head around it. I can't...'

'Trust?'

'Exactly.' She shook her head. 'I'm sorry.'

'No, I'm sorry,' he said gently. 'Maybe if I hadn't met your family I wouldn't have understood, but I do. Penny, let's give this time.'

'I won't...'

'You might,' he told her and he came back to take her hands. He tugged her forward and kissed her. It was a light kiss, a fleeting touch of lips, but it was enough for her to know she was in serious trouble. But then he put her away and the smile he gave her was rueful.

'Saturday,' he told her. 'Wedding. What time?'

'Four. But...'

'I'll pick you up,' he told her. 'If I see you sweep out in one of the bridal limousines I'll know you don't want me to come but if you decide you want me then I'll be there. But no pressure, Penny, love. Lily and I will fly to Adelaide and check out this new school but we won't make any decisions and you shouldn't either. We'll see you Saturday—or not.'

'Matt...'

'No decisions,' he said again and he turned to Lily. 'Ready to go?' he asked her. 'Penny's suggested a new school you might like. Are you ready to try again?'

'I don't know whether I'm brave enough,' Lily whispered.

'That makes all of us,' Matt told her. 'Where can we buy courage?'

CHAPTER TWELVE

IT'S A HAPPY bride the sun shines on...

Felicity should be gloriously happy, Penny decided, as she fiddled with a recalcitrant wrap and gave her reflection one last glance before heading downstairs. The sun had been shining all day.

She doubted Felicity had noticed. Felicity's six perfectly matched and beautiful bridesmaids had filled the house since morning and the place had been chaotic.

Penny had snuck out at dawn and taken a long walk around the harbour front. She'd come back an hour before they had to leave.

Even that was too early. She'd taken half an hour to dress and now she was pacing.

Matt had said he'd come, but why would he? He'd gone to Adelaide with Lily. Why would he come all the way back?

There was a faint tap on her door. Her mother was there, looking magnificent. And anxious.

'Is he coming?'

'I don't know,' Penny said shortly. She glanced at her watch. 'But we should go. It'd be nice to sneak into place before the media gets its hype together.'

'There won't be hype over me. I'm not exactly mother of the bride,' Louise told her. Felicity's mother would be sitting in the front pew with George. Penny suspected she and her mother would be relegated to a pew quite a way back.

But, even now, Louise was still trying to keep her family happy, Penny thought. She'd made the decision to leave George but she wouldn't do it until after the wedding. Instead she'd stay in the background and try and smooth things over.

'You're a very nice woman,' Penny told her and kissed her and Louise blushed and gave her a tentative hug back. But she still looked worried.

'I was sure Matt would be here.'

'It doesn't matter that he's not.'

'But Penny…'

'We can manage on our own, Mum,' she told her. 'Who needs men?'

'Yes, but Matt…'

'He's just another guy,' Penny said airily and swallowed her pride as best she could and hooked her arm into her mother's. 'Let's go slink into our back pew. You want to ride in my little pink car? Come on, Mum, let's get this thing over and done with and then we can get on with the rest of our lives.'

And she propelled her mother out of the room, down the stairs, out of the front door—where Matt was waiting.

He took her breath away.

He was standing in front of probably the world's most beautiful—and expensive—four-door sports car.

The gleaming white car looked as breathtaking as the guy leaning nonchalantly beside it. Or almost.

Because this was Matt.

He was wearing a deep black dinner suit, a suit that seemed to have been moulded onto him. It screamed Italian designer, bespoke quality. His crisp white shirt accentuated his gorgeous tanned skin, his hair seemed even darker than usual and his shoes gleamed almost as much as the car.

And his face… It was strong, angular and weathered. His crinkly eyes were smiling straight at her.

'Good afternoon,' he said formally to both of them but

oh, his eyes were only for her. 'You're a little earlier than we expected but we came prepared.'

She managed to tear her eyes from Matt and saw Lily in the back seat. The window was down. 'H...hi,' Lily managed and emerged to join her father. Matt took her hand and led her forward.

The girl was wearing a pale blue frock, deceptively simple. Strappy white sandals. A single pearl necklet and earrings.

She looked very young and very lovely and also very nervous.

'Louise, this is my daughter, Lily,' Matt told her and there was no disguising his pride. 'Lily, this is Mrs Hindmarsh-Firth.'

'Lily, call me Louise. Oh, my dear, you look perfectly beautiful. And how brave of you to let your father drag you to a wedding where you know no one.' And Lily was embraced in a cloud of expensive perfume.

Matt gave Penny a grin and a thumbs up that said a grandma-type figure was what he'd hoped for. And Penny thought this was just what her mother needed, too. Someone to mother. And then she thought—they'd arrive at the wedding *en famille*.

This was a day she'd been dreading, and her mother must have been dreading it just as much.

Louise would have walked up the aisle as a second wife, the odd one out. Penny would have walked up the aisle as a jilted bride. Now, they'd arrive at the church in this car. With this man. Together.

'Ready to go?' he asked and she managed to smile back. 'Oh, Matt...'

'Don't say a word,' he told her and he kissed his fingers and then put them gently on her lips. 'Let's just soak up our first family wedding.'

And that was breathtaking all over again.

* * *

Penny had expected to walk down the aisle as the ugly duckling. The sister who'd been dumped for the more beautiful model. She'd thought people would be looking at her with sympathy.

But as she walked down the aisle with Matt beside her she felt as if she were floating, and who cared who was looking at her?

She almost felt like a bride herself.

Louise was right behind them, holding Lily's hand. Somehow it had seemed natural to do it this way. Matt and Penny. Louise and Lily.

They slid into the pew reserved for Stepmother. As Penny had predicted, it was well back. Felicity's mother had decreed the seating arrangements for the bride's side and it was a slap to Louise. Louise was used to such slaps, as was Penny, but now it didn't affect them.

It made it harder for all the necks craning to see who they were, but Penny didn't care about that either.

Penny and Matt and Lily and Louise.

Mum and Dad and Daughter and Grandma?

She peeked a look at Louise and her mother was beaming. *Oh, Matt*... Of all the ways to dispel sympathy. They'd have the church agog as to this new order.

Had Matt known?

She dared to look up at him and found him smiling.

'You knew,' she breathed. 'The car.' She looked at him again. 'The suit.'

'I figured it might help,' he admitted. 'A bit of bling.'

'I can't begin to tell you…'

'Then don't,' he told her and grinned and held her hand tighter.

And turned to watch the wedding.

* * *

It was the perfect wedding. It was orchestrated to the last minute detail.

It was faintly…boring?

'I'm sure we can think of a better way to do this,' Matt whispered as the groom kissed the bride and six perfect bridesmaids and six beautiful groomsmen lined up to march out of the church—and Penny almost stopped breathing.

'Matt…'

'I know. It's far too soon,' he told her cheerfully and went back to watching the truly impressive bridal procession. And Penny tried really hard to start breathing again.

And then they were outside, still in a tight family group. Louise was clutching Lily's hand as if she were in danger of drowning, and Penny thought how inspired had Matt been to organise it this way.

For Lily was intelligent enough to know she was needed. The memories of her week at her horrid school had obviously been put aside. She looked lovely and she knew it. She was even beaming at the cameras.

And there were plenty of cameras. Media attention should have been on the bride and groom but it wasn't.

For, as the crowd clustered round in the sunshine, someone twigged.

'Isn't that…? Surely it's not… No, I'm certain…'

It started as a ripple, a rumour, but in seconds it was a wave of certainty.

'Matthew Fraser! Owner of Harriday Holdings!'

'Surely not!'

'I'm sure. My dear, he's possibly the richest man in the country. But he's intensely private. Oh, my heaven… Didn't they say it was Brett who dumped Penelope? Goodness, maybe it was the other way around.'

Penny could see the wave of amazement, the wash of speculation—and the absolute switch of attention.

The media was suddenly all over them.

But it still didn't matter. Matt's hold on her hand tightened. He kept Louise and Lily in his circle.

The feeling of family deepened.

She'd dreaded this wedding but the dread had gone.

This wedding felt like her own.

The reception was on the Harbour, in a restaurant with a view to die for. But of course they were seated right at the back, on a table with others Felicity's mother had deemed insignificant. They were placed with the vicar who'd conducted the marriage service and his lively wife and three great-aunts.

For someone who lived alone, Matt did an extraordinary job of pulling people together, and Louise helped. She hadn't been meant to sit with them—that would have been too big an insult to seat her so far back—but she insisted on staying. She and Matt were determined to make their table lively. The great-aunts rose to the occasion. The vicar's wife announced that she'd attended Lily's new school in Adelaide and proceeded to tell scandalous stories of the teachers.

Lily visibly relaxed and so did Penny. She sat back and watched Matt weave his magic, and the feelings she had for him grew stronger and stronger.

Who was he doing this for? His daughter? He'd turned her into a princess for the night.

Penny's mother? Louise was charmed and charming. This day had turned out to be so different to the one she'd dreaded.

The great-aunts? These were three spinsters, insignificant aunts of Louise, but Penny and Louise both loved them. And they loved Matt.

They were having fun.

They had people at the other tables staring, and Penny was starting to see an almost universal wish. Theirs was suddenly the party table.

The dancing started. Bride and groom. Then the groom's parents—and Felicity's mother with George.

This was the moment when it would have truly sucked to be Louise, but suddenly Matt was on his feet, propelling Louise to the dance floor to be the fourth couple, and if Penny hadn't been in love with him already she fell right then.

Her mother wasn't the insignificant other. Matt was heart-meltingly handsome, and he swirled her mother round the dance floor as if she were a queen.

As other couples poured onto the floor she tugged Lily up and they had fun. The vicar and his wife came out to join them and then they swept down on the great-aunts.

'We can't dance if we don't have partners,' the great-aunts said in horror, but Lily put them straight.

'That's so last century,' Matt's daughter pronounced. 'Waiting for a guy to ask you is sexist and dumb. Get with it.'

So then they were all on the floor, and the great-aunts were teaching Lily to jive and Matt and Louise joined them—and then somehow Matt had hold of Penny, steering her effortlessly away from the giggling jivers—and somehow everything around them seemed to slide into oblivion.

The music changed to a rhumba and Matt was good. Very good. Penny could dance a mean rhumba herself and it felt as if she was almost part of him.

His hand held hers, tight, strong, warm. He tugged her in and out again, swung her, danced effortlessly, held her gaze the entire time.

She felt like Cinderella at the ball, she thought wildly, and then she wondered: *Is there a midnight?*

Surely there had to be a catch.

'Where did you learn to dance?' she managed as they swung. She was breathless, laughing, stunned.

'My mum,' he said simply. 'I think she had me dancing before I could walk.'

'You do still love her then?' She said it wonderingly.

His smile faded a little but the warmth was still there. 'She was an appalling mother, but I couldn't stop loving her.' The dance had him tugging her into him, and he brushed her hair with a fleeting kiss before the moves pushed them apart again.

'It seems once I give my heart, it breaks me apart to get it back,' he said simply. 'Loving seems to be forever. Is that scary? Yes, it is. Is it contagious? I hope so.'

Out she swung and then in again, but this time his arm didn't propel her out again.

Instead he held her close, closer, and closer still.

He kissed her.

It was her sister's wedding day. The focus of the entire day should be on Felicity.

Penny stood in the middle of the dance floor and melted into Matt's arms and let him kiss her.

For how could she pull away from Matt?

The kiss was plundering, deep, hot, a public declaration but a private vow. The music faded to nothing. There was only each other.

And half Australia's polite society.

She didn't care. She kissed him back, with all the love in her heart, and she thought: *If this night is all I have, then I'm Cinderella.*

And finally, when the kiss stopped, as all kisses eventually must, when she finally stood at arm's length, when he smiled down at her, just smiled and smiled, she knew where her heart was. She knew there'd be no midnight.

As the dancers around them erupted into laughing applause she blushed, but Matt held her hand and she held his hand back.

'Hey, Penelope.' It was a reporter from the biggest society tabloid in the country, calling from the side of the room as Matt led her back to the table. 'How's it feel to be the jilted bride?'

And there was only one word to say to that.

'Perfect.'

Because it was.

Lily wilted. Matt needed to take her home and the entire table decided to follow.

'I know you're supposed to wait for the bride to leave,' one great-aunt grumbled. 'But these days they stay until three in the morning and if *you* leave, young man, there's not a person in this room who can criticise us.'

'And you don't know your way around this part of town,' Louise declared. She wasn't about to let the night end on a whimper. 'Let's make the grand exit.'

So they said their goodbyes—politely, but *en masse*—and departed and Matt thought the bride and groom would be pleased to see them go. Brett had been sending him dark looks all night. Felicity had been carefully avoiding looking at her half-sister.

They'd have much more fun without them.

'But drop in tomorrow,' Penny's father said to Matt, clapping him on the shoulder. He'd learned by now who he'd patronized five days ago.

'Thank, you, sir, but I'm heading back to Adelaide tomorrow,' Matt told him. 'I have a daughter to settle into school.'

He smiled and held Lily by one hand and Penny with the other and led them out. It was a defiant little team and it felt great.

And then they were outside, breathing in the warm night

air of Sydney Harbour, and he felt Penny almost slump beside him.

'Done?' he said gently. 'Not so bad at all, really.'

'Thanks to you,' she whispered. 'Matt, if you knew what you've done... For Mum... For me...'

'Sort of like charging in and cooking for a shearing team of twenty,' he told her. 'But with far less work.'

'Are you really heading back to Adelaide tomorrow?'

'Um...no,' he told her. The great-aunts and Louise were at his back and Lily was beside him. He needed to choose his words with care. 'I thought I might head back tonight, if it's okay with you.'

'Tonight?' Her face became still and he thought, he hoped, it was disappointment. But the expression was fleeting. Penny had herself under control.

She'd been verbally slapped too many times, he thought. He wouldn't mess with this woman again.

Ever.

'Of course it's okay with me,' she was saying but he shook his head.

'Don't say that until you hear my plan.'

'What plan?'

'I thought I'd take you with me.'

There was a gasp from the great-aunts and from Louise. Not from Lily, though. His daughter was grinning. She'd been in on this plan and was loving it.

'What...why?'

'I have things I need to show you,' he told her. 'Important things. Lily and I have been busy.'

'I thought you were looking at schools.'

'We have been,' he told her. 'Lily's planning to try out the school you recommended as a day kid, before deciding to try boarding. Boarding there looks fun but we're taking this slowly. Meanwhile, we have a master plan and I want to share it with you.'

'So…you'll both fly back tonight.'

'Not Lily,' he told her. 'Lily's exhausted, aren't you, Lily?'

And Lily looked at him and grinned. She'd made an excellent show of wilting inside the wedding venue, but now she was all smiles.

'I'm so tired,' she said meekly.

'So we're taking her back to the hotel on the way to the airport,' Matt told Penny.

'You can't leave her alone!'

'Who said anything about leaving her alone? Noreen's booked in with her. It took a bit of trouble to track her down but we managed it. Staying in the Caledonian, all expenses paid—Noreen thinks it will be awesome. Tomorrow they're taking the ferry over to Manly to check out the beach. They'll have two nights together while Lily recovers from her very exhausting night tonight…'

'I'm so exhausted,' Lily added, her smile widening. She looked so like her father!

'And they'll both fly over to Adelaide on Monday,' Matt told the speechless Penny. 'How about that for a plan?'

'Hey,' Louise said. 'What about me?'

'Hey, yourself,' Matt told her and grinned. He was no longer holding Penny's hand. He'd tugged her in so she was hugged against him. 'You're included anywhere you want to be included.' But then he reconsidered. 'Though not tonight. Not with us. But the girls would love a chaperone tomorrow.'

'I could take them to my very favourite restaurant for lunch,' Louise told him and smiled at Lily. 'My friend Beth has a son who's a lifeguard at Manly. Do you think you and Noreen would like surfing lessons?'

'Wow,' Lily breathed. 'Wow!'

Louise hesitated. 'I might stay at the Caledonian too. If that's okay with you.'

'Come over to Adelaide on Monday with the girls,' Matt told her. 'I think Penny would love it.'

'Hey, what about us?' one of the great-aunts demanded. 'This sounds fun.'

'Any and all of you are welcome,' Matt said, hugging Penny tighter. 'As of Monday, but not before if you don't mind.' He glanced at his watch. 'Apologies, folk, but I have a private jet chartered in an hour. My plan includes sweeping Penny away...'

'Sweeping?' Penny gasped.

'Sweeping.' He smiled broadly. 'But not without a plan. I'm sweeping you up in my jet and taking you off to places unknown and I'm keeping you only unto me until Monday. And, before you start with the practicalities, I had a conversation with your father's esteemed butler and it turns out he's a romantic at heart. He has a bag packed and one dog, brushed and fed and ready to go. A confirmation phone call from you, and they'll be on the tarmac waiting for us.' And then he couldn't help himself. He swept her up into his arms and held her close. His dark eyes gleamed. 'If that's okay with you, darling Penny.'

She thought suddenly of her lonely drive across outback Australia in her little pink car. Woman and dog.

I am woman...

She'd thought she was strong. She'd thought she'd cope alone.

And she was, she thought mistily. Except right now she was woman in the middle of...love.

Her family. Her mum, her great-aunts. Lily.

Her man.

'*I am woman*,' she whispered to Matt as he held her close. 'I can do anything I want.'

'I'm sure you can,' he told her. 'So what do you want?'

'I want to be with you.'

CHAPTER THIRTEEN

PENTHOUSE SUITE. Adelaide's most prestigious hotel. Gorgeous, gorgeous, gorgeous.

They'd arrived at two in the morning and Penny had hardly noticed her surroundings.

She didn't notice them now. She was spooned in the great wide bed, her body moulded, skin to skin, with the man she loved with all her heart.

She had no idea where this was going. She had no idea how their lives could mesh, but for now all she cared about was that she was with Matt. And somehow things had been taken out of her hands. The great swell of loneliness she'd felt practically all her life had suddenly been lifted.

Last night had been fun, she thought dreamily. Her sister's wedding, an event she'd been dreading, had turned out to be an event where she'd felt she'd belonged for the first time in her life.

Because of the man who held her in his arms right now.

A sunbeam was playing on her face. She felt warm, loved. She had no intention of stirring, but somehow Matt must have sensed her wakefulness.

He opened his eyes, tugged her closer and she felt him smile.

She wriggled around so she faced him, looping her arms around his neck and she thought: *If I could hold this moment... This is where I want to be for the rest of my life.*

But there was a whimper from the floor beside them and the outside world broke in, in the form of one small dog.

'I need to...' she started but Matt tugged her tight with one hand and reached for the phone with the other.

'You don't need to do anything,' he told her, and a minute later a discreet hotel employee arrived. Matt donned a bathrobe, and Samson and his leash—and a discreet bank note—were handed over. Matt returned to bed, his dark eyes gleaming.

'Now, where were we?'

It took them a while to surface. Samson was obviously being taken for a very long walk.

'He's having breakfast downstairs,' Matt told her when she managed to ask. 'Speaking of breakfast, we need room service. Can I interest you in croissants? An omelette? Champagne? Okay, maybe not champagne. We have things to do, you and me.'

'Really?'

'Or things to see,' he told her. 'Though how can I look at anything else when you're right here?' He kissed her and croissants were put on the back burner for a while.

An hour later, dressed in her very favourite jeans and sweater—*how had Brian managed that?*—they were in an open-topped roadster heading for the hills. Literally.

'It's where Lily's school is,' he told her and that was where she thought he was taking her. But instead he pulled up outside an eclectic, fashionable village-type shopping centre, lined with trees, full of enticing cafés and Sunday morning visitors.

He helped her out of the car, tucked Samson under one arm, took her hand and led her to the end of the street. Then he paused.

He stopped in front of a building that looked like an old warehouse. It was built of clinker brick, weathered with age, long and low and looking as if it was part of the land around them. It had only one storey, but the roof rose in the middle to form a rectangle of clerestory windows.

Huge barn-like doors looked as if they were built of solid oak. A smaller entrance door was built within, so one person could go in, or twenty.

It was beautiful.

There was a 'For Sale' sign out the front. A notice had been plastered over it: 'Contract Pending'.

'Want to see?' Matt asked and Penny turned her attention from the gorgeous old brick building and looked up at Matt. He looked anxious.

'Matt…'

'Nothing's final,' he said hurriedly. 'This is your decision. But come inside.'

And he opened the small door and ushered her in.

Outside it was lovely. Inside it was perfect.

It took her breath away.

It was already set up as a commercial kitchen. Great wooden benches ran along the middle of the hall. Sinks were inserted at regular intervals. More benches lined the walls with a bank of commercial ovens. There were massive dishwashers, heating banks, storage…

There was a loading ramp at the back so vans could back in. A rear door could be opened and food loaded.

'There's parking for six trucks at the rear,' Matt told her and he still sounded anxious.

'It's perfect,' Penny breathed. Samson was down on the floor, investigating smells left from a hundred years of baking. 'Wow.'

'It's an old bakery,' Matt told her. 'The original ovens are still out the back.'

'So I could make wood-fired bread. I could…'

He put a finger on her lips. 'Wait until you see the rest,' he told her. 'It's a package deal.'

And he led her out the back, across the car park and through a small garden. There were two small cottages, side by side. Built as a pigeon pair.

He opened the door of the first and she saw perfection. Two bedrooms. An open fire. Sunlight streaming through the windows.

Modern touches, subtly adding every comfort.

'It's a package deal,' Matt repeated as she prowled in wonder. 'Two cottages or nothing. Penny, it's only five minutes' walk from Lily's school.' Suddenly he sounded almost apologetic. 'I thought… I hoped…'

And then he stopped, as if what he was about to say was too big to put into words.

She turned and held his hands and smiled up at him, and she thought her heart might burst. But she waited for what he might say.

'I thought…for the first few months, until she's settled, I could stay here,' he told her. 'Well, I'll stay in Adelaide anyway. I'll pay someone to manage Jindalee but I'll go home at weekends. I can organize a chopper to go back and forth, daily if needed. If Lily's a day kid she can come back and forth at weekends too. I thought…you could have one cottage and Lily and I could have the other. Unless…'

'Unless?' She could scarcely breathe.

And then she stopped breathing entirely, because he had both her hands in his and his smile was uncertain, tremulous, but filled with such hope…

'It's too soon to ask you,' he told her. 'I know that. It's unfair to put pressure on you. But Penny, my feelings won't change. I've figured that out about myself. My heart seems to have a will of its own. I figured I'd be alone for ever but I was wrong. Penny, if you allow me to buy this…'

'I…allow…!'

'This is your place,' he told her. 'Lily and I both knew it the moment we saw it. I have no doubt you could raise the capital to buy it yourself, but it would be my very great honour to buy it for you. With no strings attached.'

'No strings?'

'Except…maybe once a month for the next six months, you allow me to ask you to marry me. No pressure to accept. Just listen to my proposal. And every month I'll think of more reasons why you should. At the end of those six months, if you're still unsure, I'll walk away. I promise. So it's a small string. One question, once a month.'

'And that's the cost of my lease?' She could scarcely make her voice work.

'Not a lease. A sale. My weekly proposal doesn't make a difference as to whether you'll own it or not.' The hold on her hands grew tighter. 'So, my love, what will it be? Do we have a deal?'

She shook her head. Somehow she made herself smile although she could feel tears welling behind her eyes.

'The cost being six proposals?'

'Yes.'

'Then how can that work?' she whispered. 'How can that possibly work when I'm answering your proposal right now. The building is sold. Of course I'll marry you, Matt Fraser. With all of my heart.'

It was a wedding with a difference. A Jindalee wedding.

Matt Fraser had been a recluse for most of his life. He wasn't a recluse any more but this was no huge wedding. This was a wedding for the closest of their family and friends and no one else.

The reception was to be held back at the homestead because the caterers—Penny's team, led by the now indomitable Noreen—couldn't cart the food all the way to the river. But the ceremony itself was held at the billabong Matt had shown Penny after shearing.

Expecting guests to arrive on horseback was too big an ask, but they'd had time to build a carefully concealed track. The wedding was twelve months in the planning.

Which wasn't quite true, Penny thought as she rode

steadily to the place where she and Matt were to be married. They hadn't spent twelve months planning a wedding. They'd spent twelve months building a life together.

For the first few months Matt had commuted back and forth between Jindalee and Adelaide. He now had his pilot's licence—and his own chopper. He'd built up his flying hours fast as he flew back and forth a couple of times a week.

He could have made his home in Adelaide but neither Penny nor Lily wanted it.

Lily boarded at her new school and loved it.

Penny had established a catering firm that was already inundated with more orders than she could handle.

And at weekends they all went home.

Home. Jindalee.

The farm looked magnificent, Penny thought, as Maisie plodded steadily on, with Ron and Harv riding side by side as her proud escorts. Matt would have bought her a younger mare, as he'd bought a lovely bay mare for Lily, but Penny and Maisie had developed a bond she had no intention of breaking. Maisie went so slowly she had time to admire the scenery, the rolling hills, the lush pasture, the contentedly grazing sheep.

This year's shearing had been the time when she'd finally handed the day-to-day running of her company over to Noreen. Shearing had been when she'd come home.

It felt good. No, it felt great.

Lily was still coming home most weekends, although Louise was now living permanently in Adelaide. The two were as close to grandmother-grandchild as made no difference. A cottage behind the old brick bakery was home for Louise and a second home for all of them.

'We're late already,' Ron warned her. 'You want to get that nag to hurry up?'

'Maisie doesn't do hurry,' she said contentedly and it

was just as well. She'd decided to do the full bridal bit, which meant she felt like a cloud of white lace, riding side-saddle with an immaculately groomed Samson up before her. She couldn't hurry.

Nor did she want to. This was a ride to be savoured.

And suddenly Lily was thinking of a wedding twelve months ago… The wedding Felicity had stolen.

How lucky am I? she thought, wonderingly. *How blessed?*

And then they reached the ridge down to the water. The newly made track made it easy. The guests were there and waiting, on chairs set up on the mossy grasses by the waterfall.

Lily was waiting to help her down, in full bridesmaid splendour. And Louise. They fussed about her dress, cluck-ing that it had crushed a little during the ride. Smoothing it down. Her mother was smiling through tears and Lily was handing her her bouquet.

Penny hardly noticed.

All she saw was Matt.

He too had ridden to the wedding—on Penny's instruc-tions. 'Because it's how I first saw you,' she'd told him. 'My knight in shining armour, on a horse to match.'

'I seem to remember I was a pretty soggy knight,' he'd told her and she'd chuckled but she'd stayed firm.

So his big black horse was calmly grazing behind the makeshift altar and Matt was standing waiting. He smiled and the world stood still.

He looked stunning. 'I'm damned if I'll wear a din-ner suit if I'm riding a horse,' he'd told Penny and she'd agreed—the Matt she loved wasn't a dinner suit kind of person. But he'd compromised.

He was wearing the breeches of a true horseman, buff, moulded to his legs. He wore glossy riding boots reach-ing to his knees, a deep black dressage jacket and a cravat, white silk, intricate, splendid. He'd do a Regency hero proud.

He'd do anyone proud, she thought mistily. He looked spectacular. Drop dead gorgeous. Toe-curlingly handsome.

Her Matt.

Music swelled in the background. She'd thought they'd have recorded music but, amazingly, Matt seemed to have organized a grand piano. *How the...?* But now wasn't the time to ask. The pianist and a cellist were playing *A Thousand Years*, a song to take her breath away. To make all eyes well.

But she was no longer hearing the music.

Matt was smiling and smiling. Their guests were on their feet, smiling almost as much as Matt.

'Are you ready, my love?' Louise asked, groping for her lace handkerchief and then giving up and sniffing.

'Of course I'm ready,' Penny told her. 'How could I not be? This is my Matt. This is the rest of my life.'

He thought of the first time he'd seen her—little, blonde, hot and cross. Bare toes covered with sand.

He'd thought she was beautiful then. How much more so now?

The dress she'd chosen—ignoring her mother's questionable advice—was perfect for her. It was mermaid style, white silk, the bodice perfectly cupping her breasts. Tiny slivers of shoulder straps made it safe for the ride. It was figure-hugging to her hips, then flared out to her feet in a gorgeous rustle of silk and taffeta.

Shoulder straps or not, how had she ridden in that?

How could he ask? There was nothing this woman couldn't do.

Her hair was caught up loosely, curls cascading from a fragile spray of jasmine and tiny white rosebuds.

How could he look at her hair?

All he saw was her smile. And her eyes. She was smiling and smiling—just for him.

And, at that moment, something in him settled. Something strong and sure.

They hadn't hurried this wedding because it hadn't seemed important but now, here, suddenly it was.

Will you take this woman...

The words had been spoken thousands, millions of times, but they'd never been spoken as they would be today.

And now she was beside him. Lily was taking her bouquet and stepping back, and Penny was smiling up at him.

'I'm sorry I'm late,' she whispered and it was all he could do to make his voice work.

'What kept you?'

'Ron found a lamb,' she told him. 'It got through the fence down the back paddock and spent the night separated from its mum. You know we had a frost? Ron brought it in just before we left, so Noreen and I had to take the meringues out of the oven and replace them with lamb. But no drama. We have mum waiting impatiently in the home paddock, baby warming up nicely and the meringues doing their final dry in the sun on the veranda.'

And she took his breath away all over again.

'Don't tell me,' he said faintly. 'You coped with a lamb in that dress.'

'I only got it a little bit smudgy,' she told him, lifting an arm so he could see a tiny smudge of mud on her waist. 'And somehow I already had a little smear of lemon icing on the hip. But it's okay. It's pretty perfect.'

And he couldn't help himself. He chuckled and then thought: *To heck with convention.* He gathered her to him and hugged her and swept her round and round until she squealed.

And then he set her on her feet again and they both stopped laughing.

Pretty perfect? She was absolutely perfect.

Life was perfect.

They turned together, hand in hand, to be made man and wife.

* * * * *

"Where have you been?"

"Getting this for you." He handed her the tissue-wrapped bundle. It warmed her hands.

Aurélie's defenses dropped, and she stared at him in disbelief. "You bought me a gift."

He frowned, which in no way diminished the potency of his chiseled good looks. "No, I didn't."

"Yes, you did."

He rolled his eyes. "Don't get too excited. Trust me. It's nothing."

With great care, she peeled back the tissue. When she realized what he'd done, she couldn't seem to utter a word. She blinked to make sure what she was seeing was real—a hot dog. He'd gotten her a hot dog.

"It's a metaphor." He shrugged as though he were right, as if this silly little gesture meant nothing at all, when to Aurélie, it meant everything. "With mustard."

She didn't fully understand what happened next. Maybe she wasn't thinking straight after getting the call from the palace. Maybe the thought of going back home had broken something inside her. Maybe she no longer cared what happened to her at all.

Because even though she knew it was undoubtedly the gravest mistake of her life, Her Royal Highness Aurélie Marchand grabbed Dalton Drake by the lapels and kissed him as though she wasn't already engaged to another man.

* * *

Drake Diamonds:
Looking for love that shines as
bright as the gems in their window!

THE PRINCESS PROBLEM

BY
TERI WILSON

MILLS
BOON

First Published in Great Britain 2017
By Mills & Boon, an imprint of HarperCollins*Publishers*
1 London Bridge Street, London, SE1 9GF

ISBN: 978-0-263-92289-9

23-0417

Our policy is to use papers that are natural, renewable and recyclable products and made from wood grown in sustainable forests. The logging and manufacturing processes conform to the legal environmental regulations of the country of origin.

Printed and bound in Spain
by CPI, Barcelona

Teri Wilson is a novelist for Mills & Boon. She is the author of *Unleashing Mr. Darcy*, now a Hallmark Channel Original Movie. Teri is also a contributing writer at HelloGiggles.com, a lifestyle and entertainment website founded by Zooey Deschanel that is now part of the *People* magazine, *TIME* magazine and *Entertainment Weekly* family. Teri loves books, travel, animals and dancing every day. Visit Teri at www.teriwilson.net or on Twitter, @teriwilsonauthr.

For my English writer friend
and fellow royal enthusiast,
Rachel Brimble.

"The pearl is the queen of gems and the gem of queens."

Grace Kelly

Chapter One

It was the pearls that tipped Dalton off.

Dalton Drake knew a string of South Sea pearls when he saw one, even when those pearls were mostly hidden behind the crisp black collar of an Armani suit jacket. He stood in the doorway of his office, frowning at the back of the Armani-clad figure. The pearls in question were a luminous gold, just a shade or two darker than a glass of fizzy Veuve Clicquot. The rarest of the rare. Worth more than half the jewels in the glittering display cases of Drake Diamonds, the illustrious establishment where he currently stood. And owned. And ran, along with his brother, Artem Drake.

Dalton had grown up around pearls. They were in his blood, every bit as much as diamonds were. What he couldn't figure out was why such a priceless piece of jewelry was currently draped around the neck of a glorified errand boy. Or why that particular errand boy possessed such a tiny waist and lushly curved figure.

Dalton had paid a small fortune for a private plane to bring someone by the name of Monsieur Oliver Martel to New York all the way from the royal territory of Delamotte on the French Riviera. What the hell had gone wrong? It didn't take a genius to figure out he wasn't looking at a *monsieur*, the simple black men's suit notwithstanding. Delicate, perfectly manicured fingertips peeked from beneath the oversized sleeves. Wisps of fine blond hair escaped the fedora atop her head. She lowered herself into one of the chairs opposite his desk with a feline grace that wasn't just feminine, but regal. Far too regal for a simple employee, even an employee of a royal household.

There was an imposter in Dalton's office, and it most definitely wasn't the strand of pearls.

Dalton closed the door behind him and cleared his throat. Perhaps it was best to tread lightly until he figured out how a royal princess from a tiny principality on the French Riviera had ended up on Fifth Avenue in New York. "Monsieur Martel, I presume?"

"Non. Je suis désolé," the woman said in flawless French. Then she squared her shoulders, stood and slowly turned around. "But there's been a slight change of plans."

Dalton should have been prepared. He'd been researching the Marchand royal family's imperial jeweled eggs for months. Dalton was nothing if not meticulous. If pressed, he could draw each of the twelve imperial eggs from memory. He could also name every member of the Marchand family on sight, going back to the late 1800s, when the royal jeweler had crafted the very first gem-encrusted egg. Naturally, he'd seen enough photographs of the princess to know she was beautiful.

But when the woman in his office turned to face him, Dalton found himself in the very rare state of being caught off guard. In fact, he wasn't sure it would have been at all possible to prepare himself for the sight of Her Royal Highness Princess Aurélie Marchand in the flesh.

Photographs didn't do her beauty justice. Sure, those perfectly feminine features could be captured on film— the slightly upturned nose, the perfect bow-shaped lips, the impossibly large eyes, as green as the finest Colombian emerald. But no two-dimensional image could capture the fire in those eyes or the luminescence of her porcelain skin, as lovely as the strand of pearls around her elegant neck.

A fair bit lovelier, actually.

Dalton swallowed. Hard. He wasn't fond of surprises, and he was even less fond of the fleeting feeling that passed through him when she fixed her gaze with his. Awareness. Attraction. Those things had no place in his business life. Or the rest of his life, for that matter. Not anymore.

"A change of plans. I see that." He lifted a brow. "Your Highness."

Her eyes widened ever so slightly. "So you know who I am?"

"Indeed I do. Please have a seat, Princess Aurélie." Dalton waited for her to sit, then smoothed his tie and lowered himself into his chair. He had a feeling whatever was coming next might best be taken sitting down.

There was a large black trunk at the princess's feet, which he assumed contained precious cargo—the imperial eggs scheduled to go on display in the Drake

Diamonds showroom in a week's time. But there was
no legitimate reason why Aurélie Marchand had delivered them, especially after other transport had been so
painstakingly arranged.

Coupled with the fact that she was dressed in a man's
suit that was at least three sizes too big, Dalton sensed
trouble. A big, royal heap of it.

"Good. That makes things easier, I suppose." She sat
opposite him and removed her fedora, freeing a mass
of golden curls.

God, she's gorgeous.

Sitting down had definitely been a good call. A surge
of arousal shot through him, as fiery and bright as a blazing red ruby. Which made no sense at all. Yes, she was
beautiful. And yes, there was something undeniably en-
chanting about her. But she was dressed as a royal bodyguard. The only thing Dalton should be feeling right now
was alarmed. He sure as hell shouldn't be turned on.

Stick to business. This is about the eggs.

Dalton inhaled a fortifying breath. He couldn't recall
a time in his entire professional life when he'd had to
remind himself to stick to business. "Do explain, Your
Highness."

"Don't call me that. *Please.*" She smiled a dazzling
smile. "Call me Aurélie."

"As you wish." Against every instinct Dalton possessed, he nodded his agreement. "Aurélie."

"Thank you." There was a slight tremble in her voice
that made Dalton's chest hurt for some strange reason.

"Tell me, Aurélie, to what do I owe the pleasure of
a visit from a member of the royal family?" He tried
not to look at her crazy costume, but failed. Miserably.

"Yes, well..." There was that tremble in her voice

again. Nerves? Desperation? Surely not. What did a royal princess have to feel desperate about? "In accordance with the agreement between Drake Diamonds and the monarchy of Delamotte, I've delivered the collection of the Marchand imperial eggs. I understand your store will be displaying the eggs for fourteen days."

Dalton nodded. "That's correct."

"As I mentioned, there's been a slight change of plans. I'll be staying in New York for the duration of the exhibit." Her delicate features settled into a regal expression of practiced calmness.

Too calm for Dalton's taste. Something was wrong here. Actually, a lot of things were wrong. The clothes, the sudden appearance of actual royalty when he'd been dealing with palace bureaucracy for months, the notable absence of security personnel...

Was he really supposed to believe that a member of the Marchand royal family had flown halfway across the world with a trunkful of priceless family jewels without a single bodyguard in tow?

And then there was the matter of the princess's demeanor. She might be sitting across from him with a polite smile on her face, but Dalton could sense something bubbling beneath the surface. Some barely contained sense of anticipation. She had the wild-eyed look of a person ready to throw herself off the nearest cliff.

Why did he get the awful feeling that he'd be expected to catch her if something went wrong?

Whatever she was up to, he didn't want any part of it. For starters, he had more important things to worry about than babysitting a spoiled princess. Not to mention the fact that whatever was happening here was in strict violation of the agreement he'd made with the palace. And he wasn't about to risk losing the eggs. Press releases had been sent out. Invitations to the gala were in the mail. This was the biggest event the Drake Diamonds flagship store had hosted since it opened its doors on Fifth Avenue back in 1940.

"I see." He reached for the phone. "I'll just give the palace a call to confirm the new arrangements."

"I'd rather you didn't." Aurélie reached to stop him, placing a graceful hand on his wrist.

He narrowed his gaze at her. She was playing him. That much was obvious. What he didn't know was why.

He leaned back in his chair. "Aurélie, why don't you tell me exactly why you're here and then I'll decide whether or not to make that call?"

"It's simple. I want a holiday. Not as a princess, but as a normal person. I want to eat hot dogs on the street. I want to go for a walk in Central Park. I want to sit on a blanket in the grass and read a library book." Her voice grew soft, wistful, with just a hint of urgency. "I want to be a regular New Yorker for these few weeks, and I need your help doing so."

"You want to eat hot dogs," he said dryly. "With *my* help?" She couldn't be serious.

Apparently she was. Dead serious. "Exactly. That's not so strange, is it?"

Yes, actually. It was. "Aurélie…"

But he couldn't get a word in edgewise. She was going on about open-air buses and the subway and, to Dalton's utter confusion, giant soft pretzels. What was with her obsession with street food?

"Aurélie," he said again, cutting off a new monologue about pizza.

"Oh." She gave a little jump in her chair. "Yes?"

"This arrangement you're suggesting sounds a bit, ah, unorthodox." That was putting it mildly. He couldn't recall ever negotiating a business deal that involved soft pretzels.

She shrugged an elegant shoulder. "I've brought you the eggs. Every single one of them. All I ask is that you show me around a little. And let me stay without notifying the palace, or the press, obviously. That's all."

So she wanted a place to hide. And a tour guide. And his silence. *That's all.*

And face the wrath of the palace when they realized what he'd done? Have the eggs snatched away before the exhibit even opened? Absolutely not. "All the arrangements are in place. I'd have to be insane to agree to this. You realize that, don't you?"

"Not insane. Just a little adventurous." She was beginning to have that wild-eyed look again. He could see a whole secret, aching world in her emerald gaze. She leaned closer, wrapping Dalton in a heady floral aroma. Orchids, peonies, something else he couldn't quite place. Lilacs, maybe. "Live a little, Mr. Drake."

Live a little. God, she sounded like his brother. And his sister. And pretty much everyone else in his life. "That's not going to work on me, Your Highness."

She said nothing, just smiled and twirled a lock of platinum hair around one of her fingers.

Flirting wasn't going to work either.

He ignored the hair twirling as best he could and shot her a cool look. "The eggs are here, as agreed upon. Give me one legitimate reason why I shouldn't call the palace."

She was delusional or, at the very least, spoiled rotten. Did she really think he had time to drop everything he was doing to babysit an entitled princess? He had a company to run. A company in need of a fresh start.

He sat back in his chair, glanced at the Cartier strapped around his wrist, and waited.

He'd give her two more minutes.

That's all.

Aurélie was beginning to think she'd made a mistake. A big one.

Granted, she hadn't exactly thought this whole adventure through. Planning had never been her strong suit. Firing Oliver Martel and demanding that he hand over his suit so she could take his place on the flight to the States had been easy enough. That guy was an arrogant jerk. He needed to go, and he'd made enough passes at her over the course of his employment at the palace for her to have plenty of leverage over him. No problems there.

Impersonating a royal courier had also gone swimmingly. It was startling how little attention the pilot had paid her. He seemed to look right through Aurélie, as if she were a ghost rather than a living, breathing person. Then again, Aurélie had lived in a fishbowl her entire life. She was accustomed to being watched every waking moment of her existence. That's what this whole charade was about—getting away from prying eyes while she still could. In a few short weeks, her entire life would change. And, if her father got his way, she'd never get this kind of chance again.

Aurélie didn't regret walking away from her royal duties for a moment. Placing her trust in Dalton Drake, on the other hand, might not have been the wisest idea. For starters, she hadn't expected the CEO of Drake Diamonds to be so very handsome. Or young. Or handsome. Or stern. Or handsome.

It was unsettling, really. How was she supposed to make a solid case for herself when she was busy thinking about Dalton's chiseled jaw or his mysterious gray gaze? And his voice—deep, intense and unapologetically masculine. The man could probably read a software manual aloud and have every woman in Manhattan melting at his feet.

But it was his attitude that had really thrown Aurélie off-balance. She wasn't accustomed to people challenging her, with one notable exception. Her father.

That was to be expected, though. Her father ran a small country. Dalton Drake ran a jewelry store. She'd assumed he would be easy to persuade.

She'd thought wrong, apparently. But he would come around. He had to. Because she was *not* going to spend her last twenty-one days of freedom staring at the castle walls.

She swallowed. These wouldn't be her last twenty-one days of freedom. Her father would change his mind. But she shouldn't really be thinking about that right now, should she? Not while Dalton Drake was threatening to pick up the phone and tattle on her.

Give me one legitimate reason why I shouldn't call the palace.

Aurélie's heart beat wildly in her chest as she met Dalton's gaze. "Actually, Mr. Drake, I have a very good reason why you and I should reach an agreement."

He glanced at his watch again, and she wanted to scream. "Do elaborate, Your Highness."

"It's best if I show you."

She bent to open the buttery-soft Birkin bag at her

feet, removed a dark blue velvet box from inside and placed it square in the center of Dalton Drake's desk.

He grew very still. Even the air between them seemed to stop moving. Aurélie had managed to get his attention. *Finally.*

He stared at the box for a long moment, his gaze lingering on the embossed silver *M* on its top. He knew what that *M* stood for, and so did she. Marchand. "One of the eggs, I presume?" Clearly, Mr. Drake had done his homework.

"Yes." Aurélie offered him her sweetest princess smile. "And no."

Before he could protest, she reached for the box and removed its plush velvet lid. The entire top portion of the box detached from the base, so all that was left sitting atop the desk was a shimmering, decorated egg covered in pavé diamonds. Pale pink, blush enamel and tiny seed pearls rested on a bed of white satin.

Aurélie had seen the egg on many occasions, but it still took her breath away every time she looked at it. It glittered beneath the overhead lights, an unbroken expanse of dazzling radiance. Her precious, priceless secret.

She hadn't realized how very strange this would feel to share it with someone else. How vulnerable. She felt as though she'd unlocked a treasure chest and offered this strange man her heart. How absurd.

"I don't understand," he said, shaking his head. "I've never seen this egg before."

But there was a hint of a smile dancing on his lips, and when he trained his eyes on Aurélie, she could see the glittering egg reflected in the cool gray of his eyes, and she knew. She just knew.

Dalton Drake would agree to everything she'd asked.

"No one has," she said quietly.

She didn't know how she managed to sound so calm, so composed, when she was this close to having the one thing she'd wanted for such a long time. Freedom. However temporary.

He lifted a brow. "No one?"

"No one outside the Marchand family."

"So there's a thirteenth egg? I don't believe it," he said.

"Believe it, Mr. Drake. My father gave this egg to my mother on their wedding day. Other than the palace jeweler, no one even knew it existed." A familiar, bittersweet ache stirred inside Aurélie. She'd always loved the idea of her parents sharing such an intimate secret. Their wedding, their engagement and even their courtship had been watched by the entire world. But they'd managed to save something just for themselves.

What must it be like to be loved like that? To trust someone so implicitly? She'd never know, whether her father went through with his plans or not.

Of course, her parents' fairy-tale romance hadn't been as real as she'd always believed. Fairy tales never were.

Her throat grew tight. "I inherited it when my mother died three years ago. Even I was stunned to learn of a thirteenth egg."

Many things had surprised her then, but none so much as the shocking details of her parents' marriage. Her mother was gone, and Aurélie was left with nothing but the egg, a book with gilt-edged pages and a father she realized she'd never really known. And questions. So many questions.

When had things changed between her parents? Or

had the greatest royal romance of the past fifty years always been a lie?

Her eyelashes fluttered shut and memories moved behind her eyes—her mother and father waltzing in a sweeping circle beneath glittering chandeliers, the whirring of paparazzi cameras and her mother's elegant features setting into her trademark serene expression. A smile that never quite reached her eyes. How had Aurélie never noticed?

She opened her eyes and found Dalton watching her intently from across the desk. "Why are you showing this egg to me, Aurélie?"

Aurélie. Not Princess. Not Your Highness. Just her name, spoken in that deep, delicious voice of his.

Her head spun a little. *Concentrate.* "Because, I'd like you to display it in your exhibition."

"You're certain?"

"Absolutely." She paused. "On one condition."

Dalton gave her a sideways glance. "Just one?"

"Give me my adventure, Mr. Drake. On my terms. No bodyguards, no notifying the palace, no press. That's all I ask." And it was a lot to ask. She had enough dirt on the courier to guarantee he wouldn't go running to the palace. But someone would notice she'd gone missing. She just didn't know when.

It would be a miracle if she got away with this, but she had to try. She wouldn't be able to live with herself if she didn't.

She stood and extended her hand.

Aurélie had never in her life shaken a man's hand before. Certainly not the hand of a commoner. In Delamotte, Dalton wouldn't be permitted to touch her. Under royal protocol, he'd be required to bow from a chaste three-foot distance. "Do we have a deal?"

"I believe we do."

Then Dalton Drake rose to his feet and took Aurélie's hand in his warm, solid grip.

Delamotte had never felt so far away.

Chapter Two

"So let me get this straight." Artem Drake, Dalton's younger brother, pointed at the diamond-and-pearl-encrusted Marchand egg sitting in the middle of the small conference table in the corner of his office and lifted a brow. "You're saying no one has ever seen this egg before."

Dalton nodded and glanced over his shoulder to double-check that he'd closed the door behind him when he'd entered. He didn't want anyone else on the staff knowing about the egg. Its unveiling needed to be carefully planned, and he couldn't risk the possibility of a potential leak.

Satisfied with the privacy of their surroundings, Dalton turned to face his brother again and noted the enormous empty spot on the wall above his desk. The spot where the portrait of their father had hung for the better part of the past thirty years.

He was a bit taken aback by the painting's absence, since Artem hadn't mentioned his plan to remove it. And Drake Diamonds had never been about change. It was about tradition, from the store's coveted location on Fifth Avenue to the little blue boxes they were so famous for. Drake Diamond blue. The color was synonymous with class, style and all things Drake. It was the shade of the plush carpeting beneath Dalton's feet, as well as the hue of the silk tie around his neck. If Dalton were to slit his wrists, he'd probably bleed Drake Diamond blue.

But time changed things, even in places where tradition reigned. Their father was dead. This was no longer Geoffrey Drake's office. It was Artem's, despite the fact that there'd never been any love lost between Dalton's younger brother and their father. Despite the fact that Dalton himself had been groomed for this office since the day he'd graduated from Harvard Business School.

He was relieved the portrait was gone. Now he'd no longer be forced to stop himself from hurling his glass of scotch at it on nights when he found himself alone in the store after hours. Which was often. More often than not, to be precise.

Dalton averted his gaze from the empty wall and refocused his attention on Artem. There was no point in dwelling on the wrongness of the terms of their father's Last Will and Testament. He probably should have expected it. Geoffrey Drake hadn't been known for his sense of fairness. He certainly hadn't had a reputation as a loving family man. He'd been shrewd. Calculating. Brusque. As had all the Drake men, Dalton included, for as long as grooms had been slipping revered Drake Diamonds on their brides' fingers. Empires weren't built on kindness.

He leveled his gaze at Artem. "That's exactly what I'm saying. No one outside the Marchand family is aware of this egg's existence. Until now, of course."

Artem reached for the egg.

"Seriously?" Dalton sighed, pulled a pair of white cotton jeweler's gloves from his suit pocket and threw them at his brother. "Put these on if you insist on touching it."

Artem caught the gloves midair and shook his head. "Relax, would you? A secret Marchand imperial egg just fell into our laps. You should be doing backflips between the cases of engagement rings downstairs."

"We're on the tenth floor. Engagements is just down the hall, not downstairs," Dalton said dryly.

It was a cheap shot. Artem actually showed up to work on a regular basis now that they'd talked things through and agreed to share the position of Chief Executive Officer. The fact that Artem was now married and expecting a baby with their top jewelry designer, Ophelia Rose Drake, didn't hurt either.

Artem was a husband now, and soon he'd be a father. Dalton couldn't fathom it. Then again, he'd never actually witnessed a healthy marriage. To be honest, he wasn't sure such a thing existed.

Artem's features settled into the lazy playboy expression he'd been so famous for before he'd surprised everyone by settling down. "I know that, brother. You're missing the point. This is good. Hell, this is fantastic. You should be smiling for a change."

Dalton's frown hardened into place. "I'll smile when the unveiling of the collection goes off without a hitch. And when I'm certain I won't be facing jail time in Delamotte for kidnapping the princess."

"She came here of her own free will." With the hint

of a rueful smile, Artem shrugged. "Besides, the way I see it, you have a much bigger problem to worry about."

More problems. Marvelous. "Such as?"

"Such as the fact that you've been charged with showing a runaway princess a good time." Artem let out a chuckle. "Sorry, but surely even you can see the irony of the situation."

Dalton was all too aware he wasn't known as the fun brother. Artem typically had enough fun for both of them. In reality, his younger brother had probably had enough fun for the greater population of Manhattan. But that was before Ophelia. Artem's face might no longer be a permanent fixture on *Page Six*, but against all odds, Dalton had never seen him happier.

"Fun is overrated," Dalton deadpanned.

Fun didn't pay the mortgage on his Lenox Hill penthouse. It hadn't landed him on *Fortune*'s "40 Under 40" list for five consecutive years. And it sure as hell didn't keep hordes of shoppers flocking to Drake Diamonds every day, just to take something, anything, home in a little blue box.

Artem's smirk went into overdrive. "From what you've told me, the princess doesn't seem to share your opinion on the matter. It sounds as though Her Royal Highness is rather fond of fun."

Her Royal Highness.

There was a princess sitting in Dalton's office. And for some nonsensical reason, she was waiting for him to take her on a grand adventure involving hot dogs and public transportation. How such things fit into *anyone's* definition of a good time was beyond him.

A sharp pain took up residence in Dalton's temples. "Aurélie," he muttered.

Artem's eyebrow arched, and he stared at Dalton for a moment that stretched far too long. "Pardon?"

Dalton cleared his throat. "She's asked me to call her Aurélie."

"Really?" Artem's trademark amused expression made yet another appearance. To say it was beginning to grate on Dalton's nerves would have been a massive understatement. "This princess sounds rather interesting."

"That's one way of putting it, although I'd probably use another word."

"Like?"

Unexpected. "Impulsive." *Whimsical.* "Volatile." *Breathtaking.* "Dangerous."

"That's three words," Artem corrected. "Interesting. The princess—excuse me, *Aurélie*—must have made quite an impression in the twenty minutes you spent with her."

Twenty minutes? Impossible. It had been precisely 10 a.m. when he'd first set eyes on those golden South Sea pearls. On that straight, regal back and exquisitely elegant neck. If the severity of the tension between his shoulder blades was any indication, he'd been dealing with the stress of harboring a royal runaway for at least two hours. Possibly three.

Dalton glanced at his Cartier. It read *10:21.* He'd need to add a massage therapist to the payroll at this rate. *If* he managed to keep an aneurysm at bay for the next few weeks.

"I dare say you appear rather intrigued by her." Artem's gaze narrowed. "If I didn't know you better, I'd go so far as to say you seem smitten. But of course the Dalton I know would never mix business and pleasure."

Damn straight. Dalton preferred pleasure of the no-strings variety, and he seldom had trouble finding it. Sex belonged in the bedroom, not the boardroom. He wasn't Artem, for crying out loud. He could keep his libido in check when the situation called for it. "I assure you I'm not smitten. I have no feelings toward the princess what-soever, aside from obligation."

"Ah yes, your bargain." Artem turned the egg in his grasp, inspecting it. Blinding light reflected off its pavé diamonds in every direction, making the egg look far more precious than a collection of carefully arranged gemstones. Dynamic. Alive. A brilliant, beating heart.

Dalton had never seen anything quite like it. The other Marchand imperial eggs paled in comparison. When it went on display in the showroom, Drake Diamonds would be packed wall-to-wall with people. People who wouldn't go home without a Drake-blue bag dangling from their arms.

If the egg went on display.

It would. The exhibition and gala would take place as scheduled. The spectacular secret egg was just what Drake Diamonds needed. When Dalton and Artem's father died, he'd left the family business on the verge of bankruptcy. They'd managed to climb their way back to solvency, but Drake Diamonds still wasn't anywhere near where it had been in its glory days.

Dalton aimed to fix that. With the egg, he could.

He would personally see to it that the palace in Dela-motte had nothing to worry about. He'd keep Aurélie under lock and key. Then, in three weeks' time, she'd pack up the eggs and go straight home. Dalton would strap her into her airplane seat himself if he had to.

Artem returned the egg to its shiny satin pedestal, peeled off the jeweler's gloves and tossed them on the table. Then he crossed his arms and shot Dalton a wary glance. "Tell me, what sort of fun is the princess up to at the moment?"

Dalton shrugged. "She's in my office."

"Your office? Of course. Loads of fun, that place." Artem shot him an exaggerated eye roll.

This was going to stop. Dalton might have agreed to escort the princess on her grand adventure, but under no circumstances would he succumb to constant commentary on his personal life. "I've asked Mrs. Barnes to get her settled with a glass of champagne and a plate of the petit fours we serve in Engagements."

"So you have absolutely no interest in the woman, yet she's in your office snacking on bridal food."

Before Dalton could comment, there was a soft knock on the door.

The brothers exchanged a loaded glance, and Dalton swiftly covered the jeweled egg with the lid to its tasteful indigo box.

Once the treasure was safely ensconced in velvet, Artem said, "Come in."

The door opened, revealing Dalton's secretary balancing a plate of petit fours in one hand and a glass of champagne in the other, wearing a distinct look of alarm. "I'm sorry to interrupt…"

Dalton's gut churned. Something wasn't right. *But what could have gone wrong in the span of a few minutes?* "Yes, Mrs. Barnes?"

"Your guest is gone, Mr. Drake."

Surely she was mistaken. Aurélie wouldn't just take off and leave the eggs behind. She wouldn't think about walking around a strange city all alone, without her security detail.

Or would she?

Dalton swore under his breath. Why did he get the feeling that Aurélie would do both of those things without bothering to consider the possible disastrous consequences of her actions?

Live a little, Mr. Drake.

"Shall I take a look in the ladies' room?" Mrs. Barnes asked.

Dalton shook his head. If he thought for one second that Aurélie Marchand could be found in the ladies' room of Drake Diamonds, he'd march in there and go get her himself. "No, thank you. I'll see to her whereabouts. That will be all, Mrs. Barnes."

"Yes, sir." She nodded and disappeared in the direction of Dalton's office.

"Calm down, brother. I'm sure she hasn't gone far. She's not going to just disappear and leave the Marchand family jewels behind." Artem waved a casual hand at the velvet box in the center of the table.

Dalton sighed. "Have you forgotten that she's in a strange city? In a foreign country. All alone."

"Exactly. She's hasn't ventured any further than the Plaza. Come on, I'll help you track her down." Artem reached for the suit jacket on the back of his chair.

"No," Dalton said through gritted teeth. He pointed at the velvet box. "You stay, and see to it that the eggs are safely locked away in the vault. I'll find Miss Marchand."

And when he did, he'd lay down some ground rules for their arrangement. *After* he'd made it clear that he considered her behavior wholly unacceptable. Princess or not.

"As you wish," Artem said. "But can I give you one piece of advice?"

Dalton glared at him. "Do I have a choice?"

"Whatever you do, don't take her to bed." Artem's mouth curved into a knowing grin. "Assuming you find her, of course."

Who did Dalton Drake think he was?

She hadn't traveled halfway across the world, and risked the wrath of her father, only to stay trapped in a closed room on the tenth floor of Drake Diamonds. Not that the surroundings weren't opulent. On the contrary, the place was steeped in elegant luxury, from the pale blue plush carpet to the tasteful crown molding. It felt more like being in a palace than a jewelry store.

Which was precisely the problem.

She didn't want to be stuck inside this grand institution. It wasn't what she'd signed on for. Did he not realize the risks she'd taken to get here? She already had three missed call notifications on her cell from Delamotte. None from her father, thank goodness. It would take him days, if not weeks, to realize she was gone. The Reigning Prince had more important things to worry about than something as trivial as his only daughter fleeing the country. Oh, the irony.

But the palace staff was another story. They watched her every move and minced no words when it came to their opinions on her behavior. Or her fashion sense. Or her hair.

Or her love life. They had plenty to say about that.

How on earth was she going to pull this off? What if her father came looking for her?

She sighed. She wasn't going to think about that now. Besides, she was lost in the maze of pale blue and the sparkle of the diamond store. How would she find her

way around New York when she couldn't even manage
to navigate the terrain of Drake Diamonds?

Every room looked the same. Row upon row of diamonds sparkled beneath gleaming glass. Chandelier
earrings. Long platinum chains with dazzling pendants
shaped like antique keys. Shiny silver bracelets with
heart-shaped charms.

Engagement rings.

Aurélie looked around and realized she was surrounded by couples embracing, holding hands and clink-
ing champagne flutes together while they gazed into
one another's eyes. Everywhere she turned, teary-eyed
brides-to-be were slipping diamond solitaires on their
fingers.

She felt oddly hollow all of a sudden. Numb. Empty.
Alone.

For some silly reason she remembered the feel of Dalton's palm sliding against her own when they'd shaken
on their deal. He had strong hands. The hands of a man
accustomed to getting what he wanted. What he wanted
right now was her secret egg, of course. She'd given it
to him on a silver platter.

And now he was gone.

Her cell phone vibrated in her pocket. Again. Aurélie switched it off and removed the SIM card without
bothering to look at the display. Without a SIM card,
the GPS tracking on her iPhone wouldn't work. At least
she thought she remembered reading that somewhere.

She really should have had a better escape plan. Or
at least *a plan*.

Her gaze snagged on a silver sign hanging on the wall
with discreet black lettering. *Will you? Welcome to the
Drake Diamond Engagement Collection.*

She rolled her eyes, marched straight to the elevator and jabbed at the down button with far too much force.

But as she waited, something made her turn and look again, some perverse urge to torture herself. Maybe she needed a reminder of why she'd fled Delamotte. Maybe she wanted to test herself to see if she could stand there in the midst of so much romantic bliss without breaking down. Maybe she'd simply left the vestiges of dignity back in her home country.

She stared at the happy couples, unabashed in their affection, and felt as though she were disappearing. Fading into the tasteful cream-colored wallpaper.

None of this is real, she told herself. She didn't believe any of it for a minute.

She wanted to, though. Oh how she wanted to. She wanted to believe that happy endings were real, that love could last, that marriage was something more than just another transaction. A business deal.

A bargain.

But she didn't dare, because believing the fairy tale would hurt too much. Believing would mean admitting she was missing out on something she'd never have. Something worth more than deep crimson rubies, cabochon emeralds and the entire collection of imperial Marchand eggs.

Why was the elevator taking so long? She pushed the button a few more times, yet still jumped in surprise when the chime signaled the elevator's arrival. The doors swished open, and she half ran, half stumbled inside.

A hand caught her elbow. "Are you all right, miss?"

She blinked up at the elevator attendant dressed in a stylish black suit, pristine white shirt and a bowtie the same hue as the Windsor knot that had sat at the base of

Dalton Drake's muscular neck. Aurélie's gaze lingered on that soft shade of blue as she remembered how perfectly Dalton's silk tie had set off his strong jawline.

"I'm fine, thank you." The elevator closed and began its downward descent, away from all those engagement rings and the quiet solitude of Dalton's office.

The elevator attendant smiled. "Do you need help finding anything?"

Aurélie shook her head, despite the fact that she didn't know the first thing about New York. She didn't know how to hail a cab or ride the subway. She didn't even have a single American dollar in her fancy handbag. She had a wallet full of euros, yet she wasn't even familiar with the exchange rate.

But none of that mattered. She just wanted to get out of there.

Now.

Chapter Three

Right around the time he was on the verge of losing his mind, Dalton spotted Aurélie on the outskirts of Central Park. She was standing beneath a portable blue awning at the corner of Central Park South and 59th Street, directly across the street from the Plaza Hotel. She was holding a dog. Not a hot dog, but an actual dog. Which for some reason only exacerbated the pounding in Dalton's temples. The woman was impossible.

What had she been thinking? She didn't want to be discovered, yet she'd walked right out the door. Unaccompanied. Unprotected. Undisguised. It was enough to give Dalton a coronary.

At least he'd been able to find her with relative ease. All told, it had only taken about a quarter of an hour. Still, those fifteen minutes had undoubtedly been the longest of Dalton's life.

To top things off, a street musician had parked himself right outside the entrance of Drake Diamonds with his violin and his tip bucket. This marked the third time in less than a month that Dalton had ordered him to leave. Next time, he'd call the cops.

He squinted against the winter wind and shoved his bare hands into his trouser pockets. He'd been in a panic when he'd spun his way out of the store through the revolving door and onto the snowy sidewalk. Filled with dread and angry beyond all comprehension, he hadn't even bothered to grab a coat, and now, three blocks later, he was freezing.

Freezing and absolutely furious.

He dashed across the street without bothering to wait for the signal at the pedestrian crossing, enraging a few cab drivers in the process. Dalton didn't give a damn. He wasn't about to let her out of his sight until he'd returned her safely to his office. And then...

What?

He wasn't actually sure what he'd do at that point. He'd cross that bridge when he came to it. Right now he simply planned on escorting her back to his store on the corner of Fifth Avenue and 57th Street while administering a searing lecture on the dangers of disappearing without giving him any sort of notice whatsoever.

"Aurélie!" He jogged the distance from the curb to where she stood, still holding onto the damn dog.

She didn't hear him. Either that, or she was intentionally ignoring him. It was a toss-up, although Dalton would have greatly preferred the former.

"Aurélie," he said again, through gritted teeth, when he reached her side.

An older woman wearing a hooded parka and fin-

gerless mittens stood next to her. There was a clipboard
in her hands and a small playpen filled with little dogs
yipping and pouncing on one another at her feet. The
woman eyed Dalton, giving him a thorough once-over,
and frowned.

"Oh good, you're here," Aurélie said blithely, without tearing her gaze from the trembling, bug-eyed dog
in her arms.

It stared at Dalton over her shoulder. He stared back
and decided it was possibly the ugliest dog he'd ever set
eyes on. Its pointed ears were comically huge, which
might have been endearing if not for the googly eyes
that appeared to be looking in two completely different
directions. And it had a wide, flat muzzle. Not to mention the god-awful snuffling sounds coming from the
dog's smashed little face.

"Hello." The woman with the clipboard nodded. "Are
you the boyfriend?"

Boyfriend?

Hardly.

He opened his mouth to say no—*God no*—but before he could utter a syllable, Aurélie nodded. "Yes, here
he is. Finally."

Dalton didn't know what kind of game she was playing, and frankly, he didn't care. If she wanted to pose
as some kind of couple in front of this random stranger
who could possibly recognize her from the tabloids, then
fine. Although, the idea was laughable at best.

"Yes, here I am." He turned sharp eyes on her with
the vague realization that he wasn't laughing. Not even
close. "*Finally*. Surely you're aware I've been looking
for you, sweetheart."

At last she met his gaze. With snowflakes in her eyelashes and rosy, wind-kissed cheeks, she looked more Snow Queen than princess.

And lovelier than ever.

Nature suited her. Or maybe it was winter itself, the way the bare trees and dove-gray sky seemed to echo the lonely look in her eyes. Seeing her like this, amidst the quiet grace of a snowfall, holding onto that ugly dog like a child hugging a teddy bear, Dalton got a startling glimpse of her truth.

She was running from something. That's why she'd left Delamotte. That's why she'd shown up in men's clothes and begged him not to call the palace. She wasn't here on holiday. She was here to get lost in the crowd.

Not that her reasons had anything to do with Dalton. He was simply her means to an end, and vice versa.

"What's our address again? Silly me, I keep forgetting." She let out a laugh.

Dalton fought to keep his expression neutral. Surely she wasn't planning on moving into his apartment. That's what hotels were for. And there were approximately 250 of them in New York.

Then again, who knew what sort of trouble she could get into unsupervised.

His headache throbbed with renewed intensity. "*Our* address?"

"Of course, darling. You know, the place where we live." Quicker than a blink, her gaze flitted to the woman with the clipboard. "Together."

Struggling to absorb the word *darling*, he muttered the address of his building in the Upper East Side. The woman with the clipboard jotted it down.

Who was this person, anyway? And why did Aurélie

think she had any business knowing where they lived? *Where* I *live. Not* we. *Good God, not we.*

He leaned closer to get a look at whatever form she appeared to be filling out. The bold letters at the top of the page spelled out *Pet Adoption Agreement*.

"Wait," Dalton said, as something wet and foul-smelling slapped against the side of his face. He recoiled and realized, with no small degree of horror, that it was the googly-eyed puppy's tongue.

Marvelous. He wiped his cheek with the cuff of his suit jacket, and aimed his fiercest death glare at Aurélie. "What do you think you're doing?"

"*We* are adopting a dog, darling." Again with the *darling*.

And again with the *we*.

"I believe this is the type of thing we should discuss," he said, trying not to imagine the dreadful dog snoring like a freight train in his office while he tried to run the company.

Or, God forbid, snoring in his bed. Because if adopting homeless animals was the sort of thing she did on a whim when he wasn't looking, she'd need to stay with him. Who knew what kind of trouble she could get into if he left her all alone in a hotel room for a fortnight?

He'd been wrong when he'd described her to Artem as impulsive. *Impulsive* didn't even begin to describe Aurélie. She was full-blown crazy. Either that or the most manipulative woman he'd ever met.

"But we *did* discuss it. This morning." Her bow-shaped lips curved into a beguiling smile that hit Dalton square in his libido, despite the deafening clang of warning bells going off in his head.

She was business. She was irritating to no end. And

what's more, she was far too headstrong for his taste. He shouldn't be attracted to her in any way, shape or form. Nor should he be thinking about that troublesome mouth of hers and the myriad ways in which he'd prefer to see her use it.

She rested a hand on his bicep and gave it a firm squeeze. "Surely you remember our agreement?"

Unbelievable. She was using the secret egg to blackmail him into adopting a dog. She wasn't crazy at all. *Cunning.* Most definitely.

Dalton Drake didn't take orders. Nor did he allow himself to be manipulated in such a manner. Aurélie would learn as much soon enough. But not until he'd taken the pathetic animal home, apparently.

"Well?" The clipboard-wielding woman tilted her head. "What's it going to be? Do you want to adopt him or not?"

Aurélie nodded furiously. "Absolutely. We do. Right, darling?" She looked at him expectantly. So confident. So certain he'd acquiesce to whatever she demanded.

He had a mind to refuse and put her on the next plane back to the French Riviera, along with the dog and all of the Marchand family jewels. Yes, they had a deal. But it didn't encompass sending him on a wild goose chase. Nor did it include sharing his apartment. With her, or the dog.

He hadn't taken a woman into his home since Clarissa. But that had been a long time ago. He'd been a different man.

Think of the egg. What it could do for business.

He looked at Aurélie for a long moment, and for some ridiculous reason, Artem's warning came flooding back.

Whatever you do, don't take her to bed.

He wouldn't. Of course he wouldn't. The very fact that Artem had seen fit to mention the possibility was preposterous. Dalton wasn't the one who'd bedded half the women in Manhattan. That had been Artem's doing. Dalton's self-control was legendary.

But looking into Aurélie's aching emerald eyes did something to him. That vulnerability that she hid so well was barely noticeable, but very much there. And it made him wonder what she'd look like bare in the moonlight, dressed in nothing but pearls.

Damn you, Artem.

Then, before he could stop himself, he heard himself say, "Fine. We'll take the dog."

What kind of person didn't like animals?

The kind who was seething quietly beside Aurélie, evidently.

Dalton hadn't uttered a word since he'd paid the adoption fee and slipped the receipt into his suit pocket. He'd simply aimed a swift, emotionless glance at Aurélie, cupped her elbow in the palm of his hand and steered her back in the direction of Drake Diamonds. Now, less than a block later, he was walking so fast that she struggled to keep up with him. She had a mind to give up entirely and pop into the Plaza for afternoon tea, but looking at the tense set of Dalton's muscular shoulders as he marched in front of her, she got the distinct feeling there'd be hell to pay if she didn't fall in step behind him.

Plus she didn't have any money. Or credit cards. Which meant she was totally dependent on the very cranky Dalton Drake.

Besides, every three or four paces, he glanced over his shoulder, probably to assure himself of her obedi-

ence. It was infuriating, particularly when Aurélie re-
called the archaic Delamotte law that stated royal wives
must walk a minimum of two paces behind their hus-
bands in public. No doubt a man had come up with such
a ludicrous decree.

She held the trembling little dog tight against her
chest and hastened her steps. She wasn't Dalton's lowly
subordinate, and she refused to act like it. Even if, as
they said in Delamotte, *la moutarde lui monte au nez.*
The mustard was getting to his nose. In other words,
he was angry.

Fine. So was she. And she wasn't spending another
second scurrying to keep up with him.

"*Arrête!* Stop it." She tugged on his sleeve, sending
him lurching backward.

Dalton's conservative businessman shoes slid on the
snowy pavement, but he righted himself before he fell
down. Pity.

He exhaled a mighty sigh, raked his disheveled hair
back into place and stared down at her with thunder in
his gaze. "What is it, Aurélie?"

She blinked up at him, wishing for what felt like the
thousandth time, that he wasn't so handsome. His intensity would be far easier to take if it didn't come in such
a beautiful package.

His gray eyes flashed, and a shiver coursed through
Aurélie. As much as she would have liked to blame it
on the cold, she knew the trembling in her bones had
nothing to do with the weather. He got to her. Especially when he looked at her like he could see every
troublesome thought tumbling in her head. "What do
you want?"

What did she want?

Not this. Not the carefully controlled existence she'd lived with for so long. Not the future awaiting her on the distant shores of home.

She wasn't sure exactly what she wanted, only that she needed it as surely as she needed to breathe. She couldn't name it—this dark, aching thing inside her that had become impossible to ignore once her father had sat her down and laid out his plans for her future.

Palace life had never come easily to Aurélie. Even as a child, she'd played too hard, laughed too loudly, run too fast. Then that little girl had grown into a woman who felt things too keenly. Wanted things too much. The wrong things.

Just like her mother.

Aurélie had learned to conduct herself like royalty, though. Eventually. It had been years since she'd torn through the palace halls, since she'd danced with abandon. She'd become the model princess. Proper. Polite. Demure.

But since the awful meeting with the Reigning Prince and his advisors a month ago, her carefully constructed façade had begun to crack. She couldn't keep pretending, no matter how hard she tried.

What do I want? She couldn't say, but she'd know it when she found it.

Dalton glowered at Aurélie.

She inhaled a breath of frigid air and felt as if she might freeze from the inside out. "Are you always this cranky?"

He arched a single, accusatory brow. "Are you always this irresponsible?"

"Irresponsible?" The nerve. He didn't know a thing

about her life in Delamotte. "Did I just hear you correctly?"

People jostled past them on the sidewalk. Skyscrapers towered on either side of the street. The snow was coming down harder now, like they were inside a snow globe that had been given a good, hard shake.

"You certainly did," he said.

God, he was rude. Particularly for a man who wanted something from her. "You do realize who you're speaking to, don't you, Mr. Drake?"

He looked pointedly at the puppy in Aurélie's arms.

The little dog whimpered, and she gave him a comforting squeeze.

If she put herself in Dalton's shoes, she could understand how adopting a dog on a whim might appear a tad irresponsible. But it wasn't a whim. Not exactly. And anyway, she shouldn't have to explain herself. They had a deal.

He crossed his arms. Aurélie tried not to think about the biceps that appeared to be straining the fabric of his suit jacket. How did a man who so obviously spent most of his time at work get muscles like that? It was hardly fair. "You said you wanted a hot dog, not a French bulldog."

What was he even talking about? Oh, that's right—her grand speech. "The hot dog was a metaphor, Mr. Drake."

"And what about the pretzel? Was that a metaphor, as well?"

"No. I mean, yes. I mean..." *Merde.* Why did she get so flustered every time she tried to talk to him? "What do you have against dogs, anyway?"

"Nothing." He frowned. How anyone could frown in

the presence of a puppy was a mystery Aurélie couldn't begin to fathom. "I do, however, have a problem with your little disappearing act."

"And I have a problem with your patronizing attitude."

She needed to put an end to this ridiculous standoff and get them both inside, preferably somewhere other than Dalton's boring office. "I could very easily pack up my egg and go home, if you like."

"Fine." He shrugged, and to her utter astonishment, he began walking away.

"I beg your pardon?" she sputtered.

He turned back around. "Fine. Go back to your castle. And take the mutt with you."

A slap to the face wouldn't have been more painful. She squared her shoulders and did her best to ignore the panicked beating of her heart. "He has a name."

"Since when? Five minutes ago?"

"It's Jacques." She ran a hand over the dog's smooth little head. "In case you were wondering."

A hint of a smile passed through his gaze. "Very French. I'm sure the palace will love it."

She wasn't sure if his praise was genuine or sarcastic. Either way, it sent a pleasant thrill skittering through Aurélie. A pleasant thrill that irritated her to no end.

Why should she care what he thought about anything? Clearly he considered her spoiled. Foolish. Irresponsible. He'd said as much, right to her face. When he looked at her, he saw one thing. A princess.

She wondered what it would be like to be seen. *Really* seen. Every move she made back home was watched and reported. Not a day passed when her face wasn't on the front page of the Delamotte papers.

"Let's be serious, Mr. Drake. We both know I'm not going anywhere. You want that egg."

He took a few steps nearer, until she could feel the angry heat of his body. *Too close. Much too close.* "Yes, I do. But not as much as you wish to escape whatever it is you're running from. You're not going anywhere. I, on the other hand, won't hesitate to call the palace. Tell me, Princess, what is it that's got you so frightened?"

As if she would share any part of herself with someone like him. She hadn't crossed an ocean in an effort to get away from one overbearing man, only to throw herself into the path of another.

She leveled her gaze at him. "Nothing scares me, Mr. Drake. Least of all, your empty threats. If you're not prepared to uphold your end of our bargain, then I will, in fact, leave. Only I won't take my egg back to Delamotte. I'll take it right down the street to Harry Winston."

She pasted a sweet smile on her face. Dalton gave her a long look, and as the silence stretched between them, she feared he might actually call her bluff.

Finally, he placed a hand on the small of her back and said, "Come. Let's go home."

Chapter Four

The next morning, Dalton woke to the sensation of a warm body pressed against his. For a moment—just an aching, bittersweet instant—he allowed himself to believe he'd somehow traveled back to the past. Back to a time when there'd been more to life than work. And his office. And yet more work.

Then an unpleasant snuffling sound came from the body beside him, followed by a sneeze that sprayed his entire forearm with a hot, breathy mist. Dalton opened one eye. Sure enough, the beast he found staring back at him was most definitely not a woman. It was the damned dog.

He sighed. "What are you doing in here? I thought we agreed the bedroom was off-limits?"

The puppy's head tilted at the sound of his voice, a gesture that would have probably been adorable if the dog weren't so ridiculous-looking. And if he weren't currently situated in Dalton's bed, with his comically oversized head nestled right beside Dalton's on his pillow—eiderdown, imported from Geneva.

Dalton's gaze landed on a dark puddle of drool in the center of the pillowcase. Eiderdown or not, the pillow had just become a dog bed.

He rolled his eyes as he strode naked to the marble bathroom at the far end of the master suite and turned on the shower. Perhaps a soggy pillow was his penance for allowing a royal princess to sleep on his sofa rather than giving up his bed. Not that he hadn't tried. But at 1 a.m., she'd still been perched cross-legged on the oversized tufted ottoman in the living room, flipping through the hundreds of channels his satellite dish company offered, like a giddy child on holiday. Dalton hadn't even known he subscribed to so much programming. In fact, he couldn't remember the last time he'd turned on the television.

Sleeping in his office had become something of a habit, especially in recent years. But he couldn't very well spend the night there with Aurélie. He wasn't about to let the staff at Drake Diamonds see her hanging about his office in her pajamas. Explaining her sudden presence in his life—and the need for a duplicate key to his apartment—to the doorman of his building had been awkward enough. Until she'd slipped her arm through his and called him darling, that is.

They were masquerading as a couple. Again.

Dalton wasn't sure why he found that arrangement so vexing. She couldn't introduce herself as a princess. That was out of the question. Posing as his lover was the obvious choice.

Dalton stepped under the spray of his steam shower and let the hot water beat against the rigid muscles in his shoulders. Every inch of his body was taut with tension. He told himself it had nothing to do with the bewildered expression on the doorman's face as Aurélie had gripped his arm with her delicate fingertips and given him a knowing smile, as if they'd been on their way upstairs so he could ravish her. Was the idea of a woman in his life really so far-fetched?

Yes, he supposed it was. He didn't bring dates here. Ever. There were too many ghosts roaming the penthouse.

It isn't real. It's nothing but a temporary illusion, a necessary evil.

In just thirteen days, Dalton's existence would return to its predictable, orderly state. He'd have his life back. And that life would be significantly improved, because the display cases in the first floor showroom of Drake Diamonds would be filled with sparkling, bejeweled eggs.

He knew precisely where he would put the secret egg—in the same glass box that had once housed the revered Drake Diamond. The 130-carat wonder had held a place of honor in the family's flagship store since the day the doors opened to the public. Tourists came from all over the city just to see the stone, which had only been worn by two women in the 150 years since Dalton's great-great-great-great-great-grandfather had plucked it from a remote mine in South Africa and subsequently carved it into one of the most famous gemstones in the world.

The loss of that diamond just three months after the death of Dalton's father had been like losing a limb.

Granted, Artem had managed to buy it back for his wife, Ophelia. But it belonged to her personally now. Not the store. The Drake Diamond's display case sat empty.

Not that Dalton despised the sight of that vacant spot for sentimental reasons. The Drakes had never been an emotional bunch, and sentimentality had been the last thing on Dalton's mind once he'd learned he'd been passed over in favor of Artem for the CEO position. His pride was at stake. His position in the family business.

He didn't want to restore Drake Diamonds to its former glory. He wanted to surpass it, to make the institution into something so grand that his father wouldn't even recognize it if he rose from his grave, walked through the front door and set foot on the plush Drake-blue carpet.

Selling the Drake Diamond had been a necessity. Geoffrey Drake had plunged the family business so far into debt that there'd been no other option. And he hadn't told a soul. He'd sat in an office just down the hall from Dalton every day for years and hadn't said a word about the defunct diamond mine that had stripped the company of all its cash reserves. About the debt. About any of it.

Dalton shouldn't have been surprised. Honesty had never been his father's strong suit. Artem's very existence was a testament to their father's trustworthiness, or lack thereof. Dalton hadn't even known he had a brother until his father had brought five-year-old Artem home to the Drake mansion. Judging from the look of hurt and confusion on his mother's pale face, it had come as a surprise to her as well. Less than a year later, she was dead. To this day, Dalton's sister blamed their mother's death on a broken heart.

If there was a bright side to any of his family's sordid past or the recent sudden death of their patriarch, it was that the brothers had made peace with each other. At long last. When Artem had made the decision to sell the Drake Diamond, he'd saved the company. Dalton could admit as much.

But that didn't mean he had to like it.

He needed to be the one to transform Drake Diamonds into something more spectacular than it had ever been. It was the only way to justify his years of mindless devotion to the family business. He needed those years to mean something. He needed something to show for his life. Something other than loss.

He switched the shower faucet to the off position with more force than was necessary, and then grabbed a towel. On any other day, he would already have put in a solid hour behind his desk by now. He dressed as quickly as possible, adjusted the Windsor knot in his Drake-blue tie and resigned himself to the fact that it was time to venture into the living room and wake Aurélie. But first he needed to get the snoring beast out of his bed.

Dalton scooped the dog up and tried to wrap his mind around how something so tiny could make so much noise. Then his gaze landed on a wet spot in the center of the duvet. The little monster had peed in his bed. Perfect. Just perfect.

"Seriously?"

The animal's googly eyes peered up at Dalton. He sighed mightily.

"Aurélie!" He stormed into the living room without bothering to deal with the mess. "Your charge requires attention."

The television was blaring and the sofa was piled with

pillows and blankets, but Aurélie wasn't there. Dalton's temples began to pound. She'd run off? Again?

The puppy squirmed in his arms and let out a little yip, so Dalton lowered him to the floor. He scampered toward the kitchen, tripping over his own head a few times in the process.

"Mon petit chou!"

Dalton didn't know whether to feel relieved at the sound of Aurélie's voice or angry. Angry about the dog. About the near heart attack he'd just experienced when he'd thought she'd run off again. About every ridiculous thing she'd done since she'd breezed into his life less than twenty-four hours ago.

He settled on relief, until he followed the dog into the kitchen and caught his first glimpse of Aurélie's appearance.

She stood leaning against the counter with her mass of blond hair piled in a messy updo, wearing nothing but her luminous strand of gold pearls and a crisp men's white tuxedo shirt. His tuxedo shirt, if Dalton wasn't mistaken. But it wasn't the idea that she'd slept in his freshly pressed formal wear that got under his skin. It was the sight of her bare, willowy legs, the curve of her breasts beneath the thin white fabric of his shirt, the lush fullness of her bottom lip.

All of it.

He went hard in an instant, and the thought occurred to him that perhaps the only ghost inhabiting the apartment in the past few years had been him.

Whatever you do, don't take her to bed.

"Bonjour." Aurélie smiled. "Look at you, all dressed and ready for work. Why am I not surprised?"

Dalton shook his head. He was aroused to the point of pain. "We're not going to the office."

"Non?"

Non. Very much *non.* Suddenly, there was a more pressing matter that required attention—clothing the princess living under his roof before he did something royally stupid.

"Get ready. We're going shopping." He lifted a brow at the puppy in her arms. "As soon as you clean up after your dog."

After more cajoling than Aurélie could have possibly anticipated, Dalton finally acquiesced and agreed to take the subway rather than using his driver. He appeared distinctly uncomfortable doing so.

Aurélie couldn't help but wonder how long it had been since he'd ridden any form of public transportation. Granted, he was rich. That much was obvious. And just in case it hadn't been so glaringly apparent, the Google search Aurélie had conducted of Drake Diamonds on her phone the night before had confirmed as much.

According to *Forbes*, the flagship store on the corner of Fifth Avenue and 57th Street was the most valuable piece of real estate in the entire country. The building and its contents were worth slightly more than Fort Knox, where America's official gold reserves were held.

So yes, Dalton Drake was quite wealthy. And as he took such pleasure in pointing out over and over again, he was also busy. But this was New York. She'd assumed that everyone rode the subway, even rich workaholics like Dalton Drake.

Aurélie was also tempted to ask him how long it had been since he'd set foot in a building that didn't bear his name. She couldn't help but notice the discreet script lettering spelling out *The Drake* on the elegant black awnings of his apartment building. He seemed to spend every waking moment inside his sprawling penthouse or his jewelry store, where the name *Drake* was splashed everywhere, including across the structure's granite Art Deco exterior.

She didn't ask him either of those things, though. Instead, she soaked up every detail of riding the city's underground—the click of the silver turnstiles, the bright orange seats, the heady feeling of barreling through tunnels. The train sped from stop to stop, picking up and letting off people from all walks of life. Students with backpacks. Mommies with infants. Businessmen with briefcases.

None of those businessmen, however, were quite as formidable as the man standing beside her. No matter how much she tried to ignore him, Aurélie was overly conscious of Dalton's presence.

As fascinated as she was by the hordes of New Yorkers, the bustling subway stations, even the jostling movement of the train, she couldn't fully focus on any of it. Her gaze kept straying to Dalton's broad shoulders, his freshly shaven square jaw, his full, sensual mouth.

If only she could ignore him properly. But it proved an impossible task, no matter how hard she tried. During the frantic disembarking process at one of the stops, someone shoved Aurélie from behind and she found herself pressed right up against Dalton's formidable chest, her lips mere inches from his. She stiffened, unable to move or even breathe, and prayed he couldn't feel the frantic beating of her heart through the soft cashmere of his coat.

She'd been so overwhelmed by the sheer closeness of him that she couldn't quite seem to think, much less right herself. Until he glared down at her with that disapproving gray gaze of his. *Again*.

Right. He was a serious CEO, and she was nothing but a spoiled, irresponsible princess. Duly noted.

"We're here," he said, as the doors of the train whooshed open.

Aurélie glanced at the tile mosaic sign on the wall. *Lexington Avenue*. "Wait, this isn't…"

But Dalton's hand was already in the small of her back and he was guiding her through the station and out onto the snowy sidewalk before she could finish her thought. As usual, he was on a mission. Aurélie was just along for the ride, but at least when he noticed how enraptured she was by the opulent shop windows, he slowed his steps. When she stopped to admire a display of dresses made entirely of colorful paper flowers, she caught a glimpse of Dalton's reflection, and it looked almost as though he were smiling at her.

Then their eyes met in the glittering glass and any trace of a smile on his handsome face vanished as quickly as it had appeared.

He cleared his throat. "Shall we continue?"

That voice. Such a dark, low sound that sent a dangerous chill skittering up Aurélie's spine, for which she heartily admonished herself. She shouldn't be attracted to Dalton Drake. She couldn't. He had too much leverage over her as it was. Besides, she had enough men in her life. More than enough.

"Yes." She breezed past him as if she knew precisely where they were headed, when in fact, she hadn't a clue. "Let's."

"Aurélie," he said, with a hint of amusement in his tone. "We're going that way."

He pointed over his shoulder. This time, he most definitely smiled, and his grin was far too smug for Aurélie's taste.

Fine, she thought. No, not fine. Good. He was much easier to despise when he was being arrogant. Which, to Aurélie's great relief, was most of the time.

They walked the next few blocks in silence until they reached a sleek black marble building that appeared to take up an entire city block. Like both of Dalton's namesake buildings, it had a doorman stationed out front. And gold-plated door handles. And a glittering, grand chandelier Aurélie could see through the polished windows. She squinted up at the sign. *Bergdorf Goodman*.

Without even setting foot inside, she could tell it was elegant. Tasteful. Expensive. Everything she didn't want.

She shook her head. *"Non."*

Beside her, Dalton sighed. "I beg your pardon?"

Aurélie pretended not to notice the hint of menace in his deep voice. "No, thank you. I'd rather go someplace else."

"But we haven't even gone inside." He eyed her.

Let him be mad. Aurélie didn't care. The rest of her life would be spent in designer dresses and kitten heels. This was *her* holiday, not his. She had no intention of spending it dressed like a royal. "I don't need to go in. I can tell it's not the sort of place where I want to shop for clothes."

The doorman's gaze flitted toward them. He'd looked utterly bored as they approached, but now his expression was vaguely hopeful. She realized he probably thought she and Dalton were a couple in the midst of some sort of domestic squabble.

Dalton lowered his voice. "Aurélie, you need clothes. This building is full of them. Dresses, blouses, pants." He cast a pointed glance at her legs. "Pajamas."

Pajamas?

So that's what this oh-so-urgent shopping spree was about. Dalton had been so horrified to find her wearing his tuxedo shirt this morning that he'd felt the need to cancel all his plans for the day and drag her to this fancy, impersonal department store.

She dropped all attempts at civility. "I'm not going in there, Mr. Drake."

Aurélie might not be American, but she'd seen *Pretty Woman*. Several times, actually. She knew precisely what would happen if she followed him inside the boutique. She'd walk out an hour from now looking like a princess from head to toe.

He crossed his arms and stared at her for a moment that stretched on too long. "May I ask why not?"

Intense much?

She felt breathless all of sudden, much to her annoyance. "I have no desire to play the part of Julia Roberts to your Richard Gere."

His broad shoulders shifted. Not that Aurélie was looking at them, because she wasn't. Not intentionally anyway. "I have no idea what you're talking about."

Of course he didn't. The man had probably never watched a movie in his life. Or done anything else fun, for that matter. "I'd prefer to go somewhere else. A vintage shop, perhaps?"

"A vintage shop?" He laughed, but somehow didn't

sound the faintest bit amused. "You're royalty and you want to wear a dead person's discarded clothes?"

"Yes. I do, even though you seem to be doing your best to make it sound disgusting."

Aurélie quite liked the idea of browsing through a vintage shop. She'd never shopped at one before, never even seen one. It sounded like fun. Or it would have, if she hadn't been accompanied by the world's most surly escort. "Come now, Mr. Drake. You and I both know you have a fondness for old treasures."

Like imperial jewels.

She very nearly said it, but she didn't have to.

"Fine, but we're taking a town car this time." He stalked to the curb, lifted an arm and a sleek black sedan materialized within seconds. Naturally. Even the traffic in New York obeyed his orders.

"After you." He held the door open.

"Merci." Aurélie climbed inside. "So where are we going?"

"Williamsburg. That's in Brooklyn," he clarified in his usual stiff tone.

The driver must have overheard, because they soon began a slow crawl across Manhattan. Aurélie had never seen such crowded streets in her life. In Delamotte, the major highway wrapped around a seaside cliff. More people drove mopeds than cars. There were sea breezes and salt air. Here, there were bike messengers zipping between automobiles, musicians on street corners and people selling things in stalls on the sidewalk—newspapers, purses, winter hats and gloves.

She felt suddenly as if she were in the center of everything and the whirling snow, the people and the cars with their blaring horns were all part of some mysterious, magnificent orbit.

So much life, so much movement—it made her giddy. A person couldn't stand still in a place like this, and Aurélie had been doing just that for such a very long time. All her life, it seemed.

"It's wonderful, isn't it?" she whispered with an awestruck tremble to her voice.

Dalton regarded her closely. Curiously. "What's wonderful?"

"This." She waved a hand toward the scene outside the car windows, where dizzying snow fell on the beating heart of the city. "All of it."

Dalton looked at her for a beat too long. Long enough for her cheeks to grow warm. Without taking his eyes off her, he spoke to the driver. "Pull over, please."

The driver's gaze flitted to the rearview mirror. "Here, sir? We're only halfway to Brooklyn."

"Yes, I know," Dalton said. He knocked on the window and pointed at something outside. Aurélie wasn't sure what. There was so much to look at, so much to take in. She didn't know where to look first.

He glanced at Aurélie. "Stay here. I'll be right back."

He was *leaving*? Unbelievable.

"Wait. Where are you going?" Had he sensed a diamond emergency somewhere? Had the store run out of those little blue boxes? She placed a hand on his forearm.

He looked at her fingertips gripping the sleeve of his coat and then met her gaze. "Let go, Aurélie. And for once in your life, could you please do as I say and stay here? I'll be back momentarily."

She released his sleeve and crossed her arms. What was she doing, grabbing him like that anyway? Dalton was free to go wherever he liked. She'd actually prefer to spend the rest of the day on her own. Of course she would. "Fine."

In a flash, he climbed out of the car and shut the door behind him. A flurry of snowflakes blew inside the cab and danced in the air, as soft as feathers. Aurélie watched them drift onto the black leather seat and melt into tiny puddles. And for an odd, empty moment, she felt acutely alone.

She felt like crying all of a sudden, and she didn't even know why.

Aurélie exhaled slowly, willing the tears that had gathered in her eyes not to fall. What was wrong with her? This was what she wanted. Adventure. Independence. Freedom. All the things her mother had never experienced.

She reached for her Birkin, removed her iPhone from the interior pocket and slipped the SIM card back inside. Now seemed as good a time as any to check her messages and see who all had figured out she'd gone missing.

The phone seemed to take forever to power up and once it finally did, the display didn't show a single voice mail message. Nor any texts.

That couldn't be right, could it?

While she was staring at the little screen, the phone rang, piercing the silence of the backseat. It startled her so much that she nearly dropped it.

She took a deep breath and closed her eyes.

Maybe it was Dalton. Maybe he was calling to apologize for running off. *Not likely.* Deep down, she knew it couldn't be him. The only people who had anything to say to her were on the other side of the world.

She opened her eyes. A glimpse of the display confirmed her deepest fears. *Office of Royal Affairs*. Her private secretary.

The palace was looking for her. Aurélie's heart beat against her rib cage like a wild bird caught in a net. She peered out the window in search of Dalton, but the city had swallowed him up.

She cleared her throat, pressed the talk button and very nearly answered in English, which would have been a massive red flag. *Focus. "Allô?"*

"*Bonsoir*, Your Royal Highness." *Bonsoir. Good night.* It was already evening in Delamotte, which made it seem somehow farther away, only not quite far enough. "Do you have a moment to go over your schedule for the rest of the week?"

"My schedule?" Aurélie swallowed. What was happening? Had her own staff not even realized she was missing yet? "Of course."

"As we discussed last week, Lord Clement will be coming to the palace the day after tomorrow to take your picture. The Reigning Prince would like a new photo for the impending press release."

Aurélie's stomach churned. *Breathe. Just breathe.* Lord Clement was the official royal photographer, one of her father's oldest and dearest friends.

"The day after tomorrow isn't a good day." *Since I'm 4,000 miles away and everything.* "We need to reschedule, *s'il vous plaît*."

"I'm afraid we can't, Your Royal Highness. The press announcement is scheduled for next Friday."

Aurélie felt like she might be sick all over the backseat. She'd thought if she left Delamotte she could slow things down somehow. She'd only been gone a day and a half, and already she felt different.

But nothing had really changed, had it? They hadn't even realized she'd gone. She might be in America, but her life in Delamotte was still proceeding as planned. With or without her.

"Your sitting with Lord Clement is scheduled for 4:00 in the afternoon in the state ballroom. The Reigning Prince would like you to wear the gold brocade dress and the Marchand family tiara." Because apparently, although Aurélie was a grown woman, she wasn't allowed even the simple freedom of choosing her own clothes.

Her throat grew tight. "I understand."

"*Trés bien*. I'll phone Lord Clement and tell him you've confirmed. *Au revoir*."

The line went dead before Aurélie could respond. She sat staring at the darkened phone in the palm of her hand. Dread fell over her in a thick, suffocating embrace.

What have I done?

Her escape may have gone unnoticed by royal staffers thus far, but failing to show up for a sitting with Lord Clement most definitely would not. Every royal office in Delamotte would hear about it. As would her father. And possibly even the press. Her face would be on the front page of every newspaper on the French Riviera, beneath the headline *Runaway Princess*.

Her heart lurched. But it wasn't too late, was it? If she caught a plane tomorrow, she could be standing in the ballroom with the Marchand family tiara anchored to her head within forty-eight hours. Then next week, she would be headline news for a different reason altogether.

She powered down her phone and removed the SIM card again. Although she wasn't even sure why she both-

ered. She should go home. Leaving hadn't changed anything. Not really. Staying in New York wouldn't, either.
She couldn't outrun her destiny. Believing that she could
was just a naïve, reckless mistake. Her mother hadn't
been able to escape, and neither could she.

The car door opened, and suddenly Dalton was back
inside the car in a flurry of snow and frosty wind. He
slid in place beside her, holding a tissue-wrapped bundle. Aurélie tried her best to focus on him without really looking at him. She couldn't face him. Not after
the phone call.

She was confused enough as it was without having to
worry about what he'd have to say if she turned tail and
ran back home. After everything she'd put him through—
the disappearing, the dog, the constant arguing—he'd be
furious. Or quite possibly relieved. Aurélie wasn't sure
which she preferred.

"Look at me," he ordered. He cupped her face and
forced her to meet his gaze. "Aurélie, is something
wrong?"

Yes. Everything is wrong.

"No." She smiled her perfectly rehearsed princess
smile, slid her cell phone back inside her purse and concentrated all her efforts on keeping her tears at bay.

But she felt his gaze on her, hot and penetrating. She
couldn't look him the eye. She just couldn't. If she did,
the truth would come tumbling out of her mouth. All
of it. Her father's plans. The looming palace announcement. If she said the words aloud, they would feel real.
And she so desperately needed to believe they weren't.

Just a little bit longer.

She focused instead on the knot in his Drake-blue tie.
"Where have you been?"

"Getting this for you." He handed her the tissue-wrapped bundle. It warmed her hands.

Aurélie's defenses dropped, and she stared at him in disbelief. "You bought me a gift."

He frowned, which in no way diminished the potency of his chiseled good looks. "No, I didn't."

She looked at the plain white package in her lap and then back up at Dalton. He seemed nearly as surprised by this strange turn of events as she was. "Yes, you did."

He rolled his eyes. "Don't get too excited. Trust me. It's nothing."

She couldn't imagine what it could be, but something told her it meant more than Dalton was letting on. He wasn't the kind of man to waste time with frivolity.

With great care, she peeled back the tissue. When she realized what he'd done, she couldn't seem to utter a word. She blinked to make sure what she was seeing was real—a hot dog. He'd gotten her a hot dog.

"It's a metaphor." He shrugged as though he were right, as if this silly little gesture meant nothing at all, when to Aurélie, it meant everything. "With mustard."

She didn't fully understand what happened next. Maybe she wasn't thinking straight after getting the call from the palace. Maybe the thought of going back home had broken something inside her. Maybe she no longer cared what happened to her at all.

Because even though she knew it was undoubtedly the gravest mistake of her life, Her Royal Highness Aurélie Marchand tossed her hotdog aside, grabbed Dalton Drake by the lapels and kissed him as though she wasn't already engaged to another man.

Chapter Five

The engagement wasn't quite official, but the royal wedding was already scheduled to take place in just under three months at the grand cathedral in Delamotte. Top secret of course, until the palace made its big announcement in twenty days.

Not that Aurélie was keeping track of the days, exactly. On the contrary, she'd been trying rather aggressively not to think about her pending engagement at all. As it turned out, though, being married off to a man thirty years her senior, a man she'd yet to actually meet in person, was something she couldn't quite make herself forget. No matter how very hard she tried.

Kissing Dalton Drake, however, proved to be a powerful diversion. Frighteningly powerful. The moment Aurélie's lips came crashing down on his, the constant ache in her heart seemed to tear wide open. It was excruciating. And exquisite. She was aware of nothing but sensation. Sensation so sweetly agonizing that there wasn't room for a single thought in her head. How was it possible to feel so beautifully broken?

His mouth was cold from the snowstorm, his tongue like ice as it moved against hers. Deep. Devouring. Delicious. God, was this what kissing was supposed to be like? Because it wasn't close to anything Aurélie had experienced before. She couldn't seem to catch her breath. And were those whimpering noises echoing in the interior of the car actually coming from her?

She should have been embarrassed, but she didn't seem to be capable of feeling anything but longing. Longing as hard and bright as a diamond. She'd needed to be kissed like this. She'd needed it so badly.

No, she realized. She hadn't needed this. She'd needed *him*. Dalton Drake.

"Oh Aurélie," he whispered, his breath now warm and wonderful against her lips.

Then he slid his hands into her hair, cradling the back of her head, pulling her closer. Closer, until their hearts pounded against each other and she could no longer tell where hers ended and his began.

If her actions had caught Dalton off guard, he certainly didn't let it show. On the contrary, the way he went about ravishing her mouth gave her the very real sense that he'd been ready for this. Ready and waiting, for perhaps as long as Aurélie had been waiting for something like this herself. Maybe even longer.

But that couldn't be true. Dalton had made it clear he was merely tolerating her until the imperial eggs went on display. And that was okay, because she'd never be a

real part of his life, and he would never be part of hers.
Nothing about her time in New York was real.

The kiss sure felt real, though. More than the crown
on her head or the white dress she'd slip over her head in
less than a month. *This is what life is supposed to be like,*
she thought. *This* was passion. Raw. Bold. Blazing hot.

And wrong. So very, very wrong.

Would her husband ever kiss her like this? Would he
twirl her gold pearls around his fingertips and use them
to pull her into his lap like Dalton was doing? Would she
thrill at the press of his erection through their clothes as
she sat astride him? Would she have to stop herself from
reaching for his zipper and begging him to enter her in
the backseat of a town car in full view of the driver and
all of greater Manhattan?

No.

Despite her staggering level of inexperience in the
bedroom, Aurélie knew how rare this connection was.
She sensed it. And as surely as she sensed it, she knew
that no man's lips would ever touch her like this again.
No other man would kiss her like she was a gemstone,
cool and shimmering. A precious object that had been
buried somewhere dark and deep, waiting for a kiss of
perfect heat to bring her volcanic heart to the surface.
Only this man. Only this place and time.

Dalton deepened the kiss, groaned into her mouth and
Aurélie's head spun with the knowledge that he wanted
her. She wrapped her fingertips around the smooth blue
silk of Dalton's tie, anchoring herself in the moment before it slipped away.

What would he say if he knew? What would he think
when he picked up the newspaper after she went back to
Delamotte and saw her photograph alongside an older

man who was her fiancé? How would he feel watching her on television stepping out of a glass coach on her wedding day? He would be furious. It would confirm every notion he'd ever had that she was spoiled, reckless and irresponsible.

At least, she hoped that was how he would feel. Fury she could handle. What she couldn't bear from Dalton was pity. She'd grown quite fond of the way he looked at her as if she were some rare exotic bird instead of a grown woman living under her father's thumb. Of course, those moments were heavily punctuated with looks of complete and utter exasperation. But every so often, when he turned his gray gaze on her, she felt herself blooming from the inside out. Like a peony unfolding before the dazzling heat of the summer sun in a tremulous display of flowering fragility.

He saw *her*. That was the difference. She didn't have to hide who she was when she was with Dalton Drake. For all the secrets she was keeping from him, he saw her for who she really was. Which was more than she could say for the entire kingdom of Delamotte.

She really should have seen the engagement coming. Women in her position had been subjected to arranged marriages since the beginning of time. But she'd been so blissfully naïve about her circumstances, she'd had no idea that something so archaic and demeaning could actually touch her perfect life.

If Aurélie hadn't found her mother's diary the day after her funeral, she would have never known the truth. Sometimes she wished she'd never opened that book and flipped through its gilt-edged pages. Then she might still believe the fairy tale, when in reality, her parents had never loved each other. Her father had one mistress after another, while her mother had no one. Theirs had been a marriage of convenience, a carefully arranged bargain of politics and power.

Now Aurélie's would be, as well.

She squeezed her eyes shut tight, and with each breath, each touch of her lips, she begged Dalton to make it stop. To somehow change the course of her future so she could always be this girl, this bold woman who could write her own destiny.

Please. Please. Please.

"Please…"

Oh God, had she really just said that out loud?

"Not here, darling. Not here." Dalton's voice was little more than a sigh, but it carried just enough of a reprimand to bring her back to her senses.

She opened her eyes and found him staring at her with an intensity that left her painfully vulnerable. Exposed. Ashamed. *Not here*. She looked down at herself and couldn't believe what she saw—her thighs straddling his lap, her hands on the solid wall of his chest, her lipstick smeared all over his mouth. What was she *doing*?

She'd all but begged him to make love to her when he'd shown no interest in her whatsoever. Actually, she may have even begged.

"Oh my God." She pulled away, horrified.

Then she heard a snap, like the sound of something breaking in two. For an odd moment, she was sure it was her heart. Until she realized her pearls were still twirled around Dalton's fingertips. Not the whole strand…only half of them. The remaining pearls were falling from her neck, one by one, dripping into Dalton's lap.

Aurélie gasped and her hand flew to her throat.

Dalton cursed, slid out from beneath her and started

chasing the gold pearls around the moving car, gathering them in his hands. But they rolled everywhere, as if refusing to be captured.

Aurélie remembered reading somewhere that pearls were a symbol of sadness and that each bead of a string of pearls represented a teardrop. She'd never given much thought to the legend before, but now she couldn't quite shake the idea of her mother's tears spilling all over the car. Lost.

What a mess she'd made of things.

By Dalton's best guess, he had $50,000 worth of South Sea pearls rolling around his feet...give or take a few thousand. The fact that Aurélie's priceless broken necklace was the least of his problems at the moment spoke volumes about the magnitude of the mistake he'd just made.

What the hell was going on? Had he seriously just had a make-out session with a princess in the backseat of a hired car while a total stranger drove them across the Brooklyn Bridge? Yes. Apparently, he had. And judging by the magnitude of the erection straining his fly, he'd quite enjoyed it.

But now...

Now Aurélie was looking around with a dazed expression on her face, her eyes shiny with unshed tears. Shell-shocked. Horrified.

Meanwhile, the driver kept shooting glances in the rearview mirror while Dalton crawled all over the car trying to save the pearls. Who knew it was possible for a simple kiss to cause this much mayhem?

Who are you kidding, you idiot? There was nothing simple *about that kiss.*

He sat up and poured a handful of pearls into his pocket. "I'm sorry, Aurélie."

God, was he ever sorry.

Dalton had done the one thing he'd promised himself he wouldn't do. Granted, he hadn't slept with her. But what he'd done might have been worse. They were in a public place. Anyone could see them through car windows. Not to mention the chauffeur!

What if the driver recognized him? What if the driver recognized *her*? There were more things wrong with this scenario than there were pearls bouncing around the car.

"No, it was my fault. I shouldn't have…" Aurélie bit her pillowy bottom lip, and Dalton had to look away to stop himself from pillaging her rosy mouth all over again.

"I'm the one who's sorry." Dalton let out a strained exhale and focused on the pearls. If he met Aurélie's gaze for even a second, surely she'd see the truth written all over his face—it had taken every last shred of self-control to stop things when he did. Part of him wondered how he'd managed it.

Please. There'd been a world of promise in that sweet whisper. Promise that taunted him now, like the perfume of hyacinths left hanging in the air after a lucid fever dream. And now every heartbeat was a knife to his ribs. His hands shook so hard he couldn't manage to piece together the necklace. Pearls kept slipping through his fingers.

Please. That word would haunt him for a thousand sleepless nights to come, which in a way would be a painful relief. He'd grown altogether weary of the regret that had been his only bedtime companion since the night Clarissa died.

He hadn't been in love with Clarissa. He'd realized that in the years since her passing. Perhaps he'd known as much all along. He'd cared about her, of course. He never would have asked her to marry him if he hadn't, despite the expectations of both their families. But his feelings for Clarissa had been closer to the brotherly affection he felt for Diana than romantic love.

If he'd felt differently, he would have picked up the phone that night. He would have been home instead of sitting behind his desk. Clarissa would still be alive, and he wouldn't be situated in the back of a car with his thigh pressed against Aurélie's, wanting, *needing*, to touch her. Kiss her. Taste her.

He blamed himself. Not just for Clarissa—that was a given. But the responsibility for what had just happened with Aurélie also rested squarely on his shoulders. He wanted her. He'd wanted her since the moment he'd seen the hope that shone in her eyes. Hope like emerald fire.

That first day in his office, she'd turned her aching eyes on him as the glittering egg sat between them. And the force of her yearning had nearly knocked him out of his chair.

Desire. It had shimmered in the air like diamond dust. He hadn't known what it was she wanted so badly. He still didn't. But that ache, that need, had kindled something inside him. He'd been numb for so long that he couldn't remember what it was like to feel, to want, to need.

One look at Aurélie had been enough to conjure a memory. His life hadn't always been this way. He'd felt things once. What might it be like to feel again?

Dalton had no idea. All he knew was that he wanted to consume Aurélie, to devour her, until he figured it out. He wanted to want the things she wanted, to feel the things she felt—life, longing.

Love.

No. Not love. Anything *but love.*

He wasn't wired that way. He wasn't capable of love. Hadn't history proved as much? He had even less to offer now, after the way he'd failed Clarissa. She'd deserved better. So did Aurélie. And Dalton refused to be like his father. He wouldn't be the kind of man who did nothing but take.

Take, take, take.

He stared ahead. He couldn't bring himself to look at Aurélie quite yet. He couldn't bear to see the heat in her gaze, the light that radiated from her as if she were a brilliant-cut ruby. Not now. Not while the taste of her scarlet lips still lingered on his tongue.

If he did, there'd be no stopping this time. Not until he'd plunged himself fully inside her and felt her exquisite body shuddering beneath him.

The city whirred past them in a blur of snow, steel and melancholy gray. Dalton breathed in and out, clenching his hands into fists in his lap. He'd let himself slip. He wouldn't do so again. Aurélie was off-limits, and besides, he was comfortable with his life now. His orderly, predictable life.

But despite every effort to regain control, to slide back into a state of numbness, he couldn't seem to still the incessant pounding of his pulse. *Please. Please. Please.*

Chapter Six

Dalton was behind his desk at Drake Diamonds the next morning before the sun came up. He'd left instructions with the doorman to arrange for a driver to bring Aurélie to the store whenever she liked. Granted, leaving her alone for any length of time was a risk, given her penchant for running away. But nothing seemed as dangerous as it would have been for Dalton to play house with her all morning.

Aurélie had come home with piles of eclectic clothing from their trip to Williamsburg, but not a single pair of pajamas. After the disastrous car ride, Dalton couldn't take watching her move about his apartment in his tuxedo shirt again. He just couldn't. Another glimpse of her willowy porcelain legs stretching from beneath the bottom of his own shirt while she peered up at him with those luminous emerald eyes of hers would have been more than his suddenly overactive libido could take. He was only human.

He and Aurélie had danced carefully around each other for the remainder of the day. At the vintage shop, she'd disappeared behind dressing room curtains with one colorful outfit after another, but never came out to model anything.

Dalton told himself that was fine. For the best, really. But he hadn't realized how much he would have liked seeing her twirl in front of the shop's floor-to-ceiling mirrors until he'd found himself relegated to a purple velvet chair in the corner. Alone. And more sexually frustrated than he'd ever been in his life.

How had his life gotten so absurdly complicated in the span of just a few days?

Enough was enough. He couldn't live like this. He wouldn't. He had work to do. Loads of it. He should be busy confirming the arrangements for the upcoming gala or working on the spring advertising campaign. Instead he was flipping through a stack of tabloids, praying he wouldn't stumble on a photo of himself ravishing Aurélie in the back of a car.

There was a knock on his office door, and before Dalton could stash his pile of newspapers, Artem poked his head inside.

"Good morning, brother." His gaze dropped to the copy of *Page Six* spread open on Dalton's desk. "Interesting reading material."

God help Dalton if he and Aurélie had been caught on film. He'd never hear the end of it. "Good morning." He flipped the paper closed and waved Artem inside.

His brother clicked the door shut behind him. "I was wondering if you were going to show up today. When you didn't turn up yesterday, I assumed you were on your deathbed or something. I can't recall when you've ever missed a day of work before. You know we have Diana's horse show in the Hamptons tomorrow, don't you?"

"Of course I do." Dalton sighed.

He'd actually forgotten about his sister's event. That would mean more time away from the store, and he'd just missed nearly two full days of work because he'd been tied up with Aurélie.

He'd never been away from the office for two consecutive days before. Ever. He'd even managed to put in a solid eight hours the day of Clarissa's funeral. It had made perfect sense at the time, but now he wasn't so sure.

Nothing made much sense at the moment.

"Have a seat. I need to discuss something with you." He shoved the tabloids in a drawer so Artem wouldn't be prompted to mention them again. Dalton would have been quite happy to forget them himself.

"Sure. I'm glad you're here. I wanted to ask you..." Artem's voice trailed off.

Dalton looked up to find him staring at Jacques who was curled in a ball on the sofa in the corner of the office. "Am I seeing things, or is that a puppy?"

He rolled his eyes. "Don't ask."

"Oh, I'm asking." Artem shook his head and let out a wry laugh. "I've known you since I was five years old, and somehow I missed the part about you being an animal lover. When did you get a dog?"

Dalton aimed an exasperated glance at Jacques, who responded by panting and wagging his entire backside. The dog was obsessed with him. The pup had responded to the pet sitter Dalton had hired the day before with overwhelming nonchalance. But he worshipped Dalton. Just his luck. "I didn't."

Artem sank onto the sofa beside Jacques and rested a hand on the little dog's back. Jacques went into an ecstatic fit of snuffling sounds as he shuffled toward his lap. "Then where did this sweetheart come from?"

Dalton cleared his throat. "He belongs to Aurélie."

Jacques flopped onto his back. The minute Artem started rubbing his belly, the puppy's tongue lolled out of the side of his mouth. A long string of drool dripped onto the sofa cushions. Naturally. "And he's at work with you because…"

"He likes me. God knows why. The feeling is definitely not mutual." The puppy was a walking train wreck. And constantly underfoot. Dalton could barely walk across the room without tripping over him, but his presence at Drake Diamonds pretty much guaranteed Aurélie would eventually show up. She'd never run off without her *petit chou*. "The homely little thing has hijacked my bed and destroyed half the pillows in my apartment."

"Your apartment?" Artem lifted a brow. "Does this mean Aurélie's staying with you?"

"It does." Dalton shrugged to indicate his nonchalance, but the gesture felt disingenuous. Forced.

Artem's gaze narrowed. "Let me see if I've got the facts straight here. You haven't been at work for a day and a half, Aurélie is living with you and you're letting her puppy—whom you clearly dislike—eat your furniture and slobber all over your office."

Sounds about right. "I realize how this looks."

"Do you really? Because it sort of looks like you're

sleeping with a runaway princess while you plan on exhibiting stolen royal jewels for your personal gain."

Dalton blinked. He'd never been on the receiving end of a lecture from his younger brother before. This was quite a role reversal, and it didn't sit well. Not at all.

"That's a gross representation of what's actually happening. For starters, she didn't steal the egg. She inherited it."

Artem stood and walked toward the desk, while Jacques grunted his displeasure at being left behind. "And do you think the palace will see it that way?"

Maybe. Maybe not.

He'd considered this complication, of course. But if things went as planned, the officials in Delamotte wouldn't know the egg was missing until its unveiling at the gala. By then, Drake Diamonds would be on the front page of every newspaper in the country. Mission accomplished. Aurélie would have a lot to answer for, but that wasn't his problem. Was it?

In retrospect, that attitude seemed rather harsh. When had he become his father?

Dalton swallowed. "Also, not that it's any of your business, but I'm not sleeping with her."

Artem looked down at him for a long, loaded moment.

Dalton hadn't slept with Aurélie. That much was true. It was also true that all he seemed to think about was how very much he wanted to take her to bed. Not wanted. *Needed.* He needed to feel the soft perfection of her curves beneath his palms once again, to feel the pulse at the base of her throat thundering at the touch of his lips, to hear that breathy whimper. *Please.*

Was it so obvious?

Judging by the look on Artem's face, yes. Apparently,

it was. "Look, do what you like with Aurélie. You're right. Whether or not you sleep with her isn't my business. Although, I can't help but mention that if I were sharing my home with the princess of a foreign principality whose most precious jewels are currently in the Drake Diamond vault, you'd have a few things to say about it."

Artem lifted a sardonic brow.

Dalton couldn't argue. He was right. And even though he had no intention of admitting as much to his younger brother, a line had most definitely been crossed.

He hadn't just crossed the line. He'd leaped right over it.

The way things stood, the two brothers had practically traded places, like they were in some third-rate comedy film.

Except Artem was married now, and he had a baby on the way. He was no longer the black sheep of the family. Apparently Dalton now held that title.

What kind of alternate reality was he living in? He was appalled at himself.

"You should probably know that while you were out of the office, you got a phone call." Artem sank into the wing chair on the opposite side of Dalton's desk. His uncharacteristically serious expression gave Dalton pause. "From the palace in Delamotte."

Great. Just great.

So they'd already found out. The palace officials knew about Aurélie. They probably even knew about the secret egg. His ambition, coupled with Aurélie's naïveté, had created an even more profound disaster than he'd anticipated.

He'd been an idiot to think he could get away with something like this. "How bad is it?"

Artem shrugged. "Not very. When Mrs. Barnes couldn't reach you on your cell, she came to me. I took the call."

When Mrs. Barnes couldn't reach you on your cell...

Memory hit Dalton hard and fast. Unexpected. Bile rose to the back of his throat, and he squeezed his eyes shut. But he could still see the notification on his phone. *Clarissa Davies, 19 Missed Calls.*

It wasn't as if he hadn't known. He'd seen the calls come rolling in, but he'd ignored them. Every last one.

Artem spoke again, his voice dragging Dalton mercifully back to the present. "Relax, brother. I handled it. Look, I know how you feel about your phone, but it's not a crime to miss a call."

"Don't go there, Artem," he said as evenly as he could manage. "Not now."

Artem held up his hands in a gesture of surrender. "Sorry. I know it's a difficult subject, but it's been six years. You don't have to be tethered to your phone twenty-four seven. Honestly, when Mrs. Barnes told me you weren't picking up, I was elated. I thought you'd actually gone and gotten yourself a life."

Dalton let out a bitter laugh. He didn't deserve a life. Not anymore. He probably never had, because he was a Drake through and through.

Like every other Drake man that had ever sat behind a desk, he was good at one thing: making money. Selling diamonds didn't leave much room for relationships, or for "a life" as Artem put it. Not the way the Drake men did it.

Dalton had tried it once, hadn't he? Never again. One dead fiancée was more than enough.

"It wasn't your fault, you know. She would have eventually found another time, another way," Artem said quietly.

They'd been over this before. The discussion was closed, as far as Dalton was concerned. What good could come of revisiting the past? Nothing. It wouldn't change a godforsaken thing. "Can we just cut to the chase? Tell me about the call."

Artem sighed. "They were calling to see if the eggs had arrived safely. It seems the palace courier, Monsieur Martel, still hasn't returned to work. There was some concern that he might have absconded with the royal jewels."

Dalton should have thought about this detail. He should have quizzed Aurélie about the courier before he'd even agreed to her terms. He was off his game. He'd been off his game since she'd walked through the door of his office. The time had come to get his head on straight again.

"What did you tell them?" he asked.

"I assured them the pieces for the exhibition had arrived, and the royal jewels were safely locked away in the Drake Diamond vault." Artem cleared his throat. "I failed to mention the treasure locked away in your apartment."

Glaring at his brother, Dalton exhaled.

Artem shrugged. "In all seriousness, have you thought about what you're going to do when they realize she's missing? Surely someone will notice."

Dalton's response rolled off his tongue before he even realized what he was saying. "With any luck, they won't before tomorrow. I'm putting Aurélie on a flight back to Delamotte tonight at midnight."

He'd been toying with the idea all morning, but hadn't realized he'd reached a decision until that precise moment. He'd known, though. He'd known all along that he should send her back. He should never have agreed to her silly plan in the first place.

Now he was just waiting. Waiting for her to show up so he could break the news that he was sending her away.

Dalton's gaze flitted to Jacques sleeping on the sofa, snoring loud enough to peel the Drake-blue paint off the walls. He frowned. What was to become of the dog? Surely she wouldn't leave the mutt behind.

Forget about the dog. This isn't about a dog.

It was about business, nothing more. At least that's what he'd been busy telling himself as he'd looked up the flight schedules to the French Riviera.

Artem leveled his gaze at Dalton. "What about the secret egg?"

"She can take it back with her. It's just not worth the risk." Something hardened inside Dalton. Something dark and deep. "Not anymore."

"What changed?"

Dalton grew still as memories moved behind his eyes in an excruciatingly slow, snow-laden waltz of wounded desire. He saw his fingers tangled in the silken madness of Aurélie's hair, her eyes glittering in the dark like the rarest of diamonds, her lips, bee-stung and bruised from his kisses as she pleaded with him for sweet relief. He saw pearls falling like teardrops, spilling into cupped hands faster than he could catch them.

What changed?

Everything.

Everything had changed.

He shrugged one shoulder and did his best to affect an indolent air. "I came to my senses. That's all."

Artem looked at him, long and hard. "You sure about this? Because I'll back you up, whatever you decide. We're a team, remember?"

All his life—from the time he'd barely been old enough to walk on the Drake-blue carpeting of the Fifth Avenue store, right up until the morning he'd listened to a lawyer recite the terms of his father's Last Will and Testament—Dalton had imagined himself running Drake Diamonds someday. Alone, not alongside his brother. Just him. Dalton Drake, Chief Executive Officer.

He'd never pictured himself as part of a team. Never wanted it. In reality, it wasn't so bad. One day, he might even grow accustomed to it.

"Absolutely." He nodded and gave his brother a genuine, if sad, smile. "I've made my decision. The princess is going back home where she belongs."

Aurélie should have been relieved to wake up alone in Dalton's pristine apartment. She still wasn't sure quite how to act around him after mauling him in the car.

What had come over her? She'd acted as if this person she'd been pretending to be in New York, this impulsive life she was leading, was actually real. It wasn't. Not at all. This was a holiday, nothing more.

But the holiday was clearly messing with her head. In a really big way.

She would have loved to blame her outlandish behavior on the hot dog. Or at the very least, the bearer of the hot dog.

She'd grown so accustomed to Dalton's straight-laced

businessman persona, that his simple act of kindness had caught her completely off guard. Every so often, he was soulful when she least expected it.

In those stolen moments of tenderness, she felt like she was seeing the real Dalton. The man behind the serious gray eyes and the Drake-blue tie. A man devastatingly beautiful in his complexity.

But really, how desperate did a girl have to be to throw herself at a man over a hot dog?

Sleep provided a temporary reprieve from Aurélie's mortification, but the moment her eyes drifted open, it all came crashing back—the cold fury of Dalton's lips, his wayward hands, the way he'd made her forget she was nothing but a virgin princess being married off to a complete and total stranger.

For one dazzling moment, she'd been more than that. She'd blazed bright, filled with liquid-gold, shimmering desire.

Until it was over.

Not here.

She'd felt herself disappearing again, falling away.

Maybe none of it had really happened. Maybe it had just been a bad dream. Aurélie's hand flew to her throat, hoping against hope that she'd find the smooth string of pearls still safely clasped around her neck, as she did every morning. But it wasn't. She found only her bare, unadorned neck beneath the open collar of Dalton's tuxedo shirt.

What was she still doing sleeping in that thing? The first night it had been a matter of necessity. It wasn't anymore.

But she liked waking up in Dalton's shirt. She liked the way his masculine scent clung to the fabric. She liked

the way the cuffs skimmed the very tips of her fingertips. She liked imagining him slipping it on sometime
in the distant future and remembering a princess who
lived on the other side of the world.

What was wrong with her? She had no business
thinking such things. She was an engaged woman. Almost, anyway.

She sat up and glanced around the spacious living
room in search of Jacques, but the little bulldog was nowhere to be seen. Aurélie sighed. He'd probably snuck
his way into Dalton's bedroom again. Jacques seemed to
be forming quite an attachment to the man, even though
the infatuation was clearly one-sided. Aurélie would
have probably found it amusing if it didn't remind her of
her own nonsensical attachment to Dalton's shirt.

The bedroom was empty, of course. No dog. No
Dalton.

On some level, she'd known. The air was calm, still.
Void of the electricity that always seemed to surround
him, like an electrical storm. He'd left a note in the
kitchen with the number to call when she was ready for
a driver to come round and pick her up. The note didn't
say where the car would be taking her. It didn't have to.

Heigh-ho, heigh-ho, it's off to work we go.

Did the man do anything else?

Judging by the looks of his apartment, no. With its
sleek lines and elegant white furniture, it was the epitome
of moneyed simplicity. Tasteful. Pristine. But more than a
tad sterile. After living there for a few days, Aurélie still
marveled at the absence of photographs. There wasn't a
single picture in the place. No candid snapshots, no family memories. It left her feeling strangely hollow. And sad
for Dalton, although she knew she shouldn't.

He'd never given her the slightest indication he was unhappy with his station in life. On the contrary, he exuded more confidence than anyone she'd ever met.

She needed to get out of here, out of this apartment that felt so oddly unsettling without Dalton's brooding presence. Even if the car took her straight to the glittering store on Fifth Avenue. At least in Dalton's place of business, she would be less likely to accidentally kiss the stuffing out of him again. Before she went anywhere, though, she needed to check the news to make sure she still wasn't a headline.

Dalton's laptop was situated on the dining room table. Perfect. She could take a look at the US tabloids and then access the Delamotte papers online. She made a cup of coffee, sank cross-legged onto one of the dining room chairs and flipped open the computer. Then she nearly choked on her coffee when Dalton's screensaver came into view.

It was a photograph—a picture of a woman on horseback, and she was quite beautiful.

Aurélie stared at it until a sick feeling came over her. A sick feeling that seemed an awful lot like jealousy.

Oh, no. She slammed the computer closed. *This cannot be happening.* But it was. It *was* happening. She was jealous of a silly little screensaver, jealous over Dalton Drake.

She was in over her head. Whether she liked it or not, what had happened the day before changed things. She couldn't stay here. Not anymore. It was time to pack up her egg and go home.

She opened the laptop back up, steadfastly refused to allow herself even a glimpse at the pretty equestrian smiling at her from the screen and logged onto the internet. Within minutes, she'd booked herself on a commercial flight out of New York that would allow her to get back to Delamotte in time for her portrait session with Lord Clement the next day.

With any luck, by this time tomorrow she'd be back home, and it would be as though she'd never come to New York, never walked through snowy Central Park, never shopped for vintage clothes in Brooklyn. Never kissed Dalton Drake.

Her flight left at midnight. Now all she needed to do was get her egg back...

...and break the news to Dalton.

Chapter Seven

Aurélie dragged her feet for a good long while before leaving the apartment. She made a second cup of coffee and drank it while she watched the New Yorkers milling about on the crowded streets below. Steam rose up from the manhole covers, and snow covered everything, from the neat grid of sidewalks to the elegant spire of the Chrysler building towering over the Manhattan skyline. From above, the city looked almost like an old black-and-white movie—the kind she used to watch with her mother on late nights when her father was out on official crown business. Or so she'd thought.

She'd been so naïve. Naïve and happy. Ignorance really was bliss, wasn't it?

How different would things be right now if she'd never read her mother's journal? Would she be dreading her arranged marriage so much that she'd actually flee the country? Would she even be standing right here, right now, in Dalton Drake's quiet apartment?

Maybe.

Maybe not.

She almost wished she hadn't. Almost.

Stop. What's done is done.

She turned her back on the window and got down to the business of preparing to leave. She rinsed her coffee cup, put it in the dishwasher. She stripped the sofa of the sheets and blankets she'd been using, washed and dried them, then tucked them away in the massive walk-in closet in Dalton's master suite. All the while, she gave the dining room and Dalton's laptop a wide berth.

His closet was meticulously organized, of course. Even more so than her own closet at the palace. Unlike her walk-in, which was packed with gowns of every color under the sun, Dalton's was distinctly monochromatic. The spectrum ranged from sedate dove-gray and charcoal designer business suits to sleek black tuxedos. The sole splash of color was the selection of ties hanging side-by-side on two sections of wooden spools that flanked his full-length mirror. All the highest quality silk. All the same recognizable shade of blue.

Drake blue.

Aurélie shook her head. The man's identity was so tied to his family business that he didn't even own a single tie in a different hue. He took workaholic to a whole new level.

She found a small suitcase tucked away behind the wall of Armani and used it to pack her new vintage wardrobe. If Dalton balked, she'd arrange to send him a new one after she got home. It wasn't like he might need it between now and then. She doubted he'd even miss it. She wondered when he'd last taken a vacation. Then she reminded herself that Dalton Drake's vacation schedule was none of her concern.

I'll never see him again.

She froze. Swallowed. Then forced herself to take a deep breath.

Of course you won't see him again. That's the whole point of leaving.

It was for the best. The longer she stayed, the harder it would be to walk out the door. She'd already had a nonsensical fit of jealousy after seeing his screensaver. How much worse could things get if she stayed longer?

A lot worse. No question. Besides, if she didn't get on that midnight plane, she'd miss her portrait sitting. She was doing the right thing. The *only* thing. She'd run out of options.

She folded her new dresses with meticulous care and tried not to think about the fact that she'd probably never wear most of them. They were wholly inappropriate for royal life. But she couldn't dwell on that now. If she did, she might just fall apart. Anyway, she loved her new clothes. Maybe she'd get to wear them again...someday.

Keep busy. That's what she needed to do. Just stay as busy as possible between now and the time she needed to head to the airport.

When at last she'd erased every trace of her presence from the apartment, she asked Sam to fetch the driver. With only a matter of hours left before her flight, she couldn't put off the inevitable any longer. She had to tell Dalton she was leaving and demand that he return her egg.

As unpleasant as such a confrontation sounded, at least it would take place at the glittering store on Fifth

Avenue, where she wouldn't be tempted to repeat yesterday's mistake.

Of course she'd forgotten that making her way to Dalton's office would involve walking through the Engagements section on the tenth floor. Tightness gathered in her chest as the elevator doors slid open.

"Welcome." The elevator attendant's smile was too kind. Aurélie recognized him as the same man who'd witnessed her last near-panic attack.

Super. Even the elevator attendant pitied her. "Thank you," she said, and forced herself to put one foot in front of the other.

The showroom was even more crowded than it had been last time. A man wearing a Drake-blue bowtie walked past her holding a tray of champagne flutes. Couples sat, two by two, at each and every display case. One of the shoppers even had the word *Bride* spelled out in rhinestones on her white slim-fit tee.

Aurélie's mouth grew dry. *Bride*. She had trouble breathing all of a sudden. Even remaining upright seemed challenging. She swayed a little on her feet.

How many engaged couples could there possibly be in Manhattan?

"It's a little overwhelming, isn't it?" said someone beside her.

"Excuse me?" Aurélie turned to find a woman, blonde, graceful and judging by the size of her adorable baby bump, a few months pregnant.

"You must be Aurélie." She gave her a conspiratorial wink. "I'm Ophelia Drake, and believe me, I know how you feel."

Ophelia Drake—Artem's wife, Dalton's sister-in-law and the head jewelry designer for the company. Aurélie recognized her from the photo in the Drake Diamonds brochure she'd read in Dalton's office on her first day in New York.

What she hadn't gleaned from the brochure was how warm and open Ophelia Drake seemed. But nice as she appeared, she couldn't possibly know how Aurélie felt. No one could.

Upon closer inspection, something in the depths of Ophelia's gaze told Aurélie that she was no stranger to heartache. Interesting.

"Come with me. I know the perfect cure." Ophelia wrapped an arm around her waist and steered her through the maze of wedded bliss and down the hall. In the time it took to leave Engagements behind, Aurélie decided she quite liked Ophelia. She liked her a lot.

"Here we go. Grab a seat," Ophelia said, ushering her into a small room filled with sleek silver appliances, trays of champagne and at least ten or twelve plates of tiny cakes.

Aurélie looked around. "Is this a kitchen?"

Ophelia nodded and slid a plate of petit fours onto the table in front of Aurélie. "I used to hide in here sometimes." She waved a flippant hand toward Engagements. "When it got to be a little much out there, I'd sometimes sneak in here for some cake. This is where I met my husband, actually."

"Here in the kitchen?" Aurélie picked up a petit four, a perfect replica of the small Drake-blue boxes wrapped with white ribbon that customers carried home everyday. It looked too pretty, too perfect to eat.

"Yes. In this very spot." Ophelia frowned at the tiny cake in Aurélie's hand. "Are you going to eat that or just stare at it? Because I'm eating for two and if it sits there much longer, I can't promise I won't snatch it right out of your hand."

Aurélie laughed. It felt good to laugh. Right. Easy. She hadn't laughed much since she'd kissed Dalton. The past twenty-four hours or so had been spent mired in regret.

She smiled at Ophelia and popped the petit four in her mouth. "Oh. My. God. This is delicious."

Ophelia shrugged. "Told you. It's a wonder what just a little bite of cake can do sometimes."

Aurélie licked a crumb from her fingertip and shamelessly reached for another petit four. "Can I ask you something?"

"Sure." Ophelia leaned back in her chair and rested a hand on her belly the way blissful expectant mothers had a tendency to do.

She was a lovely woman. Aurélie remembered reading in the brochure that Ophelia's first designs for Drake Diamonds had been a dance-inspired collection because she used to be a ballerina. Her training showed. Even pregnant, she carried herself with the grace and poise of a former dancer.

But it wasn't her willowy limbs that made her beautiful, nor the elegance of her movements. It was the way she glowed. Ophelia was happy. Truly happy.

Aurélie couldn't help but feel a little envious. "Isn't Artem the CEO? How is it that you first met him here instead of on the sales floor?"

Ophelia's lips curved into a smirk. "Let's just say Artem wasn't always so serious about this place. It took a while for him to adjust to the role." She tilted her head and gave Aurélie a puzzled look. "I'm surprised Dalton hasn't mentioned it to you. You're staying with him, right? Artem's work habits used to bother him to no end."

"*Oui.* I'm staying with him. But we don't really talk much." *We just argue. And kiss. Then argue some more.* "I'm not sure if you've noticed, but Dalton isn't exactly the chatty type."

"Oh, I've noticed." Ophelia grew quiet for a moment. Pensive. "I've also noticed he seems a bit different since you arrived."

Aurélie sighed. "If he's been extra cranky, I'm afraid that's my fault. We rub each other the wrong way." A bigger understatement had never been uttered.

Ophelia's brow furrowed. "Actually, I was thinking the opposite."

Aurélie opened her mouth, and for a few prolonged seconds, nothing came out of it. *The opposite?* Meaning that she and Dalton somehow rubbed each other the *right* way? Impossible. No. Just…no.

Yet her heart gave a rebellious little lurch all the same.

She cleared her throat and reminded herself that in a matter of hours she'd be on an airplane headed halfway across the world. As she should. "I have no idea what you're talking about."

Ophelia smiled. "I'm talking about the dog in his office, for one thing."

Oh yes, that.

"And his scarcity around here the past few days. Dalton doesn't take time off. Ever." She shrugged. "Unless Diana has a horse show in the area, like she does tomorrow."

Aurélie's heart stuttered to a stop. So the horsewoman had a name. Diana.

Well whoever Diana was, Aurélie pitied her. She

couldn't imagine being in a relationship with a man who was so clearly addicted to his work, was pathologically allergic to fun and hated rescue puppies.

For some reason though, the storm of emotions brewing in Aurélie's soul felt very little like pity. She swallowed around the lump that had taken up swift residence in her throat. "I…um…" *Don't ask about Diana the horse lover. Do* not.

"Diana is Artem and Dalton's younger sister," Ophelia explained. "The third Drake."

"Oh, I see." It was ludicrous how delighted she sounded. Borderline thrilled. She prayed Ophelia didn't pick up on it.

Judging by her amused expression, she did. Mercifully, Artem strode into the kitchen before Ophelia could comment. He took one look at the empty plate in the center of the table and aimed a knowing grin at his wife. "Busted. Again."

Ophelia lifted a challenging brow. "I'm eating for two, remember?"

As Aurélie watched Artem bend to give his wife a tender kiss on the cheek, she was struck by how different he appeared from Dalton, despite the fact that they had similar aristocratic good looks. Same dark hair, same chiseled features. But Aurélie had grown so accustomed to the thunder in Dalton's gaze and the underlying intensity of his movements that witnessing Artem's casual elegance was like seeing the flip side of a silver coin.

"Sweetheart," Ophelia said. "Have you met Aurélie?"

Artem straightened and shook her hand. "Not officially, although I've heard quite a bit about you. It's a pleasure to meet you."

"*Enchanté.*"

Meeting Dalton's family felt strange. She'd known Drake Diamonds was a family institution, but Dalton sure didn't seem much like a family man. Probably because he so obviously wasn't, the photograph on his laptop notwithstanding.

His sister.

Diana is Artem and Dalton's younger sister. The third Drake.

The woman's identity didn't change a thing. It didn't change the fact that she had no business kissing Dalton. And it most definitely didn't change the fact that Dalton had put an abrupt stop to her advances in the car. Or that she had a real life with real responsibilities on the other side of the world.

Which made the extent of her relief all the more alarming.

Where the hell is she?

Dalton checked the hour on his Cartier for what had to be the hundredth time. 8:45 p.m. Outside his office window, the sky had long grown dark. The store would be closing in less than fifteen minutes. Aurélie's plane was due to board in just under three hours, and he still hadn't managed to tell her she'd be on it.

He sighed mightily. According to Sam, she'd left the apartment building an hour ago. She should have breezed into his office by now, but of course, she hadn't. Dalton didn't know why he was surprised. Aurélie wasn't exactly a paragon of predictability. A rebellious spike of arousal shot through him, and he was forced to acknowledge that he found her lack of predictability one of her most intriguing qualities.

Too bad it also drove him batshit crazy.

By this time tomorrow, she'll be out of your life for good. He just had to make it through the next few hours and see that Aurélie got on the plane. Surely getting her strapped into a first-class airplane seat on time was a doable task. Of course, it would help if he knew where she was.

"What now?" Dalton groaned as he felt an all-too familiar nudge on his shin. He looked down to find Aurélie's dog staring up at him with its big, round googly eyes. Yet again. "You can't be serious."

The puppy pawed at him again and let out a pitiful whine. Dalton had already been forced to have Mrs. Barnes walk the blasted thing twice since lunchtime when he'd done the honors himself. There had also been an unfortunate accident on his office floor, evidenced by a wet spot on the Drake-blue carpet that belied the dog's small size. Tempted as Dalton was to ignore the persistent pawing on his shins, he knew better.

He buzzed his secretary's desk, but the call went unanswered. Which didn't come as much of a surprise since she'd been officially relieved of her duties at 6:00. Sometimes she stayed late in case Dalton needed any after-hours assistance, but he figured puppy-sitting didn't exactly fit into her job description.

"Fine," he muttered, scooping the tiny bulldog into the crook of his elbow. "Let's do this."

The dog buried his oversized head into Dalton's chest, made a few of the snuffling noises that Aurélie somehow found endearing and left a smear of god-knows-what in the middle of Dalton's tie.

Splendid. "Thanks for that," he muttered.

Jacques snorted in response. Dalton rolled his eyes and stalked down the hallway, intent on getting the business over with as swiftly as possible. But as he approached the kitchen, Jacques's sizeable ears pricked forward. His stout little body trembled with excitement, and when they reached the doorway, the reason for his elation came into view.

"Aurélie." Dalton stopped in his tracks.

There she was—sitting calmly at the kitchen table nibbling on petit fours like Marie Antoinette while her dog slobbered all over his Burberry suit. Why hadn't he been notified of her arrival? And why were Artem and Ophelia chatting her up like the three of them were old friends?

"You're late," he said without prelude or ceremony.

Artem cleared his throat.

"How is that possible when I don't even work here?" Aurélie popped the remaining bit of cake in her mouth, affording Dalton a glimpse of her cherry pink tongue, a view that aroused him beyond all reason.

She made no move to stand, instead remaining regally seated in her chair wearing one of the vintage dresses she'd chosen the day before— pale blue with a nipped in waist, voluminous skirt and large white polka dots. Wholly inappropriate for winter in New York, yet undeniably lovely. Dalton found himself wishing the dress were a shade or two darker. He'd like to have seen her dressed in Drake blue. His color...

His.

Mine. The word pulsed in his veins with a predatory fervor.

He needed to get her out of his store, his life and back to Delamotte where she belonged. The fact that she'd yet to so much as look at him, focusing instead on the squirming puppy in his arms, did nothing to suppress his desire. Much to his frustration.

The ways in which she vexed him were innumerable. He smiled tightly. "Apologies, Your Highness. I forget that work—or responsibility of any kind—is a foreign concept for you."

When at last she met his gaze, thinly veiled fury sparkled in the depths of her emerald eyes.

"Okay, then," Artem said with forced cheerfulness. "It's getting rather late. I need to get my pregnant wife home. We'll give you two some privacy, because don't you have something you need to discuss with Aurélie, Dalton?"

Artem shot Dalton a loaded glance.

"Is that right?" Aurélie stood, and the folds of her pale blue skirt swirled around her shapely legs. "I have something to discuss with you as well. Something important."

"Very well." Dalton nodded. "But at the moment, your dog requires attention. Shall we?"

She reached for Jacques, and the dog went into a spastic fit of delight. Dalton was all but ignored, which should have been a relief. The fact that he felt the opposite was every bit as mystifying as it was infuriating.

He smoothed down his dampened tie and waited as Aurélie gathered the puppy in her arms and walked past him, out the door. He glanced at his brother and sister-in-law, still sitting at the kitchen table, looking mildly amused. "Good night, Ophelia. Artem." He nodded.

Artem arched an expectant brow, but said nothing. He didn't need to. Dalton got the message loud and clear. The time had come to tell Aurélie she was leaving. It was now or never.

Chapter Eight

Aurélie's hands were shaking. Thank goodness she could hide them beneath the solid warmth of Jacques's trembling little form. She'd rather die than let Dalton see the effect he had on her, especially after his dig about her work ethic. Or lack thereof.

She really couldn't stand that smug look in his eye, but what she despised even more was the fact that he'd been right. She'd never worked a day in her life. Not technically. Of course she'd always considered being royal a job in and of itself. But being here in New York and seeing how many people it took to keep Drake Diamonds running day in and day out, made her painfully aware of how easy she had it, her dreaded arranged marriage notwithstanding.

Like it or not, Dalton had been right about her to some extent. She'd come to New York for a taste of real life, but holing up in a workaholic diamond heir's luxury apartment wasn't any more real than life in a palace.

It feels real, though. At the moment, nothing in the world felt as real as the forbidden heat of Dalton's palm in the small of her back as he escorted her down the hall. A tremble coursed through her, and for some ridiculous reason she felt like crying as the Engagements showroom came into view.

"Are you all right?" he asked, much to her horror.

Get it together, Aurélie. She refused to break down in front of Dalton Drake. She'd have nine uninterrupted hours to cry all she wanted on her flight back to Delamotte.

"I'm perfectly fine," she said as Jacques licked a tear from her cheek.

Dalton stared at her for a beat, and a dangerous-looking knot formed in his jaw. He looked like he could grind coal into diamonds with his teeth. Tears made him angry? It figured, seeing as he seemed allergic to the full scale of human emotions.

"You're fine. Clearly," he muttered and jabbed at the elevator's down button.

The elevator attendant, who felt almost like a friend by now, was nowhere to be seen. He must have gone home for the day. Aurélie stared straight ahead as the doors slid closed, despite the array of sparkling diamond engagement rings assaulting her vision. She didn't dare venture another glance at Dalton while they were trapped together in a small, enclosed space. Not after what she'd done the last time they were in a similar situation.

"Is it true that Gaston Drake invented the concept of

the engagement ring?" she asked, purely for something to say to pierce the sultry silence.

She wasn't even sure where she'd picked up the bit of trivia about Dalton's great-great-great-great-great-grandfather. Probably from one of the brochures she'd had time to all but memorize while Dalton left her unattended in his office.

"Been reading up on the company, have you?" His voice carried a note of surprise.

"I *can* read, you know. I have a master's degree from the Sorbonne." Granted, she'd completed most of her coursework long-distance. But Dalton didn't need to know that. "Does that surprise you, Mr. Drake?"

She couldn't help herself, and glanced up at him for the briefest second. Big mistake. Huge.

Instead of finding a superior glint in his eye, as she'd come to expect, he was appraising her with a penetrating stare. As if he could see every part of her, inside and out, and despite his penchant for mocking her, he liked what he saw.

The corner of his lips curved into a half grin. "You have a habit of surprising me on a daily basis, Princess."

Aurélie blinked, and despite every effort to maintain respectable, chaste eye contact, her gaze dropped straight to his mouth.

It was happening again. She was thinking about kissing him. She was thinking about his hands in her hair and the cold fury of his lips and the delicious ache that was beginning to stir low in her belly. Just under five minutes in the man's presence was all it had taken.

They didn't even like each other. What on earth was wrong with her?

Thank God for the squirming puppy in her arms. He

was the only thing keeping her from making a complete and utter fool of herself. Again.

Somewhere amid the fog of arousal, she was vaguely aware of a bell ringing and a whooshing sound, followed by Dalton's voice saying her name.

"Hmm?" she heard herself say.

"We're here. The ground floor." He stood beside her, holding the elevator door open, eyeing her with concern. She'd been so lost in illicit thought that she hadn't even noticed the elevator had come to a stop. "Are you quite sure you're all right?"

No. Not one bit. "Yes, of course."

She brushed past him, out of the elevator and into the gleaming lobby. She was immediately taken aback by the unexpected serenity of the showroom. There wasn't a soul in sight, not even a salesperson. As soon as she set foot on the marble foyer floor, the overhead lights flickered and dimmed.

The store was closing? Already?

She still hadn't uttered a word to Dalton about leaving. Nor had she even seen her egg since the day she'd arrived.

"You forgot your coat." Dalton paused in front of the revolving door and frowned down at her bare arms.

She sighed. Time was running out. There was no way she was going to go all the way back to the kitchen for her coat, especially if it meant another ride up and down the elevator with Dalton, filled with sexual tension.

She plopped Jacques on the floor, wrapped his leash around her wrist and crossed her arms. "I'll be fine like this. We'll hurry."

Thankfully, Dalton didn't look any more inclined than

she was to get back into the elevator. He glanced at his watch and his frown deepened.

"Don't be ridiculous." Dalton slipped out of his overcoat and placed it around her shoulders. "Here."

Despite the stormy disapproval in his gray gaze, or maybe because of it, an undeniable thrill coursed through Aurélie at the intimacy of the gesture. She turned her head as she obediently slid her arms into the sleeves of his coat, because it was just too much, this sudden closeness. His coat was impossibly soft— cashmere, obviously—and warm from the heat of his body. Dalton's face was right there, just inches away from hers as he buttoned her up, and all at once she was enveloped in him. His woodsy clean scent. His sultry warmth. All of him.

Aurélie's heart thundered against her ribs, and she prayed he couldn't hear it. She didn't trust herself to look at him, so she focused instead on the dazzling array of jewels behind him, sparkling and shimmering in their illuminated display cases. Treasures in the dark.

"There," Dalton muttered with a trace of huskiness in his voice that seemed to scrape Aurélie's insides.

She had to say something. If she didn't do it now, she might never go through with it.

The revolving doors were flanked on either side by two large banners advertising the upcoming exhibit of the Marchand imperial eggs. The first and oldest egg of the collection, known as the jeweled hen egg, was pictured on a pristine white background. This particular egg stood out from the rest as the simplest in design. On the surface, it looked almost like an actual egg. But in reality, it had been crafted from solid gold and coated in creamy white enamel. Upon close inspection, a barely discernible gold line was visible along the egg's center, where its two halves were joined. Once the hidden fitting was opened, a round gold yolk could be found nestled inside. And inside the yolk, a diamond-encrusted platinum crown. A precious, priceless secret.

Aurélie stared at the image of her family heirloom looming larger than life over Dalton's shoulder. *So many secrets.*

She was thoroughly sick of all of them.

"There's something I need to tell you," she heard herself say.

Dalton arched a single eyebrow. "So you said."

She swallowed. The words were gathering in her throat. She could taste their ripeness on the tip of her tongue and still she wasn't quite sure what form they would take.

You're right about me. I'm every bit as silly and irresponsible as you suspect.

I'm engaged to be married.

I'm leaving.

"I…" she started, but a sharp bark pierced the loaded silence. Then another, followed by a wholly impatient canine growl.

Aurélie looked down at Jacques, who'd stretched himself into a downward dog position that would have made even the most die-hard yogi green with envy. He woofed again and wagged his stump of a tail.

"Hold that thought," Dalton said. "I've already cleaned up after your little monster enough times today."

He strode toward the revolving door with Jacques nipping at his heels, and Aurélie had no choice but to follow. They made their way down the block to Central Park and back without uttering another word. There was something about the gently falling snow and the quiet city streets awash with white that forbade conversation.

A chill coursed through her, and she slipped her hands in the pockets of Dalton's overcoat. The fingertips of her right hand made contact with something buried in the silk pocket lining. Something small. Round. Familiar.

She knew without even looking at it that the object in her hand was one of her mother's pearls. A broken reminder of their kiss.

Aurélie was painfully aware of each passing second. Time seemed to be moving far more quickly than usual, in a twilight violet-hued blur. She couldn't help but wonder if Dalton felt it, too, especially when the echo of his footsteps on the bluestone slate sidewalk seemed to grow further and further apart.

They could walk as slowly as they wanted, but they'd never be able to stop time. Midnight was approaching, and if she didn't ask for her egg back now—right now—it would be too late. Even if she wanted to stay, she couldn't.

She glanced up at the amethyst sky and the billowing snow, like something out of a fairy tale, and told herself to remember this. Remember the magic of the bustling city. Remember what it felt like to be wrapped in borrowed cashmere with frost in her hair. Remember the music falling down from the stars.

Music?

She blinked. "Do you hear that?" she whispered.

"Hear what?" Dalton paused alongside her.

"Music." Aurélie slowed to a stop, and Jacques plopped into a lopsided sitting position at her feet. "Listen."

She couldn't quite grab hold of it, and for a split second she thought she must have only imagined the plaintive sounds of a violin floating above the distant blare of horns and the thrum of city's heartbeat center. But then she closed her eyes and when she did, she found it again.

"Do you hear it? Vivaldi." Her eyelashes fluttered open, and beyond the puff of her breath in the frosty air, she saw Dalton watching her with an intensity that made her cheeks go warm. She swallowed. "Where do you think it's coming from?"

He looked at her for a moment that seemed to stretch far too long, then he took her hand. "I'll show you."

She started to protest before she realized they were covering familiar territory, treading the now-familiar path back toward Drake Diamonds. They passed the entrance to the Plaza Hotel with its grand white pillars and crimson steps, and as they walked beneath the ghostly glow of gas lamplights, the music grew louder and louder. It swelled to a crescendo just as the violinist came into view.

He was situated right beside the entrance to Drake Diamonds with a tip bucket at his feet. Eyes closed, hands covered with fingerless mitts, he moved his bow furiously over the instrument. He was just a street musician, but Aurélie had never seen a violinist play with such passion, not even at Delamotte's royal symphony. He was so lost in his music that a lump formed in Aurélie's throat as she stood watching him, grinning from ear to ear.

For a perfect, precious moment, she forgot she was supposed to be saying goodbye. She forgot she shouldn't be standing in the dark, holding Dalton's hand. She forgot that when she looked up at him, she'd find the sculpted planes of his face so beautiful that she'd go breathless. He reminded her of all those diamonds glittering in their lonely display cases in the dark. Hard. Exquisite. Forever beyond her reach.

"It's lovely, isn't it?" she breathed.

At the sound of her voice, the music abruptly stopped.

"I'm sorry, Mr. Drake." The violinist bent to return his instrument to its case.

Clearly he'd been forewarned against occupying the precious sidewalk space in front of Drake Diamonds. As if Dalton owned the entire walkway where they were standing.

He probably does.

"Don't stop, it's okay. Please continue." Without tearing his gaze from Aurélie, Dalton reached into his suit pocket for his wallet, pulled out a thick wad of bills and tossed them in the musician's tip bucket. He angled his head toward her. "Anything in particular you'd like to hear, Princess?"

Princess. His voice didn't have the bite to it that she'd grown accustomed to. On the contrary, he said the word almost as if it were an endearment.

Tell him. Just say it—I'm leaving.

Maybe she could have if his gaze hadn't gone tender and if he'd looked less like a tragic literary hero all of a sudden rather than what he was—a ruthless, self-contained diamond heir. Instead, she heard herself say, "How about some Gershwin?"

His handsome face split into a rare, unguarded grin. "Gershwin? How very New York of you." He shrugged and called out to the violinist. "You heard the lady. I don't suppose you know any Gershwin?"

The familiar, sweeping strains of "Rhapsody in Blue" filled the air, and Aurélie couldn't even bring herself to look at Dalton, much less utter a goodbye. So she focused intently on the violinist instead.

"He's quite good, isn't he?" Dalton said.

She nodded and pretended not to notice the overwhelming magic of the moment. "Perfect."

The song had always been a favorite of hers, but she'd never heard it like this before. Not with the notes rising and floating over the city as snowflakes danced and spun in the glow of the streetlights. It was at once altogether beautiful yet hauntingly sad.

She turned toward Dalton. He had that look about him again, a fleeting tragic edge that drew her fingertips to her throat in search of her mother's pearls even though she knew they were no longer there.

"About earlier…in the tenth floor showroom," he said, his gaze searching.

The tenth floor showroom. Engagements. So he'd noticed her unease at being surrounded by all those wedding rings? Of course he had.

He smiled, but it didn't quite reach his eyes. "For what it's worth, Engagements isn't my favorite department, either."

She wasn't sure what she'd expected him to say, but it certainly hadn't been that. *"Non?"*

He shook his head. "I despise it, actually."

They had something in common after all. She couldn't help but wonder why he felt that way. *Despise* was an awfully strong word. But she didn't dare ask, lest he reciprocate with questions of his own.

She offered only a wry smile. "Not the marrying type?"

He didn't respond, just stared straight ahead. Whatever tenderness she'd seen in his gaze earlier had evaporated, replaced by the cool indifference she'd come to know so well over the past few days.

She rolled her eyes. "Right. Why am I surprised when you're so clearly married to your work?"

"Something like that." The coldness in his voice made her wince, and he kept his gaze fixed on the musician. Then, as if the awkward exchange had never happened, he said, "Shall we dance?"

She let out a laugh. Surely he'd meant the offer as a joke. "Isn't there a spreadsheet somewhere that needs your attention?"

His eyes flashed in the darkness. "I'm dead serious. Dance with me."

He slid one arm around her waist and took her hand with the other. He pulled her close, so close that she could feel the full length of his body pressed against hers. A tight, hard wall of muscle. She wasn't at all prepared for such sudden closeness. The confidence with which he held her and the warmth of his fingertips on her wrist was disorienting, and before she knew what was happening, they were floating over the snowy sidewalk.

The world slowed to a stop. In a city of millions, it felt as if they were the only two people on earth. Aurélie was scarcely aware of the violinist's presence, nor of Jacques's leash winding itself slowly around their legs. Tears gathered in her eyes. She had to stop herself from burying her face in his chest and pressing her lips to the side of his neck.

She wanted to cry, because how could she possibly walk away now, when this would undoubtedly be the most romantic moment of her life?

"You've gone awfully quiet all of sudden," he whispered, and his voice rumbled through her like distant thunder.

It was strange the things people remembered when they found themselves at an impasse. Aurélie's mind should have been on the pink enamel egg coated in seed pearls that was sitting inside the Drake Diamonds vault. She should have been trying to figure out a way to get herself back home. Instead, she suddenly remembered something Artem had said earlier in the kitchen.

Don't you have something you need to discuss with Aurélie, Dalton?

She'd been so nervous about announcing her early departure that she'd forgotten the way Dalton's jaw had hardened in response to Artem's question. She glanced up at him now. "Wasn't there something you wanted to tell me?"

He fixed his gaze with hers, and Aurélie saw something new in his eyes. A fleeting hesitancy. Above them, the darkness of the night sky felt heavy, swollen with so many words left unspoken between them. Everything they wouldn't, couldn't, say.

"It can wait," he said.

She nodded, and somehow she knew there would be no goodbyes. Not now. Not tonight.

Their legs became too entangled in the dog leash to keep dancing, so they slowed to a stop until they were standing still in one another's arms. The music may have gone quiet. Aurélie wasn't even sure. She'd slipped into a hazy, dreamlike state, drunk on music and sensation.

Dalton reached, wove his fingers through hers and brushed his lips against the back of her hand. "Let's go home."

Aurélie took a deep breath. If she didn't leave for the

airport right now, she'd miss her flight. She'd never get to Paris in time to catch a connection to Delamotte. She'd miss her appointment with Lord Clement.

The palace would undoubtedly come looking for her, and there would be no turning back. Not this time.

One more day. Just one more day.

Dalton released her hand and bent to untangle Jacques's leash. He walked a few steps in the direction of his apartment building with the little bulldog trotting alongside him, then turned and stopped. Waited. "Are you coming, Princess?"

"Oui. Une seconde." She reached into the pocket of Dalton's coat for the lonely gold pearl, held it tightly in her closed fist then dropped it in the violinist's tip bucket, where it swirled to an iridescent stop in the moonlight.

No turning back.

Chapter Nine

This is a mistake.

Dalton was fully aware of what would happen when he made the fatal choice to take Aurélie back to the apartment instead of to the airport. He knew what he was doing was wrong. Reckless. Probably even downright dangerous.

He'd been so prepared to tell her it would be best if she went back home. He'd waited all day for her to show up so he could break the news to her in person. Her little holiday was over. He was a busy man. He didn't have time to babysit a princess. Especially a princess who wore her heart on her sleeve the way that Aurélie did.

She wasn't anything like the other women who'd been in Dalton's life. More specifically, the women who'd been in his bed. If the problem had been as simple as sex, and sex alone, he would have broken down and succumbed to temptation by now.

But he had the distinct feeling that sex with Aurélie would be anything but simple. She got emotional over street musicians and homeless puppies and hot dogs.

To Dalton's complete and utter astonishment, he found it charming. Sexy. Altogether irresistible, if he was being honest.

Which was precisely the problem. Aurélie wasn't a woman he could just sleep with and then move on. She'd only been in his life for a few days, and in that small span of time, she'd thrown his entire existence into an uproar. She was sentimental to her core. She was also a runaway royal princess.

But he couldn't seem to resist taking her hand and leading her home. He had to stop himself from kissing her on the grand steps of the library under the watchful gaze of the stone lions, their manes laden with snow. Patience and Fortitude. Dalton had neither at the moment. But he knew if he kissed her then, beneath the moon and the stars and the ethereal lamplight glow, he'd be unable to stop.

At his building, the doorman nodded a greeting. Dalton must have said something in return, but he couldn't imagine what. He couldn't hear a thing over the roar of blood in his ears and the annoying howl of his conscience.

This is a mistake.

Dalton no longer believed in mistakes. Not tonight. Not now, when Aurélie was looking at him with eyes full of bejeweled longing. Not when it seemed as if the walls of the cool marble lobby hummed with desire and the wild percussion of their hearts.

He didn't wait for the elevator to deposit them on the penthouse floor. Couldn't. The doors slid closed with a sultry whisper, and he held Aurélie's glittering gaze until he was sure—absolutely certain—that she wanted this as badly as he did.

Then he moved toward her with a growl—a deep, primitive sound he'd never heard himself make before—and crushed his mouth to hers.

Aurélie melted into him with a slow, drawn-out inhale and slid the palms of her hands languidly up his chest. He closed his eyes and lost himself in the warm wonderland of her mouth and the quickening flutter of her breath as the kiss grew deeper.

More demanding.

The ground beneath them stirred as the elevator lifted them closer to the stars, farther and farther from the real world down below. Aurélie's delicate form felt weightless, feather-light in his arms, and he was hit with a momentary panic at the thought that she might float away.

He leaned closer, closer, until he'd pressed her against the elevator wall. His hands moved to her slender wrists and circled them loosely like bracelets. Her body softened. The dog's leash slipped from her fingers and fell to the floor. She whispered his name, and the aching hunger in her voice was so raw, so sweetly vulnerable, that it nearly brought him to his knees.

Everything went white hot. Like a diamond burning away to smoke.

Dalton was harder than he'd ever been in his life. He was seconds away from sliding his hand under her dress, up the luxurious length of her thigh, and stroking his way inside her with his fingers.

He wanted to make her come. He wanted to watch her go someplace she'd never been, knowing he was the one who'd taken her there. The only one.

He was fairly certain she was a virgin, which only

multiplied the severity of the mistake he was about to make. She was a princess, and seemed to have lived a sheltered existence. She had an air of innocent charm about her. He could still think coherently enough for that fact to register somewhere in his consciousness. But he no longer gave a damn about right and wrong. About who either of them were.

If she was a virgin, though, he needed to slow down. Be gentle. And he certainly shouldn't be on the verge of undressing her in an elevator. She deserved better than this.

"Aurélie," he groaned, pulling back to rest his forehead against hers and twirl a lock of her spun-gold hair around his fingertip.

He could see her pulse hammering in her throat, and he wanted to kiss it. To press his mouth, wet and wanting, against the life teeming beneath her porcelain skin.

"Please," she pleaded, just as she'd done in the car on the afternoon she'd kissed him, and Dalton knew he was done for.

Mistake or not, he couldn't let her down again. Perhaps a better man could, a more honorable man. But Dalton had never felt less honorable in his life.

For each and every one of his thirty-three years, he'd done exactly what was expected of him. Where had it gotten him? The empty place he currently occupied— nowhere. Nothing was as it should be.

He'd had enough. Enough of duty. Enough of restraint. Enough of denying himself what he wanted. It had been a long, long time since he'd wanted anything. Anyone. So many lost years.

And now he wanted Aurélie.

At last he remembered what it was like to want and

need and ache. But the way he felt when he looked at her, when he touched her, wasn't anything like a memory. It was better. It was intoxicating.

The elevator came to a stop. Finally. Dalton took Aurélie's hand and led her inside the apartment. Somehow, he kept his wits about him long enough to get the dog settled in his spacious laundry room with a rawhide chew and a stuffed toy that would no doubt be disemboweled by morning. Which was perfectly fine with Dalton, so long as the little troublemaker was content.

He found Aurélie waiting for him in the darkened living room. The sight of her standing there with her ruby-red lips slightly parted and swollen from his kisses, eyes bright, made him want to tell her all kinds of truths. He had to clench his jaw to keep them from spilling out.

Her back was to the window, where snow beat against the glass in a dizzying fury. The night was steeped in winter white, but Dalton had gone summer warm.

"Let me look at you," he said as he approached. "I want to see you."

Without a trace of shyness, she reached for the hem of her dress and slipped it over her head. If she was nervous, she didn't let it show. On the contrary, her knowing smile gave him the impression that she was well aware of the effect she had on him.

She knew, and she quite enjoyed it.

Her dress landed on the floor in a polka-dot whisper. With her generous waves of hair tumbling over one moonstone shoulder, she lifted her bowed head and raised her gaze to his.

Dalton had to pause for a moment and collect himself. It hurt to swallow. It hurt to breathe. Every cell in his body screamed in agony, waiting and wanting to touch her.

He stared at her too hard and too long—at the willowy length of her legs, the captivating dip between her collarbones, the generous swell of her breasts covered in pale pink lace, a prelude to her softness.

The space between them shimmered with promise.

Everything about her was heavenly. Dalton would have loved to drape her bare body in ropes of pearls, to adorn her glorious curves with the precious treasures of the South Sea. Aurélie deserved such adoration. She deserved everything.

What was it about this woman, this near stranger who filled him with such decadent thoughts and so thoroughly shattered his reserve?

She's not just a woman. She's a princess.

She was royalty. And for tonight, she was his.

Aurélie had been waiting for this moment for what felt like an eternity.

Days ago, if she'd known she would be standing in Dalton Drake's living room in nothing but her bra and panties while he, fully clothed, looked his fill, she wouldn't have believed it. The very idea would have made her blush.

She wasn't blushing now. It felt natural, right, predestined somehow, that she should be here at this exact place and time. A rare and precious moment that had somehow been lost. Forgotten. Waiting for Aurélie to step into it when time had reached its fulfillment.

Dalton's gaze was serious. Grave even, as his gray eyes glittered with intent. He wasn't just looking at her.

He was studying her, and she felt every hard stare as surely as if he'd reached out and touched her.

Why hadn't he touched her yet? How long was he going to stand there and watch her burn? The slow simmer that had begun the morning he'd first set his gaze on her from across the chaste expanse of his desk had become intolerable. Liquid heat pooled at her center, and fire skittered over skin in the wake of his gaze.

She needed his hands on her. His mouth. On her. Inside her. She thought she might die if he made her wait much longer, and she couldn't hide her desperation. Her pride had fallen away with the whisper of her dress dropping to the floor. She was too inflamed to feel any sense of embarrassment.

Eyes locked with his, she walked toward him. One purposeful step—that's all she remembered taking, because he moved toward her at the exact same time. And suddenly his hands were everywhere—in her hair, cupping her bottom, sliding beneath the wispy lace cups of her bra and skimming over her sensitive nipples with the softest of touches. Her body all but wept with relief.

He kissed her again, and this time his lips were deliberate. Knowing. She realized every other kiss had been nothing but a prelude. This time, he took her mouth, possessed it as if he were already buried deep inside her. She kissed him back, arching toward him without even realizing she'd moved.

Her arousal astounded her. Shocked her to her core. Aurélie Marchand, the dutiful princess, had vanished and been replaced by a stranger. A stranger whose body was crying out for relief. A stranger who did things like slip out of her bra, reach for Dalton's hands and place them on her bare breasts.

"So beautiful," he whispered.

She loved the way he touched her. The way his big, capable hands cradled her as if he were holding a bone china teacup. Graceful with purpose.

He lowered his mouth to her nipple and at the first touch of his warm, wet tongue, Aurélie's knees went weak. She fell against him, and he wrapped an arm around her waist, holding her in place as he devoured her.

His hands slipped inside her panties, pushing them down until she was completely naked. She wanted him to undress, too, so she could see him, touch him, feel the hard ripple of his muscles beneath her fingertips. But as her hands sought the lapels of his suit jacket, one of Dalton's hands slid between her thighs.

She opened for him, and he stared down at her without breaking his gaze as he slipped a finger inside.

Oh my God.

"Aurélie, princess, have you ever been with a man before?"

She bit her lip to keep the truth from spilling out. She could never lie to him, not when those devastating eyes of his saw straight through her the way that they did. But she was afraid to tell him the truth, to admit there'd never been another.

She wanted him to be her first. She needed this more than Dalton ever could, or ever would, know. Right now a plane was bound for Delamotte, and her seat was empty. But the palace was waiting, and it wouldn't wait forever. She would never have a chance like this again.

Still, she was terrified to actually go through with it. Because somewhere beneath her quivering need, the truth shined bright. A fire opal of awareness.

This was more than just physical. She cared for Dalton. She might even be in love with him.

No. No, I'm not. I do not love him. I can't.

She squeezed her eyes shut tight, but it was too late. The truth had settled itself in her bones, in the liquid embers flowing through her veins. She wasn't just giving her body to Dalton. She was giving him her soul, her heart, her everything. And God help her, she had no idea how she was going to walk away and take it all back.

Dalton's hand grew still, and his fingers stopped the delicious thing they were doing between her legs. She could feel him waiting, willing her to answer him. "Tell me, princess. I need to know."

There's never been anyone else. Only you. Always you.

"No." She reached between them and slid her hand over his, holding it in place as she ground against him, crushing her breasts against his chest until he released an agonizing moan. What had come over her? *Don't stop. Please don't stop. Please.* "I haven't, but…"

"Shh. It's okay." His voice was a tortured whisper, his breath hot against the curve of her neck. "We'll go slow."

She nodded, unable to form words. Unable to do anything but feel. Feel and sigh her surrender.

She was a virgin, but she wasn't completely naïve. She knew what went on between a man and a woman.

She'd thought she did, anyway.

She realized now that she knew nothing. How could she have possibly anticipated how overwhelming this would be? How utterly sublime?

Because this is special. This is love.

"No."

Dalton tilted his head. "No?"

Had she actually said that out loud? She swallowed and with trembling fingertips, unfastened the Windsor knot in his Drake-blue tie. "I don't want it slow. I want you inside me. Now."

In a single, unhesitating movement, he tossed the tie aside and shed his jacket. The desire in his eyes hardened, grew sharp, until it was a blazing, furious thing. Aurélie's breath caught in her throat, and the first traces of nerves fluttered low in her belly.

This was the end, the dying embers of the moment in between. They were going someplace else now. Someplace new. A place with no means of return. He swept an arm beneath her legs, scooped her against his chest and carried her there.

Behind a lacy veil of snow, moonlight streamed in through the bedroom windows. Dalton deposited her in the center of his massive bed, and before her eyes were fully adjusted to the cool blue shadows of the semidarkness, he'd pulled his shirt over his head and unfastened his belt.

She rose to her knees, reaching for him. She was afraid—not of what was about to happen, but about how it would end.

He was so beautiful. Beautiful and male and daunting in his intensity. She craved this intimacy far more than she feared its consequences, what it would do to her when the time had come to leave. She lifted her mouth to his, hungry and desperate, and he groaned into it as her hand slid inside his trousers, finding his steely length.

He was far bigger than she'd imagined. Big and diamond hard. She didn't know how in the world she could accommodate his size, couldn't even fathom how it would work, but she didn't care.

His breath had gone ragged, his eyelids heavy, and it thrilled her to know she could make him feel this way. That just by touching him the right way, she could make him let go of even a little bit of his steadfast control.

"Darling," he whispered, pushing her back on the bed, covering her body with his.

At last they were skin to skin, limbs intertwined, hands exploring. The weight of him on top of her was exquisite, and his erection pressed hot and wanting between her legs. Then he was pushing inside, past the bittersweet whisper of pain, and she was rising up to meet him. Wanting, wanting, wanting, until at long last, she was full.

He paused, giving her time to adjust, and finally he began to move. Thrusting, gently at first, with slow, measured strokes.

"More," she heard herself say, and she wrapped her legs around him, pulling him closer. And closer still. She wanted it all. Everything he could give. Even the parts of him he wouldn't.

He groaned, pumped faster, and something hot and wild gathered at Aurélie's center. Stars glittered behind her eyes, and she rested a palm on Dalton's chest, searching for something solid. Steady. A pulse to keep her grounded.

But she was too far gone, lost to sensation. She could only breathe and give herself up to the wondrous free fall of the climax bearing down on her. Beneath her fingertips, Dalton's heart pounded a constant beat.

Mine.

Mine.

Mine.

A rebellious tear slid down Aurélie's cheek. The snow spun its gentle dance and Dalton gazed down at her with a look so tender that she was certain she felt her heart rip in two even as she found her shuddering, shimmering release.

Chapter Ten

It couldn't happen again. Of that, Aurélie was absolutely certain.

She was certain of it in the middle of the night when she found herself tangled in the bed sheets with Dalton's head between her thighs. She was certain of it when she cried his name again and again to the diamond-studded sky. And she was *especially* certain of it when she woke in the morning reaching for him, tears welling in her eyes.

He wasn't there. The bed was still warm where he'd been. His heady, masculine scent still clung to his pillow. Aurélie closed her eyes, inhaled and lifted her arms over her head, stretching languidly. A cat who'd gotten the cream.

But the cat had no business tasting the cream. The cream was off-limits. And now that the cat had indulged, she wouldn't be satisfied with just a bland drop of milk. Ever.

Aurélie's eyes flew open, and she sat up, panicked. She began to tremble deep inside, as if her bones were trying to shake off the mistake she'd just made.

What had she done?

This was bad. She'd given herself to Dalton in every possible way. She'd meant to offer him her body, but somewhere along the way, she'd accidently given him her heart. And now she was rolling around in his bed like she belonged there when she clearly did not.

From the spacious master bath, she could hear the shower running. The rich scent of espresso hung in the air. She leaped out of the bed, determined not to let Dalton find her here when he returned. *If* he returned.

Would he come looking for her before he left for work? Would he cradle her face and claim her mouth as he'd done the night before? Over and over again, until her lips felt bruised. Taken.

A ribbon of liquid longing wound its way through her at the mere thought of his wicked mouth, his capable hands. Of his lean, hard muscles and the way her head fit perfectly in the space between his neck and shoulder.

Her body was deliciously sore from their lovemaking. It was almost as if she could still feel him inside her. And that phantom sensation made her want him all over again. Just thinking about it made her go all tingly inside.

Her heart gave a little lurch.

What was she going to do?

She couldn't bear to leave. Not now. But the longer she waited, the harder it would become. She should have never slow-danced with Dalton. She should have never made love with him. Because that was what it had been. Not sex—making love. At least that was what it had been for her. She wholeheartedly doubted Dalton felt the same way.

Even if he did, what difference would it make?

She glanced down at her bare ring finger and tried to imagine what it would look like adorned with a diamond engagement ring. Her vision grew blurry behind a veil of tears and she clenched her fist until nails dug into her palm.

Breathe. Just breathe.

Her lungs burned, and her throat felt scratchy. She climbed out of bed, looked around and found her lingerie in a lacy, decadent trail leading to the living room. The pretty new polka dot dress was pooled on the floor by the window. Scattered shoes, coats and Dalton's discarded tie painted such a vivid picture of what had gone on the night before that a lump formed in her throat as she gathered them all up.

She could straighten as much as she wanted. She could put the room back together again, even toss the clothes in the garbage, but it wouldn't change anything. There was no way to undo what she'd done. She couldn't take it back.

Even if she could, she wouldn't. Not in a million years.

Which was precisely why it wouldn't, *couldn't*, happen again.

Fresh from a cold shower, yet still inexplicably aroused beyond all reason, Dalton strolled naked toward the bedroom.

His appetite for Aurélie was insatiable. He couldn't quite understand it. Didn't want to. He'd think about it later. Much later, after he'd taken her to bed once more.

Just one more time.

Then he'd end things before they got too complicated. *Right.* They'd passed *complicated* ages ago. He thought of the pink enameled egg. Their bargain. Artem's warning.

In all seriousness, have you thought about what you're going to do when they realize she's missing? Surely someone will notice.

How had he allowed things to get so far out of hand?

He needed to end it. Now. For Aurélie's sake as much as for the sake of Drake Diamonds. Because she didn't know what Dalton knew all too well—leaving New York and returning to Delamotte was the best possible thing she could do. A blessing, really. If she stayed, he'd hurt her. He didn't want to, but he would.

He'd done it before, and he couldn't risk doing it again. Not to Aurélie.

The mere thought of it caused a familiar darkness to gather inside him. Like a terrible smoke. A black, suffocating fog that threatened to swallow him up.

With each step Dalton took to the bedroom, though, it lifted. Because when he was with Aurélie, when he was buried deep inside her, he could almost forget the things he'd done. The mistakes he'd made.

He could breathe again.

Almost.

The darkness descended again when he found his bed empty. Not just empty, but completely made.

Dalton glowered at the crisp white duvet, pulled so neatly over the king-size mattress that there wasn't a wrinkle in sight. His gaze drifted toward the headboard. He couldn't believe what he was seeing. Where had Aurélie learned the art of hospital corners? He would have bet money she'd never even made a bed before. He probably would have found such a surprise amusing if it hadn't rubbed him so entirely the wrong way.

He was profoundly irritated, and the very fact that he felt this way irritated him further. Because it forced him to admit the truth he'd been trying so hard to avoid—his control was beginning to slip.

The cold shower…the coffee…neither had done a damn thing to snap him back into reality. Sunlight streamed through the bedroom windows. At his feet, the city was waking up beneath a fresh blanket of snow. Morning sparkled like an upturned sugar bowl.

But Dalton wasn't ready. Not even close. He was still lost in the opulent darkness of the night before.

This wasn't as he'd planned. He'd allowed himself one night, and one night only. One night to get Aurélie out of his system so he could get back to business.

Of course the fact that she'd indeed been a virgin gave him pause. He should have stopped things the moment she'd confirmed his suspicions in that regard. He couldn't have, though. Not if his life had depended on it.

What had he done?

An aching tightness formed in his chest. He took a deep breath, but the feeling didn't go away. It lingered, much like the memory of Aurélie's touch, her taste. The sweetness of her voice in his ear.

I don't want it slow. I want you inside me. Now.

He stared down at the neatly made bed, wondering what it meant. Nothing probably. He was overthinking things, as he'd always been prone to do.

It was getting late, anyway. The driver was scheduled to pick them up in less than half an hour. Dalton dressed quickly, then strode into the living room in search of Aurélie. He found her perched on one of his kitchen barstools reading yesterday's *New York Times* with Jacques sitting regally in her lap. The fact that she was fully dressed wasn't lost on him. He hadn't realized how badly he'd hoped to find her in a state of undress until now. Seeing her again, now that he'd been inside her, now that he knew what it was like to have those lithe legs wrapped around him, was like getting punched hard in the solar plexus. He swayed a little and gripped the edge of the countertop before he lost his head and gave in to the impulse to kiss her.

He thought of his neatly made bed and its damned hospital corners, but still his gaze found its way to Aurélie's mouth. Her pillowy lips were darker than usual, as red as the deep crimson center of a ruby. Swollen from his lavish attention.

His cock throbbed to life. Again. "Good morning," he said coolly.

"Good morning," she said, barely looking up from the newspaper.

The dog, on the other hand, stared straight at him. Dalton could have sworn he saw a trace of mockery in the French bulldog's big round eyes.

Dalton suppressed a sigh.

Jealous of the damned dog? Yet again? Pathetic.

He was losing it. But he'd be damned if he was going to stand there and pretend nothing had happened between them.

"Shall we talk about last night?" He crossed his arms, leaned against the counter and waited.

Jacques sighed and dropped his chin on the countertop as if the sheer weight of his head was more than he could handle. Which wouldn't have surprised Dalton in the least.

Aurélie rested one of her elegant hands between the dog's ears. There was a telltale tremble in her fingertips.

She devoted too much care to folding her newspaper into a tidy square, took a beat too long to meet his gaze. "If you'd like."

She was pretending.

Dalton wasn't sure why, but she obviously wanted to act like nothing had changed. When in fact everything had.

"I enjoyed it." *Don't touch her. Do not.* He shoved his hands in his trouser pockets. "Very much."

He could hear the catch in her breath, could see the pink flush rise to her cheeks.

She kept up her charade, clearing her throat. "As did I, but…"

He lifted his brows. "But?" he repeated, sounding harsher than he intended.

The dog rolled its eyes, or maybe that was just Dalton's imagination.

Aurélie lifted her chin. "But I don't think it should happen again."

He looked at her, long and hard, as the darkness gathered in him again. Thick and suffocating. And for the first time, he realized it had a name. Regret.

"I understand." But he didn't understand. Not at all.

He had no business feeling as frustrated as he did. This was for the best. It was precisely what he'd wanted, wasn't it?

Yes. Yes, it is.

He was far from relieved, however. On the contrary, he was furious.

Aurélie's gaze flitted to the digital clock display on the microwave. "I suppose you're off to work now."

He would have liked nothing more than to escape to the quiet solitude of his office on the tenth floor of Drake Diamonds. But today of all days, he couldn't.

Perfect. Just perfect.

He shook his head. "No, actually."

Aurélie blinked. "No?"

"No." Dalton's cell phone buzzed with an incoming text message. He glanced down at it and cleared the display. "In fact, that's our ride."

"*Our* ride," she repeated with a telltale wobble in her voice.

Dalton nodded, stalked past her and reached for his jacket in the coat closet. He was half tempted to leave her behind. But something told him if he walked out the door, she might not be here when he returned.

Sure enough, as he pulled his Burberry wool coat from its hanger, he spotted a suitcase tucked away at the back of the closet. *His* suitcase, he noted wryly.

He looked pointedly at the bag and then at Aurélie, waiting for her to say something. If she wanted to go, he certainly wouldn't stop her.

That's right. Run away, Aurélie. Run away from me, just like you ran from whatever it is you're trying to escape in Delamotte.

He didn't know why he hadn't seen it coming. Of course she wouldn't stick around to honor their agreement.

Wasn't it just yesterday you wanted to send her away?

Dalton's jaw hardened. His hand twitched. He should pick up the suitcase and hand it to her. Along with a plane ticket.

He wasn't sure why he didn't.

If she left, he'd have the Marchand eggs to contend with. Articles about the exhibit were in every newspaper in New York. Banners were up in every showroom in the store. The Marchand eggs could be returned after the exhibit, as planned.

But what of the secret egg? What of their bargain?

A day ago he'd been prepared to let it go, to forget he'd ever set eyes on Aurélie and her glittering treasure. Now he refused to make that concession. Not when it wasn't his call, his choice. He controlled what went on at Drake Diamonds, not an impulsive princess who'd never worked a day in her life.

Aurélie's gaze flitted anywhere and everywhere *except* at the suitcase. She swallowed, and her hand fluttered to her throat.

Dalton did his best to ignore the flash of heat that rioted through him at the memory of his mouth upon her neck, the wild beat of her pulse beneath his lips.

"Where are we off to, then?" she asked, like they were a couple about to leave on holiday. Like the suitcase meant something that had no basis in reality.

Dalton shut the closet door. Out of sight, out of mind.

"We're going to the Hamptons."

Chapter Eleven

If Aurélie wasn't mistaken, Artem did a double take when she entered the Winter Hamptons Equestrian Classic's massive white tent on Dalton's arm.

"Aurélle, what a surprise," Charming as ever, Artem smiled. Astonishment aside, he seemed genuinely happy to see her. "How nice of you to join our family gathering. Dalton neglected to tell us you were coming along."

"Thank you so much for having me." The words left a bittersweet taste in her mouth.

Her voice felt raw, rusty. Probably because she and Dalton had only exchanged a handful of words during the tense ride to the Hamptons from the City. She'd sat beside him in the backseat of the town car while he pounded away on his laptop, and she felt it had been the longest three hours of her life.

She'd been so relieved when they'd pulled up to the

show grounds. She couldn't breathe with Dalton so close, not when every cell in her body was mourning the loss of his touch. She'd needed air. She'd needed space.

What she most definitely did *not* need was to be treated like a card-carrying member of the Drake fold.

Ophelia threw her arms around Aurélie and gave her a tight squeeze. "I'm so glad you're here. Wait until you see Diana ride. She's amazing."

Tears gathered behind Aurélie's eyes. She hadn't realized Artem and Ophelia would be there. Of course they were, though. It was a family event.

What am I doing here?

"I can't wait," she said, pulling away from Ophelia's embrace, aware of Dalton's gaze on her. Too aware.

This was almost worse than the car ride.

She glanced around, trying to get her bearings. Being inside the heated tent was like stepping into another world. If a fine layer of snow flurries hadn't still dusted Dalton's imposing shoulders, Aurélie might have forgotten they'd just come in from the cold.

The ground was covered in rich red dirt, a striking contrast to the snow piled outside. A course had been arranged in the large oval in the center of the tent with sets of rails painted stripes of red and white, flanked on either side by lush greenery and bright white flowers. Magnolias. Their sultry perfume hung heavy in the air, an unexpected luxury in the dead of winter.

Riders in breeches and glossy black boots walked around the outskirts of the arena, weaving between waiters holding silver trays of champagne flutes. An enormous gray horse strutted by, with its mane tightly woven in a braid snaking down its thickly muscled neck, and hooves so shiny Aurélie could see her reflection in them.

So this is the Hamptons.

Aurélie had never seen anything quite like it. Not even in Delamotte.

"It's something, isn't it?" Artem said, turning his back on all the opulence. A look Aurélie couldn't quite decipher passed between him and Dalton. "Diana is an Olympic hopeful, but I'm guessing my brother probably told you all about it."

Actually, no. We're not exactly speaking at the moment.

She forced her lips into a smile. "I'd love to hear more."

Aurélie wasn't about to admit that the man she'd slept with the night before—the man she thought she might be in love with—hadn't shared a single personal thing about himself in the entire time she'd known him. She didn't even want to admit such a thing to herself.

Fortunately, she'd been a princess all her life. Faking a smile was one of the job requirements.

That quality should come in handy when you're married three months from now.

Her gaze strayed rebelliously to Dalton. It hurt to look at him, to see the anger in his stormy eyes. It hurt even worse when she realized it wasn't only anger looking back at her, but disappointment as well.

She couldn't blame him. Not this time.

"Here she is now." Artem waved at a petite young woman making her way toward them.

She wore immaculate white breeches, a midnight-blue fitted riding jacket and a pair of neat white gloves. An elegant black horse pranced alongside her at the end of a blue lead rope. Drake blue.

She was definitely the woman from the screensaver

on Dalton's laptop. Same rich auburn hair twisted into a tight chignon. Same perfectly proportioned figure. Same confident smile. Dalton's sister.

Aurélie turned toward Dalton.

He lifted a brow. "Yes?"

"Are you going to tell your sister who I am?" she whispered.

Dalton frowned and muttered under his breath, "No. The fewer people who know, the better. Artem and Ophelia are involved with the business, so it makes sense for them to know. Let's leave Diana out of it."

"Good. I agree." They agreed on something. Miracles never ceased. "How are you going to explain my presence?"

"I'll introduce you as my friend, Aurélie." His *friend*. He looked down at her, and she saw too much on his face then—the fury and the heat still simmering between them. "She won't have any idea who you are. I doubt she's picked up a tabloid in years. Diana's life revolves around horses twenty-four seven."

"I see. So you typically bring dates to her horse shows, then?" Her face went hot with the effort it took not to sound like a jealous mistress, even though that was precisely what she was at the moment.

Pull yourself together.

Dalton's gaze strayed to her lips and lingered there. Long enough for Aurélie to grow breathless before he looked away without answering her question.

Diana greeted Artem with a warm embrace, gave Ophelia's tiny baby bump a gentle pat, then turned her attention to Dalton.

"Hi there, big brother. Thanks for tearing yourself away from the office to come see me jump." She threw her arms around him, all the while glancing curiously at Aurélie.

"Diana, this is Aurélie." Dalton's arm slid around Aurélie's waist, and she was immediately too aware of his palm resting against the curve of her hip. She fought the overwhelming impulse to melt into him.

Pathetic.

Dalton, on the other hand, seemed perfectly at ease. Impassive even. But when he looked down at her, she saw a spark of triumph in his gaze. He knew. He *knew*. He was all too aware he could drive her mad with the simplest touch, and he intended to use it to his full advantage.

"Aurélie, this is my sister, Diana Drake." His hand moved lower, his fingertips sweeping ever so lightly against her bottom.

"I'm delighted to meet you, Diana." She extended a hand and did her best to ignore her thumping heart and the way her skin suddenly felt too tight, like it could barely contain the riot of sensations skittering through her.

She wanted to strangle him.

Right after she kissed him again.

"The pleasure is all mine, I assure you." Diana ignored Aurélie's outstretched hand and pulled her into an enthusiastic embrace instead. The horse stood beside her, perfectly still other than the flicking of its glossy black tail.

"Diana," Dalton said, his voice tinged with warning.

"Ignore him," Diana whispered in Aurélie's ear. "He's all bark and no bite, in case you haven't noticed. Besides, I've been waiting for this for a long time. I haven't met one of Dalton's girlfriends since…"

"Okay, that's enough." Dalton pried the two of them apart.

Artem and Ophelia stood by, watching with amused interest.

Since when? Since whom?

Aurélie glanced at the suddenly firm set of Dalton's jaw and the flat, humorless line of his mouth. He steadfastly refused to look at her. Maybe she was just imagining the tension in the lines around his eyes. Then again, maybe not.

"We should take our seats. Surely you have last-minute things to attend to," he said, sounding more detached and robotic than Aurélie had ever heard him before.

Nope. Definitely not imagining things.

"Actually, Diamond and I are just about ready." Diana rested a hand on the horse's broad back.

Diamond's hide twitched and he stamped one hoof in greeting. His mane was braided into a graceful plait, and he'd been brushed and groomed to such an extent that he looked like a darkly elegant mirror.

"Your horse's name is Diamond? That certainly seems appropriate," Aurélie said.

"He's perfect. In showjumping a rider is only as good as her horse." Diana grinned. "Dalton bought him for me, actually. He had Diamond shipped over for me all the way from Europe."

"Did he?" She didn't quite know what to make of this news. The man was full of surprises.

"We can discuss something else now." The mysterious man in question cleared his throat.

Diana shot Aurélie a wink. "Excellent. Aurélie, why don't you tell me how you met my brother?"

Artem let out a hearty laugh.

"That wasn't what I had in mind," Dalton said flatly.

"Fine. Keep me guessing. I should probably get Diamond warmed up, anyway." Diana reached for Aurélie again and gave her another tight hug. "Thank you for coming. It was really a treat to meet you."

Aurélie wasn't accustomed to being embraced like that, especially since her mom had died. It caught her off guard.

And most of all, it made her realize what all she'd be leaving behind when she finally forced herself to leave New York. Not only Dalton, but a family. *His* family.

She'd miss seeing him like this.

She'd miss *him*.

"Good luck," she said, her breath growing shallower by the minute.

Then Diana was gone, and Artem was saying something. Aurélie wasn't sure what. A distant ringing had begun in her ears, and she had trouble hearing anything else.

What had she done?

She glanced at Dalton, at the planes of his handsome face and the dark layer of stubble on his jaw. But it was impossible for her to look at him without touching him, without wishing he would touch her in return. And she'd made it abundantly clear to him that was something she no longer wanted.

Now he would barely even look at her.

This is your doing. You did this.

She swallowed around the lump in her throat. How had she messed things up so badly? She'd been acting out of self-preservation, but suddenly she wanted to tell Dalton the truth. All of it.

She wanted to explain that she'd packed the suitcase the day before, not this morning. She wanted to confess why she'd left Delamotte. She wanted to tell him what she'd learned about her parents' marriage and about the fate that awaited her when she returned to the palace.

She wanted to tell him how she felt about him.

She wouldn't, of course. Couldn't. Not here. Not now. "I can't."

Dalton swiveled his gaze toward her. Finally.

Artem's brow furrowed. "Pardon?"

Oh God. Had she said that out loud?

Dalton slid his hand around her waist, and to her utter mortification, the tenderness in his touch nearly made her weep. "Why don't we go sit down?"

"Wait." Artem held out a hand. "Can I have a word with you, brother?"

Dalton gave a terse shake of his head. "There's no time. The show is about to start."

"Diana's class doesn't compete for another half hour. Why don't we go fetch drinks for the ladies and discuss a little business as well?" Artem's mouth curved into one of his charming smiles, but his eyes went dark.

Dalton sighed under his breath. "Very well. If it absolutely can't wait..."

"It can't." Artem reached for Ophelia's hand, gave it a squeeze. "Darling, why don't you show Aurélie around for few minutes?"

Ophelia slipped a willowy arm through Aurélie's. "I'd be happy to. Artem's right. The show doesn't technically start until ten o'clock. It's only 9:30."

9:30.

If it was 9:30 in New York right now, that meant it

was 3:30 in Delamotte. Her portrait sitting with Lord Clement was scheduled in less than an hour.

She swallowed.

Across the world, her gold dress was no doubt hanging in her dressing room with her glittering silver Jimmy Choos set out beside it. The Marchand family tiara would have been removed from its vault. Her old life was ready and waiting for her to slip back into it.

Like a dress that no longer fit.

Once they were out of earshot, Dalton didn't bother waiting for Artem to speak. He knew what was coming.

"Again, this isn't how it looks," he muttered under his breath as they fell in line at the bar.

"So you've mentioned," Artem said drily.

Clearly, Artem didn't believe him. Maybe because this time things were *exactly* how they looked.

Dalton's jaw clenched. A dull throb started up in his temples. He shouldn't have brought Aurélie here. It had been a mistake. Obviously.

Dalton didn't make mistakes. Not when it came to business. Rather, he hadn't until the past twelve hours or so.

Now he couldn't seem to stop.

And he'd tried. By God, he'd tried to get a handle on himself.

He'd intentionally spent the better part of the three-hour ride to the Hamptons on his laptop rather than interacting with Aurélie. He was woefully behind on plans for the Drake Diamonds gala. Mrs. Barnes had emailed him three menu options for review, along with photographs of floral arrangements in various sizes and shades of Drake blue, and she'd been pressing him for a response for days. He hadn't even given the guest list a cursory glance since the invitations had been mailed out. And of course the most important detail still required his attention—the arrangement of the Marchand eggs.

As much as he'd told himself he was simply doing his job, Dalton knew better. He'd wanted the distraction. Needed it. Because having Aurélie situated right beside him in the backseat of the town car, wearing another one of her quirky vintage getups, was killing him.

There was the faintest hint of lace peeking out from the hem of her dress today, and her legs were covered in opaque tights. Or perhaps they were stockings… Dalton had spent far too much time pondering the possibility of a garter belt beneath the swish of her full skirts. There wasn't a big enough distraction in the world to rid himself of his curiosity regarding that particular matter. It had consumed the majority of his thoughts during the entire stretch of I-495.

And then there'd been the matter of the email.

Less than an hour away from Manhattan, Dalton's tablet had dinged, indicating he'd gotten a new email. He'd glanced at the notification and his gut had tied itself in knots.

From: The Office of His Majesty,
The Reigning Prince, Delamotte
Re: Her Royal Highness, Aurélie Marchand

He'd switched the tablet off before Aurélie could see it. There was no reason to alarm her until he'd had a chance to read the message. It didn't necessarily mean they'd figured out where she'd gone.

But things didn't look promising. His fists clenched

at his sides and he cursed himself—yet again—for not sending her home last night. Last night…before things had gotten so carried away. Before he'd danced with her in the street. Before she'd undressed for him in that shaft of immaculate moonlight.

He'd remember how it felt to look at her beautiful body for the first time until the day he died. Like time had somehow reversed itself. He'd felt young again. Alive. Whole.

Artem stared at him long and hard, turning his back on the course where the riders and horses were warming up, preparing for competition. He shook his head and sighed. "When are you going to admit what's going on, brother?"

Dalton shrugged. "There's nothing to admit."

It was a half truth, at best. At worst, a full-fledged lie. Dalton had so much to confess where Aurélie was concerned that he'd lost track. But he didn't care to discuss it. Especially not with Artem, whom Dalton had so often chastised for failing to control his libido. The day his brother had slipped a diamond on Ophelia's hand, he'd become a different person.

Maybe you can become a different man, too.

"Who is it you're trying to fool?" Artem said. "Me? Or yourself?"

"The exhibit is going forward as scheduled. I have things under control." But that wasn't even the whole truth, was it? He still had no idea what was in the email from the palace. Even now, the cell phone in his pocket vibrated against his leg.

He reached for it and checked the screen. Incoming call: Drake Diamonds. Whatever was happening at the store could wait. For now.

He powered down the phone and slid it back in his pocket. He was having enough trouble concentrating on what was happening around him today as it was.

He took a deep breath and refocused his attention on Artem, who was still standing there. Watching. Waiting. Apparently, he wasn't going to let the Aurélie thing go.

Dalton cleared his throat. "Look, I appreciate your concern, brother. But I don't need a heart-to-heart about my sex life."

He wouldn't be taking Aurélie to bed again, anyway. His feelings on the subject no longer mattered.

Except they did matter. The fact that he couldn't stop thinking about that damned suitcase told him his feelings mattered a whole hell of a lot.

Aurélie should have been back in Delamotte by now. He'd lain awake half the night trying to figure out why he hadn't put her on the plane when he'd had every intention of doing so, and he'd been unable to come up with anything remotely resembling a logical explanation. Then again, the decadent sight of Aurélie naked in his bed might have had something to do with his inability to think.

It had taken every shred of self-control in his arsenal not to kiss her, to touch her—right here, right now—when every time he closed his eyes he saw her sitting astride him, heavy-lidded with desire.

"I'm not talking about sex," Artem said. "You have feelings for Aurélie."

Dalton couldn't believe what he was hearing. "Don't be ridiculous."

Artem rolled his eyes. "I'm not the one being ridiculous here. You're in love with her. Ophelia sees it. I see it. Why can't you?"

"Listen, I'm happy for the two of you, happy about the baby. Thrilled. Delighted. But just because you've suddenly become a family man doesn't mean I'm one."

"But you are. You always have been." Artem threw his hands up. "Look around, for crying out loud. You're at a horse show."

Dalton didn't need to look around. He knew perfectly well where he was. The Winter Hamptons Equestrian Classic was an off-season event, although most serious jumpers like Diana competed year-round. Diana participated twelve months a year, and since both their parents were now deceased, Dalton tried to attend every show within driving distance of Manhattan.

Not that their father had ever displayed much interest in his only daughter before his fatal heart attack. Geoffrey Drake had been writing checks since Diana began taking riding lessons at the age of four, but that had been the extent of his support for her career. He'd never attended a single horse show.

As far as Dalton knew, his sister hadn't considered this at all strange. The Drakes had always expressed affection via their checkbooks, after all.

Family man. Right. Dalton didn't even know what a family man looked like.

Dalton himself had never seen Diana ride until after Clarissa died. To this day, he wasn't sure why he'd turned up in the grandstand at that first show he'd attended. Maybe he'd been looking for an escape. Maybe he'd simply needed a place to go on Sunday morning before the store opened in those early days when he couldn't bear the stark white interior of his apartment.

He wasn't sure. All he knew was that it had made him feel better knowing that at least one Drake had managed to build a life that didn't revolve around the family business. He would have gladly flung himself on Diamond's back and galloped far away if he could.

If it hadn't been too late.

If he hadn't already devoted his entire existence to Drake Diamonds.

"You deserve to be happy, Dalton. Whatever is happening between you and Aurélie has nothing to do with the past." Artem's gaze shifted to the packed dirt floor. "It's got nothing to do with Clarissa."

Dalton glared at his brother. "You're out of line. And for what it's worth, categorically wrong."

You're in love with her.

In love?

Impossible.

He wanted Aurélie. He didn't love her. There was a difference. A big one.

Falling in love with Aurélie Marchand would make him the biggest idiot on the island of Manhattan. Possibly even the entire continent.

Although if he was being honest with himself, he *had* been acting rather idiotic lately.

"I'm wrong, am I?" Artem glanced at the box where Ophelia and Aurélie were chatting with each other like two old friends. Like sisters. "Then why haven't you sent the princess packing?"

Dalton wished he knew why. Oh, how he wished that.

Chapter Twelve

Aurélie did her best to make conversation with Ophelia as they sat in the Drake Diamonds private box in the front row. She listened patiently to Ophelia's explanation of the rules of showjumping, nodding in all the right places and making note of which riders were serious contenders for the Winter Hamptons Equestrian Classic Grand Prix title.

Diana was one of them. Dalton's sister rode with a passionate confidence that took Aurélie's breath away, as if she and the horse were one.

But as she followed their movements around the ring during the warm-up and Ophelia kept up her merry chit-chatting, Aurélie couldn't shake the knowledge of what was going on 4,000 miles away.

Her time was up.

Palace officials may have discovered her absence earlier this morning. In all likelihood, they had. Perhaps even yesterday. But so long as Aurélie didn't know for certain, she could hold onto the hope that she was still flying under the radar. She could choose to believe that no one would come looking for her. But once Lord Clement arrived at the palace, there would be no denying the truth. In just a few short minutes, she'd no longer be able to lie to herself.

No matter how badly she wanted to.

She couldn't stop glancing at the digital time display beside the judge's table, couldn't stop herself from counting down each minute, each precious second of freedom. Yet, she felt oddly calm. The minutes ticked by, and her pulse remained steady. There were no nervous butterflies, no panicked heartbeats. On the contrary, a detached serenity seemed to come over her.

She was dangerously calm. Numb. So much so that it frightened her.

"I wonder what's taking Artem and Dalton so long. The show is about to start, and Diana and Diamond are the first team up." Ophelia glanced around the crowded tent. "Do you see them anywhere?"

Aurélie scanned the area by the bar, and spotted them on the way to the box. Both of them carried a champagne glass in each hand, and both of them wore grim expressions. Although Dalton's was significantly grimmer than Artem's.

"Here they come," she said.

The closer they came, the clearer she could discern the barely contained fury in Dalton's posture. She wondered if something terrible had happened back at the store. A robbery perhaps.

Or maybe…

No. She shook her head, unwilling to even consider the possibility that the palace had somehow already found out where she was. *Not that. Please not that.*

She still had a few minutes left until the palace realized she was missing. At least she thought she did.

Artem's expression softened the moment he set eyes on his wife again. He handed a glass to Ophelia and winked. "It's just water, darling. But I had them put it in a fancy glass for you."

"Thank you." They exchanged a kiss that lasted just long enough to make Aurélie clear her throat and look away.

Dalton took the seat beside her. "Your champagne."

Bubbles rose from the pale gold liquid in the glass that Dalton handed her—a saucer-style glass with a delicate stem. A *Marie Antoinette glass*, as it was known in Delamotte.

Stop. Just stop.

She vowed to quit thinking about Delamotte and what might be going on back at the palace, yet still found herself lapsing into French. *"Merci beaucoup."*

Dalton barely looked at her. He kept his gaze glued straight ahead, yet didn't seem to follow the gallop of Diamond's hooves as the horse swept a wide loop around the course. His jaw hardened into a firm line.

Something was definitely wrong.

She glanced at the clock again. 9:58.

Two more minutes.

She took a large gulp from her champagne glass and slid her gaze toward Dalton. "Is everything okay?"

"Fine," he said under his breath.

"Clearly." She took another sip of champagne and watched Diana trot into the ring on Diamond's back.

The buzzer rang, signaling the start of her run, and Diamond shot forward in a cloud of red dust. His glossy black tail streamed straight out behind him. The ground shook as he thundered past the Drake box.

Horse and rider soared over the first jump, clearing the rails by such a large height that it looked like they were flying. Diana rose out of the saddle and leaned forward. Aurélie could see the dazzling smile on her face clear across the ring.

What must it feel like to be that fearless? She wished she knew. "Wow."

Her heart leaped to her throat as they approached the second obstacle, which was a water jump. Diamond soared over the partition and then seemed to hang suspended over the glistening pool. Without thinking, Aurélie gripped Dalton's arm and held her breath until the horse touched down gracefully on the other side.

She let out a relieved exhale. Then she realized she was still holding onto Dalton's sleeve.

Her face went hot. "Sorry." She let go. "You don't get nervous watching Diana ride?"

"No. She's an excellent competitor," he said stiffly.

Okay then.

Diana and Diamond galloped past the box again. Artem, Ophelia and Aurélie all cheered while Dalton remained silent.

Aurélie stared at him. "Are you sure everything is okay?" *Other than the fact that we slept together last night and today has been awkward on every possible level.* "Because you seem awfully cranky all of a sudden. Even for you, I mean."

"Quite sure. Artem can be a real pain in my ass sometimes. That's all," he said.

Then he turned and looked at her. *Really* looked at her for the first time since he'd sat down. Possibly even for the first time since she'd so bluntly informed him that she wouldn't be sleeping with him again.

His gaze softened, and his mouth curved into a smile. But it was a sad smile. Bittersweet. All at once, memories from the night before came flooding back—the reverent expression on his face as her dress fell to the floor, the tenderness of his lips on her breasts, the exquisite fullness as he'd entered her. Tears gathered behind Aurélie's eyes, and he said, "Then again, every once in a while my brother is right about some things."

She bit her lip to keep from crying, blinked furiously and did her best to keep her attention on the ring where Diamond was gathering his front legs beneath him to soar over another set of rails. But Dalton's gaze was a palpable force.

She turned to him again.

"Dalton." Her voice was a broken whisper.

He cupped her cheek. "Princess."

And for the briefest of seconds, she felt it again—the tenuous connection they'd shared the night before, as precious as a diaphanous dream.

It was real. This *is real.*

A hush fell over her heart, and in that sliver of a moment, everything slipped softly into place. There was no faraway palace, no royal wedding. Just him. Just her.

Just us.

Then a tinny clang pierced the quiet and it all fell apart. Like pearls slipping from a string.

Dalton seemed to realize something was wrong before he saw it. His smile faded, lips compressed. In the final moment their eyes were still locked, Aurélie saw fear in his gaze. Raw, primal fear that made her blood run cold.

Her throat went dry, and she realized the sound she'd heard had been Diamond's front hooves hitting the rail. *Diana.*

The world seemed to move in slow motion as Aurélie's head swiveled in the direction of the course. Already Dalton was scrambling to his feet, climbing out of the box, as the horse's back feet sent the rails flying and the big, graceful animal crashed into the dirt with a sickening thud. He hit the ground with such force that Aurélie's chair pitched forward and she had to grab onto the railing in front of her to keep herself from falling.

Diamond's leg twisted into a horrific angle, and a terrible sound came out of him. A sound that would haunt Aurélie's dreams for weeks to come. She wanted to close her eyes, to block it all out. But she couldn't. Not until she found Dalton's sister in the wreckage.

The horse tried to scramble to his feet, and when he did, Diana's petite form rolled out of the way.

She's okay. She's all right.

But Diamond couldn't support himself on his broken leg and fell sideways, his big, beautiful head smacking down squarely on top of Diana's helmet.

Her body went limp. A gasp went up from the crowd. Time sped up again and somewhere in the periphery, Aurélie was vaguely aware of the clock flashing 10:00.

"Oh, my god." Ophelia's hand flew to her throat.

"Let's go," Artem said, helping Ophelia up.

Aurélie wasn't sure if she should follow or stay put, but Ophelia grabbed her hand and held on tight as she walked past. So she followed the two of them out of the box and to the entrance to the ring, where Dalton stood as pale as a ghost.

"I'm so sorry, Dalton. She'll be okay. She will," Aurélie said, knowing full well it might be a lie.

But sometimes people needed to believe in lies, didn't they? Sometimes a lie was the only thing that kept a person going. At least that was what Aurélie's mother had written in her diary.

She swallowed, not quite sure what to believe anymore.

Diana was already surrounded by EMTs, since qualified medical personnel were required to be on hand at all equestrian events that included showjumping. A siren wailed in the distance, and Artem was talking in terse tones to the show chairman, worried that the ambulance would have trouble reaching the tent through the maze of horse trailers and cars parked outside in the snow.

Through the chaos, Dalton remained stoic. He didn't move, didn't say a word. He scarcely seemed to breathe.

When at last Diana had been lifted into the back of an ambulance—strapped onto a gurney with her head still in its riding helmet—Dalton seemed surprised to find Aurélie standing beside him. It was as if he'd been in a trance and forgotten she was there.

"Come with me." He placed his hand in the small of her back and escorted her out of the tent, to the edge of the parking lot where two sleek black cars sat idling, waiting to follow the ambulance to the hospital.

The sky had turned an ominous gray, heavy with snow. The cold air hit Aurélie's face like a slap. She ducked her head against the wind.

"We'll meet you there," Artem called, nodding sol-

emnly as he and Ophelia climbed into the back of a
sedan.

Dalton nodded and held the door open to the town
car. Aurélie slid inside and scooted across the seat to
make room for him. But he didn't get in right away. Instead he leaned into the opened window and murmured
something to the driver.

"Yes, sir," the chauffeur said and shifted the car into
Drive.

What was happening?

"Wait!" Aurélie scrambled to open the door.

"*Miss*," the driver said in a firm tone. "Mr. Drake has
given me instructions…"

She didn't wait for him to finish. She pushed her way
out of the car and ran to catch up with Dalton, who'd already begun walking away.

"Where are you going?" She could hear the panic
in her own voice, but she didn't care how desperate it
sounded. Didn't care how desperate she looked, slipping and sliding on the icy pavement. Because she knew
what he was going to say before he even turned around.

"Aurélie." He gripped her shoulders and held her at
arm's length. "Get back in the car."

She shook her head and opened her mouth to object,
but no words would come out. They stuck in her throat.
She couldn't seem to make a sound.

Dalton's expression hardened, and she was hit with
the realization that it didn't matter what she said. Or
what she didn't. There were no words that could make
him change his mind.

"I want you to go, Aurélie," he said, and she wished
with her whole heart that he would call her princess
again. Just one more time. "Go home."

Home.

The word hung in the space between them, ominous with meaning.

He wasn't talking about his apartment back in Manhattan. He didn't mean *his* home. He meant *hers*. Delamotte.

"I can't go, Dalton. Not now." How could he expect her to walk away at a time like this?

"I'm not asking you, Aurélie. I'm telling you." He paused, took a deep breath. He suddenly didn't look so stoic anymore. Or angry, either. Just tired. So very tired.

"I want you to go. It's time."

Chapter Thirteen

Dalton hadn't set foot in a hospital since the day Clarissa died.

He'd managed to avoid the beeping machines, the drawn curtains, the memories steeped in antiseptic perfume for six long years. Even in the wake of his father's heart attack, he'd stayed away. At the time, it had been alarmingly easy to explain his absence as a necessity. While Diana sat vigil at their father's bedside and Artem had gone MIA doing God knows what, no one had actually expected Dalton to show up.

They'd expected him to be sitting at his desk. Just like always. It was what their father would have wanted, after all. This expectation had of course been partially instrumental in the events causing Dalton to despise hospitals to begin with.

Oh, the irony.

Dalton had been at the office until 2 a.m. the night Clarissa slit her wrists. What no one knew, either then or now, was that he'd put away his spreadsheets and emails sometime around 10 p.m. After scrolling through all the notifications of Clarissa's missed calls on his cell, he'd opted to sleep on the sofa in his office rather than going home.

He hadn't been in the mood for another argument about his work schedule. Or his inattentiveness. Or anything, really. Whatever feelings he'd had for Clarissa had long since faded. He'd been going through the motions for months. A year perhaps. He just hadn't gotten around to officially breaking things off, in part because he'd had too much on his plate at Drake Diamonds. But mainly because Geoffrey Drake would have been livid when he found out Dalton was calling off his engagement. It had been his father's plan all along to have Clarissa join the Drake dynasty with the diamond empire her grandfather ran.

And like the obedient son that he'd always been, Dalton had fallen into step.

Until he couldn't.

He didn't love her. He was quite sure she didn't love him, either. They'd been thrown together like two animals in a cage, and each in their own way, they'd begun fighting for a way out.

With hindsight had come the benefit of clarity. Dalton could see the arguments, the tantrums, even the suicide, for what they were. Clarissa had wanted to escape. And she'd done just that.

Nevertheless, knowing why she'd done it hadn't lifted the mantle of regret. Dalton should have seen what was happening. He'd always prided himself on his atten-

tion to detail, his keen sense of accountability. Whether
they'd loved each other or not, Clarissa had been his fiancée. His responsibility. He should have gotten her the
help that she needed.

He should have picked up the godforsaken phone.

Instead, he'd woken up sometime in the middle of the
night and finally headed home. But only after checking
his phone first and seeing that the calls had stopped.
He'd assumed Clarissa had finally given up and gone
to bed. He wished to hell and back that he'd been right.
He wished so many things.

"Mr. Drake, your sister's room is right this way." A
nurse wearing mint-green scrubs and holding a clipboard
led him down a corridor on the third floor of Southampton Hospital.

Dalton fell in step behind her.

A sign on the wall announced he was in the Head
Trauma unit. Just up ahead, Dalton saw a young man
in a wheelchair with his skull immobilized in a halo
brace, eyes staring blankly into space. He couldn't have
been more than sixteen or seventeen years old. Dalton
dropped his gaze to the nurse's feet in front of him and
her soft-soled white shoes padding silently down the
hospital corridor.

"Here we are." She stopped in front of a closed door.
Room 367.

She extended a hand to push the door open, and Dalton stopped her. "Wait. Before we go in…"

"Yes?" She smiled politely at him, her kind eyes full
of concern. She was being so nice. Everyone was. The
paramedics. The ambulance driver. Even the damn Uber
driver who'd come to pick him up at the horse show.

It made Dalton want to scream.

"How bad is it?" he asked, hating himself for sounding so desperate.

Clarissa's death should have prepared him for this. What good was the cement wall he'd so carefully constructed around his soul if it didn't protect him from falling apart in the face of tragedy?

"We're still waiting on the results of the CT scan, so I'm afraid I can't really say. She's conscious, and that's a great sign. Her head hurts, though, so she's drifting in and out. The doctor should be in to speak with you shortly. In the meantime, Diana is resting comfortably. Her monitors will alert us if her vital signs change. But if you need anything—anything at all—we're right down the hall, Mr. Drake." She smiled again. Too big. Too nauseatingly nice.

"Very well. I understand." He nodded, and pushed the door open himself, needing to feel as in control of the situation as he could.

As if such an idea were remotely possible.

The nurse checked the beeping machine by Diana's bed and made a few notations on her clipboard while Dalton shifted his weight uncomfortably from one foot to the other. The room was huge. Private. What good was all that time spent at the office if the Drake money couldn't be put to good use? The sheer size of it, along with the huge bay window overlooking the beachfront of Southampton, made the mechanical hospital bed in the center of the room seem absurdly tiny. Resting in a hospital gown and sterile white sheets with her eyes shut tight, Diana looked pale and dainty.

Dainty was a word Dalton had never associated with his sister before. *Strong*, yes. *Fearless*, most definitely. *Dainty* had never been part of the equation.

Even now, it didn't seem right. Dalton frowned, struggling for the right adjective. It was a relief to have something to concentrate on. Something concrete and logical. Until he realized the word he was looking for was *broken*.

His chest seized, and he let out a cough.

The nurse rested a comforting hand on his shoulder. "Give us a shout if you or your sister need anything."

Her voice was a soothing whisper. Dalton nodded, wondering when he'd sunk into the overstuffed leather recliner at Diana's bedside. He had no memory of it. Nor of taking his sister's hand in his own. He wondered if he might be in shock, medically speaking. Not that it mattered. Only one thing mattered right now, and it most definitely wasn't him.

Wake up.

He'd feel a lot better about her prognosis if she'd simply open her eyes. He didn't say it aloud, though. He didn't dare, lest it come out as harshly as it sounded in his head.

Wake the hell up.

Dalton didn't want to be that guy—the angry one screaming orders at an unconscious young woman. Even though deep down, he knew that was exactly who he was. The moment Diana's horse went down, the second his hooves hit the rail and his slender ebony legs buckled beneath him, something had come unwound inside Dalton. Something dark and ugly.

Anger.

Six years of bloody, blinding anger that he'd buried in numbers and sales figures and marketing strategies. But like a diamond buried in a mine, his fury hadn't crumbled during its time in the darkness. It had grown exponentially sharper. Stronger. Dazzling in its intensity.

She wasn't in a coma. She'd been alert when they'd taken her away in the ambulance. She needed rest. He knew that.

But once she'd closed her eyes, Dalton worried they wouldn't open again. After all, that's what had happened last time he sat beside a hospital bed.

His fists clenched in his lap. He was furious. Furious at the horse. Furious at Diana and whatever terrible impulse drove her to hurl herself in harm's way over and over and over again. He was even furious at poor Clarissa.

And his father. Always.

Was there anyone he wasn't angry at?

Unbidden, Aurélie's lovely face came to mind. The pull of the memory was irresistible, dragging him under. He closed his eyes and let himself drown. Just for a moment. Just long enough to summon her generous lips and the elegant curve of her neck. Regal. Classic. A neck made for ropes and ropes of pearls.

But then he remembered her expression when she'd climbed out of the car and come running after him—the bewildered hurt in her emerald eyes, coupled with the painful knowledge that such damage had been his doing.

He opened his eyes and pushed the memory back into place.

I want you to go, Aurélie. It's time.

It had been past time for her to return to Delamotte, gala or no gala. He'd done the right thing.

For both of them.

Then why does it feel so wrong?

"Dalton?"

His heart crashed to a stop. He blinked in relief at the sight of Diana's opened eyes, wide and searching.

He forced himself to smile. "You're awake."

"I am." She nodded, winced and closed her eyes again. "My head hurts. I keep drifting off."

"It's okay. I'm here." He gave her hand a reassuring squeeze.

There was a smudge of red clay on one of Diana's cheeks. Dirt from the riding arena. He wiped it away with a brush of his thumb and pondered the fact that they hadn't cleaned her up. Yet there was a startling lack of blood, given the seriousness of her condition. She didn't have so much as a bruise.

Relief flooded through Dalton's veins and he swallowed. Hard. He could taste the rusty fragrance of blood in his mouth, a sensory memory of the last time he'd sat at a bedside like this one.

With Clarissa, there'd been so much blood. Red everywhere. Afterward, he'd had the apartment painted top to bottom and all the furniture replaced with nothing but white.

Again, his thoughts drifted to Aurélie. Aurélie, with her porcelain skin and windswept hair. Aurélie, swaying to Gershwin in his arms. Aurélie, adopting a dog on a whim. The ugliest one of the bunch.

He shouldn't be thinking of her at a time like this. He shouldn't be thinking of her at all. She didn't have anything to do with his family or his life. She was business. She was temporary. She was royal, for God's sake.

Yet when Diamond's hooves hit the rail with a sickening clang, when he'd watched his sister's head slam into the ground, Aurélie had been the one he'd wanted at his side. Not wanted. Needed. Needed with a ferocity that terrified him.

He didn't want to need anyone, least of all a princess.

You're in love with her. Ophelia sees it. I see it. Why can't you?

Dalton half believed Artem had been joking. Maybe. Maybe not. But his words had touched a nerve.

Out of the question.

He couldn't have feelings for Aurélie. Absolutely not. Not before Diana's accident, and most definitely not now. Not when he'd been reminded so vividly of all the reasons why he was better off on his own.

He wasn't made for this. He never had been. He was his father's son, through and through.

The door swung open again. Dalton turned, hoping with every fiber of his being to find a doctor standing in the doorway. A shining beacon of hope. Instead, he took in the tear-stained face of his sister-in-law, followed closely by his brother.

He dropped Diana's hand and stood. "Artem. Ophelia."

"Dalton?" Ophelia's brow furrowed. "How on earth did you get here so fast?"

"I gave the driver an incentive to get me here in a hurry." Again, the Drake money had come in handy.

"Marvelous." Artem rolled his eyes. "Don't you think we've had enough accidents for one day?"

"I got here in one piece, didn't I?"

"Stop. Both of you." Ophelia's voice wobbled a little. Great. He'd reduced a pregnant woman to tears. That might be a new low, even for Dalton. "This isn't the time for bickering. Diana needs us. All of us."

Diana needs us.

Dalton sank back into the chair and dropped his head in his hands. He wanted to tear his hair out by the roots. The door opened again, and it took superhuman effort for him to look up.

A man wearing green scrubs entered the room and extended his hand. "Hello, I'm Dr. Chris Larson."

Dalton shot to his feet. "Doctor."

Artem and Ophelia introduced themselves, then Dr. Larson cut to the chase. "I have the results from your sister's tests. As you know, she took a nasty spill. Fortunately, she was wearing a helmet. A good one, by all appearances."

This came as a relief, but not as a surprise, to Dalton. As fearless as Diana was, she'd always played by the rules. She had ambition, not a death wish.

The doctor nodded. "It looks like the safety precaution did its job."

Dalton frowned. "Are you sure? She's lying in a hospital bed and can barely keep her eyes open."

"Diana is suffering from a concussion, which is to be expected after taking a hit the way she did. But she's going to be fine. I'm sure she's got a monster of a headache, but now that we know there's no permanent damage, we can start administering something stronger than Tylenol. Still, we'll want to keep an eye on her at least overnight. We'll take her vitals every hour and make sure she's doing well. But those should be precautions. Barring any unforeseen complications, I expect your sister to make a full recovery."

"Thank goodness," Ophelia said. Artem wrapped his arm around her and pulled her close.

"A full recovery?" Dalton tried to focus on the doctor's face, but he couldn't seem to tear his gaze from his sister. "You're sure?"

The doctor nodded. "The scans show no structural damage to the brain tissue. She needs time to rest, but soon she'll be able to do all the things she loves to do. Including showjumping."

"That might be a tough call," Artem said under his breath. "Her horse had to be put down today."

Dalton's gut clenched. He hadn't known what happened to the horse. He'd been so worried about Diana that he hadn't even asked about the animal.

Diamond was dead. *Shit.*

His sister would be devastated. Dalton sighed and wished he could go one day, just one, without thinking about loss. Then again, he had, hadn't he? While Aurélie had been there, he'd been able to let go. Just a little bit.

He'd lived.

And now she's gone, too.

"So what happens next?" Artem asked.

The doctor assured them the hospital staff was doing everything it could to make Diana's stay comfortable. He'd given instructions for the night nurse to call him if anything changed.

Diana woke up briefly. Just long enough to register Artem and Ophelia's presence and to answer a few questions for Dr. Larson.

When her eyes fluttered closed again, he gave her arm a pat. "You're a lucky girl, Miss Drake."

Dalton knew the doctor was right. Diana had been lucky indeed, but he doubted she'd see it that way when she found out Diamond was dead. Part of him wondered if she'd avoided asking about her horse because deep down she knew.

They all knew.

No matter how things looked on the outside, the Drakes had never had luck on their side.

Aurélie sat in the backseat, still trying to absorb Dalton's words as the snowy stretch of Long Island flew past the car windows in a melancholy blur.

I'm not asking you, Aurélie. I'm telling you. I want you to go. It's time.

How could she leave without knowing if Diana was going to be okay? And the horse?

And Dalton.

He didn't mean it. He couldn't.

He'd sure sounded like he meant it, though. Everything about his tone, his stance and the glittering determination in his gaze had been resolute. He'd made up his mind. He wanted her gone.

She had to leave, obviously. She couldn't stay. Not now.

Even if she did, what could she possibly do to help? Her presence would only do more harm than good.

Aurélie had never felt so useless in her entire life, which struck her as profoundly ironic considering she was a princess. She should have been accustomed to not being particularly useful by now, especially in view of the fact that the last time she'd had any communication with the palace, they hadn't even noticed she'd fled the country.

Surely they've noticed now.

It was nearly 6 p.m. in Delamotte. Lord Clement had no doubt come and gone in a royal huff. Everyone would be looking for her, including the Crown Prince.

Any temptation to put the SIM card back in her cell

phone and check her messages had died the moment Diana's horse went down. Aurélie couldn't think about the palace right now. Or her impending engagement. Or even her father. All those people, all those worries, seemed so inconsequential compared to what she'd just witnessed. How could she possibly be thinking about something as silly as a press release after seeing Dalton's sister fall headfirst to the ground?

She couldn't.

Aurélie squeezed her eyes closed and leaned her head against the backseat of the town car. The fall kept running through her mind in an endless loop of catastrophic images and terrible sounds. The thunder of hooves. The thud of Diamond's elegant legs crashing into the rails. Those same slender bones buckling and twisting into unnatural angles. Diana's helmet bouncing on the packed red clay.

But worse than the fall itself had been the look on Dalton's face when his sister failed to get up. In a shadow of a moment, Aurélie had seen a lifetime of pain etched in the lines around his eyes. Stories he'd never told her, never would. Something had happened to Dalton Drake. Something terrible.

Diana had to be okay. She *had* to.

Aurélie would have given everything she had to be at the hospital with the Drakes, but Dalton had made his wishes clear when he put her in the town car.

He doesn't want you there.

He doesn't want you. Period.

It stung. Aurélie knew it shouldn't. She wasn't one of them. She and Dalton weren't a couple. They were two people who'd been thrown together for a few days. Nothing more.

And now she had no idea what was going on, what had become of his sister or even the injured horse. Not knowing was torture. She thought about asking the driver if she could borrow his phone, but decided against it. If Dalton wanted to get in touch with her, he would.

Aurélie spent the entire ride back to the city in agonizing silence. At last the steely skyscrapers of Manhattan came into view. "Can you drop me at Drake Diamonds before we go back to the apartment?"

She no longer wanted the secret egg. Dalton could keep it for all she cared. She hated it now, hated what it stood for—the cheating, the lies. The egg had served its purpose. It had gotten her a few days of freedom. It was her bargaining chip, and now the bargain was over.

But her mother's pearls were at the store. Dalton had given them to Ophelia to be restrung. The last time Aurélie had seen them, they'd been lined up on a velvet tray on Ophelia's desk.

She prayed they were still there.

"Very well." The car rolled past the horse carriages lined up on the curb by Central Park and turned onto Fifth Avenue.

They passed the elegant entrance to the Plaza Hotel and too soon, the imposing façade of Drake Diamonds came into view.

"Thank you." Aurélie climbed out and paused in front of the store, blinking against the snow flurries drifting from the dove-gray sky.

Just walk inside, get your pearls back and then you can go home and put all of this behind you.

Her feet refused to move. It felt strange being here without Dalton. Wrong, somehow.

This had been a mistake. She would just ring Mrs.

Barnes when she got back to Delamotte and ask her to return the pearls by post.

She turned to get back in the car, but it had already been swallowed up in the steady stream of yellow cabs snaking their way through upper Manhattan. That's right. Even Dalton's driver couldn't just park by the curb indefinitely.

She considered staying put and waiting for him to make a loop around the block and return. It could take mere minutes. Or, given the erratic nature of New York traffic, she could be stuck standing here for half an hour.

Okay then. She took a deep breath, turned and pushed through the revolving doors.

"Oh, thank goodness." Mrs. Barnes pounced on Aurélie the moment her kitten heels hit the showroom floor. "Where's Mr. Drake?"

Aurélie blinked. "Dalton?"

"Yes." Mrs. Barnes, whom Aurélie had never seen with even a single hair out of place, looked borderline frantic. She shook her head and tossed her hands up in the air. "Or Artem. Or Ophelia. Any of the Drakes, for that matter. I've been calling all three of them for hours and can't reach anyone."

Aurélie wasn't sure how much she should divulge. It didn't appear as though Dalton's assistant knew about Diana's accident. Or maybe she did, and was hoping for more information about Diana's condition. "They're… um…unreachable at the moment."

"Yes, I know. They're in the Hamptons. But I need to speak to Mr. Drake. Now." Barnes's gaze narrowed. "I'd assumed he was with you."

"No." She shook her head. Clearly Mrs. Barnes didn't

know what was going on, and it wasn't Aurélie's place to tell her. "Is there a problem?"

"You could say that, yes. A multitude of problems, actually. We were so busy that we had lunch brought in for the staff this afternoon, and now half of them have fallen ill with food poisoning. The store has never been this shortstaffed."

"Oh, no. That's terrible."

"I've been working the sales floor all afternoon." She waved a hand around the showroom, which upon closer inspection, had a rather frantic air about it. "I've tied over 400 white bows since two o'clock."

"What can I do to help?" Aurélie knew nothing about selling diamonds. Or anything else about working at a jewelry store. But she could learn. And she was pretty sure she could tie a bow.

Mrs. Barnes eyed her with no small amount of skepticism.

"Seriously, I want to help." *Please, let me.* It was a chance to be useful for once in her life. At a time when she needed it most of all.

Mrs. Barnes's apology was swift. "No, no, no. You're Mr. Drake's guest. That's not necessary."

"From what you said, it sounds very necessary." Even an ocean away from Delamotte, people still didn't think she was capable of doing anything useful. It made Aurélie want to scream. "Please. *Please.* I'll do anything."

Dalton's secretary bit her lip and looked Aurélie up and down. "Anything?"

"Yes." Aurélie nodded furiously. "You name it."

"Okay. I hope I don't get fired for this, but they're absolutely desperate for help upstairs. Anything you could do up there would be appreciated."

Aurélie swallowed. "Upstairs?" A trickle of dread snaked its way up her spine.

Mrs. Barnes flicked a hand toward the ceiling. "In Engagements."

Not that. Anything but Engagements.

She'd rather clean the toilets than spend the rest of the day neck-deep in diamond engagement rings.

But what could she possibly say? She'd begged to help. Refusing would mean everyone was right about her. Her father. Dalton. And as much as she hated to admit it, even herself. How could she fight her destiny if she couldn't even make herself get off the elevator on the tenth floor?

"I think every bride and groom in the city decided to shop for rings today," Mrs. Barnes said. *Oh joy.* "They need champagne. And petit fours. And gift wrapping. Find the floor manager, and he'll put you to work."

"Right." Aurélie nodded.

She could do this. Couldn't she?

"I'll be up to check on you in a bit."

Aurélie watched as Mrs. Barnes crossed the showroom floor with purpose in her stride. It would have been so easy to turn around and walk back out the revolving door. So easy to get back in the car, collect Jacques from the pet sitter at Dalton's apartment and head straight to the airport.

Too easy.

She'd had enough of taking the easy way out. She squared her shoulders, marched straight toward the elevator and stepped inside.

"Tenth floor, *s'il vous plait*," she told the elevator attendant.

He eyed her warily. Not that she could blame him. "Yes, ma'am."

The elevator doors swished closed. When they opened again, she exited as swiftly as possible. Maybe she could simply outrun her panic.

Then again, maybe not. As soon as she found herself surrounded by the glass cases of sparkling diamond solitaires, the familiar tightness gathered in her chest. Her knees went wobbly, and she had trouble catching her breath. Aurélie squeezed her eyes shut, and when she did, she no longer saw herself in a white gown walking down the aisle of the grand cathedral in Delamotte. Her recurrent nightmare had been replaced. Instead, she saw Diamond barreling toward the double-rail jump. She saw him stumble and fall. She saw Diana slamming into the ground headfirst.

Aurélie's eyes flew open. This was absurd. Diana was lying in a hospital bed, possibly even fighting for her life. Surely Aurélie could tolerate a few giddy brides and grooms.

There were more than a few. There were dozens. Under the direction of the acting floor manager, Aurélie brought them flutes of champagne. She served them cake. She oohed and ahed as they tried on rings. She offered her congratulations, wrapped more rings than she could count in little Drake-blue boxes and tied white bows.

And it wasn't altogether terrible.

Granted, she got a little misty eyed if she paid too much attention to the way the grooms looked at their brides-to-be. So much unabashed adoration was a little much to take, especially when she almost allowed herself to believe Dalton had looked at her in the same way during the quiet moments before Diana's accident.

But that was just crazy. Wishful thinking, at best.

Delusional, at worst. She didn't want to fool herself into believing Dalton cared about her, maybe even loved her, when he so clearly didn't.

Dealing with the grooms got easier when she focused her gaze on their foreheads rather than their lovey-dovey expressions. Before long, the smile she'd plastered on her face began to feel almost genuine. She'd just wrapped a satiny white ribbon around a Drake-blue box containing a cushion-cut diamond solitaire in a platinum setting when the overhead lights flickered and dimmed.

"What's happening?" she asked the salesman as she handed him the box.

"It's closing time." He sighed. "Finally. It's been a day, hasn't it? Thanks for all your help, by the way. What's your name, again?"

Her Royal Highness Princess Aurélie Marchand. "Aurélie."

He nodded. "Thanks again, Aurélie. Good work."

Good work.

No one had ever uttered those words to her before. It gave her a little thrill to be praised for something other than showing up at an event with a tiara on her head. "No problem. Can I do anything else?"

He shrugged. "I've got to close out the registers and get the place cleaned up, then we can all go home."

Home.

Aurélie's throat grew tight. She'd managed to stay so busy for a few hours that she'd forgotten she was supposed to be on a plane right now.

She let out a shaky breath. "I'll help you. I'm not in any hurry."

"Suit yourself," he said and handed her a bottle of Windex and a roll of paper towels.

One by one, the customers left. It was strange being in Drake Diamonds all alone after hours, peaceful in a way that caught Aurélie off guard. After so much noisy activity, there was a grace to the sudden silence. The gemstones almost looked like holy relics glowing in the semi-darkness, the sapphires, rubies and emeralds like precious stained glass.

It was soothing, therapeutic. Almost hypnotic. Aurélie didn't realize how lost she'd become in the simple act of dusting until she heard the salesman's footsteps again.

She gave a start as he walked up behind her. "Sorry. I'm afraid I'm a bit startled."

"As am I."

She froze, unable to move. She could barely even breathe.

That voice.

She knew the particular timbre of that voice. It didn't belong to the salesman. It belonged to the person she wanted to see more than anyone else on earth.

Heart beating wildly in her chest, she turned around. "Dalton."

Chapter Fourteen

Dalton thought he might be hallucinating at first.

He was bone-weary. Diana's accident and its aftermath had exhausted him on every possible level—physically, mentally, emotionally. When he passed through the darkened corridor of Drake Diamonds and glanced toward the Engagements showroom, he didn't think for a second that what he was looking at could possibly be real.

Aurélie was supposed to be on a plane. She couldn't be standing in his store after closing time. Even if she'd ignored his request and stayed in New York, she definitely wouldn't be milling about in Engagements, of all places. When his gaze landed on the dust rag in her right hand, he was sure he was seeing things.

He was wrong of course. But what surprised him even more than Aurélie's presence was the wave of relief that washed over him when she turned around and said his name.

Dalton had never needed anyone before, and that was no accident. He'd arranged his life so that he was self-reliant in every way. He always had been. He didn't want to need anyone or anything.

But right now, he needed *her*. Aurélie. He needed her so badly it terrified him to his core.

He didn't know why she was here. Or how. All he knew was that he felt like falling to his knees in gratitude that she'd ignored him when he'd sent her away.

He shoved his hands in his pockets to stop himself from reaching for her. He couldn't be trusted. Not in the state he was in. If he touched her now, he wouldn't be able to stop. "What are you doing here?"

"I could ask you the same thing." She fiddled with the rag in her hands, nervously wadding it into a ball.

What on earth was going on? It was like he'd stepped into some weird reverse Cinderella scenario.

"I own this building," he said. "I have every right to be here."

"I suppose you do." Her gaze darted toward the empty hallway.

"You can stop looking around. I've sent everyone home already." Almost everyone.

"Oh." She swallowed, and Dalton traced the movement up and down the length of her regal neck. His will-power was crumbling by the second. "How's Diana? Is she going to be okay?"

He nodded. "Yes, thank God. She's awake. Mostly anyway. According to the doctor, she didn't suffer any permanent damage."

He dropped his gaze to the display case and the diamond rings shimmering in the darkness, like ice on fire. "Her horse had to be put down. She didn't know. I told her about an hour ago, and she didn't take it well."

His voice broke, and something inside him seemed to break right along with it. Giving Diana the news about Diamond had been the most difficult conversation he'd ever had in his life. Even more difficult than telling Clarissa's parents about her suicide.

He was just so sick of loss. Of death and dying. He couldn't carry it with him anymore. Not another damned minute.

His gaze slid back to Aurélie, standing in front of him looking so beautiful. So alive. So real.

It was enough to make him lose his head.

"I was engaged once," he said, nodding at the neat row of rings beneath the glass.

What was he doing? He hadn't planned on telling Aurélie about Clarissa. He hadn't even considered it. But once it slipped out, he felt instantly lighter. Just a little bit. Just enough that he could breathe again.

"She died," he continued. "By her own hand, but I was to blame."

He took a deep inhale and paused. He wasn't sure why. Maybe he was waiting for her to respond in horror. Maybe he'd held onto the words for so long that his voice was rebelling. But he forced them out. If he didn't say them now, he knew he never would. To anyone. He'd carry his horrible secrets to his grave, and he couldn't bear the weight of them any longer.

"She called me for help, but I didn't answer. If I had, she might still be alive today." He covered his face with his hands. It hurt to be this open, this vulnerable.

"I should have been there for her, but I wasn't. I was here. Right where I always am." He forced himself to look at Aurélie. As much as he feared seeing a look of disappointment on her face—or worse, pity—he needed to gaze into those glittering green eyes.

The compassion he saw in their emerald depths kept him going. And once he began, he couldn't get the words out fast enough. His tongue tripped over them, and he told her the entire story. He even told her little details he'd thought he'd forgotten, like the shooting star he'd seen on the way home that night and the way he'd felt like the world's biggest fraud when the mourners at Clarissa's funeral offered their condolences. He talked until there was nothing left to say.

Then he finished, breathless, and waited for her to say something. He hoped to God she didn't try and tell him it wasn't his fault. He'd been having that argument with himself for six years. He didn't want to have it with her, too.

She didn't tell him he was blameless, though. She didn't try to make him feel better, nor did she look at him like he was some kind of monster. She said the only thing he was willing to hear. The right thing. The perfect thing.

"Dalton, I'm so sorry." She placed a gentle hand on his forearm.

His name was like a prayer on her lips, her touch like a balm. The tenderness of the moment ripped him open, crushed what was left of his defenses. Without the shelter of his secrets, he was no longer capable of hiding his desperation.

He a*ched* for her.

Keeping his distance from her had been torture. The only thing stopping him from kissing her right here, right now, were those six words he'd been trying to forget since the moment she'd uttered them just hours after he'd taken her to bed.

I don't think it should happen again.

Dalton had never once come close to forcing himself on a woman. He thought men who did that were despicable. He couldn't...wouldn't...kiss her without her consent. But by God, if he stood much longer in that room, drowning in engagement rings, he was liable to do something he'd come to regret. He may already have.

"Princess," he whispered as he reached to cup her face, drawing the pad of his thumb across her lovely lower lip.

She didn't say a word, didn't even breathe as far as he could tell, just gazed at him with her sparkling emerald eyes.

Dalton remembered a story his grandfather had told him when he was a little boy. He'd said that in ancient Rome, the Emperor Nero watched gladiator battles through a large emerald stone because he found the color soothing. Since the very first emerald had been dug out of the ground, people believed healing could be found in their glittering green depths. They were once called the Jewel of Kings.

It was a fitting thing to remember in the presence of royalty.

Dalton could have been Nero in that moment. Soothed and whole. Everything he wanted, everything he needed was right there in those eyes. Acceptance. Life. Passion.

He wanted her. He wanted her again. And again and again.

Walk away.

Walk away while you still can.

"Kiss me." She turned her head just slightly, just

enough for his thumb to make contact with the wet warmth of her mouth. "Please."

Please.

Dalton went rock-hard even before his lips crashed down on hers. Had it only been a day since he'd been inside her? Impossible. It felt like years since he'd buried himself between her thighs and felt her lithe body shuddering beneath him. Too long. Much too long.

He circled an arm around her, pulling her against him as her lips opened for him and he licked his way inside her mouth with teasing strokes of his tongue. He kissed her with all the dark intensity that made him who he was. A shock of pure, primal pleasure shot through him when she whimpered and melted into him.

This, he thought.

This right here was what he wanted. What he'd missed.

She tasted like promise and hunger and hope, things Dalton had given up on long ago. And the way she responded to his touch was enough to bring him back to life.

He pinned her against one of the taller display cases and kissed her until she began to tremble violently. Until the diamonds behind her shook on their glass shelves. He liked it. He liked it far too much.

He wasn't going to rush things this time. Not even if she urged him to hurry. Not even if she begged. Hell, he *wanted* her to beg. He wanted her wet, helpless and desperate for him by the time he pushed inside her. He wanted this to mean something, so when daylight came, it would be impossible for her to look him in the eye and call this a mistake.

"Dalton," she whispered against his mouth. Her hand

moved from his chest to his fly, finding him through his clothes. Exploring. Caressing. Stroking with just the right amount of pressure.

His vision blurred. He groaned. For a moment he thought he saw stars, but then he realized it was the light from the diamonds shimmering softly behind her.

"I want you," she murmured. The next sound he heard was the slide of his zipper, then her delicate hand was around his shaft, pumping slowly. He closed his eyes, lost to the pure, hot bliss of her touch. Only for a moment. Only long enough for his desire to take on an edge of desperation.

He opened his eyes.

"Not now, princess. Not yet." *Not even close.*

He dropped his lips to the curve of her neck and worked his way down, down to the hollow of her throat, casually unbuttoning her dress as he went.

"Turn around," he said in as even a tone as he could manage.

She released her hold on his cock and obeyed, turning slowly, peering at him coyly over her shoulder. But there was heat glimmering in her emerald gaze. Molten desire.

"Put your hands over your head," he told her, his voice raw with need.

Again she did as he said without a moment's hesitation, and that alone was nearly enough to make him lose control. His hands shook as he gathered the soft folds of her dress and lifted it carefully over her head. He tossed it aside, and waves of golden curls spilled over her shoulders and down her supple back.

So gorgeous.

He drank in the sight of her exquisite curves, surrounded by the luminous diamond glow and clothed in nothing but tiny wisps of lace. She was the most beautiful woman Dalton had ever set eyes on. Always would be. He couldn't say how, or why, but he knew with absolute certainty that there would never be another woman in his life like Aurélie. Whatever this was between them came around only once in a lifetime. If that.

"Be still," he said. "Be very still."

Her hair rippled gently beneath his breath. He twirled a long, lovely lock of it around his fingertips before trailing his hand ever so softly down the length of her spine. His touch left goose bumps in its wake.

She shivered.

He leaned in, pressed a tender kiss between her shoulder blades, and a slow smile of satisfaction came to his lips when she arched her back.

So needy.

Now we're getting somewhere.

What was he doing to her?

This wasn't like before. This was something different entirely. Something far more intense.

He'd been holding back last night. She realized that now. She'd asked him not to be gentle, not to go slow. And he hadn't. But tonight, Dalton was the one in control. He was setting the pace. And the deliberate slowness of his movements seemed designed to send her into sensual distress.

Aurélie could barely keep herself upright. Her legs were on the verge of buckling, and Dalton had barely touched her. There'd been just a few brushes of his fingertips and one or two lingering kisses, but it was the wicked edge to his voice that was reducing her to a quivering mass of need. He sounded so serious. So imposing.

It shouldn't have aroused her. It absolutely shouldn't have, but it did. It inflamed her in a way she didn't understand. Couldn't, even if she'd been capable of trying. Which she wasn't. Not by a long shot.

She couldn't think. She couldn't speak. When he ran his hands down her sides, grabbed hold of her hips and gently turned her around so she was facing him again, she could barely even look at him.

She peered up at him through the thick fringe of her lashes and her face went hot. His lips curved into a knowing grin as she struggled to catch her breath. She glanced down. Her breasts were straining the lacy cups of her bra, arching toward him. Her thighs were pressed together in an effort to quell the tingling at her center. This was too much. Too much heat. Too much sensation. It didn't matter that she couldn't speak. She didn't need to say a word. Her body was pleading with him, begging him to touch her. Take her. Fill her.

She would have been mortified if she hadn't been so violently aroused.

He raised a single, dark eyebrow and pushed the hair back from her eyes. Her pulse rocketed out of control, and his gaze dropped to her throat. He knew. Dalton Drake knew perfectly well what he was doing to her.

She licked her lips and willed herself not to beg. *Please, Dalton. Touch me.*

Love me.

Love me.

At last he moved closer, unhooked her bra and slid its satiny straps down her arms. Before it even fell to the floor, his mouth was on her breasts, licking, sucking, biting. Then he pressed a languid, openmouthed kiss to her belly. She was vaguely conscious of her panties sliding down her legs. Everything had gone so seductively fuzzy around the edges. She looked around, and she saw Dalton's image reflected in the cool facets of the diamonds twinkling under the shimmering lights. Everywhere. Like a starry winter's night.

Her legs trembled as he parted her thighs, his mouth moving lower, lower still.

The scrape of his five o'clock shadow along the soft flesh of her inner thigh was nearly enough to send her over the edge. What was happening? This was too intimate. Too intense. There would be no coming back from this. She'd never be able to pretend this didn't matter. Not to herself. Not to him.

He'd told her his deepest, darkest secret. And now he was uncovering hers, exposing her desire for the wanton, yearning thing that it was. She couldn't be this vulnerable to him. Not when she would eventually have to walk away.

She'd stolen another day. But this wouldn't last forever. It couldn't. She'd be lucky if it lasted until the gala.

The impossibility of the situation bore down on her. She looked at Dalton settled between her thighs, pleasuring her with his skillful mouth and she felt like crying. But instead she heard herself crying out in pleasure, saying his name as though she had a right to it. As though it belonged to her.

He's not yours.

He's not yours, and he never will be.

"Dalton," she murmured. She had to tell him. He'd been so honest with her. So real. And he still didn't know why she'd been so desperate to leave home.

"Let go." There it was again—that unflinchingly authoritative tone. Her favorite sound. "Just feel, princess."

Surrender was her only choice. It was too late for anything else. She clung tightly to him, her hands moving through his hair as she writhed against him.

Just feel, princess.

Her head fell back as she fully, finally gave herself up to him. She couldn't fight it anymore. It was no use. He slipped a finger inside her, moving it in time with his mouth. She gasped, blinking in shock at the astonishing pleasure. Her mind had caught up with her body, stripped bare and open. Everything around her shimmered. Her eyes fluttered shut, and the row of dazzling engagement rings in the case beside her was the last thing she saw before her climax slammed into her and she came apart.

Dalton caught her as she slipped toward the floor. He tucked an arm beneath her legs and carried her out of the room, down the hall to his office. She tried to wrap her arms around his neck, but they'd gone impossibly heavy. Instead she nestled her head in the warm space between his neck and shoulder.

He set her down gingerly on the sofa and undressed while she watched, memorizing every detail of his sculpted body and the way it glistened like fine marble in the moonlight streaming through the window. She wanted to hold onto what she was feeling right then— the heady thrill she felt when he looked at her bare body.

He sees me.

He always has.

He stretched out next to her, and she moved to sit astride him. She gazed down at him, this man who'd found her when she hadn't even realized how lost she'd been. He rose up to kiss her, his mouth gentle and seeking. It was a reverent kiss. Worshipful, almost. The tenderness of it caught her off guard. A wistful ache squeezed her heart.

She reached for him and guided him to her entrance. She needed him to fill her again. Now, before whatever was happening between them slipped through their fingers like her mother's golden pearls.

With an excruciatingly sweet ache, he pushed inside her. Slowly, slowly, and she arched to take him in. He curled his strong hands around her hips, thrust harder. And harder. Until the sweetness gave way to blazing heat, and fire bloomed between them once again.

Diamond bright.

Chapter Fifteen

Dalton slept like the dead.

With Aurélie's head on his chest and his fingers buried in her hair, he slept the peaceful, dreamless slumber of a man who'd managed to outrun his demons. His eyes didn't open a fraction until he heard voices. Familiar voices.

"Good morning."

"I understand. There's been a family emergency, but the moment I'm able to reach Mr. Drake, I'll let him know you're here."

Was that Mrs. Barnes? What was his secretary doing in his apartment?

He pressed his eyes closed, determined not to care. He wasn't waking up. Not yet. He wanted to stay right where he was, wrapped in Aurélie's graceful limbs as long as he could. He turned, slid behind her and burrowed into her soft orchid scent. Memories from the night before came flooding back. Tastes. Sounds. The glorious sight of her sitting on top of him with her hair tumbling over her shoulders and moonlight caressing her beautiful breasts. He ran his hands over the soft swell of her hips, pulled her close to grind against her bottom and was rewarded with a sultry moan.

"Good morning, love," he whispered, already hard, already wanting her. God, what was happening to him? He was insatiable.

"I understand the urgency of the situation, but it's really not best that you come here, Your Highness."

Somewhere beneath the liquid heat of his arousal, a prickle of unease snaked its way into Dalton's consciousness.

His eyes drifted open, and he took in his surroundings. His desk. His chair. The Drake-blue walls.

Shit. They weren't in his apartment. They were in his office.

"Aurélie, wake up. We've overslept." Sunlight and the crystal reflection of snowfall streamed through his office windows.

What time was it? He never slept past 6 a.m. From the looks of things, it was far later than that. And if Mrs. Barnes was already here...

He cursed and jerked upright. The store was about to open for business. The hallways were teeming with his employees. And he was naked in his office.

With Aurélie.

She blinked, then as the reality of the present circumstances dawned, her eyes went wide with panic. "Dalton. Oh my God."

"Don't worry." He glanced at the halfway open door,

lcapcd off the sofa and slammed it closed. "Everything will be okay."

Her gaze darted around the room. "But my clothes…"

Shit. Shit. Shit. Her dress was still pooled on the floor of Engagements, right next to her lingerie. Not to mention the fact that there were cameras all over that room. He needed to get his hands on the store's surveillance videos. Immediately, before anyone saw them. But first he needed to get her dressed.

He laid his hands on her shoulders and pressed a kiss to the top of her head. *Don't panic.* "It will be fine. I promise. I'll go get your clothes."

She nodded, looking every bit as dazed as he felt.

How had he let this happen? He'd had sex in the store. Even Artem had never done something this outrageous. That Dalton knew of.

He shook his head. If this wasn't the first time a Drake had been in this situation, he really didn't want to know.

He grabbed his pants from the floor and pulled them on. They were wrinkled as hell. Everyone in the building would be able to recognize his stroll through the store as a walk of shame. Marvelous.

At least he had a selection of pressed shirts from the dry cleaners in one of his desk drawers. He reached for the one on top of the stack and pulled it on, fumbling with the buttons.

"Let me," Aurélie said, unfolding her legs from beneath her and walking toward him.

He allowed himself a brief glance of her bare body, even though he knew good and well it would only make him forget why he was in such a hurry to leave the room. Sure enough, one look, one glimpse of her porcelain skin, her perfect breasts and their rosebud nipples, was all it took for him to forget about everything on the other side of the door.

"Stop looking at me like that, or we'll never get out of here." She rolled her eyes and smoothed down his collar.

He felt himself grinning. "Would that be so bad?"

"You tell me, Mr. CEO."

"It might be a tad inappropriate." His hands found her waist and slid lower until they cupped the decadent softness of her bottom. "Not that I care much at the moment."

She smiled up at him and something came unloose in his chest. "But you will. Eventually."

He was beginning to doubt it.

"There. You're all buttoned up."

A pity. "How do I look?"

"Like you've been ravaging women on the sales floor." She lifted an amused brow.

"*Woman,* not *women.*" He slid his arms around her, not quite willing to tear himself away despite the absurdity of the situation. "Only the one."

The one.

The One.

"Good to know, Mr. Drake." She rose up on tiptoe and kissed the corner of his mouth, and for a moment his feet stayed rooted to the floor. He couldn't have budged for all the diamonds in Africa.

The intercom on his office phone buzzed, piercing the intimate silence. "Dalton, it's Artem. If you're in there, we need to talk. It's urgent."

He took his hands off Aurélie. Came to his senses.

"I'll be right back," he said.

Artem was waiting for him directly on the other side

of the door, holding Aurélie's clothes and wearing a grim expression.

Perfect. Just perfect.

"Whatever you're going to say, I really don't want to hear it right now. Can we talk later?"

Artem thrust Aurélie's things at him. "No, it can't."

"Fine. Lecture me all you want." God knows, he deserved it.

Artem lowered his voice. "Brother, I'm not here to lecture you. Believe me. We've got a situation on our hands."

"It's not Diana, is it?" That couldn't be it, though, could it? Otherwise, Artem wouldn't be here.

"No, she's fine. I just spoke to her doctor this morning." He sighed. "It's the palace. They've been calling. And calling. Mrs. Barnes is in a panic. Have you checked your messages?"

Dalton's gut churned. After Diana's fall, he'd forgotten all about the unread email. He hadn't even turned his phone back on.

He shook his head. "Is this as bad as it seems?"

"It's not good." Artem raked a hand through his hair. He seemed to be doing everything in his power to remain calm. "Get her dressed, and we'll deal with it. Together. Sound good?"

He nodded. "Thanks."

"That's what family's for." But there was a gravity in his expression that Dalton couldn't ignore.

"Wait. What aren't you telling me?"

Artem shook his head. His gaze dropped to the floor, and Dalton suddenly didn't want to know. He just wanted to rewind the clock to the night before and stay in that dazzling place forever.

"She's engaged." Artem sighed. "Aurélie. She's getting married. It's on the front page of every newspaper in the world."

Dalton shook his head.

There had to be some kind of mistake. He was talking about some other princess. Not her. Not Aurélie.

The one.

The One.

He swallowed hard. "No." Just…no.

She would have said something. She would have told him, wouldn't she?

A dark fury began to gather in his chest, like a rising storm. So thick, so black he choked it on it. He cleared his throat, swallowed it down, as he remembered how lost she'd been when she first arrived in New York, how she'd pushed him away after the first time they'd made love…how she'd hated even setting foot in Engagements. She *had* told him, hadn't she? Not in so many words, but he'd known. On some level, he'd known. She'd been telling him all along.

Artem reached into the inside pocket of his suit jacket and pulled out a neatly folded square of newsprint. "Here. Read it for yourself."

He didn't want to look. He really didn't. But he forced himself to unfold the paper, because he'd been blind enough for the past few days. It was time to wake up to reality.

Her Royal Highness Princess Aurélie Marchand of Delamotte to Marry Duke Lawrence Bouvier on April 20 in Lavish Royal Wedding

* * *

Aurélie knew something was horribly wrong as soon as Dalton crossed the threshold.

There was a sudden seriousness in the firm set of his jaw, and he seemed to look right through her when he handed her the folded pile of clothes. Suddenly acutely aware of her nakedness, she wanted to hide. If anything, to shield herself from the coolness in his gaze.

"Thank you," she said and slipped into her dress as quickly as she could.

He said nothing, just stood there waiting with a large Drake-blue shopping bag in his hands while she pulled on her panties.

What was going on? What had happened in the handful of minutes since she'd seen him last?

She swallowed and smoothed down the front of her dress. She knew, even without the benefit of a mirror, that she looked like a mess. A complete and utter disaster. "Dalton, what's wrong?"

"Nothing's wrong." He shrugged with a casual air of nonchalance, but the impassivity of his gaze shifted into something darker. More dangerous. "I should probably offer my congratulations, though."

For a moment, she was confused. She couldn't imagine what he was talking about.

Then she realized…

Somehow he'd found out about the wedding. He *knew*.

No. He couldn't. That wasn't feasible. How could he possibly know when it wasn't even official?

"I'm not sure I know what you mean." But her words sounded disingenuous, even to her own ears.

She hated herself.

"Save it, Princess," he snapped.

With exaggerated calmness, he pulled a newspaper from the top of the shopping bag and handed it to her.

She was afraid to take it, but she didn't dare refuse him. Not when she'd already given him every reason in the world to despise her.

Her stomach plummeted when she read the headline. The palace had made an announcement. Without even consulting her. Without her knowledge. She supposed it didn't matter after all that she'd been a no-show for the sitting with Lord Clement. They'd simply used an older picture.

She stared at herself, smiling like an idiot below the awful headline, and realized that her absence *had* mattered. It mattered so much that the palace had gone ahead and released the news. They'd played the ultimate trump card. She had no choice but to go home now. She'd never be able to move about New York, or anyplace else now, without being recognized. Not after this.

She folded the newspaper and dropped it on Dalton's desk. She couldn't stand to look at it another minute. If she did, she might vomit.

"Dalton, please. Let me explain. I wasn't engaged when I came here. I'm not…"

But she was.

She knew it. And so did he. So did everyone. She was getting married, and it was front-page news.

Someone knocked on the door, and Aurélie wished with everything in her that Dalton would tell whomever it was to go away. She needed to talk to him. She needed to fix things. She didn't know how it was possible, but she had to try. She'd never be able to live with herself if she didn't.

"Come in," he said.

The door opened, and in walked Mrs. Barnes, followed by an older gentleman wearing a dark suit and a grim expression. Aurélie's father.

Her legs gave way, and she sank onto the sofa. Her father had come all this way, just to drag her home. It was over—her holiday, Dalton, their bargain.

All of it.

"I'm sorry, Mr. Drake." Mrs. Barnes was wringing her hands, and fluttering about between Dalton and her father. "I apologize, but Mr. Marchand insisted on seeing you. I know he doesn't have an appointment…"

Dalton held up a hand. "It's okay. He doesn't need one."

Of course he didn't. The Crown Prince of Delamotte always got his way.

Bile rose to the back of Aurélie's throat.

"Father," she said.

"Aurélie." He looked her up and down, from the messy hair atop her head to the tips of her barefoot toes. Her face burned with shame. Her father didn't say a word about the meaning of her disheveled appearance. He didn't have to. He swiveled his gaze toward Dalton. "Mr. Drake, I presume?"

"Yes." Dalton nodded. The fact that he refused to bow was a major breach of royal etiquette. Aurélie suspected he knew this. She also suspected he didn't give a damn.

"My office has been trying to reach you, Mr. Drake. Aurélie failed to show up for an important engagement yesterday, so we tracked her cell phone." His lips straightened into a flat line. "Imagine my surprise when it was brought to my attention that she's been here in New York. For days, it seems."

They must have tracked her phone before she'd taken out the SIM card. They'd known where she was all along.

The air in the room went so thick that Aurélie couldn't seem to catch her breath. Her father was giving Dalton a warning. He didn't care if Dalton was her lover. He was nothing to the Crown Prince of Delamotte. No one.

Dalton shrugged. "Forgive me, Your Highness, but your daughter is a grown woman. I believe she can make her own decisions."

He glanced at her, but she couldn't even look at him. This was so much worse than anything she'd ever imagined taking place. What had she done?

"Aurélie," Dalton prompted.

If ever there was a time to stand up to her father, it was now.

She took a deep breath and met his gaze, but when she did, she didn't see the man who'd bounced her on his knee when she was a little girl. She saw her sovereign. She saw the crown. She saw everything her mother had written on the gilt-edged pages of her diary about the tragedy of fate.

"I don't want to go, and I can't marry the duke." The words came out far weaker than she'd intended.

"Nonsense. You can, and you will. I won't allow you to embarrass me, Aurélie. Nor the throne." Her father glanced at his watch. "Come along. We can discuss this when we get home. We have a plane to catch."

She shook her head. "But my things…" Her dog. Her mother's pearls. *Her heart.*

If Dalton hadn't stepped forward and handed her the shopping bag, she may have found the strength to stay. She liked to believe that she would have been able to make that choice, that she would have been strong enough to stand up for what she wanted. Love. Life. Freedom. But when she looked down and saw what Dalton was offering her, she lost her resolve.

At the bottom of the bag sat a black velvet box, embossed with the Marchand royal crest. She knew what was inside without opening it. It was the secret egg. He was giving it back to her. He wanted her gone, no matter the cost.

"I've made arrangements for Sam to deliver Jacques and the rest of your things to the airport," Dalton said coolly. He nodded at the bag.

Take it from him. Just take it.

She dug deep and summoned her pride. If he didn't want her, she wouldn't stay. He'd already sent her away once. Twice was more than she could take.

She lifted her chin and reached for the bag. Only then did she notice the small glass box on top of the velvet egg carrier. Inside were her mother's gold pearls, restrung and perfect.

Just as perfect as she was expected to be from now on.

Chapter Sixteen

Dalton operated on autopilot until the night of the gala. Those seven days were the longest of his life. He spent all day, every day at the office, preparing for the party. He talked to the caterer, the florist, the baker and the linen rental company. He gave press interviews. More press interviews than he'd ever conducted before. He didn't particularly enjoy talking about the Marchand family over and over again. But he was determined not to let it show.

He spent his evenings at the hospital, sitting at Diana's bedside, until she was discharged. After Dr. Larson released her, Dalton insisted she come stay at his apartment so he could keep an eye on her. He worried about her. He didn't like the thought of her grieving for Diamond alone, in her tiny Brooklyn walk-up. At least that was what he'd told Diana. And the rest of the Drakes.

And himself.

The truth of the matter was that he was the one who couldn't handle the solitude of an empty apartment. Everywhere he turned, he saw reminders of Aurélie: Central Park, the New York Public Library, the sidewalk outside of Bergdorf Goodman. His office. His apartment. His bed.

God, how he missed her.

He missed her quirky clothes. He missed the way she never once allowed him to tell her what to do. He even missed her snoring, silly-looking dog. The enormity of her absence may not have fully hit him until one afternoon when he and Diana were walking through the park and he stopped beneath the blue awning at the pet adoption stand.

"Um, what are you doing?" Diana asked, crossing her arms and gaping at him in disbelief as he scooped a scrawny Chihuahua from one of the pens.

Was he going crazy, or had those been his exact words to Aurélie when he'd found her standing in the same spot on the day she'd first arrived?

We're adopting a dog, darling.

"I remember you." The animal shelter volunteer narrowed her gaze at him. She was the same woman from before, wielding her clipboard in the same annoying manner. "You're the one who adopted the little French bulldog."

"The *what?*" Diana let out an astonished laugh. "You have a dog? Where is it?"

The pet adoption counsclor stared daggers at him. "You've re-homed the dog? You can't do that, sir. You signed an agreement."

"I didn't re-home the dog. Look, this is all just a misunderstanding. I assure you."

But even the Chihuahua seemed to be giving him the evil eye.

Marvelous.

He set the little dog back down in its tiny playpen and moved on before he got arrested for dognapping or something equally ridiculous.

He and Diana walked the length of the park in silence. They passed the zoo, and the roar of the lions sounded strangely lonely in the snowfall. Then they made their way down the Literary Walk, and when they had to dodge out of the way to avoid a dog walker and her tangle of half a dozen leashes, Diana finally said something.

"Are you going to tell me about the missing dog? Because the suspense is killing me." She stopped in front of the statue of William Shakespeare.

The Bard peered at Dalton over her shoulder, looking every bit as serious and judgmental as the pet adoption counselor. *Or maybe I really am losing my mind.*

He sighed. "There's nothing to tell. The dog didn't belong to me. Aurélie adopted him, and she took him with her when she left. End of story. Can we keep walking now? The gala is tonight, and I've got things to do."

"No, we can't just keep walking and pretend nothing is going on." She shook her head and brushed back a loose strand of hair that had escaped from her hat.

She looked good. Healthy. But she still had a definite air of sadness about her. Dalton wished she'd start riding again, but he supposed getting back on a horse would just take time.

She crossed her arms. "You're in love with her, aren't you? You *love* her, and you miss her. That's why you wanted me to move into your apartment. That's why you were just mooning over a Chihuahua, isn't it?"

Yes. Yes, God help me. That's exactly why. "No. Don't be ridiculous. You gave us all a scare. I'm your brother, and I want to keep an eye on you. And the dog has nothing to do with Aurélie. Who wouldn't fall for that tiny little face?"

She rolled her eyes. "You're not fooling me, brother dear. You hate dogs."

Used to. He used to hate dogs. It seemed he'd developed a soft spot for them lately. But that was beside the point, especially since it looked as though the animal rescue community had probably blackballed him now.

"Anyway, don't try to change the subject. This isn't about the dog. It's about you." Diana jabbed her pointer finger into Dalton's chest. "And Aurélie."

It hurt to hear her name almost as much as it hurt to say it. "Drop it, Diana. There's nothing to discuss. She's getting married, remember?"

"But she's not." Diana shook her head.

"Yes, she is. On April 20. To a duke or a king or something like that. She'll be wearing a crown on her head, and she'll probably arrive in a damned glass coach."

"Stop yelling."

"I'm not yelling." A passerby pushing a baby carriage gave him an odd look.

Maybe he was yelling. Just a little bit.

"Calm down and listen to me for two seconds, would you? She's not getting married. I read it in the paper this morning."

"How many times have I told you that you can't believe everything you read in *Page Six*?" Artem had only actually participated in half the debauchery he'd been accused of in that rag. At least that was what he'd insisted at the time.

"Sheesh, give me some credit. I didn't read it in *Page*

Six. It was on the front page of the Books section of the *New York Times.*"

He paused for a second and glanced at William Shakespeare while he tried to absorb what his sister was saying. He thought of star-crossed lovers and fate and destiny. Then he remembered how that particular story ended.

"You're mistaken," he said flatly. The one thing he wanted less than pity was false hope. "Why would news about a royal wedding appear in the Books section?"

She lifted a knowing brow. "You know what? I'm not going to tell you. You're going to have to read it for yourself."

"Diana." He meant it as a warning, but despite himself, the faintest glimmer of hope stirred in his chest.

Stop. It's over. She's not even in the country anymore.

"This is what you get for only looking at the Business section of the *Times*, by the way. There's a whole world out there that you know nothing about."

"Thank you for the sisterly advice," he said wryly.

"You're welcome, my dear brother." She rubbed her mitten-covered hands together and looped an arm through his. "Shall we walk home now? It's freezing out, and like you said, we need to get ready for your big gala."

Clearly she wasn't going to tell him anything else. And suddenly the gala seemed like the furthest thing from Dalton's mind. "Fine."

"There's a newsstand on the corner of Central Park South and 50th Street, you know. We'll pass right by it on the way home."

"Indeed. I know." He'd already made a mental note of that very fact. It was the same newsstand where he picked up his paper nearly every morning. Not that his nosy sister needed to know any more about his personal life.

He managed to grab a copy of the *Times*, pay for it and walk the rest of the way home without tearing it open and poring over the Books section. He wanted to do so in private, even though the cat was already apparently out of the bag and Diana knew how much Aurélie meant to him. Now that the possibility that she might not be going through with the wedding had been dangled in front of him, he was consumed by the idea.

He didn't see how it was possible, yet with everything in him, he wanted to believe. He wanted to believe so badly that when he'd finally closed himself off in the privacy of his bedroom, he was almost afraid to spread the newspaper open on his bed.

He tossed it down beside his Armani tuxedo and Drake-blue bowtie and told himself if Diana had been wrong, or if she'd simply been playing some cruel joke on him, nothing would change. He didn't need Aurélie in his life. He hadn't crumbled to pieces after she'd left. He was a Drake. He was perfectly content.

Liar.

He poured himself a glass of scotch, took a generous gulp and finally sat down on the edge of the bed. His hands were shaking, and the paper rattled as he tossed aside the front page and the Business section. Then there it was, emblazoned across the header of the Books section.

Her Royal Highness Aurélie Marchand
of Delamotte Calls Off Wedding Following
Announcement of New Book Deal

Oh my God.

Diana was right.

He read the headline three times to make sure he wasn't seeing things. Then he dove into the article, which said that Aurélie had sold the publishing rights to her mother's diary. Due to overwhelming public interest in the book, the publication of the diary had been fast-tracked. It was due to hit shelves on April 20, what would have been Aurélie's wedding day.

Dalton sat very still and tried to absorb the implications of what he'd just read. There was much the article didn't say. Was Aurélie staying in Delamotte? How had her father reacted to this extreme act of defiance? Would she be stripped of her crown?

Does she still love me?

Did she ever?

He told himself what he'd just read had no bearing on his life whatsoever. It was about Aurélie taking control of *her* life.

Not about him.

Not about them.

But damned if it didn't feel like a second chance.

Dalton folded the newspaper and slowly sipped the rest of his scotch. He dressed for the gala with the utmost care, slipping into his waistcoat and fastening his Drake Diamond cufflinks. He caught a glimpse of himself in his bedroom mirror as he reached for his tie and paused, marveling at how composed he appeared on the outside when he couldn't seem to stop the violent pounding of his heart.

He stared down at the Drake-blue tie in his hand and realized he couldn't put it on. *This is where the charade stops,* he thought. *This is where it ends.*

If Aurélie could choose, then so could he.

Thirty minutes later, he barged into Artem's office without bothering to knock. "I need to talk to you."

He'd walked straight through the first floor showroom without even a cursory glance at the display cases that housed the Marchand eggs. He should be overseeing the arrangement of the collection. The Drake Diamonds staff had strict instructions that Dalton was to have final approval before the doors opened for the gala. But he and Diana had only just arrived and what he had to say to Artem couldn't wait.

"Perfect. Because there's something I need to tell you before the gala begins." Artem glanced at his watch. "Which is in just fifteen minutes, so I may as well come out and say it."

Dalton shook his head. If he didn't do this now, he might never actually get the words out. "I'd really rather go first."

Artem raked a hand through his hair and sighed. "But…"

"I quit," Dalton blurted at the exact same moment that Artem leveled his gaze and said, "You're fired."

The brothers stared at each other for a beat, shocked into silence.

Finally, Artem cleared his throat. "Well this works out rather nicely, don't you think?"

"Wait a minute." Dalton sank into the leather chair opposite Artem. "You can't fire me. You don't have the authority. We're co-CEOs, remember?"

He didn't even know why he was arguing about it when the bottom line was the same—he was finished at Drake Diamonds. He'd had enough. If Aurélie could be brave enough to take hold of her future and change it, then so could he.

Except that he'd never been fired from a job in his life. And he also owned one third of the family business.

"Yes and no." Artem shrugged. "We agreed to share the position, but never drew up paperwork to make the change official."

"It was a gentleman's agreement." How could Dalton have anticipated the need for paperwork? Artem had always been the one constantly threatening to turn in his resignation.

My, how things change.

"Exactly." Artem shrugged and brushed an invisible speck of lint from the shoulder of his tuxedo jacket. When had he gotten so casually adept at running the company? Dalton had nothing to worry about. Drake Diamonds would be in safe hands. "As far as the paperwork goes, I'm the sole CEO of Drake Diamonds, which means…"

"You can fire me." Dalton smiled. Who smiled as he was being fired? By his own brother, no less?

I do, apparently.

"Right." Artem tilted his head and slid his hands into his pocket as he examined Dalton. "And might I say, you're taking it awfully well."

It was Dalton's turn to shrug. "That's because I quit, effective the moment this gala is over."

"You're still fired. Don't take it personally, but you can't be trusted to stay away. You've done an excellent job here. You've poured everything you have into Drake Diamonds, but it's time for you to get an actual life." He had the decency to wince, but only for a second. "No offense, of course."

"None taken." Dalton rolled his eyes.

"Come on, you know I'm right. If Diana's accident taught us anything, it's that life is precious."

Exactly.

Except Dalton should have learned that lesson years ago. Six years ago, to be exact.

How had he allowed himself to waste so much time? So much life? Aside from Diana's accident, the handful of days he'd spent with Aurélie had been the best he'd ever experienced. But he hadn't fully appreciated them, had he? Save for the times they'd made love, he'd held her at arm's length. It was time to hold her close. Now and forever.

If she'd still let him.

"Yes, you're right. That's why I'm leaving for Delamotte first thing in the morning. Or tonight, if I can arrange a flight." He had no idea how he'd even get an audience with a royal princess. But he'd figure it out. He'd kick down the palace doors if necessary.

"I'd hoped Her Royal Highness might have something to do with your decision." Artem's face split into a huge grin. "Let me be the first to congratulate you."

Dalton shook his head. "Not so fast. I don't even know if she's still speaking to me."

He'd sent her packing. Twice. That was a lot to atone for.

"I see." Artem nodded and glanced at his watch. "As much as I'd like to give you a brotherly pep talk right about now, there's no time. You should probably go take a look at the eggs and make sure everything is in order, no?"

"Will do." Dalton rose to his feet, buttoned the jacket of his tux and turned to go.

He was nearly out the door when he heard Artem say, "Nice tie, by the way."

Dalton just shook his head, laughed and headed for the elevator.

The first floor was abuzz with activity. Every member of the Drake Diamonds staff was on hand. Through the glass revolving door, he could see photographers and other members of the press lined up on the snowy sidewalk, waiting for the official start of the unveiling.

Excellent. After the many professional mistakes he'd made over the course of the past month, it was comforting to know he was leaving on a successful note.

Except as he approached the exhibit and spotted the Marchand jeweled hen egg in the first glass case, he sighed. Something wasn't right. The hen egg was the oldest piece in the collection. It had been the egg featured on all the banners and advertisements. Dalton had left instructions for it to be placed in the center of the room, in the illuminated glass case that had once housed the revered Drake Diamond.

Someone had screwed up.

He really didn't need this now. Not when the gala was set to begin in less than five minutes, and not when he had far more important things on his mind. Like how to woo a princess.

"Excuse me." He beckoned the closest employee he could find. "Who arranged the eggs this way?"

"Your brother did, sir." The salesman gestured overhead, toward the upper floors of the building. "We followed the exhibit map you'd drawn up, but Mr. Drake came down about half an hour ago and changed everything."

Dalton's fists clenched at his sides. What the hell was

going on with Artem? Firing him after he quit was one thing. Completely usurping him before he was even gone was another matter entirely.

The salesman shifted uneasily from one foot to the other. Clearly he wasn't thrilled to be the bearer of such news. Not that Dalton could blame him. "He said you might be upset, and he indicated if you wanted to discuss it, you should go upstairs to Engagements."

"Engagements?" Had his brother had an aneurysm or something? They weren't even opening Engagements up to customers tonight. Everyone was to stay on the first floor.

The salesman cleared his throat. "But first he said you should take a look at the exhibit's centerpiece, Mr. Drake."

The centerpiece.

He'd been so thrown by the obviously incorrect placement of the jeweled hen egg that he hadn't even ventured a glance at the big case in the center. Who knew what Artem had stuck in there?

He turned, and what he saw stole the breath from his lungs.

On a pedestal in the center of the room, in the very heart of Drake Diamonds, sat a pink-enameled egg, covered in shimmering pavé diamonds and tiny seed pearls.

The Marchand secret egg had found its way back to New York.

Is this a mistake?

The question had followed Aurélie all the way across the Atlantic Ocean. It nagged at her for the duration of the twelve-hour flight, as she sat sleepless in First Class, clutching the black velvet egg box like a security blanket while Jacques snored in his carrier.

Would Dalton be happy to see her? Had he thought about her at all over the past seven days?

God, she hoped so.

She'd thought of little else but him. At night when she closed her eyes, she dreamt of his sighs of pleasure as he'd touched her, kissed her...loved her. When she woke in the morning, his name was the first word on her lips, the memory of him the first tug in her heart.

She'd prayed for it to stop. She'd pleaded with God to make the memories fade.

They hadn't.

If anything, her feelings for Dalton had only grown stronger. No matter what happened now, though, she was grateful for the persistence of memory. She knew that now. Knowing Dalton had changed her. Permanently. Profoundly. If she'd never met him, never fallen in love, she would have never had the courage to stand up to her father. She would have never done what she had to do in order to take control of her own destiny.

She'd paved the way for her own future. All because of him. Because of Dalton Drake.

So even if coming back to New York turned out to be a mistake, even if he took one look at her and told her to go back home, she wouldn't regret a thing.

But she hoped it wasn't a mistake. She hoped he loved her even a tiny fraction as much as she loved him.

The elevator dinged, and her knees grew weak. Jacques yipped in her arms.

This is it.

The doors swished open, and there he was. Aurélie had to bite her lip to keep herself from crying with relief at the sight of him. He looked so handsome. Even more handsome than she remembered. His exquisitely tailored tuxedo showed off his broad shoulders to perfection. Formal wear suited him.

There was just a hint of stubble on his jawline, and his eyes were even steelier than she remembered. They glittered like black diamonds as his gaze swept over her.

Aurélie's breath caught in her throat. She felt like she might faint. Jacques squirmed with such enthusiasm at the sight of Dalton that she had to set him down on the floor. The little dog bounded toward Dalton as if he hadn't seen him in a century. Aurélie wished she could do the same, but she couldn't bring herself to go to him.

Why was this so difficult? She hadn't even been this nervous when she'd finally confronted her father and told him she'd sent her mother's diary to the biggest publisher in Europe. Sad, yes. But nervous, no. Handing over her mother's diary had been bittersweet. She hated to hurt her father, but after the way he'd treated her in New York, he'd left her no choice. It was the only way she could buy her freedom.

It was what her mother would have wanted.

She leaned against one of the glass cases of diamond rings and willed herself to stay upright. But as Dalton scooped Jacques into his arms and moved toward her in the darkness, she noticed something that gave her a tiny glimmer of hope.

Is that...

No, it can't be.

Her gaze locked on the bowtie around Dalton's neck. She couldn't believe what she was seeing. The tie was red. Not Drake-blue, but *red*. Brilliant, blazing red. She couldn't seem to stop staring at it as he made his way toward her.

"Do my eyes deceive me, or is there a princess standing in front of me?" He stood about a foot and a half away. Just out of arm's reach, but close enough to see a hint of the dimple in his left cheek that only seemed to make an appearance on the rare occasions when he laughed.

Aurélie lifted an amused brow. "Is that a red tie, or am I hallucinating?"

"Touché." A smile tugged at his lips, and swarms of butterflies took flight in Aurélie's tummy. Then as quickly as the smile appeared, it was gone. In its place was an ardent expression she couldn't quite decipher. "You brought the egg back."

"You noticed."

"Indeed." He set Jacques down and took a step closer. Aurélie felt herself leaning toward Dalton, as if even gravity couldn't keep them apart. "You didn't need to do that, you know."

"But I did. We had a bargain, remember?" She needed to touch him. She needed to feel him again. It felt like a century had passed since he'd devoured her in this very room.

But her body remembered. She felt divinely liquid just standing in front of him, steeped in memories and decadent sensation. He'd loved her in this room, between these hallowed walls. He'd shared his deepest secrets. He'd done things to her that made the diamonds blush.

"You don't owe me a thing. Our bargain fell apart." He swallowed, and a rather fascinating knot flexed in his chiseled jaw. "That was my fault, Aurélie. I'm sorry."

"Don't. Please." She shook her head and realized too late that she'd started to cry.

She didn't want tears. Not now. She just wanted to throw herself into his arms and end the aching torture of being so close to him without feeling the warmth of his skin beneath her fingertips. She just wanted to kiss him again. And again.

"I…"

But he didn't let her finish. Before she could say a word about ending her engagement, his hands were in her hair, tipping her head back so that his lips were angled perfectly over hers.

"My perfect, precious pearl," he whispered. "Don't cry."

At last he kissed her, gently at first. Then as a tumultuous heat gathered in her center, the kiss grew deeper until she trembled with need. *Please. Please.* He groaned in response to her silent plea and pulled her closer. She could feel every inch of him through the lilac chiffon of her evening gown.

He pulled back slightly, his gaze fixed on her with a new intensity. "Tell me it's true. Tell me you're not marrying him."

"It's true." She nodded, dizzy with desire. Drunk with it. It was frightening how much she wanted him, needed him. She was finished with trying to protect her heart from getting hurt. She'd tried it already and had made a spectacular mess of things. She was all in now. No fear. No regrets.

"The thought of you with another man nearly killed me, princess. Have you come back to stay?" he asked, his voice rough. Questions shone in his diamond eyes.

It was time for answers. Past time.

Her heart pounded wildly. *Do it. Do it now. Say what you came here to say.* "I can't stay. I'm just here for the gala."

Dalton nodded, and the light in his eyes dimmed. "I understand."

For a fraction of a second, the silence between them expanded, threatening to choke them both. Jacques whimpered at their feet.

"My father is abdicating." She blurted it out without preamble. *So much for finesse.*

"What?"

"He wouldn't agree to end the engagement. I tried to reason with him, but he wouldn't back down. You met him. You saw what he's like."

"I did. He reminded me of my own father." Dalton rolled his eyes. "More than you know."

"Publishing my mother's diary was my only option. He knows once her words go public, the people of Delamotte will turn on him in a flash. He wants to step down before that can happen." Her father's pride came before anything. It had come before her mother. And in the end, it had been his downfall. He'd made the choice. Not her.

She'd done the only thing she could do. Letting go of the diary was her only option for getting her life back.

"Does this mean what I think it means?"

Aurélie nodded. "I'll be the Crown Princess. I'm going to rule Delamotte."

She took a deep inhale, did her best to ignore the hummingbird beat of her heart and said what she'd traveled 4,000 miles to tell him. "And I want you there with me. You and Jacques, of course."

Dalton Drake shot a glance at the dog and smiled the biggest smile she'd ever seen him display. "As luck would have it, I was already planning to visit your principality."

Is this truly happening? Is this real? "If you come…if you stay…it will mean leaving Drake Diamonds."

"Again, your timing is impeccable. I happen to be unemployed at the moment." He hauled her hard against him and brought his mouth down on hers in a powerful kiss that robbed her legs of strength.

Would she ever grow accustomed to this, she wondered. *Never.* There was magic in his touch. She was powerless against it. And she wouldn't have had it any other way.

She'd waited a lifetime for this kiss. She'd crisscrossed the globe and nearly toppled a kingdom.

It had been worth it. *He'd* been worth it.

"Excellent," she whispered against the wicked wonderland of his mouth. "Because I think you'd make a perfect Prince Consort."

"Are you asking me to marry you, Your Highness?" His eyes were shining. They seemed lighter than when she'd first met him. Soft pearl gray. "Right here in the Engagements showroom of Drake Diamonds?"

She nodded. "I am. And I just happen to know the cathedral is available three months from now."

He slid his hands down her arms, wove his fingers through hers and guided her gently backward, until she felt the cold press of a glass case against her bare back. He couldn't be serious. Half the city was downstairs. They didn't matter, though. No one did. Not now. Only them.

"No, princess." He reached behind her and slowly unzipped the bodice of her strapless gown. "Three months is far too long to wait to marry the woman I love. I want to make you my wife as soon as possible. Any chance we could get the cathedral sooner?"

Her dress slid down her body in a whisper of lilac, and she found herself naked once again in this glittering room, dressed in nothing but the cascade of gold pearls around her neck. "I think I can pull some strings."

"That's my princess."

My princess.

His princess.

His.

Dalton reached for her necklace, twirled the pearls slowly around his finger and used them to reel her in for a kiss. This time, the priceless string held tight, binding them together.

Forever unbroken.

* * * * *

Love awaits the Drake siblings in the glittering world of jewels and New York City.

Don't miss Artem and Ophelia's tale
HIS BALLERINA BRIDE
and Diana's story in the final installment of
the DRAKE DIAMONDS trilogy
out July 2017 wherever Mills & Boon Cherish
books and ebooks are sold.

MILLS & BOON®

Cherish™

EXPERIENCE THE ULTIMATE RUSH OF FALLING IN LOVE

A sneak peek at next month's titles...

In stores from 6th April 2017:

- **His Shy Cinderella** – Kate Hardy *and*
  Fortune's Surprise Engagement – Nancy
  Robards Thompson
- **Conveniently Wed to the Greek** – Kandy Shepherd
  and **The Lawman's Convenient Bride** – Christine
  Rimmer

In stores from 4th May 2017:

- **Falling for the Rebel Princess** – Ellie Darkins
  and **The Last Single Garrett** – Brenda Harlen
- **Claimed by the Wealthy Magnate** – Nina Milne
  and **Her Kind of Doctor** – Stella Bagwell

Just can't wait?
Buy our books online before they hit the shops!
www.millsandboon.co.uk

Also available as eBooks.

MILLS & BOON®

EXCLUSIVE EXTRACT

When Greek tycoon Alex Mikhalis
discovers Adele Hudson is pregnant
he abandons his plans to get even and
suggests a very intimate solution:
becoming his convenient wife!

Read on for a sneak preview of
CONVENIENTLY WED TO THE GREEK

'What?' The word exploded from her.

'You can't possibly be serious.'

Alex looked down into her face. Even in the slanted
light from the taverna she could see the intensity in his
black eyes. 'I'm very serious. I think we should get
married.'

Dell had never known what it felt to have her head
spin. She felt it now. Alex had to take hold of her elbow
to steady her. 'I can't believe I'm hearing this,' she said.
'You said you'd never get married. I'm not pregnant to
you. In fact you see my pregnancy as a barrier to kissing
me, let alone marrying me. Have you been drinking too
much ouzo?'

'Not a drop,' he said. 'It's my father's dying wish that
I get married. He's been a good father. I haven't been a
good son. Fulfilling that wish is important to me. If I
have to get married, it makes sense that I marry you.'

'It doesn't make a scrap of sense to me,' she said.

'You don't get married to someone to please someone else, even if it is your father.'

Alex frowned. 'You've misunderstood me. I'm not talking about a real marriage.'

This was getting more and more surreal. 'Not a real marriage? You mean a marriage of convenience?'

'Yes. Like people do to be able to get residence in a country. In this case it would be marriage to make my father happy. He wants the peace of mind of seeing me settled.'

'You feel you owe your father?'

'I owe him so much it could never be calculated or repaid. This isn't about owing my father, it's about loving him. I love my father, Dell.'

But you'll never love me, she cried in her heart. How could he talk about marrying someone—anyone—without a word about love?

Don't miss
CONVENIENTLY WED TO THE GREEK
by Kandy Shepherd

Available May 2017
www.millsandboon.co.uk

Join Britain's BIGGEST Romance Book Club

- **EXCLUSIVE offers every month**
- **FREE delivery direct to your door**
- **NEVER MISS a title**
- **EARN Bonus Book points**

Call Customer Services
0844 844 1358*

or visit
millsandboon.co.uk/subscription

* This call will cost you 7 pence per minute plus your
phone company's price per minute access charge.

BKCB3